HEARTLESS

AN OPTION ZERO NOVEL

CHRISTY REECE

D0912631

Heartless
An Option Zero Novel
Published by Christy Reece
Cover Art by Kelly A. Martin of KAM Design
Photography by NeonShot (DepositPhotos), chagpg (DepositPhotos), stevemc
(DepositPhotos), PantherMediaSeller(DepositPhotos), dvoevnore
(Shutterstock)
Copyright 2022 by Christy Reece
ISBN: 978-1-7337257-7-4

To obtain permission to excerpt portions of the text, please contact the
author at *Christy@christyreece.com*.

HEARTLESS

AN OPTION ZERO NOVEL

The biggest secrets are often held by those we trust the most.

Nicholas Hawthorne, code name Hawke, has lived in the shadows most of his life. The night he met Olivia Gates, a bright light pierced the darkness, and his life was never the same. Opposites in everything except what mattered, they formed an extraordinary bond based on mutual goals, unfailing trust, and most of all love. Their partnership was legendary, their devotion to each other unshakable. They believed nothing could tear them apart. But evil has a way of seeking out perfection with the intent to destroy.

Evil thought it had won.

Olivia Gates learned betrayal at an early age, and life had taught her that nothing was permanent or perfect. When she met Hawke, all those lessons went out the window. He was her soul mate, the other half of her heart. She would love him forever, no matter what. But forever is a long time. How could she have forgotten that betrayal can shatter a heart in an instant?

Returning from the dead was never Hawke's intent. The elaborate ruse was staged for myriad reasons, but now he has no choice but to come in from the cold. Enemies he's spent years hunting are on the move, and catching them is his sole focus. The woman he loves—the woman he would die for—is their primary target, and he'll do whatever it takes to keep her safe. The fact that she hates him cannot hinder his goal.

As enemies surround them, Hawke and Olivia have a choice to make—let the past destroy them forever or join forces and fight the enemy together.

Their love is eternal, but survival is optional.

"Show me a hero, and I'll write you a tragedy."
–F. Scott Fitzgerald

"In the process of letting go, you will lose many things from the past, but you will find yourself."
–Deepak Chopra

PROLOGUE

Nashville, Tennessee
Twenty-eight months ago

He would be here soon.

Excitement zoomed through her, and she could only laugh with sheer joy at the feeling. How long had it been since she'd felt this young and carefree? Years?

Silly, really. She wasn't all that old, but in many ways, she felt ancient. Having seen more death and destruction than one should see in a hundred lifetimes had done that. Well, that along with running for her life more times than she could count. A person in covert ops didn't get a lot of downtime to think about dating and the more enjoyable things of life.

That was going to change, though. She was out of that business for good. No black ops. No hiding in an underground bunker for days on end, waiting for rescue or a way to escape. No more MREs and bad coffee, and no more bedbugs! She could go where she wanted to go, eat what she wanted to eat, and sleep all day long if she so desired. Not that she would do that. A lifetime of discipline would have her up before dawn each day, but at least it wasn't to go out to some hellhole filled with blood and grief.

Yes, from now on, life would be filled with joy, not sadness.

Her team had been surprised that she'd left the spy game. She had been in the business since she was twenty years old. She had loved parts of it. There was nothing more challenging than outwitting evil. But it was time for her to live—time to see how normal people lived. She had to say that, so far, it didn't suck.

Layla Templeton stood in front of the mirror and preened. She was a pretty woman, no one could deny that fact. Obtaining intel from people sometimes involved seduction, and she had often used her looks to get what she needed. No more, though. When she dressed up now, it would be for herself—and perhaps her lover, maybe even a husband someday. But using her beauty for anything devious was in the past.

The summer dress was feminine and on the frilly side. She twirled, enjoying how the material danced around her legs like gossamer clouds. Her legs, among her best features, looked spectacular in the three-inch pale peach heels. Her thick auburn hair—also one of her assets—had grown longer over the past couple of months, now reaching almost to her shoulders. She wanted to grow it out, long and flowing. She'd always worn it short for convenience and time. But now she had all the time in the world.

She leaned forward and examined her face. Was she wearing too much makeup? She had wanted to look fresh and natural, which surprisingly took more time than she'd anticipated. She took a step back, deciding she didn't care. She liked her look, and that was all that mattered.

Olivia would be so pleased to know that Layla had a date.

She hadn't talked to her friend in weeks, but as soon as this date ended, she would grab a burner phone and spend hours chitchatting the way girlfriends were supposed to talk.

The other team members didn't yet know she'd moved to Nashville. She wasn't sure why she hadn't told them. It wasn't as if she didn't love all of them—well, most of them— but she and Liv had been the only two women on a seven-person team. They had shared secrets their male counterparts would never understand. Someday soon, she might let the others know, but for right now, it was just between the two of them.

The doorbell rang. She glanced at the clock on her dresser. Yikes, he was fifteen minutes early. It was a good thing she was always early, too. Being late in the spy game was never a good thing. She grinned at her reflection then turned away. Feeling ridiculously giddy, she headed to the door.

She was anxious to see if he was as cute as she remembered after meeting him yesterday. The mysterious man with the engaging grin and studious glasses had bumped into her at the coffee shop, causing her to spill her latte all over him. He had apologized profusely, and before she'd known it, they'd been sitting across from each other, talking like old friends. Never had she felt such an immediate connection.

Two hours later, they'd taken their leave from each other, but not before making a date for the next night. This was going to be a brand-new adventure for her. New city. New home. New man.

Happy for the first time in forever, she opened the door. In an instant, she jerked back, the smile of welcome freezing on her face as she stared up at her worst nightmare.

"What…"

· · ·

"Whaaaat?" he said mockingly. "You used to be much more verbose."

She took another step back, and he watched as she prepared to spring into action. She was one of the most lethal women he'd ever known. He'd had a hand in helping her get that way, so he knew what to expect.

He was on her before she could make her next move. Twisting both her arms behind her back, he slammed the door shut with his foot. And then he just looked down at her, grinning. "It's been a long time, baby."

"Not long enough," she gritted out.

"Is that any way to treat an old lover? I just knew you'd be overjoyed to see me."

A smile spread across her face, erasing her earlier antipathy. "I am. Let me go, and let's have ourselves a little reunion."

He marveled at her skill. Instead of looking terrified, she now seemed calm, almost happy to see him. It was a lie, of course. They hadn't parted as friends. Had never been friendly even during their short stint as lovers. But all of that was water under the bridge now. He had a job to do—and she was the job.

"Sorry, sweets. No time for hugs and kisses."

He had her body locked so those lethal arms and legs of hers were rendered useless. He took a moment and stared down into her fathomless eyes. Hatred, pure unadulterated hatred, spat from their depths. She truly was an exceptional-looking woman. So much life and fire in her animated features. What would those features look like when she was no longer breathing? He squeezed tighter, suddenly eager to find out.

The glimpse of fear he saw in her face was a powerful motivator. It took less than a minute to do the deed. Her broken body slipped from his arms and collapsed onto the floor.

He looked down at her. He'd once felt affection for her. Maybe he'd even been in love. Since he'd never loved anyone, maybe he just hadn't recognized the emotion. He'd never killed a friend before. Yeah, he'd killed people he knew, but none of them had been people he'd actually felt anything but hatred for. But this one? Yeah, she had been different.

Not that it mattered. A kill was a kill. He'd been sent to take her out, and he'd accomplished his objective. It'd been harder to find her than anticipated. Which was one of the reasons he'd been brought in to do the job. Having an intimate knowledge of the target was always a good way to find your prey.

She'd drunk tea every night before she went to bed. A common enough occurrence, with one exception. It was a special brand of tea. So special that only one shop—in Kolkata, India—carried that specific blend. Few people knew about her preference, which was why she'd probably felt so safe when she had ordered a new batch last week to be delivered to Nashville. Hacking into the shop's files to get her address had been ridiculously simple.

No one else would have even known to do this. He had proven himself a loyal soldier, a valuable ally. Just one more way he was demonstrating his worth to his employer.

Glancing around the small apartment, he noted she'd actually started nesting here. Colorful throw pillows, some fragile-looking knickknacks on the mantel, and even a photo of her family when she was a child. In her former life, that would have been a no-no. Even though her family was long dead, revealing the slightest bit of personal data could spell disaster. So yeah, she'd definitely begun to feel at home here. Safe.

Pity.

With a shrug, he turned toward the door. Even though he'd gotten the job done, completing the first step in the mission, he felt little satisfaction. He'd once had a fondness for the girl, so the triumph was bittersweet at best. But the next ones? Oh yes, the next ones would definitely bring him the satisfaction this one was missing.

Closing the door, he left the apartment, cheerfully anticipating what lay ahead.

The next kill would be on the other side of the country. With three safe houses already set up, he'd have no problem moving from one state to the other. His targets were professionals, so there would be surveillance needed to ensure he made the hit sudden and unexpected. No one would see him coming.

He'd parked two blocks away in a large store parking lot. It was a lazy, late summer afternoon in downtown Nashville. People were getting off work, headed to restaurants and clubs, eager to put their day behind them. No one noticed an attractive, albeit rather scruffy-looking, man ambling down the sidewalk. He was just one of many.

He was half a block away from the parking lot where he'd left his car when he realized he was being followed. Instinctively, he moved his hand toward his gun, but before he could reach it, two giants shoved him into an alleyway. He half turned to get a quick view, and the bullet caught him in the temple. He never got the chance to wonder who would want him dead or why he had been betrayed. He was dead in an instant.

It took seconds to load the man into the van and speed away.

CHAPTER ONE

Present Day
Mexico City, Mexico

The bearded man moved through the zealous, celebratory crowd. No one paid him attention. No one saw anything he didn't want them to see. He noticed everyone…aware of every movement, every nuance. Every face, every gesture was observed and measured. Threats could come from anywhere, anyone. Some of the most lethal came wrapped in silk and satin. He knew this all too well.

His face was obscured by a heavy beard, a baseball cap covered his brown hair, and his clothes were dark, unassuming. Everything about him said he was alone and wanted to stay that way. No one would dare approach him. He was barely a face in the crowd.

Nicholas Hawthorne, or Hawke to everyone who knew him, had been moving through cities and countries like this for half his life. It was second nature, and if a part of him felt as if this was his destiny, another part believed it was his punishment. He had glimpsed heaven, and instead of hanging on to it with all his might, he'd allowed it to drift away. Now it was merely a memory—perhaps even a fantasy. Had it ever been real?

The pain had been real, that was for damn sure.

A flash of golden hair caught his eye. The din around him ceased to exist. He held his breath. His only awareness was the hard pounding of his heart followed by an ache so deep and raw he felt it to his bones.

The woman slowly turned, and for a scant moment, his heart and breath stopped. An odd combination of joy mixed with rage surged through him. She shouldn't be here… It was too dangerous. How had she found him? How did she know—

Seconds later, his mind acknowledged that he was looking at the face of a stranger.

Breath rattled through his chest in an exhalation of both relief and disappointment. And if that wasn't the stupidest reaction, he didn't know what was.

He shook it off, and life around him resumed.

He was long past seeing her face every time he spotted a golden-haired woman, but on occasion, the steel that encased his heart weakened, the longing would seep inside, and he would see her everywhere. The flash of a slender hand as a woman spoke with animation. Husky laughter that sounded both joyous and sensuous. And the hair—glorious golden hair, which had often draped over his bare chest when they'd lain in bed. He used to complain, jokingly, that she slept on him more than she slept on the bed. He hadn't minded, though. Opening his eyes first thing in the morning and seeing her head nestled against him, her hair splayed over him, had been one of the delights of his life.

Cursing himself for getting lost in the memories, he continued toward his destination. The clock was ticking. If this didn't pay off this time, if he didn't get the intel he needed to put these bastards down once and for all, then he would have to do what he had sworn he would never do. He was going to have to return from the dead.

Being dead had held many advantages. He could see events no one thought he could see, do things no one could imagine could be done—all because he didn't exist.

Some part of him was desperate to return—it was a need he fought against daily. He wanted answers. A no-holds-barred, face-to-face confrontation until truth bled all over them. He'd been waiting too long.

Another part, though, told him he already knew the truth, and he'd gotten exactly what he deserved.

He stopped a half block from his destination and studied the area. Not the safest neighborhood, but not the worst either. Tall buildings with offices for various businesses blended with smaller structures holding tattoo parlors, delis, and pawn shops. At half past one in the morning, this area of the city was quiet except for those looking to cause trouble.

According to his intel, the meeting was to take place in one of the taller buildings up the block. He noted that the building was dark with the exception of the third floor. Understandably, a meeting between a major drug cartel and the Mexican Mafia needed secrecy as well as privacy. With no visible vehicles or people around, the light could simply be evidence of a cleaning crew. But Hawke knew that was not the case. There were likely more than a dozen hidden soldiers from both sides looking for threats.

Since he didn't have his own army—or a death wish—he had no intention of causing any problems. As far as he was concerned, the meeting could go on without a hitch. He was, in fact, happy that it was taking place. It was the aftermath of the meeting that most concerned him. Because in there, in the midst of the meeting of evil, there were answers. And he was damn well going to get them or die trying.

Knowing any kind of sudden movement this close to the building would attract attention, Hawke ducked into an alleyway. He still had a good line of sight, but any lookouts wouldn't be able to spot him from here. Leaning against the wall, he crossed his arms and waited. The meeting was likely about to commence. Who knew how long it would last? Hell, he wasn't completely sure what the meeting was supposed to accomplish. He knew only that the Gonzalez cartel had envoys inside, and one of them was about to have a really bad night.

Shifting his leg, he winced at the twinge in his knee. Last night's workout had been rougher than usual. His physical therapist had warned him not to overdo, but it had felt good at the time. Now, not so much. A twisted, bitter part of him relished the pain. It was a grim but good reminder of everything he'd lost and every single lie he had believed.

His eyes stayed focused on the third floor. He could see shadows moving by the windows—guards, most likely. He spotted a few on the ground level. Their cigarettes glowed like beacons in the dark. Arrogant idiots thought they were invisible.

An hour later, he spotted more activity. SUVs rolled in front of the building, and multiple people piled inside. Hawke inched closer. Thanks to his informant, the vehicle his target was driving would have a fluorescent glow on the left rear tire.

If one individual knew the goings-on of the major new player in drug trafficking, it would be the head of security for the Gonzalez cartel. The man would have attended every meeting. He should be able to tell Hawke exactly where the cartel was getting its funding and who was running the operation.

His stride swift but steady, he stayed in the shadows and moved toward his target. Ten feet away, he spotted him.

Dressed in dark clothing, his head covered with a hoodie, the man definitely didn't want to attract attention. Two odd things struck Hawke simultaneously. One, the man was surprisingly smaller than he'd anticipated. The guy couldn't be over five seven or weigh more than one thirty soaking wet.

Second, this was way too easy. The man was alone—all other security personnel had sped away. Was this a trap? Had he been set up once again?

He had a split-second decision to make—call off this op and try again some other time, or take his chances and complete the capture. There really was no decision to make, though. This had been going on for way too long. He wanted answers, and this man had them.

Hawke sprang into action. Grabbing hold of the man's arm, he jerked him backward and threw a hood over his head. The man let loose a string of muffled curses and kicked back. Hawke managed to avoid a groin kick, but the kick to his knee almost took him to the ground.

Growling furiously, he said, "Calm down, or I'll knock you out."

The man stopped struggling and went ominously still. Hawke didn't loosen his hold, but a new knowledge was hitting him, and his mind scoured for answers. Before he could comprehend the ramifications, a sharp elbow jabbed his gut.

Cursing softly, he held his captive tight with one arm, and with his other, he grabbed the syringe in his pocket. He hadn't planned on being this gentle. A concussion, bloodletting, or a few broken bones had been part of his plan. Not anymore.

His hold tight, he pressed the syringe into his captive's neck, making sure only half its contents were dispensed. At half the weight he'd expected, the smaller dosage should be more than enough to ensure unconsciousness for several hours.

As the body in his arms slumped, he loosened his hold and then lowered his captive to the ground. His curiosity piqued, he ripped off the hood, wanting to see just who he had captured.

What the hell?

Breath caught in his lungs, and a gnawing pit of dread developed in his gut. While a whole new set of questions whirled in his thoughts, the question of whether he would have to return from the dead had just been answered.

There was no way he could stay away now.

CHAPTER TWO

Charlottesville, Virginia

They say you heal. They say that over time, the pain somehow lessens. They say you eventually remember just the good times, that the jagged edge of agony is diminished and softened. Wounds heal. They scab over and form scars. There's evidence of past pain, of trauma, but the agony of the wound no longer exists.

They say that someday you'll smile again and be grateful for the time you spent together.

Olivia Gates knew all these things very well. She'd read the books, watched all the self-help videos. They had said a lot of things. That didn't mean they were true. Not for everyone. Especially not for her.

Death was part of life. It came to everyone, and we either accepted it and moved on, or let it destroy us. Olivia knew exactly where she was on that particular spectrum, and it wasn't on the good side.

Her mother, on the other hand, held the opposite position. She was a big proponent of the moving-on philosophy.

When her husband, Glen, Olivia's father, had been killed in the line of duty, Iris had continued working as though nothing untoward had happened.

Olivia was not her mother. That was something she had strived to avoid her entire life. But in this instance, she actually wished she had a little more of Iris Gates's coldheartedness inside her. It would have been very helpful, especially right about now.

Her hands shaking, Olivia had to concentrate to get the key into the lock. When it finally clicked and she turned the knob, the tension lessened in her muscles. It was almost as if the house were welcoming her home after all this time. No one lived here. The house had been empty for weeks, had been on the market for months. The family who had lived here had relocated, leaving it in the hands of a realtor. The downturn of the economy promised that it would likely stay empty for a while longer.

She pushed open the door, and in her mind's eye, she could see everything the way it used to be. The way it had been before all was lost. Even though the living room was empty, she saw the massive sofa in front of the fireplace. The sofa had been so large that two grown adults could fall asleep in each other's arms. Snuggled together in front of a roaring fire, they could forget the world existed. Something they'd done numerous times. As long as they'd had each other, they hadn't needed anything or anyone else.

A chair had sat a few feet away from the sofa, a small table with a good reading lamp beside it. Back then, she'd been a voracious reader, and that had been her reading spot. Directly across from that chair had been a large recliner, one that a big male body could sprawl out on and catnap after a long hard day. How many times had she been reading and looked over to see him snoozing in that chair?

It all sounded staid and boring, but it hadn't been. Their

jobs were demanding and dangerous, so when they were home, comfort and relaxation had been their top priority.

She took another step inside and then stopped. Seriously. What was she doing here? What did any of this do but remind her of what she'd lost? What she could never have again? Grief had consumed her for over two years, and just when she'd almost come to terms with what had happened, she had decided to come back here and bring it all back again? Just what kind of masochist was she?

Even as she lectured herself on the sheer stupidity of her actions, she closed the door behind her and took several more steps into the house.

Memories swamped her, and she automatically reached for the doorknob behind her in an effort to escape the pain. A voice in her head stopped her. That voice, gravelly and low, whispered softly, *What are you afraid of, Livvy?*

He had said that to her the day she'd finally admitted her feelings to him. She had denied them for so long, and he of infinite patience had finally grown tired of her denials and confronted her. She had been afraid to admit her love. Having grown up in a household where expressing affection was tantamount to admitting you were human, she had resisted. Even as every fiber of her being was shouting at her to tell him, still she had resisted.

If she had known what was to happen, would she still do it? Would she have given her heart to him, given her everything to him, knowing that in only a few years it would be crushed to dust? She wanted to say no, but she was unfailingly honest and could give herself only a little leeway by admitting that she just didn't know.

Nicholas Hawthorne had been larger than life. From the moment she'd met him, he had fascinated her. *Dynamic* and *forceful* were two of the adjectives she'd heard used to describe the man named Hawke, so when she'd met him, she had been prepared. The description had been true, but that wasn't what had stunned her. What she hadn't been able to get her head around was his lack of ego. Others might have held him in high esteem, but for Hawke, his heroic actions were all in a day's work.

She would never forget their first meeting. They'd both been on an undercover job, though neither of them had known it at the time. The instant she'd heard his voice, something happened inside her—something she had never been able to explain. She only knew her life had changed in that moment.

She hadn't learned who he was until months later. She had taken an assignment to liaise with an off-the-books special ops unit in the US. It turned out Hawke was the team leader and was not remotely happy to have her in his unit. She had felt the same way...for a while.

Even now, after all these years and after all the pain, she could smile at how very much she'd disliked Nicholas Hawthorne that first day on the job.

It hadn't been long before he'd changed her mind.

Shaking off those memories, Olivia continued through the house. The interior had been updated quite a bit, with a kitchen remodel, new bathroom fixtures, and light gray wall colors as opposed to the ice blue she remembered. The hardwood floors had a nice sheen to them, but the scuff marks from the dining room table were still there, as was the dent left from when the movers set her piano down too quickly. She hadn't noticed the dent until they'd moved out of the house eighteen months later.

Time had flown in the tiny house, and love had grown. Here, they had been Livvy and Nic. So crazy in love, so wild for one another, they had needed nothing but each other. There had been an abundance of laughter and a minimum of tears here. She could count on one hand the number of times they'd argued.

That had come later.

Her footsteps now at a steady, even pace, she peered into each room she passed. Memories swept over her of small, seemingly inconsequential events. Looking back on them now was a reminder of how love was supposed to be. How had they messed it up so badly? A twisted, self-condemning voice whispered inside her, *You know.*

Shaking off the pain, she reached the bedroom and stopped at the doorway, unable to make herself walk any farther. This was too much. Too many memories. This was the place of love and passion. So many wonderful memories, more than passion—even more than love. Devotion, tenderness, an all-encompassing commitment to each other that she would have sworn with her last breath could never be broken. Until it was. The happy times of the past couldn't erase the hideous pain that came after.

Backing away quietly as if to avoid disturbing those glorious memories, Olivia backtracked to the front door. Once there, she opened it, stepped onto the porch, and let loose a long, gasping breath. She closed the door, and leaning her forehead against the wooden frame, she whispered softly, "Happy anniversary, my love."

As if demons were chasing her, she turned abruptly and ran as fast as she could to her car, hitting the remote starter on the way. She threw herself into the driver's seat, shifted into drive, and spun out of the driveway.

She never looked in the rearview mirror. If she had, she might've seen the shadow of a man at the edge of the yard— an ominous warning that the past could never be truly buried.

CHAPTER THREE

Alexandria, Virginia

Fighting a yawn, Olivia pushed open her apartment door. It had been an exhausting day of running down leads and research. She enjoyed that part of her job at Last Chance Rescue—it was like solving mysteries with clues she dug up from nothing. However, it could be as exhausting as kicking down doors and rounding up human traffickers, just in a different way. Her mind, more than her body, needed a break. All she wanted to do was pour a glass of wine, slip into a fragrant bubble bath, and relax.

Part of the problem was the trip she'd taken three days ago. The sadness she kept inside her, which she had never shared with anyone, had been exacerbated. Why she had done that, she didn't know. It had been her first time back there since she'd lost Nic, and it had done nothing but cause more nightmares. Last night's had been especially harrowing. Not having answers caused her unconscious mind to work overtime, creating the most horrific scenarios and events. Would she ever know the truth?

She opened the fridge and grabbed the bottle of Riesling she'd uncorked yesterday and halted abruptly. Telling herself she should leave the past behind was one thing. Actually living it was something else. The contents of the refrigerator told the tale. Half the fridge was filled with foods that only Nic would have eaten. His favorite kind of cheeses, red grapes—instead of the white ones she preferred—and his favorite kind of mayo. And why, oh, why did she continue to purchase his brand of beer when she didn't even like beer?

She turned and took in the kitchen and living room area. The furniture was the same. The sofa was much too large for the small space, and the chair she'd loved to read in was stuck in a corner because that was the only place it fit. Even the few knickknacks—a crystal vase they'd picked up in Madrid, the carving of a bird from Tibet—that she and Nic had accumulated in their travels, were displayed the way they'd been when they'd lived together.

She hadn't moved on. Yes, she lived somewhere else and worked for only one employer, but those two things were the only real changes she had made. She was living in limbo, as if expecting Nic to walk through that door any minute. Those days of hope had ceased, yet she was still living as though she had some.

That had to stop. She had to let go of everything—let go of him. It was time she accepted that he wasn't coming back. All the searching, all the begging for information, and all the tears were not going to bring back a dead man. Nic was gone, and she had to accept it.

Grim determination driving her, she grabbed a box from the hall closet and began to fill it with items from the past. A few she couldn't let go of—the wood carving of a couple embracing that Nic had given her on their first anniversary, the blown glass jar of emerald she'd fallen in love with on their honeymoon in Germany, and the ugly purple and orange stuffed orangutan she had felt sorry for in an open-air market in Tanzania. She had remarked on how sad and lonely it looked, and he'd gone back and purchased it, surprising her with it the next day. Those things were too precious, too dear to give away. But the rest… Yes, the rest could go.

It was two thirty in the morning before she turned off the lights. She fell into bed and into the deepest sleep she'd had in years, feeling lighter and less burdened by the sadness that had haunted her for so long.

The click of the door lock woke her. In an instant, Olivia was on alert. Her hand went to the gun on her bedside table. Sliding out of bed, her feet bare and swift, she went on the hunt.

The intruders were quiet. She had a brief moment of regret that she'd left her phone on the nightstand. One press of a button would have alerted her LCR team that she was in trouble. They would have come running. That's what she got for always trying to handle things by herself. She could practically hear Nic's gruff words in her ear. *Being a one-woman army can only get you so far, baby.*

Since she'd set the security alarm when she'd walked into the apartment, it was apparent that her visitors were also professionals. Her alarm system was state-of-the-art. They obviously knew what they were doing.

But so did she. Not only had she been trained by the best, she had been doing mixed martial arts for over half her life. She knew how to take care of herself, and she knew how to turn a surprise attack around.

Total darkness surrounded her, but she knew every inch of the apartment, had committed every squeak in the floor and every creak of a door to memory. Having been hunted for a good part of her adult life had given her the impetus of preparedness.

They were in the living room, skulking toward the bedroom. Four of them. Their footsteps might sound silent to them but not to her. They were moving swiftly, which told her they were wearing night-vision goggles. She judged each one weighed a good one eighty to two twenty.

Four men would be a challenge even for her. Her best bet was to attack first—getting them off their game was a must.

With her back nestled in the corner of the hallway, she waited. Her heart raced, her adrenaline pumped. The instant they entered the bedroom, she flipped the light switch. Curses flew, and so did she. Striking the closest one, she went for a double punch—face and gut—followed by another kick to the gut. A hand tugged at her shoulder, and she whirled, punched, and kicked. He barely grunted and returned her assault with a slug to her jaw. She heard her gun fall and skitter across the hardwood floor. Seeing stars from the blow, she barely registered the pain as she came back at him full force, kicking and punching. She knew she was losing, but she wasn't going to go down without causing some major pain.

The approach of the third attacker barely registered. She turned to confront the new threat but stopped short when a searing pain electrified her entire body. A small part of her brain recognized she'd been tasered, but doing anything other than riding out the pain was impossible. Her entire body was not her own for several agonizing seconds.

Large, rough hands picked her up, and she fought with all her might to make her limbs move. They were taking her somewhere. The very idea that she was being abducted was stunning. This was something she had been prepared for, and part of her brain was infuriated at her inability to fight back. Another part of her brain analyzed her chances of survival. She had to hold her ground here. She could not leave this apartment with them.

Her muscles still stunned with immobility, she ground her teeth until her jaws ached as she managed to throw up a fist and make contact with one of the men carrying her. She heard a grunt, but there was no stopping their progress.

Surprising her, they didn't carry her out the door but stopped in the kitchen. She heard a chair being pulled out from her kitchen table. One of the men pushed her down to sit, while another held her body still. Her hands and then her feet were tied to the chair, and a slab of duct tape covered her mouth.

Her eyes spitting fire, she looked up at her tormentors. Their faces were covered with ski masks, so their intention wasn't to kill. She, however, wanted to see their faces. Because she did intend to kill.

One of them, the most slender of the four, squatted in front of her. Though she couldn't see his face, his eyes were gleaming with what looked like amusement. The tone of his voice confirmed this. "I was told you were a wild hellcat. I am pleased that the intel was accurate."

His accent was Albanian, northern province. Elite education in the US or possibly England. Age between thirty-five and forty-five. She had a master's degree in linguistics and over a decade of real-world experience in parsing the nuances in speech patterns.

"I'm sure you are wondering why we are here. However, as we are short on time and our needs override yours, I will be brief. You are Olivia Gates. Your aliases are Sonia Gomesky, Daniela Rostov…"

As she listened to the list of aliases she'd used in the past, she learned something intriguing. She hadn't used any of those in years. They were over a decade old—some older. Sonia had been her first alias. When he stopped at six, she learned something else. He knew nothing about her current work. This was all related to her former job—her former life.

"You see, we know who you worked for and what you did. What we don't know are the names of your assets. That's what you're going to tell us."

Now she was even more confused. Those assets were either long dead or out of the spy business. Why would they be important after all this time?

"I can see your confusion, and while I would love to sit and chat about the why of things, I'm afraid there just isn't time."

Ripping the tape from her mouth, he said softly, "Speak, and then we'll be gone."

Old intel or not, there was no way she would give these bastards any information. Her eyes cold, she stared straight ahead.

The man released a sigh and then swung the back of his hand across her face. As punches went, it wasn't particularly hard, but it hurt like hell. She'd definitely have bruising, but nothing was broken yet.

"That was a mild taste of what you can expect if you continue to be noncompliant. Again, I ask you, what were the names of your assets when you worked for the British government?"

Remaining silent was an effort, as she wanted to turn the tables and ask some questions of her own. What did these people know? Were they Nic's killers? Adrenaline surged through her at the fantasy of loosening her bonds and finding out the truth.

Another slug came… This time much harder. Her eyes watered, and blood filled her mouth. Might've loosened some teeth with that one.

"Speak!" the man shouted.

Instead of speaking, she gathered bloody saliva and spat it at him. Blood covered the man's ski mask. A roar of outrage followed, and then new agony began as fists came at her left and right. Disassociating oneself from pain was a learned skill—one that required constant honing. She hadn't practiced lately, and it was showing.

"Stop!" a man barked.

The blows ceased, but the pain continued. Bruised ribs, maybe a dislocated jaw.

"She isn't going to talk without incentive," someone said.

Through bleary, watery eyes, she watched one of the men open a black bag and remove a needle filled with liquid.

Oh hell no.

Her struggles began in earnest. She couldn't let them drug her. She could fight pain, but she had no way to control her tongue under the influence. Somebody slapped more tape over her mouth, and while three men held her still, the fourth jammed the needle into her arm.

Warmth flooded her body, and behind the tape, she screamed obscenities and threats. Seconds later, an icy coldness replaced the warm flush, and she began to shiver.

"I'm told that's the worst part. First the heat and then the cold."

She glared up at the beast who'd done this, shooting murderous thoughts from her eyes. She might not be able to do anything now, but if she survived this ordeal, she wouldn't rest until these bastards were dead.

Blurred images appeared before her eyes, and her mind muddled with the bizarre and obscure. Holding a thought in her head for more than a few seconds became a challenge, and she chased after them as though she were running for her life. A dull flash of pain in her face brought her head up briefly. A monster in a mask stood before her, and she opened her mouth to scream. Only a moan emerged.

Olivia dropped her head, her chin on her chest, her entire body limp.

"She's under."

"Good."

Her dulled mind recognized the voice was one she hadn't heard before.

The sound of thundering feet penetrated her consciousness, but she couldn't make herself raise her head. Voices came and went. There were shouts, curses, grunts of pain.

A hand touched her neck, and she heard a soft, growling curse. Despite her drugged state, her heart leaped at the sound.

"Sorry, boss," a man said in a breathless voice. "They all got away except this one."

"Take him back to the house and find out what was in the needle they gave her."

"You want me to stay?"

"No. I'm good."

Voices cut in and out of her consciousness. Her mind was still, filled with white noise, the pain in her body dulled, but she heard something...someone. The sound came knocking at her brain, telling her to wake up, to pay attention. She fought the sluggishness, the need to just drift away.

Her hands and feet were released. Strong, muscular arms lifted her, and she was floating through the air. Her head nestled against something hard and warm, something familiar. She heard a thud—the thud of life. A small voice in her brain told her that the sound was significant, but her brain wouldn't function, couldn't reason why.

The world whirled as her mind struggled to comprehend. Blurred images swirled around her, and she blinked rapidly, fighting against the need to close her eyes. She had to see... She needed to see. Her eyes refused to cooperate, and she muttered a frustrated moan.

"Shh," the voice said. "You're all right now."

Though she couldn't comprehend what was happening,

that deep voice assuring her that she was all right lessened the agitation building within her.

Softness beneath her and the familiar smell of lavender-scented sheets brought more comfort. Pain continued to be present but distant—a dull reminder that something had happened and wasn't right.

With a sigh, she succumbed to the lethargic pull of the drug and drifted away. A second before unconsciousness took her, she felt warm lips against her forehead and heard an achingly familiar voice whisper, "I'm sorry, Livvy."

CHAPTER FOUR

F rustration fueling every step, Hawke strode out of the house where he'd been living for the past few days. Wasn't much to look at, but it had a big basement, which served as an excellent interrogation room. This wasn't the first prisoner they'd questioned here, nor the most annoying. However, they needed answers, and no matter how many times he asked, Hawke knew he wasn't going to get what he needed. The man was a mercenary, hired to do a job without any real idea of why. Hawke had run across hundreds like him, and they were rarely given any intel. They didn't want it. They wanted only to do the job, get the money, and move on. This guy was worthless to him. He'd keep him here, under guard, and decide later what to do with him. For now, he had bigger fish to fry.

His heart told him to go to Olivia and assure himself she was okay. The beating she'd taken had been mostly surface injuries, but that didn't still his need to see for himself. One would think he'd be past caring, but one would be wrong. When it came to Olivia Gates, there was no such thing as not caring. Even when he had hated her, he had cared.

But his head—which he told himself was a lot saner than his heart—told him she was fine. She'd been dealt worse and had gotten up the next day to do it all over again.

So he was going to follow what his head told him to do. He would go to Montana and face the OZ team. It was not going to be pleasant. First, they'd be shocked, and then they'd be pissed. They had every right to feel that way.

He had never been one to hold back intel. Had always been of the philosophy that if you trusted a person with your life, then you sure should trust them with your secrets. In this, he'd had no choice. If they had known what was going on, nothing would have stopped them from getting involved, making them targets. One or more of them could have gotten killed. He couldn't have risked that. Yeah, they faced death every day, but this had been his mess to clean up. Unfortunately, it had just gotten messier.

Despite his seemingly sound reasons for not telling them his plan, he had no choice but to involve them now.

Olivia would come to Montana soon, too. She would arrive, demanding answers. That was fine. He'd give her some, but he was going to get some answers of his own.

She would take extra precautions now that she knew she'd been compromised. He'd had security on her, and they'd managed to get to her anyway. They hadn't wanted to kill her. Information had been what they were looking for, but she'd had none to give them. Dammit, he should have seen this coming…should have put even more security on her. This was all on him, because what they wanted was something only he could give.

And if they knew he wasn't dead after all, he was living on borrowed time. And so was Olivia.

~

OLIVIA WOKE GRADUALLY, her eyes so heavy she was sure rocks were sitting on them. When she finally got them open, her vision was blurred for several seconds. Whatever she'd been given had delivered a powerful punch. She made herself lie still for several long moments as she tried to regain her sense of self. Shadowy memories of pain and anger swirled around her. Then she remembered a gravelly, masculine voice and strong, sure hands, both achingly familiar. Nic—he had been here. She knew his touch, knew his voice. He had rescued her.

Her husband was *alive*.

Willing herself not to think about that right now, she forced her body to move. She made it to the bathroom where she didn't bother to undress before stepping into the shower and turning the cold water on full force. After a couple of minutes, she switched to warmer water and yanked off her wet nightgown. The cold water had woken her, and now the hot water eased the pain from the multitude of bruises. She stood beneath the flood for a full five minutes, her mind deliberately blank.

Feeling almost human again, she turned off the water and snagged the towel hanging on the peg beside the shower door. She dried off quickly and, catching a glimpse of herself in the mirror, groaned out loud. Yeah, they'd done a bang-up job. A black eye, bruises on both jaws, and an extra dark one on her chin. The bruises on her ribs were thankfully not as bad as she'd feared. Breathing wasn't too painful, so no cracked ribs this time. Various bruises on her thighs, an ugly one on her left shoulder.

She looked like an abuse victim. But she was no victim.

Who these people had been and what they'd wanted was still a mystery. Their questions had been both specific and bizarre. Why would they want names of assets that were almost a decade old? Nothing about this made sense.

Turning from the mirror, she pulled a large T-shirt from the closet and slipped it over her head. She'd dress fully later. For now, she needed three things—a gallon of black coffee, ibuprofen for her aches, and a clear, focused mind.

Two cups of coffee later, her mind was now clear and alert. She shoved aside questions about the reason for last night's attack and allowed herself to face the miraculous truth—her husband was alive. Despite the hurt, the anger, the soul-rending sense of betrayal, she could not stop the rush of relief and joy at the knowledge.

Nic was alive!

Another cup of coffee later, she reviewed the facts. What she had been told. What she knew to be true. What she suspected.

How many people knew he was alive? Kate, most definitely. Kate Walker, friend and ally, had been their go-between. She and Nic had brought Kate in on their plan from the start. Had Kate been played, too, or were she and Nic both in on the deception?

If so, why? What could be the reason to keep her out of the loop? She had been a major player and had as much, if not more, to lose if the plan had gone awry. Why would she have been kept in the dark?

Was it because of what had happened before? Their personal lives had been in shambles, their marriage essentially over. Had the hurt neither of them had been able to get past colored Nic's perspective so much that he had deliberately shut her out? Had he hated her that much?

Pushing back the pain, she continued to grapple with questions. What about Ash? Did he know, too? Asher Drake was the head of Option Zero. Though she and Nic had agreed to keep him out of their plan, she couldn't help but wonder if she was the only one who'd actually been in the dark.

It had been two years, three months and seven days since she'd last seen her husband's face. She remembered that moment like it was yesterday. He had walked into the small cabin. Seconds later, the cabin had exploded. But seven seconds before the explosion, she had seen him exit out the back, just as they had planned.

From the moment she'd met Nicholas Hawthorne, he had never stopped surprising her. Their first encounter in Munich had been epic. They had both been on missions and had used each other for cover without even knowing why. As if an invisible force were working, they'd been drawn to each other. She'd stolen a kiss from him that night, believing she'd never see him again.

Six months later, she had asked for an assignment as a liaison to a covert government agency in the US. By that time, she had been desperate to get away and had looked upon the opportunity as a godsend. When she arrived and saw that Nic had been in charge of one of the teams, she had been immediately suspicious.

Neither of them had been keen on working together. Even though she had been training for years, she'd had almost no real field experience. Hawke, as everyone called him, had been a seasoned professional, having run numerous missions as both a Navy SEAL and then team leader for several different covert agencies. Having a neophyte on his team had not been his idea.

To his credit, he had never berated or humiliated her when she'd messed up, which she had in those first few months. She had been trained to accept harshness, and when it hadn't come from him, she had somehow believed that he hadn't cared enough to berate her. In time and with the help of her teammates, she had learned that Hawke was not that kind of leader. Because of that, she had become a valuable member of the team much sooner than she had expected.

The team. She had loved them, and they had loved her back. It had been the first time she'd ever felt she was part of a family. The one she'd been born into had been the antithesis of *family.*

The heartache of what had happened to Layla would haunt her till she died. Hawke had felt the same way. In those last days before he had disappeared, that had been the one thing they had both agreed on.

Rising from the kitchen chair, she put away the few kitchen items, allowing her mind to go into neutral. Working out problems in this way was an old routine, and she desperately needed that normalcy today. She dressed for comfort in a pair of cotton pants and a long-sleeved blouse. With all the bruises on both her body and face, there was no way to hide them all. However, she did what she could with makeup and decided that would have to do. Staying inside until they healed was out of the question. She had places to go and people to confront.

Her first call was to Noah McCall. He was head of Last Chance Rescue and her boss. She owed him an explanation. Not only was she going to be out of commission for a while, he needed to know that she had been compromised. She had believed she'd been off the radar and couldn't be found. Now that she knew that wasn't true, he needed to be aware. The last thing she wanted was to put LCR at risk.

Half an hour later, she was standing in front of a hotel room. When she'd requested a meeting away from LCR headquarters, Noah had known immediately something was wrong. In his fashion, he hadn't demanded an explanation. One of the many things she appreciated about Noah McCall was his steadiness.

Taking a breath, she knocked, and Noah opened the door. He was tall, dark, and ruggedly handsome. His coal-black hair had silvery threads running through the thickness that he jokingly attributed to his two children and not to his job as head of Last Chance Rescue.

Years ago, Noah had made rescuing human trafficking victims his life's goal. During that time, he had created an organization that had successfully rescued hundreds of people and brought thousands of traffickers to justice.

His eyes were wide with concern as he took in Olivia's appearance. It was probably good that he had detected that something was wrong earlier. Otherwise, he might've been even more shocked. She had covered up the damage as best she could, but no amount of cosmetics was going to cover everything. The bruised ribs and multiple bruises on her arms and legs were hidden but a painful reminder when she moved too abruptly.

"What the hell happened?" he asked.

She went to one of the chairs in the sitting room and gratefully sat. Despite the pain meds, her head was still pounding from whatever drug she'd been given, and her body felt as though she'd gone a couple of rounds with a heavyweight boxer.

"That's hard to say."

She started from the moment she'd heard the intruders and ended with the moment she'd woken up this morning.

"Did you see any of their faces?"

"No. They all wore ski masks. One of them was Albanian. I'd never heard his voice before. The others had mottled accents—American— but nothing distinct."

"What did they want?"

"They asked me about intel going back to when I worked for the British government."

"That was a long time ago."

"Yes. Most of the people involved are either dead or don't exist in the same roles. It makes no sense."

"And you say some other men rescued you?"

"Yes. I don't think it was long after I was injected with the drug. All the images were blurred, but whoever they were, took care of my attackers fairly quickly."

"Have you seen a doctor yet?"

"No… I—" How to say this without sounding insane?

"You what?"

"One of the men who rescued me… He took care of my injuries."

She only vaguely remembered waking up to the feel of a warm, damp cloth bathing her face and firm, gentle fingers testing her ribs to check for fractures.

"Did you see him?"

She had tried, but her eyes had refused to cooperate. Every time she had told herself to open them, they had opened in little slits, giving her only a blurred glimpse of a tall, broad-shouldered man with a full beard.

But she hadn't needed to see him to know his identity. She had recognized him the moment she'd heard him speak.

"I didn't see him. I heard him, though."

"You know him?"

"Yes."

"Who was it?"

"My husband, Nicholas Hawthorne."

"But I thought—"

"That he was dead? Yes, so did I."

For every second she told herself it wasn't possible, the next second she reminded herself that it was. People faked their deaths all the time. Everything could be faked these days.

Telling herself that he wouldn't have done that to her… that the love they'd once shared, the commitment they'd made to each other, wouldn't have allowed such a betrayal would be a gigantic lie. What they'd had had already been destroyed before he disappeared. She had just not been willing to accept it. With his reappearance, she had no option now but to accept it. All this time, he had been alive and had never contacted her. He had let her believe he was dead.

Noah broke into her tortured thoughts. "We've never talked about his death. I assumed you didn't want to, that it was too painful."

"The official story was that he was killed on a mission."

He raised a brow. "Official?"

"It's complicated."

He settled back into his chair. "All right. Tell it your way."

She explained the plan, the reasons they'd implemented it, and how it was supposed to have worked.

"The ruse was simple and a realistic one. We told everyone we were called back to consult on a previous mission. A terrorist, well known in the intelligence community, had resurfaced. Nic was always good at deep cover and had a lot of experience with this type of op, so the mission looked legitimate. Nic was to go under deep cover again and meet with this terrorist. He would draw him to a meeting place. I would then blow the building, killing the terrorist. The op supposedly went sideways, and the building blew before Nic could get out."

"But that's not what happened," Noah said.

"No. There was no terrorist. We created an entire back-story, complete with photos, family history…the whole nine yards. I had footage showing the building exploding. No one could have survived the blast. If anyone dug deeper, they would only see what we wanted them to find."

"Impressive."

She gave a grim, half smile. "It took some work, but it all went off like clockwork. We needed everyone to believe I was responsible for his death."

How many times had she practiced how she would tell the OZ team what had happened? At least a dozen, if not more. By the time she'd actually said the words, she had sounded as unemotional and uncaring as she had planned. Their regard for her had turned to hatred in an instant.

"I'm sorry, Noah. I probably should have told you all of this long ago."

"When I hired you, I told you I didn't need to know everything about your life, past or present. You've been an exemplary operative, saving lives on almost every mission. I trust you, and as you know, I don't do that easily. Whatever happened, there's a good reason for what you did."

"I thought so at the time. Nic and I were in a bad place. Some things had happened that neither of us was able to get past."

Those last few days had been some of the most painful moments of her life. She and Nic had barely spoken to each other. And that last day, the day before he'd disappeared, he hadn't even been able to look her in the face as he had delivered the final blow.

Had that been part of the plan? Had she missed all the nuances because she'd been hurting so much? Now she would question everything. Every word, every glance, every promise—had they all been lies?

She looked away from Noah's penetrating gaze. There were details she couldn't share and some she was too ashamed to voice. But when your heart was breaking and every breath felt as if shards of glass were clawing at your lungs, you forged ahead and hoped for the best.

Had Nic known that? Counted on that? Had he planned all of this from the outset?

No. Nic had never been one for revenge or pettiness. He was too laser-focused on the job to fall into that trap, but that didn't mean he wouldn't use others' weaknesses against them. Had he used hers? Knowing how she was hurting, had he set her up?

When he had missed his first check-in, she had been concerned but not overly so. Things happened, and in this line of work, you had to improvise. But when he had missed the next one a week later, she had known something had gone sideways. Problem was, no one could, or would, tell her anything.

Kate had assured her that she hadn't heard from him either. They had discussed what might have happened. Kate had told her that she'd sent people out looking for him—that she was doing everything she could to find him.

Olivia had gone on her own several times. Starting from where he'd planned to be that first week, she had searched, asked questions, dug as deep as she could. Nothing had come up. It was as if he'd dissolved into thin air. That was the problem with searching for a man with Hawke's skills. If he didn't want to be found, he wouldn't be. Her husband was a master of disguises, and his deep-cover talents were second to none. She had just never considered that he would use them against her.

"How long has your husband been gone?"

"A little over two years."

"Does anyone else know he's alive?"

"Yes, but I don't know how many."

Olivia accepted the other betrayals with equanimity. Why shouldn't she? When you'd been deceived by the one person you trusted most in the world, what did another, lesser betrayal matter?

NOAH HEARD the pain behind the words. Olivia Gates was the coolest, least emotional of all his operatives. He had always clocked that up to her upbringing. Being raised by spies to be a spy would definitely make one wary to reveal anything one didn't want to reveal.

But the pain showed now. In her face, her voice. The clenched fists she made as she relayed her story told a tale of extreme emotional trauma.

He could only imagine the pain and loneliness she must have felt. He rarely went more than a few hours without talking to his wife. A year or so back, Mara and their children had been abducted. Each breath he'd taken until they were returned to him had felt like razor blades slicing into his heart. Olivia had been living with this pain for over two years.

"I'm sorry," he offered. "I wish you had shared what was going on."

She gave a halfhearted shrug, and he wondered if she knew how even that little gesture showed the depth of her hurt.

"I was taught that sharing information, especially personal, was tantamount to being a traitor. Stupid, I know, but what you grow up with sticks with you, whether you tell yourself to get over it or not. It always seems to be there, hovering."

Noah knew that was all too true. It was something he'd fought against his entire life, until he'd met his Mara. She had changed everything for him. Not a day went by that he didn't know how blessed he was.

Olivia went on, the emotion in her voice almost painful to hear. "Our marriage was over long before Nic disappeared. I didn't see it for a long time… Didn't want to see it. Then I… We…" She swallowed hard, gave a quick shake of her head. "Something happened that brought it to a head, making us both realize that what we'd had no longer existed."

Noah was no marriage counselor. He'd screwed up too many times to even consider himself wise in the way of wedded bliss. But he happened to know someone who excelled in such things. He knew her very well, in fact.

"Will you do me a favor?"

Olivia blinked up at him in surprise. "Of course. If I can."

"After you called this morning, I thought you might need someone to talk to. I asked Samara to come with me. She's in the next room. Will you talk with her?"

Her smile gave him her answer before she said, "Thank you for that, Noah, but I have a plane to catch. I've got some cleanup to do, and it can't wait."

"Of course."

"I'd like to talk to her at some point, though. Would you tell her that for me?"

"Of course I will. Just let her know when you're ready."

"Thank you. And also…I wanted to tell you this…before I left. Working for Last Chance Rescue has been one of the greatest joys of my life. I want to thank you for that opportunity."

His brow furrowed with concern. "This sounds a lot like a goodbye. Are you resigning?"

"No. Not unless you want me to. I just won't be able to work any ops for a while."

"Take as much time as you need. But understand that you are a vital member of our team. I don't want to lose you. None of us does. We value you, Olivia. Know that, if you know nothing else. You are important to us. Not just as an operative, but also as someone we care deeply about."

The gleam of moisture in her eyes told him he'd said the right thing. He'd meant every word. Olivia was often harder to read than anyone he'd ever known. Seeing her relief at his words was a revelation.

"Would you explain to the team that I'm just taking a few weeks off for personal business, but I'll be back as soon as possible?"

"Of course. And let us know if there's anything we can do."

"Thank you, Noah. For everything."

Noah watched Olivia leave with a strange heaviness in his heart. She was about to face her demons, and he knew from personal experience that no matter how hard you fought, sometimes those demons won.

CHAPTER FIVE

Option Zero Headquarters
Montana

A sher Drake sat at the head of the conference room table. The day he'd anticipated and dreaded had arrived. Would it all fall apart, or would they weather this storm as they had so many others? The truth would be revealed very soon, and the chips would fall one way or the other.

As far as he knew, no one suspected what was about to take place. He wished that wasn't so. Keeping secrets from his team was an abomination to him. The reasons behind the deception were many and varied, but the number one root was the need to keep people alive.

He already knew the team wouldn't see it the same way—at least not at first. In fact, these people would have a huge problem with the concept. They faced danger on a daily basis. Telling them the deception had taken place for their own good would not go over well. He didn't blame them. If he had been left in the dark, he'd be mightily pissed, too.

He was prepared for the anger. It should be directed at him—he was a big boy, he could take it. He refused, however, to let it fall on anyone else. He was the one who'd agreed to the deception. Only one other team member knew about it, and that was only by default. He had never intended to involve anyone else. This had been his secret to keep.

Serena Donavan walked into the room, and he could see the dread in her eyes. Guilt weighed heavily on Ash's shoulders. She had happened upon the intel by chance—something he should have anticipated but hadn't—and found out that Hawke was still alive. When he had explained the situation, she had volunteered to aid them. While he felt remorse for having her involved, he also knew they'd accomplished much more with her help.

But now they were both going to pay the piper.

"The others on the way?" he asked.

"Yes."

"You say anything to Sean yet?"

"No. He needs to hear it with everyone else. It'll be better this way."

He wasn't so sure about that, but Ash didn't argue. Since Jules was on bed rest for the remainder of her pregnancy, he had told his wife the truth this morning before he'd left the house. She had been supportive and had understood his reasons but agreed that the other team members might not be as generous. She didn't know Hawke. The rest of the team had known him for years. He'd been a member of their family. When they thought he'd died, it had hurt them deeply. Had almost destroyed them. What would his reappearance do?

And what about Olivia? His guilt on that matter was tripled. What they had done to her, what he had allowed to be done, hit him square between the eyes. He had been harder on her than almost anyone else, and when he'd had the chance to make it right, to tell her the truth, he had chosen not to. Yeah, there had been reasons—good ones. That didn't clear his conscience, though. Not by a long shot. No matter his reasons, Olivia would have every reason to hate him when she learned the truth.

Another hurdle they would have to jump was Hawke's opinion of Olivia. Ash thought because his own emotions weren't involved, maybe he could view things as an impartial observer, see things in a way Hawke could not. If nothing else, having Olivia and Hawke in a room together for the first time in years would definitely crack something open. Hopefully, it wouldn't be someone's head or heart.

Ash glanced up as the OZ team came into the room, one by one. Each operative was impressive in their own right, but as a team, he'd never seen their equal. Their success rate was phenomenal. Ash valued each of them as a co-worker and as a friend. The fact that the latter could be obliterated today was no small concern. But this could wait no longer.

Since he hadn't given them any idea what the meeting was about, they were laughing at one of Liam's stories about his honeymoon. He and Aubrey had just returned two days ago, and from the sound of it, they had enjoyed every moment. The contentment on Stryker's face was a direct contrast to how he'd looked a few months back.

The rest of the team looked surprisingly content as well. Things were getting back on an even keel, and their focus was on the future. The shadow organization they were pursuing had gone deeper into the shadows, but that wouldn't stop them. Someday, someway, they would find the head of that evil entity and end them.

If there was a ray of light in all of this mess, that was it. Hawke was bringing them a spark of hope where none had existed. But first, Ash had a fiery hell to confront.

Might as well get started.

"Have a seat, everyone."

Ash waited until they were all seated. The room became quiet, and he noted that everyone's expressions had changed to tense and wary. Yeah, they were picking up on the bad vibes.

Even though it was a well-known fact among them, Ash began the meeting with an explanation of sorts.

"As you know, when Option Zero first started up, we agreed that not only would we work as a team to bring down as much evil as we could, we each had our own personal agendas. That hasn't changed and won't change. A couple years ago, a member of the team came to me, asking a favor regarding a delicate project. After listening, I agreed. We both believed involving the rest of the team would jeopardize the project."

"That's not how our team works."

The words came from Sean Donavan, and though Serena's expression never changed, Ash saw her shoulders go rigid. Yeah, this was going to be rough.

"The argument was sound," Ash continued. "It was a time-sensitive matter, so I agreed to the plan."

There was silence as each of them looked at one another, trying to determine who had made this radical request.

When no one spoke up, Xavier said, "All right. So somebody's been working on their own without us. Apparently, whoever it is, needs the team's help now, so who was it, what's going on, and what do we need to do?"

That was Xavier Quinn to a T—*tell me the problem, and let's get on it.* If only this one were that simple.

"It wasn't anyone in this room," Ash said.

"What do you mean?" Gideon Wright asked. "Who else is —" He cut off, and realization flashed on his face. "It was Hawke, wasn't it? Is that what got him killed?"

"Yes and no."

Moving restlessly in her chair, Eve Wells sighed. "These cryptic comments are getting frustrating, Ash."

"You're right. But before we go any further, I want to make sure everyone understands. This was my decision, no one else's. If you're looking for someone to be angry with, you don't need to go any further than me. It was my choice."

"Since no one knew about it except you, that shouldn't be hard," Liam said.

Ash opened his mouth to agree, but before he could, a calm voice said, "I knew about it."

All eyes targeted Serena. True to her nature, she didn't flinch or back down.

"What are you talking about?" Sean asked.

Even though she hadn't flinched, her chin wobbled slightly at her husband's terse question.

Regaining the little composure she'd lost, she said evenly, "I've known for over a year."

Now all eyes were back on Ash, all accusing. Yeah, he figured they'd be even more pissed when they realized another one of the team members had not only known about it, but had apparently found out much later. Leaving the rest of them in the dark.

"Serena came upon the intel by accident," he explained. "She came to me and asked. I chose to bring her in—she's been a valuable asset to the project."

"Somebody want to fill us in on what the project is, or was?" The worry in Jazz McAlister's eyes was telling. She was the youngest member of the team, and whether she wanted it or not, every one of them felt protective of her. Ash still remembered how she'd reacted when they'd been told Hawke was dead. He never wanted to see that look on her face again.

Ash took a breath. "I'll let someone else fill you in."

"Who would that someone else be?" Liam asked.

"That would be me."

All heads turned toward the door where a tall, broad-shouldered man stood. A man almost everyone had thought dead.

It had been over two years since Ash had seen Nicholas Hawthorne. Any communication they'd shared had been via texts and encrypted emails. The man had changed—so much so that Ash might not have recognized him if not for his distinctive silver-gray eyes.

"What the—" Eve snapped.

Chairs scraped back as both Sean and Xavier lunged to their feet.

Ash watched each operative's initial reaction with interest. Sean and Xavier appeared both stunned and not a little angry, while both Gideon and Liam stayed seated. Gideon had a small smile on his face, and though Liam wasn't smiling, there was no anger in his expression.

The reactions of Sean, Xavier, Liam, and Gideon had concerned Ash the most. These men had known Hawke the longest, and over the years, all of them had worked under his authority. When they thought he'd died, they had taken it hard.

Jazz's expression was one of both confusion and joy. Thankfully, she appeared, at least initially, to be relieved.

Serena sat quietly, taking it all in, but her eyes never strayed far from her husband. Ash knew she had worried how Sean would react when he learned that she had kept this secret from him.

Eve Wells's reaction was the most interesting. Her eyes narrowed into slits, and her voice held a quiet fury as she said, "Does Olivia know?"

"Hawke will take care of filling you in on Olivia."

Eve rose to her feet, fire flaring from her eyes. "Oh, will he? The way he took care of making us believe that she was responsible for his death?"

Ash wasn't going to defend Hawke or himself. Olivia had been in on the initial plan, but there had been reasons to keep her in the dark about certain things. Hawke had explained his reasons, and while they'd been valid, Ash had lost more than a few nights' sleep over that decision. Olivia Gates was a courageous, intelligent, and extraordinarily kind person. She hadn't deserved what had happened. Question was, when the team members learned that she had been in on Hawke's disappearance initially, would they extend grace to her for that, or would the anger continue?

There were still questions Olivia would need to answer herself. She acted like she knew nothing about what really happened with Hawke, which was the biggest reason Ash believed in her innocence. No one could act that heartbroken or destroyed and it not be real.

"That's why I need to talk to all of you before Olivia arrives," Hawke said. "She's going to need your help."

Standing, Ash waved Hawke into the room. "We all need to hear this."

Surprising everyone but Ash, Hawke entered the room with a noticeable limp. A full beard covered half his face, and there were more than a few visible scars on his neck. No one had come out of this unscathed, especially Hawke.

All eyes were on their former teammate as he made his way to the front of the room. Though Hawke's expression never changed, Ash wondered what was going through his mind. These people, all of them, had been his friends—his best friends—and he had lied to them.

HAWKE MET each person's eyes as he said, "I know I have a lot to explain—a lot to make up for—but this can't wait."

They had every right to their anger, and it was there. One

of the many things he'd always appreciated about his OZ brothers and sisters was their forthrightness. They didn't hold back with their opinions.

They were men and women who would have died for him without a second thought—just as he would have for them. They had been as close as a family. Didn't take a psychic to see that had changed. Everyone was looking at him with either animosity or distrust. He didn't blame them. All of this was on him. He'd had his reasons, but that didn't diminish the harm he'd caused.

There were a lot more details he needed to share, but that would have to wait. For now, he focused on one issue. "Olivia was attacked in her apartment last night."

"Is she okay?" Ash asked.

Okay was a relative term, but he nodded. "Bruised up, but no major damage."

"Who was it?" Ash asked.

"Don't know that yet." Although he had a pretty good idea, and it pissed him off that he hadn't stopped it before it happened. He should've seen it coming. "There were four of them. We caught one, but he's not giving us much."

"We?" Gideon said.

"My people stopped them."

A wry tone to his voice, Xavier said, "Not to sound too much like a jealous teenager, but weren't *we* your 'people'?"

Hawke had known there would be a rub there. The people who'd been helping him weren't the same as his OZ brothers and sisters. They were good, but they weren't *these* people.

"They weren't 'my people,' per se. They were on loan."

"From who?" Sean asked.

It was the first time he'd spoken, and Hawke knew that when this was over, there would be a reckoning. He understood why, but it didn't make it any easier.

"Kate."

"So Kate was in on this from the beginning?" Liam said.

"Yes."

Sean's chair squealed as he pushed it away from the conference table and stood. "Are we even a team anymore, Ash?"

"We are," Ash said.

Hawke looked into the face of each OZ member and wondered if they could come back from this. He had caused this. He had known their anger and hurt would be there, and while he could tell himself all day long that he'd been justified in his actions, the consequences of those actions were difficult to bear.

"I know you have questions, and I want to address each one. I promise I will."

A chime sounded, alerting the entire room that someone had driven into OZ territory. Hawke met Ash's gaze, confirming what he already knew.

"But we'll have to put off the rest of the explanation for a little longer," Hawke said.

"Why?" Jazz asked. "Who's here?"

Before Hawke could respond, Eve gave her the answer for him. "Olivia."

CHAPTER SIX

Olivia walked into OZ headquarters as if she were still one of them. Not one person tried to stop her. In fact, she'd spotted zero people. Even when she'd been an OZ operative, she had never walked into headquarters without seeing someone. Even Rose Wilson, OZ's general factotum, who'd always seemed to be everywhere at once, was noticeably absent.

She wondered if she could walk through the entire building without being confronted. The house, though large and quite lovely, was actually a front for an entire world below ground. A dozen or so people gathered intel, working in a maze of rooms beneath the house. As one of the most secretive spy and intel organizations, Option Zero moved silently throughout the world, solving problems most people never knew existed. It was one of her proudest moments when she'd been allowed to join Option Zero.

Most of the members had known each other for years, and it had warmed her heart that she had been so readily accepted. Of course, the fact that she was married to Hawke at the time had had a lot to do with it.

She shook her head quickly, forcing the memories down. She wasn't here to relive the past. She was here for answers and would not be leaving until she had them.

She continued through the seemingly empty house. If she hadn't known better, she'd say the place was empty, but she did know better. They were expecting her. They knew she was here.

She approached the largest conference room where she had attended many OZ meetings. This was where missions were planned. This would be where everyone would gather. And apparently they had—before they'd scattered. Several coffee mugs sitting on the conference table still steamed. They'd likely been alerted to her arrival and had exited quickly.

She didn't need to wonder why. It was the reason she'd come here. She'd known what she would find. Which was why, as she moved to look out a window, the sound of footsteps behind her also came as no surprise.

A dichotomy of emotions swirled within her. Thousands of cutting words and stinging accusations came to mind, garbled and incoherent. The hurt was so overwhelming, she had to grip the edge of the windowsill. And while fury surged, there was an even bigger urge to throw herself into his arms and celebrate that he wasn't dead. That he still breathed.

She told herself to turn, give him a frozen, uncaring smile, and act as if her heart hadn't been torn to shreds. After all, she was the queen of frozen smiles. She was Iris Gates's daughter—her mother had taught her from infancy that you never revealed an emotion you didn't want to show. She knew how to do this.

Using every bit of that poise she'd been instilled with from birth, Olivia turned to face her husband. Only by maintaining that poise was she able to keep from gasping in shock. He had aged years, and no matter how angry she was with him, it hurt her heart to see him looking so ravaged by his experience. Wherever he'd been and whatever he'd been doing, it had not been easy.

"Hello, Livvy."

The cool, casual greeting bolstered her, lessening her anguish and reminding her that he was still the man who had deserted her, lied to her.

"You bastard," she said softly. "How could you?"

"How are you feeling? Any residual effects from the drug they gave you?"

"No, you don't get to ask the questions."

"I'll give you answers, but I need to know if I missed anything. The injection was a light dose of scopolamine. Not damaging, but you might have some aftereffects, like dizziness and blurred vision."

"I'm fine," she bit out.

"You might want to see a doctor, just in case."

"I said I'm fine. Now answer my question. How could you disappear like that? I thought you were dead."

"There were...extenuating circumstances. It wasn't all by choice."

She released a choked, unbelieving laugh. "The great Nicholas Hawthorne dancing to someone else's tune? No way in hell."

"Not exactly someone else's tune. As I said...extenuating circumstances."

"No matter how much it hurt me."

He stared at her for the longest time, as if he could divine what she was thinking without asking questions. Finally, he said, "It was never meant to be that way."

"And how did you think it would be? I thought my husband was dead."

"Ex-husband."

A wave of relief rushed through her. He didn't know. She was glad of that. Pride was all she had left. She didn't think it could take another blow.

"You think that made a difference?"

"No." His sigh was heavy and deep. "No, I don't.

They had once shared everything—so in sync with each other that a look between them could communicate what other people might use a hundred words to convey. How had it all gone so horribly wrong?

She shut down that thought. She knew exactly what had gone wrong. No way could she delve back into that hellish memory.

"We had an agreement. The only reason I consented to the plan was because you promised me that you would stay in touch. You never contacted me again."

"Livvy, I know this. But explanations are going to have to wait. I—"

"No. You don't get to just brush this away."

"I'm not brushing it away. I will explain everything soon, but the team is coming back in here."

"Of course they are." She tried her best to keep the bitterness out of her voice and knew she wasn't going to be able to. "How many of them have you been in touch with before today?"

"Ash and Serena."

"And Kate."

"Yes. And Kate."

The admission didn't surprise her, though it did sting. How many times had she gone to the woman she had called friend, begging for information? Pleading for anything. Each time, Kate had sworn she hadn't seen or heard from Hawke. She'd said she had no idea where he was or what had happened to him.

And now Olivia knew that Ash and Serena had also

known he wasn't dead. They had never let on, treating her like a murderer, just as the others had.

"I see."

"No, you don't. But in time, I promise you will." He paused, then said with a harshness she could not begin to comprehend, "I have questions, too, you know."

"Well, please." Her hand flew out in an angry gesture. "Don't let me stop you. You're the man of the hour. Ask your damn questions. I have nothing to hide."

Again, one of those silent, searching looks crossed his face. At one time, she would have been able to read him, but with that beard and the hardness in his icy eyes, she hardly recognized him as her husband.

"Everyone is waiting to come back in."

She pulled out a chair at the end of the large conference table and sat. "By all means, have the team return. They hate me and won't want me to be here, but they'll just have to deal with it."

"They don't hate you. If they hate anyone, it's me."

"They blamed me for your death."

"Our plan worked, then."

She drew in a shaky breath. Yes, it had worked. Despite the fact that one part of the plan had gone exactly as they'd intended, it could not erase the memory of the hurt. The people she'd thought of as family had treated her like a pariah. The lame excuse she'd given for Hawke's death had not flown with them. They had believed her when she'd told them that he was dead. And they'd believed it was her fault. As she had intended.

Just because she and Hawke had set the scenario in place, and it had worked the way they'd planned, didn't mean it hadn't been without cost.

Seconds later, the OZ team walked into the room. She didn't acknowledge any of them. A part of her felt childish for not doing so. Acting this way made it clear to them that she was still hurt by their attitude. She wasn't sure how to act, so she went with her fallback—when hurt, she shut down. She'd gotten even better at that over the years.

Ash went to the head of the table and addressed the room. "I know everyone has questions. I have them, too, but Hawke said there was some urgency. So let's hear him out."

HAWKE STOOD in front of the group again. Even though they were furious with him, he couldn't help but feel lightness in his heart. This was his family. They'd had one another's backs in some of the most dangerous situations imaginable. He hoped they would forgive him someday.

He shot a look at Olivia. She looked so alone and miserable. The bruises on her face and neck were painful to look at, but he knew they were only a small representation of what her entire body looked like. She had bruises everywhere. She had fought four men, all of whom were twice her size. He had never known anyone tougher or braver in a fight.

Everyone was looking at her now, and she looked more uncomfortable than he'd ever seen her. She had never liked the limelight. Even when she'd done extraordinary work, she would always brush it off and give credit to the team and not herself. But he wanted these people to remember the good she had done and what she had once meant to them. They owed her that.

And what did he owe her? He simply did not know. They needed to talk, but he wasn't sure how to go about it. At one time, there was nothing they couldn't discuss and work out. Now, they were like strangers. Question was, were they also enemies?

Someone cleared his throat, bringing Hawke's attention

back to the fact that he had nine very pissed-off people waiting to hear his story.

"Ash is right," Hawke said. "I know you all have questions. Now that Olivia is here, I'll do my best to answer them."

Gideon turned to Olivia, his tone unthreatening, almost tender. "How are you feeling, Liv?"

She gave him a quick look and said, "I'm fine. It's mostly superficial."

"Did you see a doctor?" Jazz asked.

"No." Apparently regretting her shortness with Jazz, she sent her a strained smile. "I'm fine. Really. But thanks." Returning her gaze to Hawke, she said, "One of the men who attacked me had an Albanian accent."

Her voice was cool and unemotional, but at least she was talking to him. That one of her attackers was Albanian was new information but corroborated what his hostage had said. Her attackers had no allegiance or cause. They were a group of mercenaries hired to do a job.

"I'm not sure what their purpose was," Olivia said. "Their questions related back to ops I worked before I came to the US. They didn't get a chance to ask much before Hawke intervened."

Hawke didn't visibly flinch, but he withered inside. Once they fell in love, she stopped calling him Hawke. When she was exasperated with him, she had called him Nicholas. All other times, he had been Nic. But now he was Hawke again.

"What did they ask?" Jazz said.

"Really obscure things." She shook her head. "I only recall bits and pieces… I was so out of it."

"Out of it how?" Jazz asked.

"I was drugged. Scopolamine, apparently." She looked at Hawke again. "Do you think they recognized you and could tell someone?"

"I don't know. I look a little different than I used to, and these men were mercenaries. I doubt they'd have known who I was. We managed to capture one of them."

"Where is he?" Xavier asked.

"In a secure spot, being questioned."

"He tell you anything?"

"Not yet. Claims he's freelance, which I believe. Said he was paid to break in and rough Olivia up. That's all."

"Who hired him?"

"Doesn't know that either. Said he's a tall, bald guy with ugly brown eyes and a scar over his left eye. Has no accent."

"Sound like anyone you know?" Ash asked.

"No."

"You believe him?"

"Yeah, I do."

Kate's people were good at interrogation, but he was better. Their captive knew nothing.

"How did you know they were going to attack Olivia?" Serena asked.

"Because I've had her under surveillance since I disappeared."

CHAPTER SEVEN

S urveillance? Olivia jerked at the terminology. Not *someone watching over her*. Not *some people keeping an eye out for her safety*. It was almost as if she were under suspicion for something. What did that mean?

And why hadn't she spotted them? She always took precautions. She switched up her routines three or four times a week. Never went directly to LCR from her house. Never ate at the same restaurant twice. Nothing she did was the norm. And yet, she had never seen anyone watching her. As angry and confused as she was, she still couldn't help but be impressed. Almost from the time she could crawl, she had been trained in covert ops. She knew how to hide, and she knew how to spot a tail.

What infuriated her more than anything was the fact that any one of those people at any time could have spoken to her. Hawke could have gotten a message to her at any time. He could have told her he was alive. The hell she'd been going through for the last two years could have been eased in an instant with just a few simple words. Instead, he had wanted her to believe that he was dead. Why? She wanted answers, and he had promised that he would give them. She intended to ensure that he kept that promise.

"How did the attackers find Olivia? And if you've had people watching her, how did the attackers get past them to get to her?" Xavier asked.

"They screwed up."

That wasn't completely true, and Hawke knew it. They might have screwed up in letting them get to her, but the way they'd found her was all on her. The realization of how she'd been found had come to her earlier. On the flight to Montana, she'd had a lot of time to think. It infuriated her that she had never even considered it. If he'd had people following her, then they both knew how she'd been found.

He was going to let her off the hook. She could see it in his eyes that he was going to blame those watching her for the screw-up and not her own stupidity. She refused to allow it. She wanted no favors from him. She wanted nothing but answers from this man—not even to lessen her embarrassment.

Olivia refused to look at Hawke as she admitted, "I went to the house in Charlottesville where we lived when we were first married. They tracked me from there."

"What?" Xavier's incredulous look went between Olivia and Hawke. "They lay in wait for years at your old house just on the off-chance you happened to stop by?"

Always the most sensitive of the group, Jazz apparently sensed Olivia's discomfort. She touched Xavier's hand and said softly, "Let it go."

"Let it go... Why?" His gaze continued from Olivia's face to Hawke's. "What's the deal? What am I missing?"

Olivia refused to allow herself the comfort of silence. It had been her mistake. A stupid, foolish error. "It was our wedding anniversary a few days ago. I imagine they had a standard practice of keeping an eye out on that particular day each year."

After her statement, the room was quiet for some time. She kept her head high. She had nothing to be ashamed of. There was no crime in being a sentimental, stupid idiot.

"All right." Eve broke the uncomfortable silence. "So you went off the grid for over two years, Hawke. You want to tell us why you faked your death, why we weren't allowed to know about it, and why the hell we were made to believe that Olivia was responsible?"

"As you know," Hawke said, "before Olivia and I came to OZ, we were working with our own team. Olivia almost died on our last op. We knew we had a traitor somewhere. Never found them. We disbanded the team, worked solo for a while, and then came here."

It was a simplistic retelling of a complicated, multifaceted story. One that seemed to become more complicated as the years went on.

Eve released a frustrated sigh. "We know all of this."

"Yes, I know you do, but this is relevant."

"Fine," Eve snapped.

A lump developed in Olivia's throat at Eve's anger. Her former friend had not yet been able to look her in the eyes. Olivia drew in a breath, trying to will her emotions to settle. Out of all the hurt she'd suffered during the faking of Hawke's death, the treatment she'd received from Eve Wells had been the most painful. Everyone had been quite mean to her, but Eve had been particularly vicious. She didn't suffer fools gladly and had felt duped by what she had referred to as Olivia's betrayal.

Even though she had enjoyed a friendship with everyone on the OZ team, she and Eve had shared a special bond. When it had been severed, something had died within Olivia. And the longer she had gone without hearing from Hawke, more parts of her heart had withered away. Now, she felt like a completely different person.

These people were no longer her family. Not like they once had been, but she still considered them some of the finest people in the world. She could acknowledge that without giving them anything back. They were her past.

Last Chance Rescue had been her saving grace, but she had never allowed herself to be fully immersed in their world. They would have welcomed her with open arms if she had allowed them. She liked and respected every person at LCR, and some of them, like Noah and Samara McCall, and Brennan Sinclair and his wife, Kasie, she would even call friends. But there was always something holding her back from getting too close to anyone. Loving meant hurting, and she had been hurt enough for a couple of lifetimes.

"I kept in touch with each former team member," Hawke was saying, "but it was hit or miss. Everyone started a new life. Deacon retired from active service and started work in the private sector. Mack went back to the Navy as a chaplain. Trevor went to work at the Pentagon. And Layla went completely off the grid. Last we'd heard, she'd moved to Fiji."

"And Rio started working for a private security company," Olivia said. "He was killed on an op in Ixtapa, Mexico."

Rio's death had been a blow. Even though she and Hawke had grieved, because, despite his faults, Rio had been a valuable team member, neither of them had been surprised. Rio had enjoyed living on the edge and could be reckless. He'd once stated that his goal was to die young and violently. He'd gotten his wish.

"A few months later, Layla…"

Hawke paused. Olivia knew it was not for dramatic effect, but because the pain was still there. He had loved Layla like a sister and blamed himself for what happened to her. Didn't matter that she was one of the most lethal women either of them had ever known. They both felt like they'd let her down.

There had been no indication at the time that Rio's death was related to Layla's. They were told he had died on a mission. But when attempts were made on other team members' lives, they had taken another look at Rio's death.

"We didn't know about Layla's death for a couple of weeks," Olivia said. "She was found in her apartment in Nashville, strangled to death. A man she'd been dating found her. He was looked at hard, but was finally cleared. There was no evidence he had anything to do with her death."

If they had known sooner, they might've been better prepared to face what had happened next.

"The other attacks were carefully coordinated," Hawke said. "A sniper tried to take Deacon out while he was driving down the interstate in Ohio. He should've been killed, but he changed lanes at the last moment, and the shooter missed. He didn't even realize he'd been shot at until the damage was assessed, and a bullet was found in his engine block.

"On the same day, Mack had lunch at his favorite restaurant in Dallas and ended up in the ER with what he thought was food poisoning. Blood samples were taken, and we later found out his food had been poisoned.

"Trevor was mugged outside his business. He's a former Marine, so they likely didn't expect the fight he gave them. They got away, but not before he broke some bones."

"And you're sure Rio's and Layla's deaths are related to the attempts on the others?" Gideon asked.

"Rio's death happened a couple of months prior to all the other incidents. But yes, we believe they're all related."

"Strikes me as strange that the last three attempts weren't successful," Liam said.

"Olivia and I considered that, but we couldn't wait

around to see if the attempts were warnings or the killers were just sloppy."

"What about you and Liv?" Jazz asked. "Were you two targeted back then?"

Instead of a direct answer, Hawke said, "Olivia and I were already off the grid. With the exception of Layla, the others weren't in hiding."

"But no one ever came after either of you?" Eve clarified.

At that question, Hawke's gaze zoomed to Olivia in a searing, searching look. Based on the scars she'd seen on his neck and the slight limp in his gait, she knew something had happened to him. But why was he looking at her like that? She was the injured party here. He was the one who'd disappeared. He was the one who'd left her alone, allowing her to think he was dead. If anyone had a right to be pissed, it was her.

"No," he finally said. "No one came after either of us back then."

"All right," Eve said softly. "We know you were being targeted, but how about telling us why we couldn't be told?"

"Because I knew what you would do," Hawke said. "You'd have jumped in with both feet and in the process, maybe have gotten yourselves killed."

"I'm not sure if we are supposed to be touched that you cared about us that much or just really honked off at you for thinking we couldn't handle ourselves," Eve said.

"It was my mess to clean up," Hawke said.

"No, it was *our* mess," Olivia snapped. "And was it even worth it? Do you know anything more than you did two years ago, or was all of this shit for nothing?"

The room went silent, and Olivia inwardly cringed. Not only had she drawn everyone's attention, but the anger in her voice had been evident. Having others see her pain went against her training. If people didn't know what you were feeling, then they didn't know what you were thinking. That was Spy Craft 101.

All the adrenaline that had been keeping her going since she'd woken this morning seemed to leave her at once. Being beaten and drugged and then finding out her husband was not dead had been a bit much to handle in such a short period of time. If she didn't get some alone time soon so she could regroup, she would be no good to anyone.

She blinked to keep her mind on what Hawke was saying.

"Everything points to the Gonzalez cartel."

The information diverted her exhaustion. That name was easy enough to remember. She had almost died on that mission. She had been protecting Tomás Ramirez, the seven-year-old son of Pedro Ramirez. Their team had made a deal with Ramirez, who had been looking to get completely away from his family's legacy of crime. He'd given them a way into Hector Gonzalez's drug trafficking empire. It had gone off like clockwork, or so they'd thought. Then someone had sold them out and leaked the location of where she was holed up with Tomás. An army had descended on the private island. Eighteen of Ramirez's people had been killed. Tomás had survived, but only because Olivia had thrown her body over his. She had taken three bullets that day.

Despite the attack, Hector Gonzalez had gone to trial and died in prison a few months after being found guilty.

"We checked that lead thoroughly," Olivia said. "After Hector was incarcerated, the cartel fell apart. There was nothing left."

"They had help we didn't know about."

"From whom?"

He shifted in his chair as if he, too, was feeling the strain from the last few hours. She thought again about his limp. What had happened to him? Was he in pain? And why the hell did she care?

"I've got intel coming here soon," Hawke said. "We need to wait for that."

"They can't send it electronically?" Jazz asked.

"No. We do this old-school."

"Seems like that would really slow one down."

Hawke shrugged. "Safer this way."

"Then we'll wait," Ash said.

There were no protests, so it seemed that everyone was content to wait until they had the intel in hand. Olivia wasn't going to argue about it either. She wanted out of here, needing fresh air in the worst way. There was no purer air than in the mountains of Montana. She jumped from her chair and made it three steps before the one person she knew would be the first to speak to her grabbed her arm.

"I'm so sorry, Liv."

She turned to Jazz and felt a tug at her heart. The young woman had tears in her eyes and an expression of extreme distress on her face.

"It's not your fault, Jazz. You believed what we wanted you to believe."

"Maybe so, but I could have been more supportive. I should have known you wouldn't have deliberately hurt Hawke."

As much as she tried not to let the emotions get to her, Jazz's apology went a long way in soothing the ache she had lived with these last couple of years.

"Thank you for saying that."

"And let me add on to that," Gideon said. "I'm very sorry, Liv."

She turned to the tall man who often reminded her of the movie version of Thor. Tall, muscular, with golden-blond hair and piercing blue eyes, he could almost be a Chris Hemsworth stand-in. Olivia had always respected Gideon, and while he, like everyone else, had believed the lie that she and Hawke created, he had never been cruel with his treatment of her. Not like his partner, Eve.

"Thank you, Gideon."

Out of the corner of her eye, she saw Eve slip out the door. Gideon followed Olivia's gaze, then gave her a wry look. "Hard for a proud woman to admit she's been wrong. Give her time."

"It doesn't matter. She bought the lie, just as we intended."

He only smiled, but she saw the knowledge in his eyes. While no one had been kind, Eve had been something else.

Needing to be alone in the worst way, she said, "If you'll excuse me, I need some fresh air."

She managed to get away from everyone else. She knew they would each come to her and apologize. She figured they needed to say the words, but she didn't need them. Not really. It had all been part of the plan. Hard to be angry when what they had worked so hard to achieve had succeeded.

But had it been successful?

Before she walked out the door, she took one more glance toward Hawke. He was in an intense conversation with Liam and Sean but looked up as if he knew her eyes were on him. The expression on his face was both inscrutable and weary. Whatever she had gone through, whatever heartbreak she had experienced, there was no doubt that Hawke had suffered, too.

It infuriated her that his suffering bothered her much more than her own did. And what was with all the harsh looks he'd been giving her? She was the one who had been betrayed. She was the one who had grieved. She was the injured party.

She would not be leaving here until he answered her questions.

CHAPTER EIGHT

Gideon found Eve exactly where he thought he would. Whenever she was emotionally upset, she retreated to dwell on her pain. He had told her more than once that she could come to him for solace, but she rarely did as he asked. His Eve was a loner. Had been since she was a child. It was one of the many reasons he loved her. For such a tough, no-nonsense, call-it-as-she-saw-it person, she had some unique vulnerabilities that cut straight to his heart.

She stood beneath the branches of a giant oak, staring up at the snow-capped mountains. He knew she sought peace, but whether she liked it or not, finding peace for what hurt her would not be found here.

"Guess we got fooled," Gideon said.

"Yeah, guess so."

"You pissed?" he asked.

"Of course. Aren't you?"

"Yes. Especially looking back on it and seeing the things that didn't add up, things I should have questioned. I'm not usually one to accept things blindly. None of us are."

"And yet, we did." She paused for a long second and then added softly, "I don't think she'll ever forgive me."

"People often surprise us. She knew your words came from a place of hurt."

"Yes, they did. But the fact is, she was hurting, too, and I did nothing but pile more on her."

"Sounds like you need to forgive yourself, too."

She looked at him then, and his heart hurt. Those beautiful sapphire eyes that he saw in his dreams were drenched with tears. His Eve didn't cry. Not anymore. She got mad, she got even, she got in your face, but she did not cry. He had seen it happen only twice in the last few years—when they'd learned Hawke had been killed and when Gideon had been shot a few months back. Both times, he had held her.

Putting his hand on her shoulder, he guided her into his arms. She pressed her face against his chest and shuddered out a shaky breath.

"How can I forgive myself? The things I said to her are unforgivable."

"Are they?"

She raised her head, the sorrow replaced with fury. "I told her she should've been the one to die, that Hawke was the best of us. I called her a stone-cold bitch who deserved to be alone."

He wasn't about to diminish her pain by telling her those words hadn't been hurtful. He had heard them himself and had winced at the venom she'd spewed. He had understood them and, in part, had agreed with her. Olivia had stood before them that day and announced Hawke's death as coolly and calmly as one announced the weather. There had been no emotion, no monumental pain in her voice. She hadn't acted like a grieving widow or the least bit sorry that her husband was dead.

Now that he knew the truth, he knew she had done that

on purpose—if they hated her, blamed her, they would be less likely to look for another explanation. They wouldn't get involved in looking for other answers. And they would stay safe.

"She gave us someone to hate."

"And we did it with a vengeance."

"It wasn't something she wasn't expecting."

"No. I'm just sorry we were so predictable."

"You're going to have to talk to her."

"I know," Eve said softly. "But you know that apologies are not my strong suit."

He smiled at that. One of the many things he admired about Eve was her acknowledgment of her weaknesses. She was a strong, proud, stubborn woman, but she was also the wisest person he knew. She could see her flaws better than anyone.

"Suck it up, Wells, and get it over with."

EVE ALLOWED herself the warmth of Gideon's embrace for a few more seconds. She had relied on this man's strength more times than she could count. He had once again offered her solace and peace. Taking a bracing breath, she pulled away and straightened her shoulders. "Thank you."

"It's what I do."

She laughed softly and kissed his cheek. "And you're so humble about it, too."

He gave her arm a quick squeeze and then nudged her forward.

There was no going back. She had faced more unpleasant things in her life. More than anyone might know. Guns and knives no longer fazed her. She'd even had a huntsman spider thrown at her once, and she hadn't flinched. But this… oh, this was hard.

She found Olivia sitting on a side porch, looking out at the same view Eve had been gazing at. She had likely seen Gideon talking with her. No doubt Olivia knew what they had discussed.

Sitting beside her, Eve stared straight ahead, working on the words.

"They're not necessary, you know," Olivia said quietly.

"Yes, they are. I was horrible to you. I'm sorry."

"Everyone reacted the way we planned."

"Really? I don't remember anyone else telling you they wished you'd died instead."

"You always did have a dramatic flair."

"You must have hated me."

"No, I didn't. I was numb for a long time."

"And now?"

Olivia shrugged. "I think I just want it over with."

"Gideon once told me that we hurt the ones we love more than anyone else. Guess it doesn't make you feel any better that I loved you that much."

Olivia cut her eyes over to Eve, a slight glimmer of amusement in the blue-green depths. "Love hurts?"

"Something like that. You were the sister I never had, Liv. When you told us Hawke was dead in that oh-so-proper British way of yours, I felt betrayed. And I let you have it with both barrels."

"Did you mean it?"

"Mean what?"

"You said the reason I would die alone was because I was a stone-cold bitch."

"No, Liv. I didn't mean it. Finding the most hurtful things to say is one of my gifts." Tentatively, she took Olivia's hand in hers and squeezed softly. "You're my family. Even when I was infuriated with you, I never stopped seeing you as my family."

Eve's heart filled when Olivia squeezed back and whispered, "I've missed you."

"I've missed you, too. So, can we go forward from here? Be what we once were?"

OLIVIA WANTED TO SAY YES, they could. But she honestly couldn't see that happening. She was a different person now. Or maybe she was the person she had been before she'd met Hawke. Perhaps she was the woman her mother and father had intended her to be. The thought infuriated her. She had worked too hard and too long to be the antithesis of her parents. Was she going to allow them to destroy her future because she was too tired to try? She was not a quitter.

"Liv? Can we?" Eve said again.

She glanced over at her friend. She had loved everyone at OZ. They were unique, gifted, opinionated, and fiercely loyal. They'd been her family. But Eve had been more. She had been the sister of her heart. They'd had so much in common that the moment they'd met, they were practically joined at the hip. That was why Eve's defection had hurt worse than anyone's.

"I'd like that. It just may take some time. Okay?"

Eve squeezed her hand again. "That's not a problem." Frowning slightly, she said, "Can I ask you a personal question?"

Exhaustion was beating at her, and she was at her limit on confessions today, but when she looked at Eve, she found she couldn't say no.

"Of course."

"Why did you agree to that plan? I know you and Hawke sometimes went on separate missions, and I know you were having some issues with him being gone so much, but for you to be separated from him for two years seems like an extraordinary ask."

"It wasn't supposed to happen like that. He was supposed to contact me the next week. When he didn't show up, I went to Kate. She said she hadn't heard from him."

And now she knew that had been a lie, too. She was infuriated the most with Hawke, but to only a smaller degree, she was also infuriated with Kate. She had trusted her, believed the lies. And Kate had known all along that Hawke was alive. Why had they kept it from her? Why had he stayed away for so long? Their marriage had been over, yes. And they'd barely been able to be in the same room with each other, but had he hated her that much?

"Hawke asked me for a divorce before he left," Olivia added.

Eve wrapped her arm around Olivia's shoulders. "Oh, sweetie, you never told me."

Of course she hadn't. Not even to her best friend could she admit the misery she had been going through. People handled emotional devastation in various ways. Her coping mechanism had always been to shut down and hope that the pain would eventually pass. Sometimes it worked, other times not so much.

What had happened between her and Hawke wasn't something she could verbalize. There was hurt, and then there was hurt that went beyond words. Pain so devastating and final could not find purchase in something as mundane as words. It was just there, shimmering in a hot mass of existence. Even now, two years later, it hovered and simmered.

She blinked, her eyes suddenly so heavy she could barely keep them open. She couldn't think straight. She needed to think about something else until she could get this figured out. She gave what she hoped was a convincing smile. "Tell me what's been going on here. I know that Ash married Juliet

Stone. And I heard that Sean and Serena finally tied the knot, too."

As if time and harsh words had never separated them, Eve jumped into the conversation with both feet. "Liam, too."

Gasping, she twisted to face Eve. "Oh my gosh, he found Cat?"

"Yes. Her name's Aubrey Starr." The beautiful smile on Eve's face lifted her spirits even more. "It was epic, Liv. I can't wait to tell you all about it. You're staying here, right?"

That wasn't something she'd even given a thought to. Normal activities like where she would sleep had not even entered her mind.

"I can find a place in town."

"Don't be silly. Of course you're staying here. Or if you'd rather, you can come home with me. We can stay up all night and talk like we used to."

That was too much, too soon. Even though she wanted to go back to her easygoing days with Eve, that was going to take time.

"That's not necessary. I'll ask Ash if I can stay here a few days."

"A few days? You *are* coming back to OZ, right?"

That would be a big *hell no*. She wanted answers to her questions, but beyond that, she was out of OZ, and she would remain out. Last Chance Rescue was where she belonged. Pretending otherwise wouldn't be smart, but if she said upfront that she wouldn't come back, would she be pushed out the door as she had been before? She couldn't let that happen. Not until she had answers.

"I'm not sure. I have a lot to think about."

"I know Ash would welcome you with open arms. We all would. And we've been crazy busy lately. Ash has talked about bringing on a couple of new people to take up the slack. Having you and Hawke back with us would be perfect."

At the thought of working with Hawke again, Olivia suppressed a shudder. That would never happen. There was too much hurt, the chasm was too huge to even consider that. It was all she could do to be in the same room with him. She was sure he felt the same way.

"I've taken a leave of absence from LCR. So for now, I'll be here."

That was as far as she would go. That way, when she went back to LCR, no one would be caught off guard.

"Then we'll just have to use that time to convince you to come back for good."

Olivia said nothing.

HAWKE STOOD in the middle of the OZ house. Indecision was not his norm. He rarely gave a second thought to anything, and when he made up his mind, he could be ass stubborn. But this... He admitted he did not know which direction to take. On one hand, he wanted to find Olivia and demand she give him answers. On the other, he wanted to find Olivia and hold her close, ensuring she wasn't hurting.

If that wasn't a dilemma, he didn't know what one was.

"Well, that went about as well as could be expected."

He turned to see Ash striding toward him. The grimness in his expression was a reflection of Hawke's turmoil.

"You're right. They could've just shot me."

"Considering how capable they all are, I think it's a positive that you're still breathing." He jerked his head toward the door that Sean had just stormed through. "You make peace?"

"Not hardly. I tried to make him understand that Serena's silence was at my request. I don't think he took that as a good thing."

"Yeah, well, Sean's got some trust issues, and this didn't help."

One more pile of crap on top of a mountain of it.

"So, tell me why we took a break when I know all the intel you need is in your head."

"Did you see Olivia? She could barely hold her head up. She needs some rest."

"I see. So you've decided to trust her?"

Had he? For over two years, that had been his nightly question. Had she betrayed him? Had she been lying all along? His gut told him she was as true and honorable as he'd always believed. But there was plenty of evidence that showed the exact opposite.

"I don't know."

"Then you need to find out. Sharing this intel with people you don't trust is a good way to get our people killed."

"You're right."

"I'm headed home to be with my wife."

"I hope to meet Jules soon." Hawke said.

The change in Ash's face at the mention of his wife was amazing. The whole time he'd known the man, grim and grim light had been his demeanor. But the peace that swept over the other man's face told the tale. "She's looking forward to meeting you, too. And hopefully, you'll be meeting my son soon as well."

A heaviness landed on his chest, but Hawke managed a convincing nod before Ash walked out the door.

"You really know how to cause a stir, young man."

Turning quickly, he faced a teary-eyed Rose. He held out his arms, and she walked into them. Out of everyone, he had known that Rose would welcome him home. Carrying a grudge was not her way. Anger and resentment were not even in her vocabulary. She embraced Hawke as she would any of the OZ members, as if he were her own child.

"I've missed these hugs," he whispered.

Rose sniffed and laughed softly. "All you needed to do was come home."

"There were reasons why I couldn't."

Pulling away, she patted his jaw gently. "I'm sure there were."

If there were a billion people like Rose in the world, peace would no longer be an out-of-reach fantasy. Her entire being embodied the word.

"I wish everyone was as accepting as you."

"They'll come around. Families never stop loving, even when you're boneheaded."

That was likely the most criticism he would hear from her.

"I understand Olivia is here, too," Rose said.

"She is."

"That girl was not treated well."

Yeah, he knew that. They'd both known she would have to pay a higher price than he would. Having your friends turn on you, especially when you'd done nothing wrong, would be devastating.

"I wasn't here on her last day, and I'm sorry for that," Rose said. "I would have liked her to know that at least one person was on her side. I tried calling her a few times, but she never returned my calls. I'm sure she wanted to move on."

She hadn't done that, though. He should know. He had been watching over her. And while she had lived her life and done good work, she had never resumed *living*. Those last few days, before he'd faked his death, had drained the life from her. And then when the OZ team had turned on her, she had retreated into her own little world. Last Chance Rescue had been her saving grace, but even there, she'd held herself back.

"I know she'll be glad to see you, Rose. You were always her favorite person."

"That's because I know the real Olivia. There's a sweetness to that girl that she does her best to cover up. I see through that façade." She gave him a hopeful smile. "Now that you're back… Are you and Olivia going to rejoin OZ for good?"

He didn't know the answer to that. He definitely needed OZ's help. But would they accept him after what he'd put them through? Olivia's status was even shakier.

"I can see by your silence, you don't have an answer."

"I could never fool you, Rose."

"Ha. Having children and then grandchildren is good training for reading people. You'll understand when you have some of your own."

He was glad she turned away and didn't see him flinch. That pain, no matter how long it had been, never ceased. He doubted it ever would.

She headed toward the stairway and then stopped. "Are you coming?"

"Where are we going?"

"I've got you set up in the blue room. I believe Eve sent Olivia to the emerald room across the hall from you."

He hadn't given a thought to where he would stay tonight. His focus had been on getting here and seeing the team. Not a surprise, since he had a tendency to be able to sleep anywhere. A hard ground and a rock for a pillow had been his bed many a night. However, he couldn't deny that the older he got, the more his body appreciated creature comforts.

He followed Rose up the stairway, enjoying listening to her tell him about her grandchildren. They reached the door of his assigned bedroom just as Olivia opened her door to step out into the hallway. For just an instant, Olivia's too-still face lit up with a smile. Rose, just as she had Hawke, wrapped Olivia into a strong, affectionate hug.

As if it was as natural as breathing, Olivia returned her hug. But when she raised her eyes to look at Hawke, the smile fell away from her face, and the cool mask of indifference slid back into place.

Knowing his presence made her uncomfortable, Hawke opened his bedroom door and slipped inside. They would eventually have to face each other, but for right now, he wanted to keep that one unguarded picture of Olivia in his mind. It had been years since she'd looked at him like that. He remembered the exact moment when her smiles for him had disappeared forever.

Was it any wonder that she might have actually wanted him dead?

CHAPTER NINE

Two thousand miles away

The Killer gave himself a mental pat on the back. Things were finally beginning to add up. As one of his foster mums would say, *This was a fine kettle to fry fish*. Yeah, it hadn't made sense to him either, but somehow it seemed to fit this situation.

When his hired men had come running out of the building like the devil himself was after them, he'd had his tool bag in hand, ready to cross the street. Telling them to rough Livvy up and get her ready had been a genius move, if he did say so himself. He'd given them a few things to say to her, most likely confusing the hell out of her. The truth would've come after she'd been dosed.

But now, oh yes, now he had more intel than he'd ever imagined. The one piece of information that made everything else click into place.

Once he'd seen that the op was blown, he'd stayed back and watched. Two big brutes had dragged one of his men, obviously unconscious, out of the building. Where they'd taken him and what they'd done with him was of no interest. The poor sop knew nothing other than what he'd been told. He was a disposable tool, and good riddance to him.

Just when he'd thought the night was over and he'd have to find another way to get the intel he needed, another man had stepped out of the apartment building and limped his way to a waiting SUV. It was as if angels had begun to sing. So many questions had been answered, and he hadn't even had to get his hands dirty.

There was some disappointment, admittedly. It had been years since he'd seen Olivia. Ever since he'd gotten this assignment, he'd been dreaming of bruising that soft, tender skin and marring her beauty. Alas, he hadn't gotten the chance, but despite the missed opportunity for some fun, he'd gotten something infinitely better.

This was a game changer. Nicholas Hawthorne, aka Hawke, wasn't dead like everyone thought.

He didn't know if he was happy or sad about that. He hated the bastard—had for years. Years ago, Hawke had taken what belonged to him. And now, he had apparently done it again. No way Hawke wasn't behind all of this. And no way his superiors weren't going to go apeshit when he told them.

Remembering what he was supposed to be doing, he scowled at the bruised and bloodied men who stood before him. "How could you let them get away?"

"It wasn't like we had a choice," one of them said. "Those men surprised us. We didn't know anyone was watching her. We barely got away with our lives. Douglas was caught."

"That's the lamest excuse I've ever heard."

These men weren't professional soldiers. But, on the upside, they had no morals either. That could be a double-edged sword, as they had no liking for him and weren't committed to any kind of higher mission. The counterbalance of having someone willing to do almost anything for money was an acceptable trade-off.

They didn't, however, have the kind of guts he'd wanted them to have. Hence, one of them had been captured, and the rest had swarmed away like frenzied roaches.

"What are we going to do to get Douglas back?"

He snorted. "You think I care about him?"

"He's my younger brother."

"He knew what he was getting into when he accepted this job. You all did. You get caught, that's on you. I'm not pulling your ass out of the fire. You're on your own."

Before any of them could protest, he turned his back on them. He waited for a few seconds to see if one of them would try anything. They always checked their weapons at the door. That was a major rule, but that didn't mean they wouldn't try something. They were street fighters and knew every dirty trick in the book. In a way, he hoped they would come after him. He had some untapped energy he needed to get rid of. Unfortunately, no one made a move.

Sighing, he faced them again. A handful of ragtag mercenaries didn't exactly inspire confidence, but that was okay. They knew how to kill and had no qualms about doing so. For what he needed, they'd do.

"So what now?" one of the men asked. Harold or Howard? Something like that.

"We lie low and wait. Another opportunity will present itself."

He had no worries about Douglas spilling any secrets. The man hadn't known anything other than their plan to break into a woman's apartment, secure her, rough her up a bit, and drug her.

He'd planned to question her himself. He had questions none of these men could fathom or understand.

The things he'd told them to ask her had been red

herrings, geared to distract. It wouldn't have taken Olivia long to figure that out. However, he now had intel that far surpassed what he might have gained from questioning her.

If Douglas talked, and he highly expected him to do so, he'd have very little to tell. The man would give a vague description of who'd hired him. That description would give absolutely no clues to his true identity. He looked nothing like he used to look.

Now that he knew Hawke was alive, this changed his focus. There was no doubt in his mind that the man had the intel he sought. Now he just needed to find him. An attack on Olivia had brought him out of the shadows the first time. Seemed likely a second attack would bring him out again.

He smiled at the thought. He had access to things few people could fathom. He knew exactly what needed to be done and how to go about doing it.

His phone chimed a text, and he glanced down to read it, cursing under his breath. Was he the only one they knew to call to get things done? He was no freaking babysitter.

Texting back an affirmative, he looked around at the shabby accommodations he'd been forced to live with for the last few days. The stink of motor oil and old sweat permeated the place, and he doubted he'd ever get those smells out of his senses. This was the last time he'd set up business in an old, abandoned car repair shop.

Turning back to the men glaring at him like they'd take his head off any second, he offered them a smarmy smile. "Go find a place to hide and lie low. I've got some business to take care of. When I get back, we'll regroup."

"What about my brother?" the man gritted out.

He huffed out an exasperated sigh. With lightning reflexes, he pulled a knife from the sheath at his belt and threw it with maximum force. The blade landed in the man's throat, slicing his jugular in two. The dying man reached toward him.

The Killer smirked, not moving.

The other men stood and watched. When the man fell dead at their feet, The Killer met the others' gazes. "Any more questions or complaints?"

The remaining men quickly shook their heads and backed away.

"Good. I'll be in touch."

The Killer strode out the door.

Nothing like a little bloodletting to make a point.

CHAPTER TEN

OZ Headquarters

Olivia eased her tired, sore body into the hot, foamy water and released a long, shaky sigh. Hawke likely wanted to talk tonight. So did she. But that would have to wait until she'd soaked her physical pains away. The emotional ones would likely take a lot longer to erase.

Leaning back against the back of the tub, she closed her eyes. The fragrant scent of wild jasmine rose up with the steam, soothing not only her muscles, but also her weary soul. She had yet to come to grips with all that had happened over the last thirty or so hours. She had been beaten and drugged, and she'd found out her dead husband was alive. That was a lot for even the most seasoned and toughest person to handle.

Hawke and the people he'd had watching her had likely saved her life last night. She knew she should feel grateful. She still didn't know what her attackers had wanted, but there was no telling what might have happened. Overshadowing that gratitude was the monumental sense of betrayal.

Her husband, the man she had loved and trusted above anyone in the world, had betrayed her trust. He had destroyed everything she had thought they'd built together. She wanted to hear the reasons, but she already knew there was no adequate excuse. No word had been invented to justify what he had done. All the promises they'd made to each other, all the things they'd meant to each other had been ground into dust. There was no way she could forgive him this. She had forgiven him other things. Terrible, rotten words that scored her soul. But this? No, there was no reason, no explanation good enough to justify why he had let her think he was dead all this time.

She told herself she shouldn't be that surprised. Betrayal certainly wasn't new to her. At an early age, she had learned that most people had an agenda, and if you got in the way, they would do whatever they felt necessary to achieve their goal. Sometimes, they would do extraordinarily wicked things.

Her first real lesson had been when she was ten years old. Not by any stretch of imagination had she ever believed her childhood was normal. Her parents had been cold and distant. Discipline had been a way of life. Even when she'd been allowed to play, it had been with a training purpose in mind. Every moment of every day had revolved around that training.

Her only outlet had been her grandmother. Her mother's mother had been the exact opposite of her daughter. Warm and loving, with the most wonderful sense of humor and adventure, Maggie Marshall had been everything good and kind. She had come to live with them when Olivia was seven. There had been no explanation of why she was there. She had just shown up one day, and much to Olivia's delight, Gram had changed her life forever.

For three years, Gram had been her touchstone. She had

gone to her grandmother for solace, for encouragement, and for the love she'd longed for from her parents.

There was so much her grandmother had taught her, but the number one thing had been the recognition that there was good in the world. Without her grandmother's influence, Olivia knew she would have become just like her mother.

Olivia hadn't known the extent of how much her mother was watching their relationship until she had returned from school one day to learn that her grandmother had been moved to a care home for the elderly. Just like that, her foundation had been shaken to the core.

She had asked her mother why and was simply told it was time. Even though her heart had been torn to shreds, she'd known that reacting to that news in a negative way would have put Iris Gates on high alert. Instead, she'd nodded calmly and asked the location of where her grandmother had been taken. Without hesitation, her mother had told her.

Olivia later decided that it had been a test. One that she failed miserably.

The next day, instead of going to school, she caught a bus and traveled the forty-six miles to see Gram. It broke her heart to see her lively and intelligent grandmother sitting in a chair by a window looking like a frail and lonely old lady. At ten years old, with no resources, Olivia didn't know what to do or how to fix anything. She spent the day with Gram, promising her she would visit frequently. She promised they wouldn't lose touch. They both knew she was lying. Before Olivia left, her grandmother took her in her arms and hugged her harder than she ever had before. It felt so final.

At the door, before Olivia walked out, Gram said softly, "Get away from them, my precious, before they destroy you."

Those words proved to be prophetic.

She walked out of her grandmother's room, and her parents were waiting for her in the hallway. She wasn't surprised. She had known her mother would find out where she'd gone. There was no place to hide, no secrets that Iris Gates could not find.

Not one word was spoken between them. She simply followed them to their car, and they traveled home in silence. Her parents didn't even talk to each other. They were on a mission, and Olivia was it.

The moment she got out of the car at home, her mother said, "Go down to the training room."

It never occurred to her to argue or protest. She was not only powerless, she had been trained to obey. Traveling to see her grandmother had been an anomaly. One that she had known at the time she would pay for. And now that time had come.

As she made her way downstairs to the large training room, she wondered what they had in store for her. She was already trained in mixed martial arts and fully expected that she would likely have to fight. Sparring with one of her parents was a weekly training activity, and she thought perhaps they would likely make it a harder, longer session. Maybe even make her take on both of them together.

She was naïve. That wasn't what they had planned at all.

The moment she stepped down into the room, a cloth bag was thrown over her head, and her arms and legs were bound. Fighting was a natural response, but she barely managed a half-glancing blow to one of her attackers before she was completely immobilized.

She was carried only a short distance. Her hands were untied, and she managed another jab to a soft body part before she was once again bound. This time, her hands were tied separately to rings on the wall she faced. The rings were the starting point of a climbing wall. She used them frequently and never once considered they could be used in another manner.

The entire time, not one word was said. She didn't even speak herself. She had known she would be punished, and no matter what they did to her, she could not regret seeing her grandmother one last time.

She remembered every agonizing moment of what had followed. She had worn a dark brown jumper that day, believing she would blend into the background, and no one would notice her. A ten-year-old traveling alone was not the norm. When she heard the scissors cutting the sweater from her body, a new terror swamped her. What happened next was something she could still, to this day, not fathom.

A fiery strip of pain zipped across her back, and she screamed in agony. Before she could catch her breath, another followed. It was on the fifth strike that she recognized the instrument of torture was a cane. She stopped counting on the eighth strike, and on the tenth, she started praying for unconsciousness to claim her. How long it went on, she didn't know. It felt like hours. She was barely conscious when she finally heard her father say mildly, "You're going to scar her."

She hadn't known for sure who was doing the beating, but she wasn't surprised when the voice that responded was her mother's. "Just enough where she'll never forget."

Whether it was her father's warning or her mother just got tired, she didn't know. There were only a few more blistering strikes before the punishment stopped.

Choking back sobs, Olivia heard footsteps and knew she had been left alone. They left her there for hours, and she wondered more than once if they were planning to just leave her to die. She needed water in the most desperate way. She could feel blood oozing down her back and over her bottom. Her legs had been hit, too, but not as badly as her back and bottom. She urinated on herself at some point, and even to this day, she could remember the sting from the urine. Her arms went from pained, to numb, to agony. How many times she lost consciousness, she didn't know.

Finally, after what seemed like an eternity, lights flooded the room, and she was cut down. She dropped to the ground, crumpling onto the floor. Her legs wouldn't work.

The bag was removed from her head, and arms scooped her up. A new torture began as she was carried upstairs, each step causing agony to the welts and open rips on her skin. She kept her eyes closed until a door was opened, and she realized she was in her bedroom. Looking up into her father's face, she wanted to ask him why, but he had no expression other than a slight pity in his eyes.

He placed her on the bed and said quietly, "Learn your lesson?"

She nodded. Speaking was beyond her at that point.

"There's water on the bedside table as well as ointment for your wounds. Your mother will be in soon to discuss your future. I suggest you listen."

He left then.

She was eventually able to get to her knees and grab the water on the table. She drank it slowly, knowing she would throw it up if she didn't. Since she didn't have the strength to walk, she crawled into her bathroom, reached up to turn on the shower, and then sat on the shower floor. The water stung her wounds, but it also did the job of waking her up. She managed to stand, turn the water off, and step out of the shower. Her mother was standing in the bathroom door.

Blond, beautiful, and lethal—even now, that's how Olivia thought of Iris Gates.

Hatred filling her every pore, Olivia acted on instinct. Swiping a pair of manicure scissors from the bathroom counter, she ran toward her mother. Seeing the look of surprise on Iris's face was something she would never forget. She tackled the woman to the floor and held the scissor point at her mother's jugular, the rage within her so fierce she wasn't sure she was even human anymore. At ten years old, Olivia barely weighed seventy pounds soaking wet. Her mother could have easily overpowered her, even killed her.

Instead, Iris gave her what could be described only as a proud look. "There's my girl," she whispered.

Those three words did something to Olivia. *This* was what they wanted for her, what they were training her to be. They wanted her as heartless and cruel as they were.

"If you ever touch me again," she snarled, "I will kill you."

Iris nodded and gave her an approving smile. "I would expect nothing less."

Olivia got to her feet, backed up, and slammed the door in her mother's face.

Three days later, her mother showed up again. The bruises on Olivia's back were still there, but the cuts were closing up, and the welts had lessened. The pain was manageable. There would be scars, as her father had said, but Olivia didn't care. Her mother had been right about one thing: She would never forget where they came from.

Iris stood at the doorway, and though Olivia doubted she feared her, she liked to think that at least the woman might be somewhat wary.

"Pack your bags. You're going to boarding school tomorrow."

Olivia didn't react. She had been standing at her window, staring out at the freshly mowed lawn and wishing for a different life.

"You'll stay there until we tell you differently. Do you understand?"

Olivia didn't bother to acknowledge the question.

"I'm sure you believe your punishment was unfairly harsh, but you need to know that life is like that. Never feel comfortable, Olivia, because in that comfort, death lurks."

Iris opened the door, and then, almost as if it was an afterthought, she said the words that she knew would devastate her daughter. "By the way, your grandmother is dead."

She refused to outwardly react to the pain that slammed into her. She just asked mildly, "Did you kill her?"

Iris huffed. "I'm not into matricide."

The door closed, leaving Olivia alone to grieve for the only person she had ever loved.

Until Hawke.

She had left home that day and never returned. Boarding school hadn't been the punishment her parents had likely meant it to be. She had made a few friends and, for a short period of time, had felt like a normal person. On the day of her graduation, everything had changed. She had once again been sucked back into a world she hadn't wanted. And somehow, she had stayed.

Blowing out a soft sigh, she raised her head from her knees, unsurprised to see Hawke sitting only a few feet away from her. She had often accused him of having feline DNA. A six-four, two-hundred-and-twenty-pound man should not be able to move as quietly as he could.

"How are you feeling?" he asked.

"Like I was beaten and drugged."

"We need to talk."

"Did you know?"

"Know what?"

"Did you know you wouldn't be coming back when you left?"

"Yes."

She supposed she'd known this since last night. His confirmation made little difference.

"That's why you gave me the divorce papers," she said softly.

She stared up at him, trying with all her might to see the

man she'd married, the man she had loved with all her heart. There were glimpses in the depths of his beautiful silver-gray eyes, but the beard obscured most of his expression. She felt as if she were looking at a stranger.

"Get out," she said.

"We have to talk."

"Whatever you have to say to me can be said in front of the team."

"Not this."

She clenched her jaw to keep from screaming. The pain from her injuries was nothing compared to the agony in her heart. "Get. Out. Now."

He gave a single nod, stood, and walked out the door.

CHAPTER ELEVEN

Hawke paced the bedroom, waiting for Olivia to emerge from the bathroom. Over the last two years, he'd had this conversation in his head a thousand times. He imagined hurling accusations at her, followed by an apology, and then, hell, maybe he'd grab her and kiss her, because, yeah, he was just that screwed up.

Except for a brief period of heaven after they'd first married, things with Olivia had always been complicated. With that first meeting, when they'd both been undercover on different ops, the chemistry had been immediate and off-the-charts electric. It had been a defining moment for him, though he hadn't realized it at the time.

Their backgrounds couldn't have been more different, but they'd both grown up hard. Her parents had been sociopaths who'd had no business having kids. His hadn't been any better—he'd been the only child of a drug-addicted mother and an alcoholic father. Both he and his mother had been punching bags for his old man. After a lifetime of misery and one punch too many, she'd taken off. He'd been about seven at the time. He had become his father's responsibility and his sole outlet for his fury. That had lasted until Hawke got big enough to defend himself. Then the brawls had begun. His old man had been quite the teacher in how to live the most miserable and useless life possible.

Even with all that, Hawke always thought he'd had it easier than Olivia. At least when his mother hadn't been high on something, she had shown him affection. Her love had been careless and selfish, but at least it had existed. Olivia had never received that from either parent. If not for her grandmother, there was no telling what she might have become.

When he and Olivia had first realized their growing feelings for each other, they'd had plenty of heartfelt, soul-deep conversations. Their determination to never have children was one of the first things they had discussed. Neither of them had wanted the monumental task of being responsible for another human being, not with their past history.

His old man still lived inside his head. His tainted blood was in his veins. There was no way in hell he planned on repeating what Cooper Hawthorne had propagated. His bloodline would die with Hawke, and good riddance.

The bathroom door opened, and Olivia emerged. Dressed in a robe that was two sizes too large, with her hair in a messy knot and bruises on her face, she was still the most beautiful woman he'd ever known.

She raised that haughty chin of hers and snapped, "I thought I told you to leave."

"And I told you this can't wait."

He knew she was close to collapse. Hell, it had been over thirty-six hours since he'd slept, and his entire body felt sluggish and worn. And he hadn't been beaten and drugged. But this had to be done. He'd put it off too long already.

"I brought you a sandwich and a pot of tea." He gestured

toward the desk where he'd set a tray earlier. "There's some ointment for your injuries and some pain meds, too."

He told himself he wasn't taking care of her like before. This was something he'd do for anyone who was hurt. Even an enemy.

"How thoughtful, Hawke. That makes up for everything."

He ignored the sarcasm. "We need to talk."

"All right. You want to talk, then tell me why you lied."

"Now's not the time for that. We have some new players in the game."

"Dammit, you owe me an explanation. Why did you disappear? We had an agreement."

"I had my reasons, Livvy."

"No. I'm not Livvy to you anymore, and you're not Nic. We are Olivia and Hawke from now on."

"If that's what you want."

"What I want is so far out of reach, it doesn't even exist on this plane."

"Liv...Olivia, we will get to the reason I disappeared, I promise. But for right now, we have bigger fish to fry. I need to know what those men asked you, what they said. You were vague before, but you must remember something."

"I told you what they asked about. All the questions were related to old cases I worked while I was still with MI6."

"Nothing current? Nothing that you didn't understand?"

Her brow furrowed with confusion. "No. Nothing like that."

"Then it was for show."

"What do you mean?"

Hawke pushed his fingers through his hair, cursing his stupidity. It was what he'd feared, and he was once again infuriated with himself for not seeing this coming. Of course they'd go after Olivia. They would think she was involved, that she likely had even instigated the whole thing.

Turning his gaze back to her, he swallowed what he'd been about to say. He could at least give her one night of rest before he pierced her already-dented armor.

"Nothing. We can talk about it tomorrow."

Moving faster than he expected, considering her battered body, she ran to the door, blocking his exit. "No," she ground out. "You will not do this to me, Hawke. Not again. Tell me why you let me believe you were dead. You're not leaving until you do."

"Our marriage was over. After what I did…what happened… I thought it would be best to—"

"That was not our agreement. Our marriage might have ended, but we were still partners. So don't give me that. There was another reason, and I'm not moving until you tell me what it was."

He could easily pick her up and move her out of his way. But damn if he didn't deserve his own answers.

Before he could respond, she huffed out a sobbing breath. "Oh my sweet heavens. Did you think it was me? That I was the traitor?"

Her eyes shimmered with tears, making Hawke feel like the lowest form of humanity. Which was damn stupid. He could show her why he'd had doubts. He had tons of proof.

Instead, because he couldn't give her any more pain now, he hedged. "I had some…questions."

"Questions? About whether or not I was a killer? These people were my friends, my family. How could you believe I would do something like that?"

He had never seriously considered that she could be involved. Yes, there had been evidence, more than enough to rouse suspicion. But both his heart and his gut had been in agreement on this. Until his entire life had literally blown up.

"Why, Hawke?" she asked again. "Why would you believe something like that?"

He threw a small amount of info her way. "You were in Mexico when Rio was killed."

"What?" she mocked sarcastically. "You thought I took a quick break from rescuing children from a human trafficking ring, jumped on a plane to go kill my friend, and then went back to work?"

He flinched at that. Yes, it sounded boneheaded, but there was more.

"A woman fitting your description was seen in the area minutes before he was killed."

"I'm sure there was more than one blond woman in Ixtapa that could fit my description."

"You were the only one who knew Layla was in Nashville. We all thought she was still in Fiji."

"So because my friend, my very good friend, wanted to keep her location private from everyone but me, you assume I used that information to kill her?" She shook her head in wonderment. "Who are you, Hawke? What happened to the man I married? How could you believe the woman you supposedly loved, the woman who shared her body and soul with you, is a cold-blooded killer?"

"I don't think you're a cold-blooded killer. Maybe you said something to someone or—"

"So which is it? Either I'm a cold-blooded, heartless killer, or I'm too bloody stupid to know how to keep secrets? Make up your mind."

This was the time he should tell her. It's the reason he'd come in here to talk to her. If he explained everything, she would see exactly why he'd made the decisions he had.

The pain in her eyes, the trembling of her mouth stopped him cold. She had plastered herself against the door, and her body looked so fragile, so tired. So crushed. The hurt in her eyes could not be faked...not like this. Knowledge stunned him into immobility, and he inhaled a breathless gasp as the truth washed through him. Olivia really was innocent. She truly had no idea what had happened. Even as his gut had told him repeatedly that she hadn't been responsible, the resulting agony had tainted his every thought.

He couldn't hurt her any more tonight. The truth would tear her to pieces, and hurting her was the last thing he wanted to do.

"We'll talk more tomorrow."

Her shoulders slumped farther, and she moved away from the door, no longer interested in trying to stop him. "Then leave. I'm tired of your vague innuendos."

He stopped with his hand on the doorknob when she said softly, "I always thought we had the perfect relationship, the perfect marriage. That nothing could tear us apart. Now I see we really had nothing but lies between us from the start."

Unable to deny her statement, Hawke walked out the door.

CHAPTER TWELVE

Dressed in running shoes, a long T-shirt, and shorts, Olivia stepped outside her bedroom. It was still early, just before six, but she had slept fitfully and had given up trying at dawn. With her mind whirling from all that she'd learned and all the questions she still had, sleep was impossible.

When she and Hawke had been with OZ, they'd stayed here frequently. The accommodations were better than any hotel. The views and hiking trails were second to none. When possible, she would wake before dawn and hike. There were several trails, but her favorite was an easy two-mile trek to one of the most spectacular views she'd ever witnessed. She'd often thought that if anyone ever doubted the existence of a creator, this view would convince them. There was no way this magnificence had happened by accident.

Since she hadn't eaten the food Hawke had brought her last night, her stomach was an empty cavern. Hoping to avoid running into anyone, she grabbed a couple of energy bars and a bottle of water from the kitchen. Rose always made sure there were plenty of supplies.

She stepped out onto the back porch and drew in a breath of fresh, crisp air. It was early September, and autumn was already peeking around the corner. Leaves were turning, and a mossy, earthy scent wafted on the breeze. Hawke used to laugh at her when she told him she could smell the seasons. Each one had its own unique scent. He'd told her she was part bloodhound.

Hawke.

She took off down the steps, running at a slow, easy pace toward the beginning of the trail. With each step, she felt freer and less burdened. If only she could outrun her thoughts. The last two days had been a revelation. Not only was her husband alive, he had believed she was a traitor. That she had killed their friends.

After all they'd shared, all they'd been through, if he could believe that about her, nothing they'd had was real. Having been trained to endure physical discomfort and pain, nothing could control the hurt she felt. She had valued Hawke's opinion above anyone else's. What did it say about their marriage that he could believe she could be that evil?

How could everything you believed about yourself, about your life, be a lie? Reaching the beginning of the trail's incline, she set a brutal pace, her legs eating up the distance as she tried to come to terms with why he believed she could be a traitor. What flaw or defect did she have that could make anyone believe she could do that, much less the man who supposedly knew her better than anyone?

Her first ten years of life had been lonely. Homeschooled by a bevy of tutors, she had never learned how to build a real relationship with anyone. Her grandmother had been the one person she had cared for, and that relationship had had a terrible ending. She had managed to forge a few friendships

at the exclusive boarding school, but none of them had been
sustaining.

When she'd begun her MI6 training, she had been part-
nered with another trainee. His background couldn't have
been more different from hers. Orphaned young, raised in a
series of foster homes, he had managed to claw his way out
of a brutal system. Even though there were differences, there
had been similarities, too.

Model handsome, with a head full of wavy, blond curls
and the sleek frame of a dancer, Simon had been fairy-tale
prince material. For a girl with absolutely no experience in
navigating the most basic of friendships, a romantic relationship had seemed like a dream come true. Their relationship
had advanced beyond mere friendship, and though there had
been passion between them, it had never felt intimate, only
convenient.

When he'd asked her to marry him, she had seen no
reason to say no. They were of the same ilk, working for the
same agency, doing the same kind of work. It had just made
sense. Within a week of saying yes, she'd regretted her decision. She'd realized she was headed in the direction of being
a carbon copy of her parents. She and Simon had been
destined to become Glen and Iris Gates 2.0.

She had explained her fears to him, and when he'd not
seen a problem with becoming like her parents, she had
known she couldn't go through with it. All her life, she had
sworn not to be like them, and here she was, willingly headed
toward that end.

After she had broken off their engagement, he had
admitted one of his biggest reasons for wanting to marry her
had been the influence her parents could have had on his
career. Saying goodbye had been easy after that. He had
gone on to make a name for himself solo, and she held no
grudges.

After falling in love with Hawke, she had realized how insignificant and lame her feelings for Simon had been.

Layla had been her very first genuine friend. She had been the lone woman on the team until Olivia had arrived. They'd taken an instant liking to each other, and Olivia had been able to talk to her about anything. After the team had disbanded, they hadn't seen each other often, but she and Layla had kept in touch.

When Layla had moved to Nashville, Tennessee, she had called Olivia and told her, but she'd asked her not to tell anyone else. One of her friend's greatest fears had been that she would be called back to work in that life again. Olivia had never told a soul.

When Layla had been found dead in her apartment, Olivia had admitted to knowing her friend's whereabouts. And somehow, that had made Hawke think she'd had something to do with Layla's death?

What kind of person did he think she was?

"Hey. Didn't think anyone else would be up this early."

She whirled around in a defensive pose, ready to strike.

Xavier held up his hands. "Whoa. Sorry I startled you."

She took a step back and blew out a breath. "I'm sorry. Guess my mind was a thousand miles away."

"No problem." He gestured to her face. "Those bruises look pretty brutal."

She hadn't bothered with makeup, and she was sure she looked like an accident victim, or worse.

"They're not as painful as they look."

"I didn't get to talk to you yesterday. I wanted to apologize for the way I treated you back then."

"There's no need, Xavier. Hawke meant a lot to you, and hearing of his death was a blow. I understood."

"That's true, but, Olivia, you meant a lot to me, too. I hope you know that."

She tried to smile but couldn't get her mouth to cooperate. Without Hawke, she never would have known these people. He had brought her with him when he'd joined OZ. She had always assumed that if anything ever happened to Hawke, they'd expect her to leave. It was one of the reasons she had never made a total commitment to OZ. She'd been Hawke's partner and his wife. She'd never believed she had much identity to the OZ team other than that.

"Thank you, Xavier. I valued my relationship with each of you."

Those words had sounded cold and unemotional. She hadn't meant them that way, but everything with her former teammates felt awkward now. The gap was too great, and she didn't think she had the strength to repair it.

Thankfully, he didn't seem to see anything wrong with her response. He swept his arm toward the mountains surrounding them. "Have you ever seen anything more spectacular?"

"No. It's perfect."

"Jazz and I usually try to run this trail a couple of times a week. I pounded on her door this morning, but she told me to go away." He grinned. "She's grouchy as a bear with a sore paw in the morning."

She had always believed Xavier and Jazz would someday realize they were meant to be together. Hawke disagreed, saying they saw each other as friends only, that, if anything, Xavier looked upon Jazz as his kid sister. Looking at his face now, Olivia decided there was nothing brotherly about the affection he had for her. She hoped they didn't let this opportunity pass them by.

Mentally shaking her head at her silly romantic ideas, she asked, "How is she doing? I know she was hurt pretty badly on an op a couple years ago."

"She's almost one hundred percent again."

"Is she still searching for her brother?"

Looking at the vista before them, Xavier said, "Yeah."

One of the things she had appreciated about Option Zero was the team's commitment to one another. With the dangerous lives they'd all led, each of them had a private agenda—someone they wanted to find, someone they wanted to bring to justice, something for which they needed to be able to feel peace. Ash had promised each of them that the team would have their backs when the time came.

Jazz and her brother had been separated when she was in her early teens. She never knew what happened to him. Hopefully, she would find him one day. When she did, the entire OZ team would be there to help her.

Olivia swayed slightly and rubbed her head where a headache was starting.

"Hey." Xavier touched her arm. "Those protein bars look awfully good. Think I could have one?"

She had forgotten that she'd stuffed them into the small bag on her shoulder.

"Sure. Help yourself."

He took two from her pack and handed one to her. She was in the middle of eating it when she realized exactly what he had done. Xavier had likely known she was low on fuel.

She took another bite and said, "Thank you."

"No problem."

Taking a swallow of water, she offered him the bottle. He took a couple of gulps and gave it back to her.

"Guess we'd better head back. Meeting starts at nine."

She took one last sweeping look at the peaceful scene before her and turned her back. She had a feeling this would be the last peaceful moment she would have for a long time to come.

CHAPTER THIRTEEN

"So you believe her?"

Turning from the window, Hawke faced Kate. He and Kate Walker had been friends for a while. When his life had turned upside down, she had pulled his ass out of the fire, literally. When she'd knocked on his door this morning, he'd known she would be demanding answers. She deserved them, but so did Olivia.

"Yes, I believe her."

"Without reservation?"

"Yes." After seeing Olivia's reaction to his accusations last night, there was no doubt in his mind. He didn't know what had happened, wasn't sure he'd ever know, but one thing he was sure of was that Olivia was completely innocent. Somebody had done an excellent job of making her look guilty, and because of all the pain, before and after, he'd allowed it to completely fuck up his judgment.

"Even after what happened?"

"She's not responsible. I'd bet my life Olivia was not involved."

"You already have," came Kate's dry reply.

"Might I remind you that your own husband had some accusations made about him at one time? You stood by him."

"Lars didn't almost kill me."

"She doesn't know about that… I don't want her to know."

"She's going to find out sometime."

"Maybe…but not yet. Not with everything else she's going to have to come to grips with."

"Don't treat her as a victim. She's a strong, intelligent woman with a backbone of steel. If she's innocent, she deserves the truth. And you need answers."

Kate was right. Olivia was all of those things, but that didn't negate his need to protect her. His every instinct urged him to take her someplace safe, away from all of this. Because she might not know that she was involved, but she was. And it was only going to get worse.

"I'll tell her when the time's right."

Kate huffed out a breath of exasperation and headed to the door. "I'll see you in a couple of hours."

"Everyone will be at the meeting. Expect fireworks."

"Do they know I'm coming?"

"No. So be prepared. They're pissed."

"Pissed-off OZ operatives?" Kate grinned. "I've faced worse."

Hawke released a dry laugh. "Yeah, I guess you have. But these people are your friends. They feel betrayed."

"I know they do, and I'm sorry for that."

"Put it on me, where it belongs."

"No, Hawke. Stop the martyr act. I was one hundred percent on board, as was Ash. We're adults, and we made the decision on our own."

"Olivia will be there, too."

Kate shrugged. "Just because you're one hundred percent

sure of her doesn't mean I am. I've seen the evidence, too. I have no regrets about what I did."

He had more than enough regrets for both of them. Everything Kate had done, all the lies she'd told Olivia, had been at his request.

She put her hand on the doorknob and turned back to him. "One last question. If with one little conversation, you've decided upon her complete innocence, why did you wait so long to talk to her?"

"I had my reasons."

She raised a brow, shrugged, and walked out the door.

Hawke stayed glued to his chair for several more moments. Why hadn't he let Olivia know he was alive? The first four months after his disappearance, he'd had good reasons. But after that?

She'd asked him last night if he had planned on not coming back, and he'd admitted that he hadn't, but it was more complicated than that. He'd had every intention of checking in with her each week. But she was right about the reason for giving her the divorce papers. They might've been working together, but that hadn't meant he intended to reenter her life. Their marriage had been over—there'd be no point in returning.

Truthfully, he was surprised that she could even stomach looking at him. After what he'd done, he had assumed she wouldn't want to even be in the same room with him. Which was one of the reasons it had been easy for him to believe that she might have tried to kill him. He had deserved no less.

But she hadn't. She had no idea what had happened, and though she was not a victim in the truest sense of the word, she had still been wronged. Someone had set it up to make Olivia look like both a traitor and a murderer.

Olivia was not his enemy. But was she his ally?

With the capture he'd made last week, the answers were close, and the lid on several issues was about to be blown. Which would cause Olivia only more pain. It couldn't be helped, but he'd make sure that he was there for her this time, whether she wanted him to be or not. He was done letting her down.

Coffee mug in hand, Olivia headed to the conference room. OZ meetings always started on time, and she had thirty seconds to go. She had deliberately waited until the last moment. Before each meeting, there was always chatting about weekend plans and back-and-forth about different things, much the way coworkers or families would behave. She wanted to skip all of that. She was no longer part of that world.

She stopped at the conference room door, glad to see that everyone was already seated. A young woman she didn't recognize sat beside Liam. She wondered if she was a new OZ operative, but then the woman gently caressed Liam's face. This must be Cat. Or Aubrey Starr, as she'd learned from Eve yesterday. The woman Liam had searched almost twelve years for and, despite all odds, had actually found.

Spotting an empty chair next to Eve, she headed her way. She was halfway there when she caught sight of another person who hadn't been here yesterday. Kate Walker was seated three chairs down.

Rage pumping through her, dispelling all the calmness she'd felt before, Olivia marched to Kate's chair.

Kate gave her a cool nod. "Hello, Olivia."

This was the woman who had lied to her face for over two years. Every time Olivia had called, pleading for information about Hawke, Kate had insisted she hadn't heard from him. She had told her she had people looking for him, that she had no idea what could have happened. Kate was the one who had finally convinced her that Hawke was dead.

"You lying bitch," Olivia whispered.

A large hand touched Olivia's shoulder. "Olivia, now's not the time."

She turned and faced Hawke. She had thought last night, after realizing he believed she was a traitor, nothing else could hurt her. But this, to have the woman who had so cruelly misled her be here, in this room, as if she was part of this operation...

She looked down at the scarred hand on her shoulder. "Get your hand off me."

His throat worked as he swallowed hard, but he removed his hand and took a step back. "I know you're angry, but that's going to have to be put on hold."

"Fine," she snapped and walked away.

Eve pulled a chair out for her, and Olivia gratefully dropped into it. Her legs were shaking, and the small blueberry muffin she'd had for breakfast was threatening to come up.

"Deep breaths, Liv," Eve whispered.

The room was silent, and all eyes were on her. She hated that. Being the center of attention always made her uncomfortable.

"All right, everyone," Ash said. "We're all here, including some additions. Jules is still on bed rest, but I'm going to get her on video chat."

Seconds later, a pretty woman with strawberry-blond hair and a tired-looking smile appeared on the television screen.

"Hey, Jules," several people called out.

"Hey, everybody. Wish I could be there in person."

"Not a problem," Jazz said. "You just take care of that bundle of joy."

The brilliant smile she gave made Olivia's heart clutch with a pang she hadn't expected. Shouldn't she be past that by now? Would the pain ever stop?

"I asked Aubrey to come along as well," Ash said, "since she has personal knowledge of what we're looking at."

Confused, Olivia couldn't resist asking, "What *are* we looking at, Ash?"

"Several years ago, we came across some kind of shadow organization. We've yet to figure out their ultimate motive or reason for existence. However, they're woven throughout various government agencies, as well as organizations, conglomerates, and businesses."

"In the US?" Olivia asked.

"Yes, and throughout the world. We've encountered them in multiple countries. We have no idea how many members there are—hundreds, maybe thousands."

"So they all work together for whom? And for what purpose?"

"We don't know. And it's not like the people we've identified work exclusively for this entity. They have normal, everyday jobs, but when their expertise is needed for something, they rise up and do the bidding."

"This is the first I've heard of such an organization," Olivia said. "How long has it been in existence? Have you actually talked to anyone within its ranks?"

"Jules and I have dealt with one member. Aubrey and Liam have close experiences, too."

"How so?"

"Remember my experience in Colombia?" Ash asked.

Olivia nodded. In a way, it was actually the starting point for OZ. Ash had just left the Marines and had been heading back home to the States when he'd gotten a call from a friend who'd offered him a chance for some fast cash. All he'd needed to do was assist with security for some fat-cat business people in Colombia. It had turned into a total disaster when locals had attacked the meeting. All the business people had escaped, leaving Ash and the other security people behind to face an army of rebels. Ash was the only survivor.

He'd been captured and knocked out. When he'd woken, he'd found himself in a Syrian prison, which was where he'd met Liam and Xavier, who'd been prisoners in the same building.

Hawke had been in charge of the covert operation that Liam and Xavier had been working. Hawke, along with Gideon and Sean, had arrived to rescue them. They had rescued Ash as well.

The rescue hadn't turned out as well as they'd hoped as their helicopter had been shot down during their escape. They'd ended up walking through the desert and, during that time, had forged a bond.

When Olivia had first met Hawke, he'd told her the story. Their survival had been miraculous, and even though each of them had gone on to pursue other avenues, they'd never lost touch. Option Zero was born a few years after that.

"Turns out," Ash was saying, "the business meeting in Colombia was being led by a woman who later became a state senator for Ohio, the late Nora Turner. She was part of this shadow organization."

"How did you find out?"

"That's where Kate comes in."

Olivia told herself to be a grown-up and look at Kate. If she thought she would see remorse in the woman's eyes, or even sympathy, she was wrong. The woman looked at her as coldly as anyone she'd ever known. What had happened? She and Kate had never been close, but they had been friendly at one time.

Olivia had understood the antipathy she'd received from the OZ team. They hadn't been in on Hawke's faked-death plan, but Kate had been involved from the beginning. They had worked closely together, ensuring everything went as intended. So why was she now looking at Olivia as if she really was a traitor?

"Yes," Kate said coolly. "I had my own suspicions about Turner. I knew Jules from an earlier time. We worked together, along with Ash, to find out just where Turner's allegiance lay."

"And we found she was connected to this shadow organization," Ash said.

"I know this is a lot to absorb, Liv," Serena said.

Olivia glanced over at the young woman. She hadn't yet talked to either her or her husband, Sean. From the expression on Serena's face, she hadn't had a restful night. She was pale, and her mouth had a pinched, sad look. Sean was sitting beside her with a similar expression. The secrets Serena had kept from her husband were obviously causing some marital strife. While Olivia could understand Sean's anger, she didn't like seeing Serena looking so sad. She and Jazz were the only two people who hadn't lashed out at her after Hawke's disappearance.

Serena pointed to a stack of pages on the credenza behind her. "Since we're trying to stay old-school with this, I printed hard copies for you of all the intel we've been able to gather so far, including all the personal experiences we've encountered." She sent Hawke a strained smile. "I have it stored in the cloud. I know you're worried we'll get hacked, but I promise it's safe."

"How can you be sure?" Hawke asked. "Ash said you were hacked last year."

"Yes," Ash said, "and for the past year, she's been working on an impenetrable firewall, and she's achieved one. No one is aware of its existence. We won't get hacked again." He looked at Olivia. "Olivia, you can get caught up on the background later. Let's talk about where we go from here."

"So let me see if I understand this correctly," Olivia said. "There is some kind of shadowy entity working behind the scenes that coordinates and manipulates events and people for some sort of devious purpose?"

"Exactly," Ash said. "From what we can tell, people can remain dormant for decades, living regular lives. Then when they're called upon, they'll do whatever they're asked to do."

"What's in it for them?"

"Based on our personal experience, they're rewarded in various ways."

Aubrey sent Olivia a smile and said, "We've not met officially, but I feel like we know each other. Liam told me you were one of the OZ team members who helped try to find me. Thank you for that."

Silly, emotional tears sprang to Olivia's eyes. After all the upheaval and sadness over the last few days, to have someone say a simple thank-you was like a balm to her soul. "I'm so glad he found you."

Aubrey looked up at her new husband, all the love in the world in her eyes. "I am, too." Turning back to Olivia, she said, "My uncle, Syd Green, was one of these people. He was a well-known movie director." Her voice thickened. "He died before he was able to tell us a lot, but from what we could discern, he received special perks and monetary gain."

"How would a movie director be able to help this shadowy organization?"

"He told us he didn't do a lot," Liam added. "He hired certain people they recommended, took on certain projects, turned down others."

"And you're sure all of these…" She pointed to the stack of pages. "All of these people are working within this entity?"

"Yes, without a doubt," Ash answered.

"And you believe the Gonzalez cartel is tied to the group as well?"

She didn't look at Hawke when she asked that question, but he was the one who answered. "Yes, I do."

Having no choice, she turned to him. "Why?"

HAWKE KEPT HIS EXPRESSION IMPASSIVE, his tone businesslike. "When Gonzalez went to prison, remember what happened to the cartel?"

"Yes. It was destroyed."

Moving his gaze off Olivia, Hawke let it roam the room. "Even though the op went sideways, we managed to destroy the cartel, which was our plan. Hector Gonzalez went to prison. His wife and son were left, but they only had a small portion of what Hector had built. Hector died in prison not long after his incarceration. It looked like nothing could resurrect their business.

"When we took Gonzalez down, he said something about having power behind him that we couldn't begin to fathom. And he bragged the same thing to Ramirez."

"Yes," Olivia said. "We thought it was the bravado and ego talking."

"Well, it's taken me more than a year, but with Serena's help, I was finally able to understand what he was talking about."

"How so?"

"The meeting in Colombia, the one where Ash was on that security detail and Senator Turner was in charge of? We've managed to track down a few people who were there with Turner. Turns out, Hector Gonzalez was one of them."

"And there's our connection," Eve said softly.

"So you think Gonzalez was referring to this shadow

group when he bragged about having power we knew nothing about?" Olivia asked.

"Yes," Hawke answered. "Over the last year, this has happened." Using the remote in his hand, he clicked it to reveal a list of warehouses, labs, and businesses on the screen at the front of the room. "All of these belong to the Gonzalez cartel."

"They had nothing left," Olivia whispered.

"Exactly. And now they're one of the largest cartels in South America, responsible for trafficking more than a quarter of the heroin, cocaine, and opioids throughout the world. They also have labs, some of which are creating lethal and highly illegal synthetic drugs. The way they're moving, they're destined to become much larger over the next few years."

"Who's running the cartel?" Liam asked.

"Hector's twenty-year-old son, Juan, is the figurehead, but I don't believe he has any decision-making power. Neither he nor his mother were involved in the cartel when Hector was in charge. Hard to imagine they've managed to develop the business savvy to create this new, even bigger cartel."

Hawke waited to see if anyone would argue with him. He was being deliberately vague about some things. He could give concrete answers later, but for now, this would have to suffice.

Surprisingly, no one demanded specifics, but Eve asked the question that was on everyone's mind.

"So, what are we going to do about this?"

"We're going to destroy the Gonzalez cartel once and for all. And then we're going to find out who this shadow group is and end them, too."

CHAPTER FOURTEEN

Taking the robe from the back of the door, Olivia wrapped herself in warm cotton. The aches in her body had eased with a hot bath, but the ache in her heart had only grown. Her reserves were almost at an end. Putting her emotions on hold for just a short while, she longed for the oblivion of sleep.

She had spent the last few hours poring over the pages that Serena had printed out for her. It was hard to imagine that such a group existed, but there was no denying that some kind of entity lived within the shadows, manipulating and controlling people and events. To what end was as murky as pond scum.

The knock on her door brought a long, exhaustive sigh. Talking to someone right now was the last thing she wanted. She knew her body. If she didn't get rest soon, she would not be able to function at all. She pulled the door open and faced the last person she wanted to see.

"What do you want, Kate?"

"We need to talk."

"Oh, really? You have more lies to tell me?"

"Either let me in your room, or we'll have this conversation in the hallway. Your choice."

She considered the woman she'd once called friend. The woman who'd repeatedly lied to her for the last two years.

Apparently reading her thoughts, Kate sighed and shook her head. "All right. I'm sorry I lied to you, Olivia. A part of me felt shitty doing it, but there were extenuating circumstances."

"There are no circumstances, extenuating or otherwise, that justify what you did."

"Let me in, and I'll prove you wrong."

Olivia stepped back, allowing the other woman to walk inside. She shut the door and went to the other side of the room. If she stayed within touching distance, she feared she would punch the woman into unconsciousness.

Kate settled into a chair by the window, her demeanor one of relaxed casualness, but the lines around her mouth belied a tension the rest of her body didn't reveal. It wasn't much, but it made Olivia feel a little better to know that Kate wasn't as at ease as she liked to pretend.

The woman was always impeccably dressed, and today was no different. Even in black slacks and a light blue silk blouse, she exuded an elegance that Olivia had always admired. With dark brown, shoulder-length hair, emerald-green eyes, and a slender build, Kate Walker was an attractive, vibrant woman.

A new worry hit Olivia, one that she had not considered until now. And one that would finish her if it was true.

"Are you and Hawke…" She swallowed, took a deep breath to better handle the blow, and tried again. "Are you and Hawke having an affair?"

The surprise on the other woman's face was authentic, and something like compassion temporarily softened her features. "No, Olivia. Hawke is my friend and nothing more."

The relief was instantaneous. Her knees trembling, Olivia dropped into a chair to avoid falling. She believed her, which might be stupid since Kate was such a good liar, but her surprise at the question had seemed genuine.

"Please tell me why, Kate."

"I had doubts about you."

"You believed it, too? You think I'm responsible for Rio's and Layla's deaths? For the attempts on Deacon, Mack, and Trevor?"

"I didn't want to."

So tired of being considered a traitor when she had done nothing wrong, she shouted, "Then why the hell did you?"

"The evidence pointed to you."

"What evidence?"

"As you know, Hawke tasked Layla with finding the person who sabotaged the Gonzalez op. She looked at everyone on the team."

Yes, they had all discussed this. The op had been compromised, and no matter that it ultimately had achieved their objectives, they'd known there was a rat in their midst. Even though the team had disbanded soon after that mission, she'd known Hawke had continued to try to find the traitor.

"When Layla went off the grid," Kate continued, "Hawke sent me her hacking programs, and all the intel she'd been able to dig up on the possible identity of the mole. I gave everything to a trusted associate for analysis. He took it and found even more intel. I then gave everything to Hawke."

For the first time, Olivia noticed a small stack of papers in Kate's hands. She held them up. "These are my copies. Hawke doesn't know I'm here, and he'll be pissed at me for bringing this to you. But if I were branded a traitor, then I'd want to know why, no matter how much it hurt. Can you handle that, Liv?"

"As it's been pointed out to me several times," Olivia said

coolly, "I'm a stone-cold bitch. That means I can handle anything that's dished out. Let me have it."

"Very well. Don't say I didn't warn you." She handed the papers to Olivia, stood, and walked to the door.

"Do you still think I'm a traitor?"

Kate looked at her for a long moment and said, "I don't know." She walked out, shutting the door behind her.

The pages gripped in her hand, Olivia went to the giant window of her bedroom. It was way past dark, and the view was no longer visible. All she could see was her reflection, a tired and bruised woman whose face showed a weary soul and a broken spirit. She was self-aware enough to know she had many faults. She was sometimes selfish, acted like a petulant child if her feelings were bruised, and on occasion, she could be bitchy. But the one thing she always relied on above all others was her integrity. Every important decision she'd ever made was with an eye toward doing the right thing.

But somehow all of that was being questioned. Somehow the man she loved and trusted above all others had doubted her. He'd actually believed she could be, for lack of a better word, evil. And she had no idea why.

The papers in her hands could well hold the key to how he'd come to that conclusion. She would read them, study them, but no matter what they said, she could not come to terms with his lack of faith in her. If the roles were reversed, there was nothing he could do, nothing anyone could say to make her believe the same of him. She had believed his love and faith in her was rock-solid. Instead, she had discovered, it was made of clay.

She went back to her chair in the corner, turned on the bright floor lamp beside it, sat, and began to read.

At first, the conglomeration of words made no sense. She rubbed her tired eyes and refocused. They were emails.

Friendly, chatty, but there was no real content or context. There were also a lot of letters used instead of actual words. Nothing made sense.

She shuffled through several pages, still not seeing anything that would condemn her or anything even related to her. She glanced at the top of one email to see if she recognized the sender or recipient's name. Her breath caught in her throat. The email handle was Dove22. That had been her code name when she'd first started working with Hawke and his team. No one should know that name except the people on her team.

With that new knowledge, she went back to the first page and reread the lines. As she read, a cold lump of dread grew in her belly. The emails referred to H, L, R, M, T, and D. Those letters obviously represented Hawke, Layla, Rio, Mack, Trevor, and Deacon. The emails also referenced locations, jobs, and degree of difficulty. One exchange in particular caught her attention.

Dove22: *H is such a hard-ass. Saved his life twice, and he's harder on me than anyone.*

Z: *Get what you need and get out. Don't whine.*

Whoever this mysterious Z was, it was obvious there was something he did not know. There was no mention of her having met Hawke six months earlier in Munich. That was because she'd told no one. She had kept that amazing connection to herself.

She scrolled through several more pages, her horror growing as she read details of missions that no one but the team should have known about. She stopped on what was obviously the Gonzalez job. This fake Dove was furious about being almost killed on that mission. And that was true. Olivia had almost died protecting Tomás Ramirez.

But what was not mentioned in the emails was how much the mission had meant to her. She had learned so much about herself during that op. It had been one of the most significant and consequential jobs of her life.

Getting to know Tomás had been a revelation. The bright, articulate, and charming seven-year-old had woven a place in her heart, and she would have gladly died for him. And she almost had.

It was also during this time that she was beginning to recognize her deep feelings for Hawke. She had kept all these thoughts to herself. This Dove22 impersonator knew nothing about them.

This person did not know the real Olivia Gates. The writer of the emails continued to complain about Hawke's harsh treatment and stringent rules. If she hadn't known better, she'd say a spoiled, bratty teenager had written them.

It was after three in the morning when Olivia turned off the light and lay down on the bed. Her mind was an active hive of thoughts, and though there was no way she would sleep, she gave herself permission to cry. If she had seen those emails when Hawke and Kate had first seen them, she could have pointed out the inconsistencies and the obvious manipulation of the intel. Yes, they contained facts and data that only someone on the team should have known. But whoever had designed this hoax hadn't known *her*. Not really.

As the tears poured out, she hugged herself tight and thought about all she and Hawke had lost. If he had just come to her, she could have proved her innocence. But he hadn't. He had assumed she was a traitor. A liar. A killer.

The last few emails she'd seen had been the most damning of all.

Dove22: *New job a bore. Got any action?*

Z: *Interested in making a killing?*

The double entendre hadn't been lost on her. The emails

had gone on to mention that R was in M, and he needed to disappear. Was she up to the task?

Dove22 had answered in the affirmative. Days later, Rio had been murdered in Ixtapa, Mexico. His killer had never been caught.

Hawke had said that someone fitting her description had been spotted close to where Rio's body was discovered. Had that been part of the hoax, too?

A gap of several months had passed before another email arrived, indicating that L was now in the Music City. Was she interested?

Layla had been killed in Nashville, known as the Music City, a few days after the date on that email.

Yes, it looked damning, and yes, she wanted answers. But dammit, it hadn't been her! Why hadn't he seen that? How could the man she had shared every intimacy with believe she was this Dove22? A cold, heartless murderer.

Around five, she got up and showered. She brushed her teeth and combed her hair, all without looking at herself in the mirror. She knew she looked like hell, and she just didn't care.

She dressed, grabbed the damning papers, and walked out the door.

CHAPTER FIFTEEN

Someone pounding on the door before dawn was never a good sign. Hawke figured he'd slept maybe forty-five minutes the whole night, and he was not ready for whatever it was. Didn't really matter, because whoever was on the other side of that door was not going to stop until the entire house was awake.

He pulled the door open. One look at Olivia's puffy, red eyes and the pages she had grasped in her hand, and he said softly, "Shit."

"Exactly."

She pushed him back and Hawke shut the door behind her.

"Kate shouldn't have given you those."

"You're right. She shouldn't have. You should have. Three years ago, or whenever this first came to light."

"Sit down." He nodded to the sofa. "You want some coffee?"

"No, I don't want coffee. I want answers!"

Instead of replying, he went to the alcove across the room and turned on the small coffee machine. Whether she wanted coffee or not, he did. He glanced back, noting the droop of her shoulders and the prominent dark circles beneath her eyes. Turning around, he took down another mug from the cabinet, grabbed a tea bag, and switched the function of the machine to hot water. In less than a minute, he was pouring steaming water into the mug.

He switched the machine back to coffee mode, then took the hot water and tea bag to Olivia. He set them on the table beside the sofa and handed her two pills and a glass of cold water.

"What's this for?"

"Headache."

She glared up at him but took them from his hand without argument.

He went back for his coffee, took a sip.

"Dammit, Hawke."

Blowing out a breath, he went to the closest chair and dropped into it. His leg ached like a sore tooth, but he refused to try to rub the pain away. She would ask questions, and hell if he wanted to get into that. Not with everything else she had to face.

"What did Kate tell you?"

"She said Layla was monitoring all of us at your request. That after the team disbanded, you asked Kate for help. She gave Layla's notes and programs to her people. These emails were found."

"And that's the way it was with one exception. A lot of those emails were found while the team was still together."

"And you didn't think the fact that I was implicated was something I should have been told about?"

"As team leader, it was my responsibility to protect each member. I believed they were bogus and had Layla digging for the truth."

She glanced down at the papers still clutched in her hand.

"A lot of the emails are dated right after I arrived to work with the team."

"They're made to look that way. Layla did some back-tracing. She said even though the emails looked like they were written in the early days, all the ones she found were actually generated right after the Gonzalez operation."

"How could she know that?"

"I don't pretend to know the technology she used to determine that. I just know it's what she believed, and I believed her."

"And it never occurred to you to tell me? Did you ever think that I might have been able to give you some ideas, some suggestions for who might be behind them?"

Hawke shrugged. She made some good points, but he refused to apologize for how he'd handled things. Nothing would have really changed, and she would soon learn why.

"As team leader, I made the decision not to."

"All right, Mr. Team Leader. Fine. But what about when you were no longer team leader? What about when you were my husband? Did you ever consider saying, 'Hey, honey, someone's trying to frame you for being a traitor. You have any idea who that might be?'"

Instead of answering, he nodded toward the pages. "You see a difference between the emails that were sent during the time the team was together and after we disbanded?"

She gave him a scathing glare and then shuffled through the emails again. He watched her demeanor change as realization hit her. "There's no real detail to them."

The emails that were sent while the team was together contained specific information about locations, dates, and times. Some even had kill and capture numbers. The ones sent after the team disbanded were vague and uninformative. Maybe to the casual observer, they would look authentic, but to someone who knew the facts, it was obvious that the writer had had no clue at that point what was going on in Olivia's life.

After the team dissolved, he and Olivia had created their own operation. It had been the best year and a half of his life. They had taken only the jobs they'd felt strongly about and had enjoyed every moment.

"Whoever created them," she said softly, "had to have been on the team."

Hawke nodded. "Note that the later ones, after we started working for OZ and you were working with LCR, are even vaguer. This person had no clue what you were doing or who you worked for."

A look of horror flashed across her face. "Mack, Trevor, and Deacon… Do they think I betrayed them?"

"No. No one knew about the earlier emails except Layla. Kate's hacker found the later ones."

"Then would you please answer my initial question? Why didn't you tell me about them?"

"Because it could have been anyone on the team. Yeah, your code name, Dove22, was being used, but all of them knew it. There was nothing that pointed directly to you other than that name. Until something did."

"Rio's death," she said.

"Yeah. Until those last emails were found, I actually suspected Rio was the mole. He'd requested his own team and got denied. There was always a little friction between him and everyone else." Hawke took a breath. He'd promised full disclosure, and this was as close as he could get. "A while after his death, I brought them with me to show you…"

"And?"

"And you had your own bombshell."

It took only a second for her to comprehend his meaning. "I can't believe we're back to that."

"No, that's not why I brought it up. It was…" He

shrugged, knowing he was making a mess out of things. "I forgave you for that a long time ago. I don't want—"

"You forgave me?" Her voice was thick with fury. "You *forgave* me? How very big of you, Hawke."

"No! That's not what I meant, Livvy. I just…" Hell, what could he say? Even today, he was gutted by what had happened. By what he'd done. It was her forgiveness he needed, not the other way around.

Her eyes dark with hurt, she said, "All right. Fine. Go ahead and blame me. I don't care. I'm a big girl. I can take it. I was the one who went through the pain. I was the one who suffered the consequences. I lost everything that day. Nothing happened to you. You lost nothing. I don't need, nor have I ever wanted, your forgiveness."

He jerked back at her words. She thought he'd lost nothing? How she must have hated him. "I'm sorry, Livvy. So sorry."

He reached out a hand to her, which she ignored. Could he blame her?

"All right." She drew in a shaky breath. "Let's refocus." She held the emails up and shook them. "This wasn't me. You knew it wasn't me from the beginning. And you didn't tell me. We were together for years, and you didn't think it was important enough…or I wasn't important enough."

"That's not why. I told you—"

"Yes, yes. You were handling it. Whatever. What else have you got?"

Feeling about twenty years older than he had ten minutes ago, Hawke stood and went to the desk in the corner where he'd left the intel, his leg aching with every step.

"What happened to your leg?"

He headed back to where she sat. If he'd thought she was pale earlier, it was nothing to how she looked now. There was absolutely no color in her face, and her eyes had a lost, empty look. He had promised to tell her everything, but no way in hell was he going to put that on her today.

"Banged up my knee. It's fine." He handed her the additional intel. "Kate's people found this, too. There's a bank account from the Bank of the People in the Cayman Islands created under one of your old aliases. It was opened a few days before Rio's death. The day after his death, there was a deposit of two hundred fifty thousand dollars. And then, the day after Layla's, another two-fifty was added."

She stared down at the pages and shook her head. "I just don't understand why anyone would go to so much trouble to frame me."

He had an idea about that, but she needed to hear the rest of it first.

"I went to the bank and managed to talk to a sympathetic bank manager." He didn't bother to explain the lies he'd told. That was the job. "He gave me a still photo of the person who opened the account."

He handed her the grainy photograph. The photo showed only the side of the woman's face, and it was slightly out of focus. This person had clearly tried to resemble Olivia Gates. She had done a fairly good job of it.

"She looks like me."

"Yeah."

"Someone went to a lot of trouble to destroy my life."

"Actually, I don't think that was the intent."

"What do you mean?"

"Have you ever wondered why you were the only team member who wasn't targeted at that time?"

"That's not true. You weren't either."

"I was. The same day as the attempts were made on Mack, Trevor, and Deacon, someone took a shot at me and missed."

"Why didn't you tell me?" She raised her hand to stop his

reply. "Don't bother. I was just your wife. Why would I need to know something like that?"

He ignored her sarcasm and said, "Ever wonder why, other than Layla and possibly Rio, all the other attempts failed?"

"No. I just…" She shook her head. "No."

"I think they were deliberate misses. I think someone was trying to send us a message."

"What was the message?"

"I don't know. Get out of town, lie low. If so, it worked. We all disappeared after that."

"And I wasn't targeted because this person wanted everyone to think I was responsible?"

"Yes, but not the way it seems."

"What do you mean?"

"I think you were being protected."

"Protected?" She gave a humorless laugh. "I was being framed for killing and trying to kill my friends, for being a traitor. That's protection?"

"I think part of the deal that Gonzalez made with this shadow organization was to target the people who brought Hector down."

"Then why the near misses? You said you thought they were deliberately botched."

"That's something I'm not sure about, but I hope to get answers soon."

"Then why was I attacked the other night? Why am I suddenly being targeted if I'm supposed to be the one responsible?"

"I don't believe that's why you were attacked."

"Then why?"

Instead of answering directly, he continued, "I got a lead that the Gonzalez cartel and the Mexican Mafia were meeting in Mexico City. I went after the head of security for the Gonzalez cartel."

"You got him?"

"Her."

"Okay, her. What did she tell you?"

"Not a lot so far. I've got her in a holding cell at a black site in Arizona."

Olivia got to her feet. "Well, then, let's go make her talk. If she knows who's behind this, then she knows who killed Layla and Rio. She might even know who our traitor was. She's got to—"

"Wait...Olivia. She's not the head of security for the Gonzalez cartel. My intel was wrong. I do, however, believe she's responsible for the missed hits on the team. I don't know about Layla's or Rio's deaths, but I'm almost sure she's responsible for the attempts on the others. And I believe she's responsible for the emails. That's why you were attacked the other night. I think they planned to question you about her whereabouts."

"But why? What would I know about this person?"

"Because of who she is."

"Who is she?"

Hawke took a deep breath and said, "Your mother."

CHAPTER SIXTEEN

Olivia looked out at the wet tarmac of the private airport. She'd learned only two hours ago that her mother was behind all of this, and she and Hawke were already on OZ's Gulfstream jet, headed to Arizona.

The clouds were gray and leaden, and rain slashed angrily against the plane's windows. The weather was a fitting companion to her mood. Was her mother a traitor? Of all the harsh things she believed about Iris Gates, treason had not been on her radar. Yes, the woman was an evil, self-centered sociopath, but she had worked for one of the premier intelligence agencies in the world. Iris and Glen Gates had been revered among the intelligence community. Their names were synonymous with loyalty and patriotism to the Crown. How was any of this even possible?

She hadn't asked Hawke for details. She hadn't needed to. He would not make this accusation without just cause. Yes, she realized the irony. Her faith in her husband had been shaken to the core, but she believed him about this. Maybe it was because she knew her mother. She had seen beyond the façade her mother showed to the world. She had lived the nightmare of Iris Gates and bore the scars to prove it.

"Pilot said that with the weather, it'll take about three hours or so to get there."

She glanced up at Hawke and nodded. She would need that time to prepare for the battle to come. She had no illusions that her mother would willingly reveal secrets. She hadn't seen Iris in years. They had no relationship, no real connection, so counting on any kind of familial bond to goad her mother into talking was not going to work. She needed another angle.

"There's a bedroom in the back," Hawke said. "Why don't you go lie down?"

Without speaking, she stood and walked toward the back. She knew Hawke watched her closely, maybe even waiting for her to fall apart. She was past that stage. She actually wasn't sure what stage she was in right now. There was numbness, but maybe also a bit of relief. Maybe at last she'd get some answers.

She opened the door, aware enough to note the serene décor of Caribbean blue and silver. She switched on the bedside lamp, turned off the overhead light, slipped off her shoes, and then dropped onto the bed. It was still early morning. The last few days had left her both exhausted and sleep-deprived. However, getting any sleep with everything spinning through her mind would be impossible. Just to lie prone for a couple hours would be helpful. A whirlwind of questions swirled through her scattered thoughts. If she could just settle for a few moments and find a moment of peace, perhaps something cohesive and coherent would arise.

The pillow was soft, the mattress firm, and the room was cool. The drone of the plane's engines created a comforting white noise that should be conducive to rest. But that wasn't going to happen. Everything she'd known in her life—all thirty-four years of it—was being called into question. Her mother could very well be a traitor. And the man she loved more than anything or anyone on the planet had believed at one time, at least, that Olivia might be one, too.

The bedroom door opened quietly, and Hawke walked in. She looked up to see him holding a glass of water. Two pills lay on his other palm.

"What's that?"

"Sleeping pills."

"No, thank you." Waking groggy and thickheaded would be worse than getting no sleep at all.

"It's a light dose. Just enough to relax you. You haven't had more than a few hours sleep in the last three days. Your body is going to give out. Not only that, you need to be sharp when you question Iris."

"I know that, but I'm not taking a sleeping pill."

"There's something else that used to put you to sleep better than sleeping pills." A small smile lifted his mouth and heat shimmered like molten silver in his eyes.

He was referring to sex, of course. Their physical relationship had been off-the-charts intimate and passionate. So much so that having sex with him had been one of the best ways for her to rest before a big mission. She would sleep like the dead after intensive lovemaking.

"Yes, well, that was a long time ago." Even as she said those words, her body was already reacting to the idea. No matter what happened, no matter the angry words and deeds between them, the very idea of this man's touch created a heat within her that nothing could match. In her heart, she knew it would always be like that.

He sat on the side of the bed and said firmly, "Sleeping pills or the other. Your choice."

Their eyes locked, and Olivia couldn't look away. This

was the man she had ached for every night for more than two years. This was this man who, despite everything, still owned her heart. This was the man she had vowed to love until death parted them. Even when she'd thought he was dead, she had never stopped loving him. And even though he'd crushed her heart, she still wanted him. Every night she would go to bed, aching for his touch, his mouth, his body covering hers.

Her heart thudding, her body flooding with a familiar throbbing desire, she said softly, "I don't want the pills."

Hunger flared in his eyes. He set the water glass and pills on the table and stood. Turning the lamp to its lowest setting, he began to strip. It was dark in the room, and she could barely make out the outline of his body. She wanted to tell him to turn the light back on—making love in the light had never been an issue for them. But her heart was beating so hard, she wasn't even sure she could get the words out. They had made love thousands of times, but this time... This time seemed so different. Almost as if they were strangers.

Once he was nude, he began to work on her clothes. She didn't offer to help him other than to shift to aid him in removing her shirt and bra and lifting her legs for him to slide her pants and underwear off.

When they were both nude, she scooted over to allow him room to lie beside her. It wasn't necessary. He straddled her hips and, propping himself on his arms, hovered over her. She looked up at him, wishing she could see his face, his beautiful eyes. Her breathing increased, and her entire body filled with warmth, softening everything within her, preparing for him. At the same time, her heart raced frantically. She didn't know why she was nervous. This was Nic, her husband, her lover. The man she had pledged her heart and her body to years ago. This part used to be as natural as breathing.

For some reason, she felt the need to say, "I haven't been with anyone since you."

He froze for a second and then answered quietly, "Neither have I."

Relief flooded her, and tears sprang to her eyes. The words were a balm to her bruised heart. She raised her hand to touch his face, but he stopped her. Taking both her wrists, he pulled her arms above her head and wrapped her hands around the railing of the headboard.

"What are you doing?"

"Living out a fantasy I've had for two and a half years."

"Of what?"

"Of making love to my beautiful wife."

He kissed her softly, his mouth moved over her face, gently, like a whisper. Olivia chased his mouth, groaning, needing more. She wanted his fiery kisses, to feel the insatiable desire that had always defined their lovemaking. Passion, bright and burning, would incinerate them, until nothing was left but two creatures writhing in pleasure, giving their all to each other.

"Nic...please. I need..."

"Patience, my love."

He moved tenderly down her neck, stopping for an occasional lashing of his tongue at an ultrasensitive spot. He knew her body better than she did. Everything within her surrendered as she gave herself over to his touch, his desire. This man was the love of her life. She didn't think about the past or what lay in their future. For over two years, her body, heart, and soul had yearned for this. She had fantasized and dreamed of this moment, creating hundreds of scenarios in her head, which always resulted in an aching, unsatisfied emptiness, longing for the man she never believed she'd see again. She wasn't about to waste a second on regret or hurt.

Nic's mouth traveled down to her chest, paying homage

to each breast, licking and sucking around each areola before moving down her midriff. He swirled his tongue into her navel, and she raised her hips, showing him exactly where she wanted him to go. As soon as his mouth covered her center, she exploded around him, crying out his name.

Barely cognizant of anything other than the ecstasy of her release, she vaguely registered that he pulled something from the drawer beside the bed. When she heard a tearing sound, she knew he was slipping on a condom.

Throbbing with the need to be filled, she writhed on the bed, and groaned softly, "Nic…please."

"I'm right here, Livvy."

He thrust deep inside, and she cried out. Wanting, longing to hold him, she released the headboard to touch him. Before she could reach him, his hands wrapped around her wrists again and held them as he moved inside her. She was so lost in him, in the passion, the soaring desire, she didn't question anything other than the next wave of pleasure that tossed her up and over and into velvet, blessed oblivion.

When his release came, he stiffened and groaned out her name as if he were in agony. His breathing heavy, he stayed inside her for a long while as if he didn't want to let her go. Aching to hold him, she tried to move her hands from his grip again. He withdrew and dropped down beside her. Pulling her into his arms, he whispered softly, "Sleep, my love."

And she did.

HAWKE DRESSED FOR POWER. Designer suit, designer shoes, designer tie. He was slightly amused that Rose had even included designer briefs. He hadn't had a haircut in a couple months, so his dark, brown hair was a little shabby, but he'd shaved his beard, leaving only slight stubble, which helped a little. Besides, Livvy had told him one time that he looked good in scruff.

Livvy. What had happened a couple hours ago had been the culmination of a thousand and one dreams and fantasies. He had made love to his wife many times, and each time had been sexy and delicious. But this last time… He could not begin to describe how special it had been. He had missed her so much. The intimacy and softness, her sweet warmth and honest passion. There was no one like Livvy, and there never would be.

He looked over his shoulder at the still figure on the bed. She had fallen asleep in his arms, like she had so many times before. They'd loved each other until they were breathless. It hadn't been a long sleep, more like a nap than anything, but it had been the best sleep he'd had in over two years, and he was willing to bet it had been the best she'd had in a while, too.

She stirred slightly, and he walked over to her. He noted her color was better, and the tension around her mouth had lessened.

He sat on the edge of the bed and watched as she opened her eyes and began to remember what happened. "Nic," she whispered.

"Good afternoon."

He leaned over and kissed her softly. Right now, they were still Nic and Livvy. When they left this bedroom, it would be different. He was under no illusion that their problems were over. No matter how passionate it had been, the past could not be erased. But for right now, he would take this.

"We're due to land in about twenty minutes."

"I need to shower."

He stood and gestured toward the bathroom. "There's plenty of hot water. I left a makeup bag on the counter, and your dress is hanging in the closet." He headed toward the door. "I'll get us some coffee."

"Wait. My dress?"

He closed the door without answering. She would understand once she saw the dress.

After responding to a couple of texts and making a call to the holding facility with specific instructions for their visit, he returned to the bedroom, coffee in hand.

Olivia was just coming out of the bathroom. She was wearing the dress he'd set out for her, and she had made good use of the makeup. Only if someone were extremely close would they be able to make out the healing bruises on her cheek and chin. Her skin looked as flawless as ever. She looked healthy and vital. Beautiful.

He had described what was needed, and once again, Rose had come through spectacularly. The dress was ultrafeminine and floaty—if that was even a word. The light blue color turned her eyes to turquoise, and the just slightly modest neckline showed more of that English rose skin. The hem fell to an inch above her knee, showing off her spectacular legs. The heels were two inches. Livvy didn't need extra height, and any more would look out of place. She wore a delicate pearl and diamond necklace, which looked lovely against her soft, pale skin, and the classic diamond studs in her ears were the perfect accompaniment. She looked exactly how he wanted—the exact opposite of what Iris Gates had tried to create.

She had put her hair up in an intricate twist, and while he considered it sexy as hell, that wasn't the look required for this visit.

"Take your hair down."

"Why?"

"She needs to see you with your hair down."

"What do you mean?"

"She needs to see she failed."

Iris Gates had tried to clone her daughter into a replica of herself—a soulless, heartless bitch who cared for no one but herself. Olivia was one of the warmest, most loving women he'd ever known. Many people didn't see that—they looked at the cool exterior and never saw the gentleness beneath.

Without asking for another explanation, she loosened her hair and allowed it to fall onto her shoulders in soft waves.

"Perfect."

He glanced at her hand, double-checking that she still wore her wedding ring. Though he knew she had never taken it off. Over the last two years, hundreds of photos had been taken of her, and every time her hand had been in the picture, he had zoomed in to check her left ring finger. He had never seen her without her wedding band. The fact that she still wore hers, even after their divorce, did something to his heart. At some point he should ask her why, but not today.

He'd taken his off the day he'd left, but he was wearing it now. Iris needed to see them as a united front against her.

"Ready?" he asked.

"As I'll ever be."

He held his hand out to her. "Let's go."

Armed for whatever came next, they walked out the door together.

CHAPTER SEVENTEEN

Yuma, Arizona

Olivia was grateful for the air-conditioned SUV waiting for them on the tarmac. The weather in Montana had been chilly, on the edge of cold. The temperature here was a sizzling ninety degrees at least.

She glanced down at the dress she wore, thankful it was made of light, breathable material. It was ultrafeminine, and she knew exactly what Hawke had meant when he'd told her that Iris needed to see that she hadn't won.

He knew everything about her upbringing and what she had endured. She remembered the first time he'd seen the scars on her back. They'd just begun to realize their feelings for each other, both of them easing into things. Well, her more than him. She had just not been able to wrap her head around falling in love. The concept had been so foreign to her.

They had gone swimming at a hotel pool where they'd been staying for a few days. She had worn a semimodest two-piece and had been thoroughly enjoying herself—until

Hawke had asked about her scars. At first, it had been a teasing question. A few days before that, they'd been laughingly talking about various scars they'd earned along the way. So when he'd touched a scar on her back and told her she'd forgotten to tell him about that one, he hadn't realized the significance. She hadn't yet told him everything.

Olivia had frozen, unable to say anything. Stupid, she'd known, but there had been such shame in her. She hadn't wanted to admit to being beaten. Even though she had been only ten years old at the time, it had been humiliating.

She had rarely thought about the scars. They were as much a part of her as her eye color or the dimple in her left cheek. But Hawke had gone quiet, and then when she'd felt him touch another scar, higher up on her side, she'd known he was realizing it wasn't just any kind of scar.

"Who did this to you, Livvy?"

The fury in his voice had been so cold, so lethal, that even now she could shiver at the sound of suppressed violence.

When she had told him, it was all she could do to keep him from flying to England to confront her mother. She had convinced him it no longer had an impact on her. She had gotten over it and had escaped that life. That was all in the past.

But she knew exactly what he'd meant with the words *she needs to see she didn't win*.

Iris had wanted Olivia to be just like her. Her mother already knew she had failed, that, despite her best efforts, Olivia was nothing like her. But this dress, this look, would emphasize that failure. She would be on the defensive, and she would reveal more than she planned.

Or that was the hope.

She glanced over at Hawke, at his rigid, unyielding jaw. "I'm glad you shaved your beard."

141

His mouth twitched in a small smile. "I decided I'd had enough of the untamed look."

Her gaze traveled over his suit, and she noted it looked as though it had been tailored just for him. Her eyes moved to his right hand on the steering wheel, and she remembered how those long fingers had trailed across her body, bringing her to pleasure over and over again. They had yet to talk about what had happened, and they couldn't right now. They needed to focus on getting as much information as possible from Iris.

He wore a wedding band on his left hand. She told herself it didn't mean anything. She told herself it didn't matter even if it did mean something—nothing could ever be the way it was. She told herself they weren't the same people they had been before.

She told herself a lot of things, but that didn't stop the gnawing ache.

"You're wearing your wedding band."

Without moving his eyes from the road, he gave an abrupt nod. "She needs to see a united front."

Of course she did. How stupid to think it was for any other reason. He hadn't worn his ring yesterday. She was surprised he still had it, though from here she couldn't tell if it was his actual wedding band or one he'd borrowed. Rose had hundreds of pieces of jewelry for OZ operatives.

Hawke sent her a quick look. "You know that, right?"

"Yes. Of course. She'll do her best to tear us apart, sow division. You forget I've had years of intensive experience with this enemy."

And Iris *was* the enemy. There was no doubt about that. Finding out who she worked for was their primary goal, but Olivia wanted other answers, too. Had Iris ever worked legitimately for MI6? How long had she worked for this shadow group? Had Olivia's father worked for them?

She wondered if they would have tried to recruit her, too, if she'd returned to England.

Hawke steered the SUV into an older residential neighborhood about five miles outside of Yuma. Not exactly the type of area where one would think enemy combatants would be held.

"You never said if you've talked with her," Olivia said.

"I have, but only briefly. I wore a mask and disguised my voice, but I imagine she's suspecting or at least wondering."

"Maybe that will give us the element of surprise."

Neither of them said what they were both thinking—Iris Gates was too savvy to not realize who'd captured her. And though Olivia didn't say it, she couldn't help but wonder if her mother had set up the entire scenario. For what reason, only heaven knew, but this woman had been around too long to be taken alive if she didn't want to be.

They drove for several more miles, weaving through the large neighborhood. Hawke turned onto a street and headed to the very last house at the end of a cul-de-sac. The structure was an eighties-style brick home, very middle class with a well-cared-for lawn and giant oak and elm trees to give it a homey, lived-in look. There was even an old clunker RV in the drive.

"Does anyone live here?" she asked.

"One guy—Bruce Gordon. Retired CIA. He keeps up the façade, steers away curious neighbors and door-to-door salesmen."

When they parked in front of the house, she craned her neck to see that the backyard led to an empty, barren field.

"Just the house?"

"It's a front. Activity goes on below."

Of course. Like OZ, it likely had a warren of underground hallways.

"How many prisoners are here?"

"Only a handful. I was going to take her to that old cabin in Tennessee we used to use, but Kate steered me here."

When they'd worked together, they'd purchased a run-down cabin in the deepest, densest part of the Tennessee hills to use for interrogations, as a holding facility, and, on occasion, as a weekend getaway.

"You ready?" he asked.

She drew in a breath, feeling stronger than she had in a while. Perhaps confronting the demons of her past, along with one very current demon, was a cathartic move for her. "Yes."

They stepped onto the front porch, and Hawke rang the doorbell. Olivia looked around, noting that the colorful geraniums and petunias in the big flowerpots had recently been watered. A porch swing swayed gently in the wind, and wind chimes played a lovely melody. From the outside, it was a comfortable abode, an excellent front for what really went on inside.

The door opened, and a middle-aged man with the buzz haircut and erect shoulders of a military man said, "Yes?"

"Sweet potato," Hawke replied.

"Sweet potato?" Olivia whispered.

Hawke grinned down at her. "You gotta have a sense of humor in this business."

The man stepped back, and they entered the place that imprisoned Iris Gates.

AFTER INTRODUCING HER TO BRUCE, the man who'd opened the door and overseer of the prison, Hawke took Olivia's hand and led her to the back of the house, into the kitchen area. The smell of cooked bacon and eggs permeated the room. Neither of them had wanted breakfast this morning, but they'd downed coffee and a protein bar for energy.

Despite the need for answers, this wasn't something either of them looked forward to. Doing this on a full stomach would've been even more unpleasant.

He opened a door in the corner that led to the lower part of the facility. At one time, it had been a simple basement. Now, a maze filled with cells, interrogation rooms, and a few bedrooms for the personnel who lived here spread out over almost a quarter mile. An exit at the other end of the area, in the middle of the empty field, enabled workers to come and go without anyone being the wiser.

"Should be the second door on the right."

Hawke opened the door and walked inside. The room was bare with the exception of a couple of folding chairs, a table with a laptop, and a couple bottles of water. On one side was a large window that looked into another room. That room was dark right now, but in a few minutes, it would light up, and Iris Gates would be led inside.

"Does the window go up?"

"Yes. Once she's brought in, we can talk to her face-to-face. Until then, she can't see inside this room."

"Okay. Let's get this done."

Hawke squeezed her hand once more and then spoke into the earbud Bruce had handed him when they'd arrived. "Bring in the prisoner."

They waited for a full minute before the lights in the other room switched on, and a door opened. A woman with blond hair that was much lighter than her daughter's shuffled awkwardly into the room, flanked by two men. Her ankles were shackled together, her hands cuffed behind her.

They seated her on a chair in the middle of the room, and Hawke watched her closely as one of the men uncuffed her hands, then secured her wrists to the arms of the chair. She didn't try to fight them, which didn't surprise him. She knew this wasn't an opportunity to run. She might try at some point, but right now, she was anticipating what came next. He saw it in the little smile on her face as she looked at the glass partition. She knew what was about to happen.

If he hadn't needed to do this, he would have grabbed Olivia's hand and taken her out of here. In a perfect world, that's what he would do. But they didn't live in a perfect world, and Olivia deserved to face down her biggest demon.

"Lower the lights, raise the window."

The light went slightly dimmer, and then the glass partition rose. For the first time, Hawke came face-to-face with his former mother-in-law. Since the other two times he'd seen her, he'd been wearing a mask, this was their first official meeting. Olivia hadn't wanted her at their wedding, which was a good thing, because he wasn't sure he wouldn't have killed her.

The resemblance between Iris Gates and her daughter was uncanny. From what he could discern, Iris had turned fifty-five last March, but she looked at least ten years younger. Even in gray prison garb and no makeup, she was a beautiful woman. If she and Olivia were standing side by side, some might even think they were sisters. There was one important element missing in Iris Gates that Olivia had in abundance, though, and that was humanity. This creature had nothing but a facial resemblance to the beautiful woman standing beside him.

The instant the glass was raised and Iris could see who was standing in the other room, a bright smile lit her face. "Olivia, what a delightful surprise."

Her tone was one of warm graciousness, as if she were welcoming a treasured friend into her home for a cozy chat.

"Hello, Iris," Olivia said.

Hawke was proud of her tone. It was cool but not unfriendly, almost as you would greet an acquaintance who meant nothing to you.

"And is that Nicholas with you? What a treat to finally get to meet my son-in-law. And, oh my, Olivia, he is a handsome one."

"This isn't a social visit, Iris," Olivia said dryly.

"You have questions, I assume."

"How clever you are. Of course I have questions."

"No need to be impertinent, young lady." The smile she sent Hawke couldn't be described as anything other than a smirk. "But it is wonderful to see you two together again. I must say, Nicholas, I'm impressed by your willingness to forgive."

Hawke stiffened at the taunt.

"Forgive what?" Olivia asked.

"Why, for almost killing him, my dear."

Olivia jerked her head up to stare at Hawke, confusion in her eyes.

Shit!

Pressing the earbud, he commanded, "Shut it down. Shut it down now!"

In an instant, the lights in the other room went out, and the window closed, leaving Olivia and Hawke alone once more.

"A/V off," Hawke said hoarsely.

Why the hell hadn't he seen this coming? He had suspected Iris was involved in framing Olivia. It wasn't much of a stretch that she might've had a hand in the explosion that had almost killed him.

Finding that out would have to wait, because Olivia was looking at him with equal parts horror and confusion.

"How did I almost kill you?"

"It doesn't matter now, Livvy. I'm fine."

"Don't patronize me, Hawke. I deserve an answer to such an accusation. How did I almost kill you?"

He should've talked to her about this already. All of this

could have been avoided. He blew out a ragged, weary sigh. "The explosion the night I disappeared."

"Yes, what about it?"

She acted as if she had no idea what he was talking about, as if things had gone just the way they'd planned.

"The bomb went off seven seconds sooner than it was supposed to."

"No, it didn't. I watched the live feed. You came out of the back of the building. I saw you exit. At exactly 4:01 a.m., the bomb detonated. It worked just as we planned."

"It didn't."

She shook her head, confusion darkening her eyes. "That's not possible. I watched it."

"It went off seven seconds sooner."

Her knees buckled, and Hawke quickly shoved a chair beneath her. "That's just not possible… It couldn't have…" She looked up at him, horror dawning in her eyes. "How badly were you hurt?"

"It doesn't matter. I'm fine now."

"It damn well does matter. I'm tired of being told only what you want me to hear, Hawke. Tell me the truth. How badly were you injured?"

She was right. She deserved to know everything.

"Skull fracture. I was in a drug-induced coma for ten days. Second-degree burns on my back. Broken hip, busted knee, and about five pins in my leg."

"Dear God," she whispered. "How did this happen? I watched the feed… I watched the clock. Someone faked it? How? Why?" Her eyes searched his face, the horror continuing to grow in them. "How did you…what happened…after?"

"Kate. As you know, she and I were supposed to meet that night. When I didn't show up, she went to the site and found me. After I was stabilized, she had me taken to a private hospital in Switzerland, where I stayed for three and a half months."

"That's why you wouldn't let me touch you," she said faintly. "You have scars."

Unable to deny that truth, Hawke gripped her shoulders and shook her gently. "Livvy, I'm fine now."

The expression on her face was one of both shock and sorrow. Hawke cursed his lack of forethought. This could not have happened at a worse time. Iris Gates had known that. Maximum damage equaled maximum payout.

"No wonder you thought I was a traitor." She said it so softly, he almost didn't hear her.

He hadn't though...not really. Even in his most excruciating moments, when agony had ripped through him with every breath, he'd had his doubts. There'd always been a gut-deep voice whispering to him that it was all a lie. That Livvy could not have done this to him.

Hawke shook her shoulders harder, his fingers digging into her skin. "I don't think you're a traitor, Livvy."

As if she hadn't heard him, she continued, "That's why you never came back. You believed I tried to kill you."

There was a distance in her eyes, an unawareness of what was happening around her. He'd seen this happen to her only one time before. It had been his fault then, too. Shame washed over him at the memory. But no, not this time. He would not lose her again, especially not to the bitch in the next room.

More out of desperation than because he had a plan, Hawke hauled her into his arms and covered her mouth with his. He ground his lips against hers until she allowed him entry. Then he devoured. Sweeping his tongue into her mouth over and over again, he kissed her until they were both breathless. How long it went on, he didn't know, but finally...finally, he felt her respond. She threw her arms around his shoulders and swept her tongue over his lips and then went deep, tasting, exploring. They were lost to everything but the magic they always created when they were in each other's arms.

SWEPT up in the passion and heat, Olivia let it overwhelm her, let it take her away from here, from this darkness that seemed to follow her. Hawke hadn't allowed her to kiss him as she'd wanted to when they'd made love, hadn't allowed her to touch him. Even through the layers of his suit jacket and shirt, she could feel the ridges of scars. Scars that he had received in an explosion she was responsible for.

She moved her hands over his back, into his hair, and then touched his face, all in an almost desperate attempt to assure herself he was here, alive. She had lived with the belief that he had been killed and had mourned him. She hadn't known that he had come very close to being dead—because of her.

Breathless, she pulled away and looked up at him. Heat and something deliciously wicked burned in his beautiful eyes, and despite the fact that it was the most inappropriate time to have these thoughts, she wanted nothing more than to find a private place and act on that promise in his eyes.

But reality zoomed back, and she had no choice but to let it take over. They had a job to do.

Gathering her wits, she said, "How could Iris know about the explosion?"

"I don't know," he said grimly. "We're going to find out."

She pulled farther away from him and reined in her emotions. Later, she would take apart that kiss and that promise. Right now, she wanted answers. Someone had almost killed her husband. That someone had taken too much from her already. They could have nothing else.

"Okay. Let's get back to our questions."

Hawke nodded. "She thinks she scored some points."

"She did, but she's not winning this game. We are."

A sexy smile curved his mouth. "That's my Livvy."

She smoothed down her hair and adjusted the shoulder of her dress that he had pulled down. "How do I look?"

The smile went wider, but his eyes heated up even more. "Thoroughly kissed."

"Maybe I should go clean up."

"No. Let her see who we are. Let her see that no matter what, she'll never destroy what we have."

She wanted to ask him exactly what they did have, but now was not the time.

"Any new strategy?"

Hawke shook his head. "Just get her talking. Her ego will bring her down."

"Okay. Let's do this."

Hawke pressed his earbud and said, "A/V back on. Reengage interview."

CHAPTER EIGHTEEN

The lights came on in the next room, giving them the view they expected. Iris still sat in her chair, hands still cuffed to the sides. But a new, very wicked smile was on her face. Hawke was right. She knew she had scored some points and was exceedingly proud of herself. No way was she going to win this. No way in hell.

The window slid up, and the interview began again.

"Who do you work for, Iris?" Hawke asked.

"What? Just like that? Can't we go back and revisit that little boom that almost tore you to pieces?" Her grin went wider as she added, "One Mississippi, two Mississippi… etcetera. Isn't that how you Americans count seconds? Seven to be exact, wasn't it?"

Olivia searched for an explanation. Iris knew the bomb had gone off seven seconds sooner than it should have. How did she know this? How had someone manipulated not only the timer but also her video feed? Who were these people?

"You seem very proud of this, Iris," Hawke said. "Were you responsible for the timing difference?"

"I do wish I could take credit for it. It would be so fitting to say I was finally able to destroy the man who corrupted my daughter, but alas, no, it wasn't me."

The taunts didn't land with Olivia as Iris had wanted. Having her mother disapprove of her marriage to Hawke was surefire proof that it was the best thing she'd ever done.

"Then who was responsible?"

"Underlings, of course. I admit I used to enjoy the wet work, but after a while, it can become tedious."

"Whose underlings?"

"Come now, Hawke. You can't expect me to reveal all my secrets. What would be the fun in that?"

They were getting nowhere. Olivia grabbed Hawke's hand below Iris's line of sight. Years ago, she and Hawke had developed their own version of sign language. It was a sort of shorthand that only the two of them understood.

She pressed her thumb into the middle of his palm, which meant, *Let me take over*.

He squeezed her wrist, indicating he agreed.

"Very well, Iris," Olivia said. "If you don't want to talk about that, let's talk about something else."

"What else is there, my dear?"

"Let's talk about my father."

She actually looked mildly shocked. "You want to talk about Glen? Whatever for?"

"Was he part of this organization that you work for?"

"What organization do I work for, my dear?"

"You tell me. Did you ever work for MI6, or was that a cover?"

"What makes you think I don't still work for them?"

"Because the purpose of MI6 is to protect England."

"I'm one of the greatest patriots England has ever known."

"Patriot? In what way?"

"I'm trying to save England."

153

"Save it from what?"

"Total destruction."

Before Olivia could comment, Iris went on, "You see, my dear, so many people live their lives unaware of the greater good. They think a certain way their entire life. The people I work for are able to see beyond the here and now. They see a future far beyond our mortal years."

"Who are *they*? Other sociopaths such as yourself?"

Iris laughed, and it was a lovely trilling sound. Olivia remembered how Iris had once told her that she had practiced this kind of laugh for years. She had tried to get Olivia to mimic the laugh, but it wasn't something she'd ever perfected.

"You have adopted some of your husband's more unpleasant attributes, Olivia. Bluntness, especially in a woman, is not a good quality."

"How should I ask you about your treasonous activities?"

"Your idea of treason is so narrow-minded. My actions might look questionable to the naïve and ill-informed, but I assure you, the cause I work for is most definitely not treasonous."

"How so?"

"It's simple, really. The people who employ me have a calling, a higher purpose than most anyone could understand."

"And what is that purpose?"

"To make the world a better place."

The idea that Iris Gates would want the world to be a better place was laughable, but Olivia kept the amusement out of her voice when she asked, "Better in what way?"

"Too many ways to count, my dear. Their ideals are lofty and quite sophisticated."

"Give me an example. Help me to understand why you

would betray your country, your government, and the people you supposedly represented."

"These questions are getting tedious, Olivia."

She was right. They were. They were going in circles and getting nothing accomplished. Time to change tactics. "Did you kill my father?"

"Why this sudden interest in Glen? You never seemed overly fond of him before. You didn't even come to his funeral."

No, she hadn't. And no, she had not been fond of Glen Gates, but she did want to know more about him.

"Answer the question. Did you kill Glen?"

Sighing, Iris shifted in her seat. "No, I didn't kill him. It was, however, time for him to go."

"Why?"

She shrugged slightly. "He was becoming useless."

Unable to help herself, Olivia asked, "Did you ever love him?"

"Love?" Iris rolled her eyes. "Did I teach you nothing, Olivia? Love is for fools. It's a silly, shallow emotion that has no place in an intelligent person's life."

"Then what does, Iris? What's more important? Greed? Avarice? Power? Control?"

"Still so innocent? Where on earth did I go wrong?"

The pitying look would have been more convincing if Olivia hadn't seen the stiffening of Iris's shoulders. They were getting into an area she didn't want to go, and Olivia was encouraged to press harder.

"Answer the question, Iris. Who do you work for, and what do they want?"

"I've given you my answers, Olivia. Just because you don't like them doesn't mean they're not true."

She'd forgotten how very infuriating her mother could be. "And Glen? Did he work with you?"

"Glen and I agreed on so many points over the years. We were once of one mind, but he later came to look at things differently."

When her father had died, Iris had told her he had recently learned he had an inoperable brain tumor, and instead of enduring months of suffering, he had walked willingly into the line of fire.

"He didn't have a brain tumor, did he?"

Iris smiled. "Of course he didn't."

"You killed him."

"No, my dear. I didn't. I simply told my superiors of his changing philosophy, and they took care of the problem. I thought it quite magnanimous of them to let him go out looking like a hero."

"Why did you marry him?"

"We were young agents. Our superiors thought it would be a good cover for us. And it was. Decades of devoted service followed. It could have continued for many more years if he hadn't suddenly turned against everything we fought for."

"You mean he finally grew a conscience."

"Such idealism. I knew sending you to work with the Americans was risky, but I told myself you could do it. I fought for you to go. You were naïve, but so very malleable. You should have given us intel we could never get on our own. But you became a traitor to your country, to your family.

"And what have you done since then? You married a man beneath you. No pedigree, no money. Zero influence. You then proceeded to roam around the world, doing God knows what. When I heard you had divorced him, I thought you had, at last, come to your senses. I even considered contacting you, but then you went to work with that rescue organization, and I knew you were a lost cause."

"How do you know about them?"

"Oh, my dear, there's nothing I don't know about you. I even know about the child you lost. Which, by the way, was a blessing, if you ask me."

Sucker-punched was the terminology that best fit how Olivia felt. Only by calling on the training that Iris herself had drilled into her was she able to keep her composure.

Hawke took her hand and squeezed in comfort, then used two fingers on her palm to tell her to take a break.

She needed one. Desperately. But if she walked away now, Iris would win. There was no way she would give her mother the satisfaction.

She pressed her thumb into his palm, letting him know she would continue. She would face the pain later. Right now, she had a job to do.

"The divorce didn't take, unfortunately." Iris sighed dramatically, and Olivia, who had faced some of the most monstrous people imaginable, knew she had never met anyone worse than this woman.

"Am I really your child?"

Iris laughed again, though there was a sharper edge to the sound than normal. Apparently, that had gotten under her skin.

"Unfortunately for me, you are."

"Why did you even have a child?"

"What a silly question, Olivia. It was part of the job. Not only did it help with our cover, we believed we could make a good spy out of you."

"Does the Gonzalez cartel work for these people?"

"Gonzalez?" She tilted her head slightly, as if confused. "I don't believe I know any Gonzalezes."

"Since you'd been at a meeting with them when you were captured, you might want to save your lies for something we'll actually believe."

She shrugged a shoulder. "It was merely a coincidence that we were in the same building."

"Was Gonzalez responsible for the attacks on my team? The deaths of Layla Templeton and Mario Kingston?"

"Now, how would I know something like that when I don't know anyone named Gonzalez?"

"Were you responsible for the emails?"

"Emails? I'm sorry, dear, you'll have to be more specific."

"The emails that tried to frame me as a traitor."

"Ahh, those emails. Yes, I'll take credit for them. I was just doing what any mother would do—protecting her child."

"Protecting me?"

"Your *team* was targeted for annihilation. As a kindness to me—a reward for all of my years of service—you weren't to be touched. And you're welcome, by the way."

"Those people were my friends."

"Oh, get a grip, Olivia. Friends are a luxury we can't afford in this life."

Hawke grabbed Olivia's wrist, indicating he wanted to ask questions.

"How did you get the intel you revealed in the emails, Iris?" he asked.

"Oh, now, Nicholas, do you really expect me to do all your work for you? It was your team. They were your responsibility. Those things happened on your watch."

Olivia spared a glance at Hawke's face. Though his expression never wavered, the tenseness in his body indicated that Iris Gates had scored another point. One of the things her mother excelled at was knowing exactly what poison dart would have the greatest impact.

"Maybe," Iris added, "you don't know your surviving team members as well as you think you do."

That was something that would have to be looked at again. The person who'd given Iris the details to use in those emails knew way too much about the missions not to have been a part of their small circle.

Moving on, Olivia asked, "Who is your superior?"

"Do you honestly think I'm going to tell you anything useful?" Her laughter was genuine and lighthearted. "That naïveté never really went away, did it?"

"How large is the organization?"

"We are in the millions. You could live to be a thousand and never find us all."

"And for what purpose, Iris? What is your main goal?"

"To make things better, of course."

"To make what better?"

"Life. The world we live in."

"You don't have an ounce of altruism in your body. The only person whose life you want to improve is your own."

"Oh, now that really stings." She blinked her eyes in mock horror. "Who knew I could raise such a cheeky girl. But you're right, you know. I don't care. Not really. I lost my idealism at a young age. Learning that no one would look out for me but me, put things in perspective. When I was recruited, it put things in perfect alignment with those goals. I make a lot of money. I have every possession I could want. And I live a life of elegance, danger, and intrigue. What more could a woman ask for?"

"You still haven't answered my question. Who do you work for?"

"You can ask the question a dozen times, my dear. It doesn't mean I'll answer."

Olivia tilted her head and let a mocking smile play around her mouth. "You don't know, do you?"

"I beg your pardon?"

"You don't know who you answer to. You're just a cog in a wheel. You follow orders like a drone, a little worker bee. Like all those others—thousands—that you mentioned. The people high up in the organization likely don't even know your name."

"Don't be ridiculous. I'm very valued. You're trying to needle me into telling you something. It won't work."

Yes, it would, but it would take some time. Shrugging, she said, "Whether you tell me anything or not, you're finished."

"You know, I used to think that virtuousness of yours was an act, but it's not, is it? You really do think in terms of good and bad."

"And in what terms do you think?"

"Not in any way you would understand." She let out an elegant sigh of exasperation. "Is the inquisition over? I'm getting quite bored, and not to be crude, but I need to use the loo."

"It's too bad you can't cross your legs, because this inquisition hasn't even started."

A smile played around her mouth. "You are much tougher than you used to be. I like to think I had something to do with that."

In many ways, Iris had everything to do with Olivia's veneer of toughness, but it wasn't something to be admired.

"You think you can keep me here forever?" Iris asked.

Olivia had no idea what Hawke's plans were for Iris. The UK authorities would want her, that was a given. Did they know she was in custody? Did they know she was a traitor?

"How about we strike a deal?"

"What kind of a deal?"

Hawke squeezed Olivia's hand, letting her know he needed her to stop.

"Let's take a short break, shall we?" Hawke said. He pressed his earbud. "Take the prisoner back to her room so she can use the facilities. Get her some water and a protein bar. She's going to need the energy."

They watched as the same two guards came inside and

unlocked Iris's wrists from the chair. They cuffed her hands behind her back. As she shuffled toward the door, she made one last parting remark that was so typically Iris Gates.

"Oh, and, Olivia, that dress is totally inappropriate for this meeting."

The comment brought a genuine smile to Olivia's mouth. "Thank you, Iris. Coming from you, that's a real compliment."

Without another word, Iris walked out the door, and the lights went dark.

"She's a piece of work, I'll give her that," Hawke said.

Feeling as though she'd just walked over hot coals, Olivia said, "I need some air."

Taking her hand, he led her out the door. "Follow me."

They went down a different hallway than when they'd first arrived. A steel door with an exit sign above it and a lighted security pad beside it was obviously his goal. He punched in a series of numbers. As soon as it beeped, Olivia shoved the door open and drew in a shaky breath. That had not been fun.

HAWKE LED Olivia by the hand down a worn path into the open field. A bench beneath a large oak tree looked both peaceful and serene. The instant they sat down, she turned to him.

"What's going to happen to her?"

"I don't know. MI6 is aware of her capture and what she's done."

"So she really was MI6? It wasn't just a front?"

"Both your parents were MI6 agents, but they were apparently recruited by this shadow organization years ago."

"Double agents?"

"So it would appear. The British government isn't very

tolerant when it comes to traitors, but this info might never reach the higher-ups. Wouldn't be the first time things get done in the dark."

Olivia huffed out a breath. "You would think I wouldn't care."

"You're a decent, compassionate person. Besides, no matter how much we might despise our relatives, they're still blood."

When his old man had finally passed away, Hawke had grieved for the lost opportunities, the loss of a life that had been destroyed by alcohol long before cancer had claimed him. But he didn't think he had grieved for the loss of the man himself. Cooper Hawthorne had been a cowardly bully who had never owned up to his mistakes.

"Were you surprised about Glen?" he asked.

"That Iris betrayed him? No, not at all. I never witnessed an ounce of affection between them. I am surprised, I guess, that he had a limit when it came to evil."

"Yes, and that got him killed."

"So what now?"

"We go back and try again. She's going to break eventually. We just need to wait her out."

"How did she know about the baby?"

She said it so matter-of-factly, anyone who didn't know her well would think she didn't care. The truth was the exact opposite. Something had broken inside her that day. He had witnessed it. And he had been the cause of it.

Matching her tone, he said, "She had to have bugged the house."

"I checked for bugs daily."

"Who knows? With this shadow organization's deep pockets, they likely had sophisticated equipment that's not on the market."

She nodded, looking out at the empty field as if mesmerized. He knew she was pulling in her strength. This had been tough on her, as he'd known it would be. The below-the-belt remark about the baby they'd lost had cost her even more.

He wanted to reach out and touch her but knew she wouldn't welcome him right now. Not that he didn't deserve it. What he'd done was unforgivable. They had been struggling already. He'd been gone for months at a time. When they were together, talking had taken a back seat to the passion that never seemed to die. If they had talked, none of that horror would have happened. And he might be able to look in the mirror without flinching.

Bringing up the painful subject right now wasn't remotely appropriate, but he couldn't help but ask, "When did you change your mind about having children?"

She huffed out a long, tired sigh. "It was a gradual thing. And definitely wasn't something I planned. I was due to get my birth control shot, and my doctor suggested if I was considering pregnancy, I shouldn't take the shot. She told me it could take a few months to get the birth control out of my system. Since you were gone so much during that time, I thought I would have time to think more on it and then talk to you about it so we could decide together."

"But I came home unexpectedly," he said softly.

"Yes." She met his gaze unwaveringly. "I never meant it to happen that way. I didn't even think about it until after you'd left again. And then when I did, I kept reminding myself of what the doctor had said, that it could take several months for the birth control to get out of my system."

"But that's not what happened." Hawke touched her shoulder, needing some kind of contact to make his point. "I want you to know I'd rather have cut my own tongue out than to have said what I did."

"I know that. And it wasn't your fault, you know," she said softly. "No one could have predicted what would happen."

"No one will ever be able to convince me of that."

This was a conversation they should have had years ago, when it had happened. But he'd been so stubborn, so furious in his self-righteous anger. He'd handled it in the worst way possible—in the way his old man might have handled it, minus the violence. If he'd ever wondered if Cooper Hawthorne still had an influence on him, that day had proved it.

His gaze moved to the open field before them, but in his mind's eye, he saw her that day. Saw the pain in her eyes because of his reaction. And then he saw her face afterward. That hurt had been a thousand times worse.

She put a hand on his arm, rubbing in comfort. "Please don't do that to yourself. It was no one's fault."

A part of him would always believe he'd been the cause. There was nothing he could say or do to erase what he'd done.

For several moments, there was only silence. He could only imagine what she was thinking or feeling. She had been put through so much, not only by him but her mother, too.

Finally, she turned to look at him, her face slightly pale, but her expression set with determination. "So, what's the plan? Do we go back in and try to negotiate some intel from her?"

Refocusing, he said, "We can't offer immunity."

"Maybe not for real." She cocked her head, smiling slightly. "I don't mind lying to her. Do you?"

"No, not at all. Those low-level insults really got to her. She didn't like your taunt about being a worker bee."

Her eyes lit up with amusement. "She didn't, did she?"

"Just one of the many reasons you're the perfect person— the only person—who should question her."

"Why's that?"

"Because you're the opposite of her in every way. She

resents that. Instead of being her clone, which is what she wanted, you became her opposite, her nemesis. That has to infuriate her."

"Then let's head back and start on her again."

"Olivia, wait."

"What?"

"I—"

The cellphone in his pocket buzzed. Sighing, he grabbed it and said, "Yeah?"

"You'd better get back here, Hawke. Iris Gates just killed herself."

CHAPTER NINETEEN

Olivia stood over Iris's lifeless body. She looked peaceful, which seemed so incongruent with how she'd lived her life. Olivia had seen numerous expressions on her mother's face, but never one of peace. She had gone out on her own terms, which was no surprise.

"We searched her," Hawke said. "Multiple times. How did this happen?"

"Tiny pill beneath one of her fake nails."

She could have done this at any point during the time she'd been incarcerated. She had waited, though. Was it because of Olivia? Had Iris known she would see her daughter one last time? Or had she done it because she'd realized there was no way out?

"Sorry, man." The medic who'd tried to revive her stood next to Hawke. "By the time I got to her, she was gone."

"What did she take?"

"Hard to say without an autopsy. No convulsions, no obvious trauma. It's like she just went to sleep and didn't wake up."

"Let me see the footage." Hawke touched Olivia's arm. "You okay?"

"I'm fine. Go ahead."

He gave her one last worried look and then walked out the door.

Olivia knew she should feel something. Grief, sadness, maybe even anger. She felt numb, as if she watched everything from afar. But that was wrong, wasn't it? This was the woman who had carried her in her womb for nine months. She tried to conjure up any memories that were remotely fond. Iris and Glen had been gone for weeks at a time. Olivia had endured a string of nannies and tutors who'd gone out of their way to make sure they developed no real relationship with her. They'd rarely stayed more than three or four months, and Olivia had always assumed the shuffling of her caretakers was to ensure no affection ever existed.

The only anomaly had been when Iris had allowed Olivia's grandmother to live with them. It was so out of character for her mother to do anything like that, and Olivia was suddenly infuriated that she didn't know the reason. Why had she never asked Iris? Had it been to bring some kind of stability to her, or perhaps even a kindness? Or had it, in fact, been just another test? Another way to try to break her? Now she would never know.

The longer she stood over her mother, the less numb she felt. From out of the blue, a rush of nausea hit her. Covering her mouth, Olivia quickly turned and ran down the hallway. She had no clue where she was going. She knew only that she couldn't stay inside this place any longer. She spotted the door she and Hawke had used earlier. She vaguely noted that the security pad was on and would likely create an ear-piercing sound, but she could do nothing about it. She was within seconds of losing the small amount of breakfast she'd managed to swallow.

Shoving the door open, she ran, ignoring the blare of the alarm. She was halfway to the big oak tree when she could no longer control the surging bile. Holding her stomach, she vomited and then, her stomach completely empty, battled dry heaves. In the middle of her misery, she felt a hard, warm embrace and a big hand holding her hair away from her face.

When she finally had her stomach under control, she straightened. Hawke held a handkerchief for her. Gratefully, she took it and wiped her mouth.

"Better?" he asked.

"A little. Thank you."

"Come on. Let's go sit down."

He led her back to the bench they'd used before. Feeling ancient, she sat and whispered, "I have no idea why I'm upset."

"Yes, you do. No matter the strife and animosity between you, she meant something to you."

"I wish I knew why she was the way she was. I knew nothing about her, not really."

"That was the way she wanted it, Livvy."

"I guess." She looked up at the clear, blue sky and wondered at its perfection. How could everything be so messed up down here and look so perfect up there? Drawing in a breath, she straightened her spine. "So what's next? Did she give us anything useful?"

"Yeah, but we need to review it, analyze it. In the meantime, we focus on the Gonzalez cartel. They're the ones responsible for targeting our team. They won't stop until we stop them. Once we have them, we'll use them to find this shadow group."

"Then let's get back to OZ and find a way to make that happen."

Hawke grabbed her wrist. "You've had several shocks the

last few days. We can take a day or two off. We don't have to go back yet."

She shook her head and headed back to the house. "I'm fine. I don't need to rest. We need to find the people responsible for killing our friends."

Setting her sights on the door ahead of her, Olivia focused on her next steps. She knew Hawke watched her, felt his concern. Yes, she'd had a few shocks, but this was what she'd been trained to do—hunt down killers and end them.

She was, after all, Iris Gates's daughter.

THE FLIGHT back to Montana was the complete opposite of the one to Arizona the day before. He and Olivia sat across from each other. She sipped a cup of tea. He drank a beer. To an onlooker, they might appear peaceful and calm, but nothing could be further from the truth. While Olivia read over the transcript of the interview with her mother, Hawke listened to the audio. He'd watch the interview later, with and without audio, but for right now, he wanted to listen to the words, hear the nuances. In the midst of that ridiculous interview, there was something there, and he would damn well find it.

When her teacup rattled, Hawke looked up at Olivia. Outwardly, she seemed serene, but the feverish look in her eyes worried him. She had received blow after blow the last few days, and at some point, everything would come to a head.

Not for the first time, he questioned his decision to not contact her after the explosion. The first few weeks, he'd barely known his own name. Then there had been surgeries and rehab, followed by more surgeries. He'd had a lot of time to think. Lying in a hospital bed for weeks on end gave a man time to build up all sorts of ideas. He'd gone from disbelief to hurt to hatred, and that had all gone on repeat for a long time. He'd ended up numb and bitter.

Over the last two years, he'd developed a hardness he hadn't been sure he would recover from. He had blamed Olivia. She'd been in control of the blast—in charge of the detonator and the timer. He thought about the anger between them, the hurt he'd caused. And yes, a small part of him had wondered if her anger and hurt had made her do something she would never have considered under normal circumstances. He had allowed his bitterness to color what he'd known to be an absolute truth. There was no way Olivia had tried to kill him. He knew her inside and out. The fact that he'd even allowed himself to get mired up in his anger only showed how messed up his mind had been.

Even so, he had still been determined to stay away from her. Their marriage had been over. What he'd said to her the day she'd told him she'd miscarried could not be undone. No matter how much he apologized, the words had been said. He could never take them back.

He'd delivered the divorce papers to her the day before their fake mission had happened. There had been too much between them—too much sorrow, too much pain. He had thought she would get on with her life. He'd thought he'd be better living in darkness anyway.

But he had been a fool. Olivia hadn't moved on, not like he'd hoped she would. And he'd been too long in the darkness. When he'd captured Iris and her organization had targeted Olivia, it had forced his hand, sending him back to her. He had known he'd have to return at some point, if for no other reason than to give her closure.

What he saw in her face right now wasn't closure, though. It was a desperate attempt to return to normalcy. Something neither of them had felt in a very long time.

"I want to see you."

Turning off the audio, which he realized he'd been only half listening to anyway, he said, "What?"

"I want to see the damage, what the bomb did to you."

"No, you don't, Olivia. It's done and over with. I survived. That's all that matters."

She stood and went to him, holding out her hand. He took it, and she tugged him forward. He acquiesced and stood.

A strange light flared in her eyes. "Show me."

He had removed his suit jacket and tie when they'd boarded the plane. Watching her closely, he unbuttoned his shirt, removed the cufflinks from his sleeves, and pulled his shirt off. The instant his shirt hit the floor, her hands were touching him. Her fingers traced the scars, created mostly from the shrapnel and a few flying objects as he'd run through the small cabin. The worst was a six-inch scar right below his heart. A piece of wood had pierced deep, missing his heart by an inch.

"How many stitches?" she whispered.

"Couple dozen."

He told himself this moment was not sexual, but the rest of his body wasn't getting the message. With each gentle touch of her fingers, desire flared hotter. Looking down, he watched the intensity of her expression. So serious, so sad.

She pressed her lips against the scar across his heart and said, "I'm sorry."

"It's not—"

Raising her head, her eyes shimmering with emotion, she whispered, "Turn around."

She was breaking his heart. "Livvy, you don't need to see this."

"Yes, I do. I need to know."

Sighing with resignation, he turned. He expected a gasp,

171

even a curse. He knew it wasn't pretty. The right side of his back was deeply scarred. Ridged and distorted, it spoke of unspeakable pain.

She touched him, and he jerked.

"Does it hurt?"

"No."

He barely even thought about it anymore. The nerves had been damaged, and other than an occasional phantom pain, he felt nothing. He'd been unconscious much of the time it was healing and always counted himself lucky, because it could've been so much worse.

"Most of it is covered with a tattoo."

"Had that done a few months ago."

She traced the soaring hawk with her fingers, and Hawke closed his eyes, willing himself to not turn around and grab her. He wanted her with a fierceness that almost scared him. How was he going to live without her for the rest of his life if one touch from her delicate hand made him want to drop to his knees and hold on to her with all his might?

She pressed her face against the most scarred part of his back and said, "I'm so sorry, Nic."

"Sweetheart, you have nothing to be sorry for. You didn't do this."

Seeming not to hear him, she said again, "I'm sorry…I'm sorry." A sound like that of a tortured animal erupted from her throat, and she sobbed, "I'm so sorry."

Turning, he caught her in his arms as her knees buckled. The dam had finally broken on her emotions. Deep, aching sobs of anguish racked her body. Hawke picked her up and carried her to the small sofa a few feet away. Sitting down with her, he cradled her in his arms as she released the sorrow she'd been living with for so long.

The sounds were harsh, ugly, and heartbreaking, and Hawke's eyes filled with his own tears. Seeing her like this, he cursed every person who had ever hurt her, especially himself. Olivia worked so hard at hiding her emotions to keep people from seeing the vulnerable, fragile creature beneath the façade. Often, the people who were hurting the most were the ones who put on the biggest smile or coolest demeanors.

He held her until her cries became little breathless shuffles of sounds. When she finally quieted, he kissed the top of her head. There were so many things he wanted to say, so many things he couldn't say, but there was one thing she needed to know.

"None of this is your fault, Livvy. You did not cause any of it."

Her voice hoarse, she said, "If you had never met me, none of you would ever have been hurt. Layla and Rio might still be alive."

"Bullshit. If your mother hadn't been around to do the deeds, someone else would have done them. Put the blame where it belongs. The Gonzalez cartel wanted its revenge and found the perfect organization to help them achieve that goal. Your mother and all the others were tools, nothing more."

"I wish I could hate her. A part of me does. Another part just... I don't know. I guess that part grieves for a wasted life."

"She chose her path, just like you have. You know what I want more than anything?"

She raised her head to meet his gaze. Her eyes were swollen and red, her nose was pink, and her mouth trembled with emotion. He had never seen a more beautiful and precious sight in his life. This woman had owned his heart from her first words to him, and he had never wanted another woman since. She was it for him, always and forever.

"I want you to see the woman I see. You are strength,

beauty, compassion, gentleness, and loyalty. You're the opposite of what Iris and Glen tried to make you. You did that on your own. That's how strong you are."

She pressed her forehead against his chest. "I don't feel very strong."

"You just need some rest."

The memory of how he'd ensured she got some sleep earlier swept through him. That couldn't happen again. Even as much as he loved her, they wanted different things. That hadn't changed.

"Why don't you go lie down? We're still a couple hours from landing."

She lifted her head and whispered, "Come with me?"

Everything within him wanted to say yes, but instead, he said, "You go on. I've got some calls to make."

She stared at him for several seconds and then stood. Adjusting her clothing, she walked into the bedroom without a backward glance. He had pretended he hadn't seen the need in her eyes, hadn't heard her invitation. It would be so easy to give in to temptation again. Follow her in there and embrace the need that would always be part of him when it came to Olivia. But it would also give her the wrong idea for the future. There was no future—not for them. Once this was over, he would return to the darkness, where he belonged.

Olivia belonged in the light. She always had.

CHAPTER TWENTY

OZ Headquarters

Her chin set at a cool angle, Olivia walked into the conference room. She met each person's eyes as she seated herself. She didn't know what she expected any of them to say. *So your mother was a traitor. So your mother killed herself. So your mother might've tried to kill your husband.*

All of it was true.

After they'd gotten back yesterday evening, she had gone straight to her room. A new awareness of who she was and what she needed to do had been foremost on her mind.

Seeing and talking to anyone was something she had wanted to avoid until she could gather her composure. She had lost it with Hawke on the plane, and though he had been gentle with her, she had gotten the message. She was on her own. Leaning on anyone, including him, couldn't happen.

After seeing the damage—his injuries—it had been all she could do not to scream the world down. She could not even imagine the agony he'd gone through. The pain would have been unbearable. And the whole time he'd suffered, she had believed he had voluntarily walked away from her. There was no way he hadn't blamed her. How could he not? She had supposedly been in charge of the blasts. She had created them. Set the timer. Calibrated to the millisecond when the explosion would go off. Everything that had happened to him would have looked intentional and malicious. How he must have hated her.

Did it help knowing that her mother had been involved in some way? That she might've even set up the whole thing? Not really—at least not for her. Hawke had endured unspeakable agony, and no matter who was at fault, she grieved for his pain.

Weariness had dogged her every step up to her room last night. A bath had helped, as had the few hours of sleep she'd managed. This morning, she'd woken with determination. They had a target—the Gonzalez cartel. That was her new goal. Once that was done, she would face the future. Hiding her head in the sand would no longer be her modus operandi, especially with Hawke. She saw her future, and he was not part of it.

"Liv." Eve came to her the instant she sat down and took her hand. "How are you?"

A fractured breath escaped her, and she put on her best smile. "I'm fine."

"Ah, babe, don't kid a kidder. You're hurting, but I'm here for you. We're all here for you. Got that?"

She glanced around the room, and instead of judgment, she saw compassion, empathy. It wasn't what she had expected. She knew they knew everything, but there wasn't an ounce of condemnation on their faces.

Realization hit her hard. She'd been so wrapped up in her own self-pity and torturous thoughts that she hadn't seen what was around her. These people were her friends. Yes, they'd turned on her at one time, but their feelings then had been justified. She had set it up that way.

She needed to get out of her own head and remember she wasn't alone. Not anymore.

"Thank you." Her gaze swept the room. "Thanks to all of you. It's weird to mourn a person I despised, but it is what it is."

"We've all been there, Liv, in some form or fashion," Eve said.

She was right. Everyone at OZ had experienced their own hell in some way. Just because hers was her own didn't mean others hadn't gone through the same, or worse.

Ash came into the room, and everyone immediately knew something was wrong. His expression wasn't one Olivia had ever seen on him. If she didn't know him better, she would say he was in a mild panic.

He went to the front of the room, and his gaze immediately went to Olivia. "I'm sorry for your loss, Liv. We all are."

"Thank you, Ash."

"I know you're hurting and need time to grieve, but we really need you on this op. Will you stay?"

"Yes, of course."

"Good…good." Ash took a deep breath and said, "Okay, even with the additions of Olivia and Hawke, we're going to be down a few operatives. Sean has asked for a leave of absence, and I approved it."

Olivia glanced over at Serena, whose face was pale but composed. She swallowed audibly and said, "He just needs a few days to decompress."

Everyone knew why. Olivia hoped Sean and Serena could work things out. One of the sweetest things she'd ever seen was when Sean had proposed to Serena in front of the entire OZ family. At that time, she remembered thinking that if anyone could make a marriage successful in this kind of environment, Sean and Serena could.

Ash went on, "Jazz and Xavier are out, too. They've uncovered some new intel on her brother that's time sensitive. And"—he glanced at his watch—"in about an hour and a half, I'm going to be a dad."

Everyone exploded with the same question. "What?"

Though he smiled, Olivia saw the worry behind his eyes. "Jules is in labor. Kate's with her right now. I just left the house for a few minutes to give you this info and to let you know that Hawke is going to run point on this op. He knows the Gonzalez cartel better than anyone. Any questions?"

"I have one," Gideon said. "What the hell are you still doing here, man? Get out of here and go have a baby."

A huge grin spread across Ash's face, and everyone laughed.

"Then I'm outta here."

"Give Jules our love," Eve said, "and call us as soon as we have a new family member."

Striding toward the door, Ash said, "Will do."

The lighthearted moment had been much needed. Seeing Ash so happy and nervous was a delight. Olivia glanced over at Hawke to share this brief moment of happiness and was shocked to see him staring at his laptop as if nothing momentous was happening. If that didn't show her that he hadn't changed, nothing would. Bringing a child into this world was nothing special to him.

To her, it was the greatest blessing.

THE INSTANT ASH was out the door, Hawke clicked the remote in his hand. "All right, everyone, let's get started. This is the Gonzalez family."

Photos of Priscilla Gonzalez and her son, Juan, appeared on the screen behind him.

He knew everyone was staring at him as if he had two heads—everyone except Olivia, who was looking away from him. Yeah, he was an ass. Not always, but when it came to a discussion of babies, he shut down. He always had, always would. They weren't a part of his world and never could be.

He pointed to the photo of a well-dressed young man in his late teens. A scar ran down one side of his face. "When Hector went to prison, Juan was fifteen. His mother…" He pointed to the photo of the woman in her late thirties. "Priscilla presumably took over the operation until her son was old enough.

"Most of the cartel was disbanded after Hector's arrest. His soldiers scattered, going to other cartels. There was almost nothing left. Somehow Priscilla found a way to hold on to a fraction of it for her son. For four years, there was nothing to indicate the remaining operation had any power whatsoever. Then, almost overnight, the Gonzalez cartel exploded on the scene again with more money and power than anyone could ever have expected. They took over the smaller cartels, killed the leaders and some of their families. The rest were allowed to live if they pledged fidelity to the new and improved Gonzalez cartel. They were richer, better connected, and twice as powerful as they were before."

"Has anyone tried to stop them?" Gideon asked.

"Yes and no. The DEA wanted to know how they got so big so fast. It all seemed to occur under the radar. The feds went after them hard, looked like they had all their ducks in a row to bring them down. Within a month, the investigation was over."

"How? Why?" Eve asked.

"My sources—the ones willing to talk—said they were told to back off. The cartel was untouchable."

"That takes a lot of influence and money to make that happen," Serena said.

"Exactly."

"And this shadow organization that OZ is after, that my mother was apparently part of, you really believe they're involved?" Olivia asked.

Hawke felt a settling, an easing of the muscles in his body. It was the first time she had acknowledged him since entering the room. When they'd gotten back late last night, she had been quiet, pensive. He knew she had taken his subtle rejection hard. He hadn't meant to hurt her. If there was anyone in this world he would give his life to keep from hurting, it was Olivia. But what she wanted and what he could give her were still worlds apart.

She had stopped at her bedroom door, and what she'd said had gutted him to his soul. *"Thank you for your help. I'm sorry for what happened, how it happened. I was angry with you when you came back, for not telling me you were alive. But now I get it. You had moved on. We were finished, and you knew that. I didn't, but now I do. Once this is over, once we've destroyed the people who killed our friends, it will be over. I'll be finished."*

She hadn't said *with you*, but those words had been implied.

Without another word, she'd opened her door and shut it in his face. A part of him had been infuriated, wanting to go in there and tell her they would never be over. But the sane part had recognized she was right. And if he cared for her at all, he needed to let her go.

"Hawke?" Olivia said.

Telling himself to get his head out of his ass and do the job, he shrugged. "Sorry, guess I zoned out. Didn't get much sleep last night."

He'd gotten exactly zero sleep because, after her words,

he had done the only thing he could do, the only thing that had ever saved his sanity. He'd gotten to work.

As if he hadn't zoned out, he answered her question, "I have no doubt that this shadow organization is involved. Once we take the cartel down, we'll get them to talk. Then we'll find these people and end them one by one."

"Sounds like a plan," Gideon said. "Let's get started."

As he revealed what he had, and laid out the plan, Hawke felt a resurgence of energy. This was what he lived for. From the day he'd joined the Navy at age eighteen, he'd found a purpose in life. In the almost twenty years since, that hadn't changed.

He and Livvy had shared that passion once. They had been unconquerable, but they'd gotten careless, taken things for granted. What once was could never be again.

CHAPTER TWENTY-ONE

Fury overshadowed heartache as Olivia watched while Hawke revealed the Gonzalez holdings. A collective gasp could be heard around the room. Olivia barely registered the sound as she stared at the screen. Really, how was this remotely possible? Outrage bubbled within her like lava. She had come to this meeting, sure of how things would proceed, sure that she knew what they were facing. But this? This was so much more than she had ever thought possible. Hawke had said the Gonzalez cartel had exploded into a huge conglomerate, but this...this...

"How on earth could this happen?" she whispered.

Though everyone else in the room was likely outraged at the sheer enormity of the cartel, Olivia's anger was much more personal. Little more than five years ago, they had brought this cartel to its knees. After Hector Gonzalez had gone to prison, the Colombian government had seized all their assets and monies. All product had been destroyed. All lieutenants and soldiers had either been captured or had retreated out of fear. The cost had been painful and devastating. There had been a tremendous loss of life. She had taken three bullets that day. She had almost died.

The injustice in this world never seemed to end. It was one of the reasons she loved working for Last Chance Rescue. There was a balance there, unlike with OZ. Option Zero took down bad people and saved lives. Last Chance Rescue saved lives and took down bad people. A subtle difference, perhaps, but it was there.

No wonder the DEA had been told to back off. The cartel looked untouchable. How many politicians and backdoor dealings had it taken to create this kind of gargantuan enterprise?

If she'd ever had doubts that a powerful organization or entity in the background was funding and manipulating world events, she no longer had them. This just did not happen without tremendous backing. What had Gonzalez promised to do for them in exchange? The mind boggled at the consequences of such an arrangement.

"As you can see," Serena was saying, "we have our work cut out for us." She clicked the remote in her hand, and a map of South America appeared. "These stars represent known warehouses. We know that in at least three of these warehouses, they have labs."

"Do we know what they're creating in these labs?" Liam asked.

"Not yet, or at least nothing is confirmed," Hawke answered. "Coincidentally, a top biochemist and two pharmacological scientists disappeared a couple of years ago. One from Chicago, the other two from Mexico. They've not been heard from since. No leads, but there's plenty of suspicion pointing to the Gonzalez cartel."

"So they could've kidnapped these scientists and forced them to create new drugs."

"That's our best guess." Hawke sent a look to Olivia that she couldn't quite decipher.

"There's got to be weaknesses," Eve said. "Something they've overlooked."

"There is," Hawke said. "OZ."

Olivia jerked her head up. "What?"

"They likely know I'm alive and are probably looking for me. But they have no idea that we know how the cartel got this big and this powerful so fast. Remember that DEA agent who went after the cartel and was told to back down? His name is Braden Pierce. He left the agency over that, and is still pissed. Turns out he and Kate know each other from when she was in the FBI. Between the two of them, they're putting together a small army. With OZ's help, we can target the cartel simultaneously and bring them to their knees."

"That's going to take some major coordinating to get all our ducks in a row at the same time," Eve said.

"Yeah, that's why I'm putting one person at the communications helm." Hawke nodded at Serena. "You okay with that?"

"Absolutely. I've already communicated with Kate and Pierce. Kate's got eight people, Pierce has five. Not a huge amount, but they're all trained professionals, and they trust them. Even with OZ's help, we'll be spread thin, but we should still be able to get it done."

"We'll work in teams of two," Hawke said. "Each team will have a targeted location. You'll need to learn about it backward and forward. What it contains, what kind of security exists… In other words, everything."

"I've sent details to each of you about your assigned target," Serena added.

"Olivia, you'll team up with Liam," Hawke said. "Eve and Gideon, you're together. Serena will coordinate from here."

Hawke glanced down at his phone, and though his

expression didn't change, the slight furrowing of his brow told Olivia he'd read something he didn't like.

Raising his head, he went on as if nothing had happened. "Read through your assignment. Make note of questions. We'll meet again tomorrow at noon."

"Oh my gosh, guys," Serena said. "Look at this."

"What?" Hawke said.

She clicked something on her phone, and the big screen that had been filled with intel on the Gonzalez cartel and all the rottenness involved was suddenly changed to a photo of a brilliantly smiling Asher Drake holding a tiny newborn wrapped in a blue blanket. "Meet Joshua Yeager Drake."

The room exploded with applause and cheers.

"Ash said Jules did great. They're both healthy, and everything went perfectly."

"Good news to end our meeting on," Hawke said and exited the room.

Pushing aside the desire to stay and share in the joy everyone except Hawke seemed to be feeling, Olivia quickly excused herself and followed him. Even as awkward as he was about discussing children in any context other than rescue, his abrupt departure had been extreme.

She caught him just as he was headed upstairs to his room. "Hawke, has something happened?"

He glanced back at her, and she could see the struggle in his eyes.

"What?"

"The toxicology report came back on your mother."

Out of all the things she'd thought he'd say, that wasn't one of them. "What did they find?"

"Nothing conclusive." He glanced down at his phone. "Looks like the pill she took was a cocktail of several ingredients. One of them is particularly suspicious."

"How so?"

"The scientist from Chicago—the one who went missing —invented a drug. It's some kind of sleeping agent. Works fast. It was designed as an alternative anesthetic for surgery. Our chemists thinks it's been altered for a more permanent effect."

"So the Gonzalez cartel might well be responsible for the drug that killed her."

"Could be."

For the first time, she wondered if her mother had resented dying that way. Iris Gates had lived a dangerous, often violent life. To simply go to sleep and not wake up was likely not the way she had wanted to go out. But who knew what her mother had thought or wanted?

"One thing," Hawke said. "They've taken all the blood and tissue samples they need. They want to know what to do with the body."

Why this hurt, she had no idea. The woman meant nothing to her.

"MI6 is all right with this? They don't want her body?"

"No. As far as MI6 is concerned, Iris Gates is alive and on a deep-cover assignment. They haven't decided when and how they'll report her death. Her treasonous activities will likely stay hidden. They did, however, indicate that you can decide what kind of burial you want."

"When do I need to let them know?"

"You can wait a few days. She's in the morgue under an alias. No one else knows."

"I'll give it some thought and let you know."

She turned to walk away.

"Olivia?"

She glanced over her shoulder. "Yes?"

"I'm sorry about last night…on the plane. I shouldn't have—"

Determined to keep her dignity intact, Olivia raised her

hand to stop his apology. "No. You were right. It was a weak moment for me. I never should have asked. It's been over for us for a long time. I was just too thickheaded to see it."

She did walk away then, not caring if he thought her weak again. She just needed to get away from him before she confirmed to him just how weak she really was.

CHAPTER TWENTY-TWO

Colombia

Juan Gonzalez stood in his office, one of his many in the region. Rows and rows of product owned by the Gonzalez cartel stood before him as far as the eye could see. This was just a small sample of what the cartel owned throughout South America.

There were factories that created the most addictive and dangerous narcotics and massive ships that delivered those products throughout the world on a weekly basis. Additionally, various laboratories were creating new potions, elixirs, deadly poisons, and toxins to aid and/or destroy at a user's discretion.

Every addictive and dangerous chemical known to man would soon likely be synonymous with the Gonzalez name.

At almost twenty years old, he, Juan Gonzalez, was being set up to be the wealthiest and most influential drug lord in the world. He had been told that his name would be whispered in awe and reverence. Men and women would lower their heads out of respect and fear. When people heard the name Gonzalez, they would be filled with the highest admiration.

He had been promised that and more. As long as he did what they told him to do, he would attain the highest goals.

Years ago, his father had made this arrangement. Before he could see it to fruition, he had been betrayed. Hector's arrest had looked like the end for Juan and his mamá. He'd been too young to know what to do, and his mamá had never been involved in the business. His papá had tried to communicate from his prison cell what should be done, but neither of them had understood.

When his papá had died in prison, the days had been darker than ever. Then his mamá had received a visit from a man who had made so many promises it had been impossible to keep up with all of them. All their troubles, he'd said, were over. They would not only honor the promise they'd made to his papá, but they would also avenge his death.

It had seemed like a dream come true. From that moment on, life had improved. So much so that it had been overwhelming and frightening. Juan had tried to keep up, tried to understand what was happening. It had soon become apparent that he had little say over anything. Yes, he was the head of the Gonzalez cartel, but he made no decisions, had no input. He reaped the benefits of wealth, power, and prestige without lifting a finger. He should be happy—he had everything any man could want.

But no one had ever asked him what he wanted. He'd been told that this was his legacy, his calling. But shouldn't he have some kind of choice? Some input on what he wanted to do with his life?

They had just assumed that since he was Hector Gonzalez's only son, that he would want this legacy. Even Mamá had thought this was what he wanted. He'd once had friends, and though he'd not had a steady girlfriend, he had dated.

Now it was as if his life was already over. His friends were attending university, they were making lives for themselves, pursuing their dreams. And he, with his expensive toys, luxurious cars, and multiple houses, envied them.

Talking to anyone about this was out of the question. He had tried to discuss his concerns with his mamá, but she could offer no solution. Juan didn't blame her. She had married his papá when she was just sixteen and knew nothing of business. She was expecting him to handle things the way his papá would expect.

He had idolized his papá, and when he'd been taken away that day, Juan had sobbed like a child. Never had he felt so lost and abandoned. But now he felt alone in a different, much scarier way. If he didn't do what these people told him to do, he and Mamá would have no future at all.

His papá had left him this legacy, and as much as he didn't want to disappoint him, he wished so very desperately that his legacy had been something else. Anything else, anything at all, other than the evil that permeated everything to do with a drug trafficking cartel.

A noise behind him was a reminder that he was being watched at all times. He was Juan Gonzalez, leader of the Gonzalez cartel. It didn't matter that he was little more than a figurehead and therefore replaceable. There were cousins who would be all too eager to step into his shoes. If they did, Juan knew that he and his mamá would be considered expendable. There would be no reason for them to exist.

He had to play the part, no matter how distasteful or frightening it was. If he did what they told him to do, acted the way they told him to act, he and his mamá would continue to live.

What other choice did he have?

"Hey, kid. Am I boring you?" The exasperated voice of the man behind him reminded him of his role. Juan didn't have to turn to see him. He easily pictured him. Something about the man made his skin crawl. Cold, dark, almost lifeless eyes, a thin, cruel-looking mouth, and a bald head so shiny Juan wondered if he polished it every night. He would like to have laughed at the thought, but there was nothing funny about the man. He had arrived an hour ago, and the moment he'd stepped into the room, the temperature had dropped at least ten degrees. The man was coldness personified, the most terrifying man Juan had ever met.

When Juan asked for his name, he'd simply said to call him The Killer. The man had smirked and told him that should be easy enough to remember.

Revenge. That was what he was supposed to care about. The people who had originally brought his father down had been targeted for termination. The promise had been made to destroy them, and they intended to keep their word. In this world, retribution was almost as important as power. Without the promise of destruction for perceived wrongs, one looked weak. Threats of retribution and death were what made the world, or at least the drug cartel world, go around.

Forget the terror, a small voice reminded him. *Play the part.*

Making himself turn, Juan faced The Killer and spoke in his most forceful tone. "Four are still alive."

Slouched in Juan's eighteen-thousand-dollar leather chair, his large feet propped up on Juan's ninety-five-thousand-dollar desk, The Killer didn't bother to look up from the paper he was reading. He said in his soft, calm voice, "You're a math genius, kid."

Juan refused to flinch. If there was any kind of hierarchy, this man was a peon, wasn't he? He was a hired killer, nothing more. But there was something not right about him. Something beyond sinister.

"I was told you were the best."

The man did look up then, and Juan's blood went cold. Eyes darker than midnight looked through him as if he didn't exist. They didn't have a glint in them like regular eyes. It was almost like they were the eyes of a dead man.

"I...I was simply pointing out what I was told."

"Thanks for the reminder."

Swallowing down the fear, Juan asked, "What is the plan to take care of the others?"

"You don't need to know."

"But I—"

Juan broke off when The Killer tilted his head slightly. The man didn't like to be questioned. He made his own agenda, his own timeline.

Stiffening his spine, Juan narrowed his eyes the way he'd seen his father do and growled, "You've had ample time to—"

The Killer dropped his feet onto the floor with a thud and rose slowly to his feet. Dressed in a black T-shirt and pants with a ridiculous amount of pockets, the man should have looked weak, even comical. But there was nothing funny about him. Juan was more than aware that he had poked a sleeping bear.

Despite his best efforts to stand still, Juan found himself backing away. Perhaps acting tough with this man was not the way to handle things. He was out of his element and could only offer his most humble apology. "I didn't mean to offend you."

THE KILLER rarely felt amused by anything, but this little pipsqueak was becoming fun. Probably weighed twenty stone, if that, and when he stood ramrod straight, as he was trying to do right now, he came up to his chin. His thirty-thousand-dollar suit and three-thousand-dollar tie were impeccable, but he'd bet his last quid that the kid's designer briefs were wet with sweat, and maybe more. Juan Gonzalez was way out of his league, and he was too stupid to know it. He was a naïve kid playing a tough man's game.

When Juan backed up, his eyes wide with fear, he revised his assessment. Maybe he wasn't completely stupid.

"I'll say this once, and then we'll put this to rest. Mack Johnson, Trevor Holden, and Deacon Marsh will be eliminated."

"But...but..." Juan swallowed audibly and tried again. "But what about the other one?"

Oh, he had plans for Olivia. Big plans. She had gotten away from him a few days ago, but he had a new plan in place. One that guaranteed her compliance. And now that he knew Hawke was alive, it was going to be even sweeter.

Little Juan didn't need to know that. His only concern was avenging his low-life father. The kid was too stupid to realize that if Hector Gonzalez were still alive, Juan wouldn't be in the position he was in now. Papá's death had paved the way for this idiot's success. He was also too naïve to realize that Hector's death in prison had been arranged. Hector had been stupid enough to get caught, which had played right into their hands. Little Juan and his mamá were much easier to control.

Pawns, all of them, and none of them was smart enough to figure it out.

The Killer gave the smile he'd once been told looked like a ravenous piranha. "You let me worry about that, Juan."

The kid nodded nervously. "Yes, all right."

The Killer headed for the door but stopped before opening it and looked back at the young man shaking in his shoes. "This will be the last time you'll see me. You'll receive notification when each person is dead."

Juan nodded again.

"Oh, and if you do ever see me again, it'll be the last thing you see. Got it?"

He watched a dark wet spot appear on Juan's expensive pants. Deciding he had gotten his point across, he walked through the door.

Ignoring the workers and the millions of dollars of drugs before him, he moved down the stairs, his mind on his next destination. He slid into his SUV, pressed the ignition, and turned the air conditioning on full blast. The heat here was unbearable. He longed for the high hills and cool valleys of his homeland, but until this job was done, he'd be forced to be here for the foreseeable future.

Shifting into gear, he worked through the mission in his head. Contrary to what Juan Gonzalez thought, he was not a contract killer. Well, he was a *killer*, but he also oversaw multiple assassinations throughout the world.

This job was a bit more personal than the others. He could admit this to himself. Several of the players were well known to him. One in particular, well, she was more than that. And even though he had been given the honor of finding and destroying her, he planned to take special care with her. When the end came, his face would be the last one she saw. It was the least he could do.

After all, he owed her everything.

CHAPTER TWENTY-THREE

OZ Headquarters

"Tell me something, brother, do you have a death wish?" Gideon asked.

Taking a long draw from his beer gave Hawke a few seconds to come up with a reply. He, Gideon, and Liam were sitting on the back porch of the OZ house, guzzling down excellent beer and reliving good times. He didn't want to think about tomorrow.

"Not a death wish, but tell me how this is a bad plan. Tell me another way, and I'll consider it."

"We could still destroy Gonzalez without you putting a big-ass target on your back."

"Maybe so, but it won't be as easy or as efficient as this." Still seeing the doubt, Hawke made his case. "Look, I'm sure they know I'm alive. I wasn't exactly discreet when Olivia was attacked."

He'd been too worried about her and too furious with himself for not seeing the attack on her coming. Staying low-key at that point had not been his priority.

"Which means their focus will be on me."

"And that's a good thing how?" Liam asked.

"With their attention on me and what I might do, OZ will have the cover we need. They'll have no clue that a small army is going to descend on the Gonzalez cartel and blow it to pieces."

"OZ already has a target on our backs," Liam said. "Don't forget they tried to kill Aubrey and me, as well as Ash. They also hacked our computers. They know we're after them."

"Yeah, but they don't know we're coming after Gonzalez."

"Do you really see the kid coming after you himself?" Gideon asked. "He's barely twenty, still wet behind the ears with pimples on his butt. He's not gonna go gunslinger on you. He'll call in the big guns, and they're a helluva lot more competent than that little pipsqueak."

No, Juan Gonzalez had no power, no control. He was being used, Hawke was betting his life on it. These people were too powerful, too full of themselves to allow a kid like Juan to have any kind of say-so or power. He might be the face of the Gonzalez cartel, but there was no way in hell he was making any decisions regarding the everyday aspects of the business.

That didn't mean Hawke couldn't use him to his advantage.

He took another swig of his beer. "Just over the last couple of months, Juan has purchased more toys than he'll ever get to play with. He's a little boy in a big man's game. He doesn't know he's being used as a pawn. The minute he does something this organization doesn't like, they'll eliminate him and put someone else in his place." He shrugged. "Kid's in over his head."

"So you're going to save him from himself?"

"Maybe. Or maybe he'll end up in a coffin."

"Or maybe you will," Liam said quietly.

Hawke took another slug from his bottle. "Maybe."

And maybe he was getting soft in his old age. When they'd taken Hector Gonzalez down, Juan had been in his mid-teens. Hawke remembered him well. He'd had a mouthful of braces and a cowlick. When he and his team had infiltrated Gonzalez's stronghold, the kid had come running out of his dad's office. Hawke remembered the shock and fear in his eyes when he'd seen his father on his knees, his hands cuffed behind his back. He'd run toward him and had fallen face first over the dead body of one of Gonzalez's men. When he'd gotten back up, blood had been running down his face. Hawke had learned later that a jagged piece of glass had sliced his cheek.

A few months after that, his father had been found dead in his cell. Hawke had seen photos of the funeral. Priscilla Gonzalez had stood stoic and proud beside her husband's coffin. Her son had been beside her, and though he had stood just as stoically as his mother, the tears running down his young face had tugged at Hawke.

Life was a cruel bitch, and loss of innocence was one of her most painful lessons.

"At twenty, most kids don't know which way is up," Hawke said.

Gideon snorted. "Unless you joined up at eighteen and got sent to Fallujah in your first deployment."

True that, but Hawke had been a different kind of kid at eighteen, having lost his innocence long before that. Facing death had been scary as hell, but he'd had few illusions. He'd known death would come for him at some point. Juan Gonzalez might think he had life by the proverbial tail. Little did he know that it could tear him to pieces like a ravenous lion.

"So what's up with you and Liv?" Liam asked.

The beer Hawke had consumed churned in his gut. "You

mean other than I disappeared for two years and let her think I was dead? Other than I captured her mother, who then killed herself while under my charge? Other than the fact that I'm asking her to work with me instead of allowing her to get on with her life?"

Not one bit fazed by Hawke's bitter questions, Liam shrugged. "Yeah. Seems like an awful lot of steam coming from you two that has nothing to do with any of those things."

Hawke blew out a ragged breath. "Yeah, well, steam has never been our problem."

"Sorry to be so blunt, but what the hell is your problem?" Gideon asked. "I've never seen two people more right for each other than you two."

Hawke snorted and sent his friend a telling look. "Oh yeah? You really want to go down that road?" The flash of pain in Gideon's eyes made him feel even shittier. "Sorry, man," Hawke said. "Low blow."

"No, you're right. I'm the last person that should question you. At least you had the balls to go for it once."

Hawke didn't take that as an insult. Gideon had been in love with Eve for years, and the only person who didn't know it was Eve.

"Guess this isn't a good time to rub your faces in it, but hell, I don't care." Liam grinned like a loon. "Aubrey and I are having a baby."

Gideon slapped Liam on the back and offered his congratulations. Hawke swallowed down the bitter lump of regret and gave Liam his sincere good wishes. For twelve years, Aubrey and Liam had fought ugly battles and held on to an impossible love. He wished them nothing but the best.

Any sadness he felt for the past was his own damn fault.

～

"Oh man, I needed this."

Olivia glanced back at Eve, admiring that her friend looked as if she'd just walked out of an air-conditioned spa.

As perspiration rolled down her back, she grinned at her friend. "Do you ever sweat like a regular human?"

"Ha. I was taught to glow, not sweat. And you're one to talk. I don't see a drop of dew on you."

Before she could answer, the woman behind them said, "Well, let me tell you. I'm not glowing, and there's not an ounce of dew anywhere on me. I'm sweating, and it ain't pretty."

They turned to see a breathless and red-faced Serena huffing about ten yards back. Eve had decided an early-morning hike was what they all needed. Olivia had to admit that the fresh air and stretching of her muscles felt wonderful. She usually did some kind of physical activity each day, but the past few days hadn't allowed her to do much more than sit.

"Come on, slowpoke," Eve said. "I see a rock with your name on it up here."

They hadn't yet reached the pinnacle, but even from here, the view was glorious. Majestic, snow-topped mountains as far as the eye could see stretched out before them.

"I've missed this," Olivia said softly.

"No place like it on earth," Eve said.

Serena finally joined them, her breathing slightly less ragged than before. The second she stopped, she took a long drink from her canteen and said, "I didn't realize how out of shape I am."

"You're not out of shape," Eve said. "You've just been working too hard." She pointed to a smooth rock a few feet away. "Take a seat and catch your breath."

"You'll get no argument from me." Sliding her backpack

from her shoulders, she dropped it onto the ground and then plopped onto the rock with an explosive sigh.

Both Eve and Olivia found their own rocks to rest on, and for the next several minutes, the only noises were the rushing of the wind through the trees and the serene sounds of nature at its finest.

Peace flowed through Olivia, and for the first time in days, she felt the constriction around her chest loosen. It was hard to imagine anything wrong in this world when beauty surrounded them at every turn.

Reality returned with the sound of Eve's determined sigh. "Okay, sweetie, how bad is it?"

They both looked at Serena who, now that she'd caught her breath, was on the verge of tears. "Pretty bad. He left home two days ago, and I haven't heard from him since."

"Did he say where he was going?"

"No. He won't answer my calls or texts." She swallowed and added thickly, "He said I betrayed our wedding vows."

Indignant for her, Olivia said, "In what way?"

"We added some things to our vows, including that there would be no secrets between us."

"Why's that?"

Eve glanced over at Olivia. "Teresa."

"Gotcha." Sean's first wife had not only been a habitual liar, but she'd had multiple affairs while he was deployed overseas. The marriage had lasted less than a year, but it had done a number on the man's ability to trust.

"This was a special circumstance," Olivia said.

"Maybe so, but that's not the way Sean sees it. I knew he would be angry. I didn't realize just how bad it would be, though."

"He'll get past it, sweetie," Eve said. "Just give him some time."

"I don't think I'll have a choice. I even called his step-mother who, as you know, is not my favorite person. In addition to saying, 'I told him you weren't good for him,' she said she hasn't heard from him."

"Would she tell you if she had?"

"Who knows?" She shook her head, her eyes sadder than Olivia had ever seen them. "I just wish he would let me explain."

"He didn't give you a chance?" Olivia asked.

"I tried, but the instant I said that it was my choice not to tell him, he gave me a look and walked out the door. I couldn't blame this on Ash. He told me if I needed to tell him, I could. But I knew if I did, he'd try to find Hawke on his own. The less people who knew, the better."

"I'm so sorry, Serena," Olivia said. "What we did… We really were trying to protect you all."

"You have nothing to apologize for. Especially after the way we treated you. And I should have reached out to you once I knew the truth. I just didn't know how to do that and keep the secret that Hawke was alive."

"Did Hawke tell you why he didn't want me to know?"

"He said you were moving on in your life and that it was for the best. I'm sorry, Liv. I should have questioned him about it."

"Did he tell you he almost died because of me?"

Frowning, Eve asked, "What do you mean?"

Olivia explained about the explosion. How they had wanted his death to look as authentic as possible, so she'd set a bomb to go off in the cabin. Hawke was supposed to escape seven seconds before it detonated.

"Somehow Iris, or someone associated with the people she worked for, was able to detonate it early. I watched what I thought was a live feed. I thought it went exactly as planned."

"He's never said anything," Serena said. "How badly was he hurt?"

Olivia closed her eyes against the tears that threatened as she remembered the horrific scars on his back. She could not imagine the pain he'd endured. "Bad. He was in a coma for several days. He has burns on his back, scars all over his chest, and his leg was almost destroyed. Iris taunted him about it in the interview."

"Bitch," Eve said softly. "She knew exactly what Hawke would think, that you did it on purpose."

"Yes."

"How did he survive?"

"Kate. She found him and took care of him."

Though she had resented Kate for not telling her that Hawke was alive, Olivia couldn't hold on to her anger. Kate had been a good friend to him. She had taken care of him, saved his life. That eclipsed any hard feelings Olivia might have for her.

"He doesn't still believe you were responsible, right?" Serena asked.

"No," Olivia said evenly. "We're past that, but we'll never get back to where we once were. That's gone forever."

"Stupid, I know, but I was going to say I can't believe he even thought you were responsible, then I think about how we believed the very same thing." Eve shook her head. "You're a helluva actress, Liv."

"I am my mother's daughter."

"You're nothing like your mother."

No, she wasn't. But she still wasn't the woman Hawke wanted to spend the rest of his life with. Not anymore. They both wanted different things now.

She thought back to yesterday when they had all gone to see Jules and Ash's new baby. The happy glow on Jules's face, the deep pride gleaming in Ash's eyes had been beautiful.

Exactly the way it was supposed to be when a new life was created.

"So let me sum this up," Eve said. "I'm sorry I treated Liv so badly. Serena's sorry she didn't tell Sean about Hawke. And Olivia is sorry that she lied to us because she wanted to protect us. Is that about right?"

"In a nutshell," Serena said wryly.

"Well, aren't we a sad sack of sorry?" Eve said. "Here we are in one of the most beautiful places on the planet, and we look like somebody just stomped all over our tender, delicate asses. Up and at 'em, ladies. Let's get our sorry butts moving."

Olivia felt another lessening of the constriction in her heart. Eve was right. Feeling sorry for themselves would solve nothing.

When she stood, Eve grabbed her hand and then Serena's and pulled them in for a group hug. *This*...this was what Olivia had missed. Even though she wouldn't be staying, she was glad she had come back. She had missed her friends.

CHAPTER TWENTY-FOUR

Colombia

"Olé! He scores!" A surge of happiness rushed through Juan as he clicked off the video game. This was the newest version on the market, and he'd been one of the first to buy it.

This was his domain, where he really felt the most confident, the happiest. He had designed his first video game when he was eleven. His papá had not been impressed. He had told him that was not his legacy. Juan hadn't understood it at the time, but after his papá's arrest, he'd been left with no doubt what that legacy entailed.

Since then, he'd created three more games. He'd told Mamá about them, and she had reminded him that was not his destiny.

Juan rubbed the scar on his face, remembering how he'd gotten it. Was that really to be his destiny? Head of an industry that destroyed people's lives? Hunted by men with guns? To have no real choice other than the ones he was allowed to make?

He was nothing to these people who had created all this wealth that surrounded him. His papá had made this deal, and his mamá had held it for him until he could take over. And now, he was merely a warm body, here to do what they said and how they said to do it. He had no real power. No one would do anything on his say-so.

The Killer's words had terrified him as nothing ever had. He had pissed himself in fear. The man had seen that and smiled as he'd walked out the door. The shame had been immense, but it was the fear that remained. If this was his legacy, his destiny, he didn't want it.

Mamá had been furious when he'd told her, but he knew it was because she was afraid, too. Had his papá really wanted him to die an early death? Because that's what he'd seen in The Killer's eyes. One mistake and he could just disappear, never to be seen again.

He had no one to talk to about this. No friends he could trust. They had deserted him when his papá had been arrested. Even his aunts, uncles, and cousins, the ones who would gladly take his place, had left them. It had been just him and his mamá. Since the Gonzalez name was now at the top of the heap again, though, they were contacting him left and right to let him know they stood with him. Did they think he was a fool? He knew exactly what they wanted. They wanted the power they thought was his. Little did they know he had nothing and no one.

So he was here, in this dark theater room where he played video games because it was the one place he felt safe.

Juan shuddered out a breath and contemplated whether he could get away with playing another game before he was forced out into the real world again.

An IM popped up on his screen.

Hello, Juan.

The username *concernedfriend* was one he was intimately

205

familiar with. The first time he'd heard from him had been a few days after his papá was arrested. The messages had come via emails, texts, and IMs. They were random, vague, but somehow always uplifting. They encouraged him to finish his education, made suggestions for an alternate career, shared motivational quotes. Once, a message had even included several places he could go for counseling if he ever felt the need.

He had no idea who this person was. He occasionally responded to the messages, but not always. This person seemed to know a lot about him, but whenever Juan had asked for identification, the answer had always come back the same. *Concerned friend.*

Over the last couple of years, the messages had disappeared. He'd frequently checked his email, but nothing more had shown up. He had assumed this person no longer cared. In a way, the silence had felt like one more betrayal.

Excited and hopeful, Juan typed, *Haven't heard from you in a while.*

Sorry about that. You okay?

He wanted to answer honestly, tell his concerned friend everything that had happened, all the things that had been going on since they'd last chatted, but he couldn't. What if this was a trick? What if the organization was testing his loyalty? If they found out how scared he was, how much he didn't want this kind of life, how much he wanted out of it, they would kill both him and Mamá. Of that, he had no doubt.

Before he could answer, another message appeared.

They're lying to you

Juan typed, *About what?*

Everything. You can't trust them. You're their pawn, nothing more.

Fear spiked through him. He knew this. Of course he

knew this. But to have it confirmed, and by this stranger, made it seem all the more real. What was he supposed to do?

Juan asked, *Who are you?*

Same person as before. A concerned friend.

What do you want?

For you to have a chance at a better life

Why?

Because you don't have to be your father's son

Furious, Juan typed a vicious reply. His father was…his father had been…his father… Tears filled Juan's eyes as he acknowledged the truth. His father had not been a good man. He had killed many people and had destroyed lives. He had been a good papá, but not a good man.

Deleting the curses and insults, Juan instead typed, *What do you want from me?*

Your trust.

How can I give it if I don't know you?

You don't have to know me to know you can trust me.

He couldn't just take this person's word for it. He typed, *Give me proof that I can trust you.*

Check your email.

Juan hadn't looked at his personal email in months. He had a business email account that he used to correspond with distributors, but his personal account was highly encrypted, and few people outside his personal acquaintances knew the address.

He clicked a few keys and logged into his email. There were dozens of spam ads, but his eyes quickly found the email from *concernedfriend*. He clicked on it. A photo of an old enemy appeared—the man who had destroyed his father. He remembered him from that day. He'd been the one in charge, the one to give the order to handcuff his father. Juan remembered yelling at him, sobbing, and pleading to leave his papá alone.

The man's name was Hawke.

Juan returned to the IM thread and typed, *He's dead.*

That's what they want you to think.

Jerking back in his chair, Juan felt his heart thud against his chest. Was this true, or some kind of cruel joke? They had promised Mamá that all the people responsible for destroying his papá were either dead or on a hit list to be killed. The one named Hawke had been of particular interest to Juan. He'd been the one who'd given orders. And he'd been the one Juan had pleaded with, had literally begged to leave his papá alone. To Juan, Hawke was the face of his family's destruction.

Could he still be alive? Had they lied about killing him? If so, why? And if they lied about this, what else had they lied about?

Quickly, Juan typed, *How do I know this isn't an old photograph?*

He impatiently waited for an answer. After several seconds, he typed, *Are you still there?*

No answer.

Surging from his chair, Juan paced around the room. Was this true, or was this a test? Were they trying to determine how loyal he was? If he questioned them, would they turn on him? His only contact was The Killer. The thought of questioning The Killer sent ice through his veins. Especially after what the man had told him—if Juan saw him again, he would be the last person he saw.

Juan glanced at his computer screen, torn between wanting another instant message from his concerned friend and wanting to never hear from him again.

Taking a breath, Juan returned to his computer and typed, *If this is true, what do you want me to do with this information?*

Is there anyone you can trust other than your mamá?

His first thought was no, he had no one. But then he rethought that. There were two men who had been loyal to his father. Two men who would protect both him and Mamá without question.

Yes.

Sending you details via email. This won't be easy, but if you want a different, better life for you and your mother, do what it says.

His hand shaking, Juan clicked on the email and read through the detailed instructions. There were no real answers there. Just five paragraphs of specific instructions on what he should do to start this process.

Juan pictured how he would tell his mamá that a stranger was communicating with him, casting aspersions on the organization they owed everything to. How could he explain that he wanted to leave this life and all it stood for? After all she'd done to preserve it for him, how was he going to do that?

She would tell him that it was a trick, a trap. And she could be right. But what if she wasn't? What if this person really was trying to help him?

Juan had never felt more helpless and terrified in his life.

Tears stinging his eyes, he powered off his computer. This person wasn't trying to help him. It was a trap, and he had almost fallen for it. He would do what he was told to do, and everything would work out fine.

Hopelessness filled him as he acknowledged that no matter what happened, there was no way out for him or Mamá. They had signed a deal with the devil, and in this business, the devil always won.

Walking out the door, his shoulders slumped with dejection, he stopped on the landing and looked around at the surrounding opulence. When his father had been arrested, everything but this house had been seized. There had been five other houses, cars, yachts, speedboats, prize-winning horses. Everything had been gone. And other than the horses, he had missed none of it. Neither had his mamá. They had talked about it, about how you could live in only one house at a time or drive one car at a time. The boats had held no appeal. At the time, he had believed he had used those excuses because they had made things easier to accept, but now he realized that was not the case. Even though he had recently started acquiring things again, none of those items held the appeal he had thought they would. He really didn't want *things*.

He wanted a life—a real life.

Taking a determined breath, he turned, went back to his computer, and powered it back on. He reread the instructions. And then, finally feeling like an adult for the first time in his life, he made a decision.

CHAPTER TWENTY-FIVE

OZ Headquarters

Her eyes narrowed in concentration, Olivia looked at the board she and Liam had created. She was expecting him at any minute to go over the final details, but she wanted to make sure she knew this op backward and forward before anything happened. This would be one of the bigger jobs, and they needed to ensure there were no holes. One slight miscalculation could spell complete disaster.

The last demolition she'd been in charge of had been a major muck-up, almost costing Hawke his life. That could not happen again. It didn't matter that she could not have anticipated what had happened—she'd been in charge of the op. The failure was on her.

The scars on Hawke's chest were a road map of that failure, but the scars on his back were a testament to the man's incredible strength. The pain would have been agonizing on its own, but that had been made worse by the fact that he had believed she had done it on purpose. She could only imagine how betrayed he had felt.

That could never happen again. She didn't care if she had to stand in the middle of the warehouse while the charges went off. She could never allow anything so disastrous to happen again.

Working with Liam was an interesting change of pace for her. Hawke was intense to the point of hyperalertness. While Liam could be intense, he didn't display the same level of extremeness that Hawke often did. Or maybe it just seemed that way because she was always so very aware when she was with Hawke.

While they'd worked, Liam had told her about his reunion with Cat, who'd turned out to be an award-winning documentary maker. Their reunion had been epic, and a little thrill rippled in the part of her soul that still carried romantic notions. A love like theirs, one that had held solid even when they'd faced the most horrific events life could offer, would last forever.

Sometimes, no matter what happened, love endured.

And sometimes, it didn't.

The knock on the door brought her out of the past. Returning her thoughts to the job ahead, she opened the door, surprised to find Hawke standing in front of her. He had been gone for almost a week. She hadn't heard from him, not even a text. The fact that she was hurt by that was down-right ridiculous. And yet, as she looked up at his face, which showed exhaustion and something else she couldn't define, she was torn between saying something hateful and wanting to throw herself into his arms. She did neither.

Opening the door wider, she said, "Welcome back. Liam is due any minute to go over some final details. You want to sit in?"

He walked in the door, glanced at the board, and then turned his eyes back to her, giving her a very thorough up-and-down look.

"You're not eating."

"I beg your pardon?"

He gave her his cocky grin, making her remember the man she'd fallen in love with at first glance. He had swept her off her feet, and even years later, he could still make her feel giddy and warm in all the right places.

She tilted her head questioningly. "Have you been drinking?"

"No. I've just missed your prissy, British way."

"Not all of us are heathens."

"You used to love my heathenish ways."

When he was in a teasing mood like this, she didn't know how to handle it. Not now. Before, she would have come back with something playful, he would have kissed her, and they likely would have ended up in bed. But now... Now she just felt lost.

His jaw clenched as if he'd realized what he'd done. Then, just when she was sure her shattered heart could someday be whole again, he said softly, "Sorry, Livvy. Sometimes, I forget."

He had apparently forgotten more than that. She didn't bother to remind him that he was the one who had turned her down on the plane. He was the one who had stayed away for two years. He was the one who had served her with divorce papers when her heart was already crushed beyond repair.

Since she was good at pretending, she gave him a cool smile. "Come look at our plans. I'm expecting Liam any minute, and we can fill you in."

"That's why I'm here. Liam's not coming."

"Why?"

"Xavier is back. Liam's going to be working with him. I've assigned them a new location."

"What about Jazz?"

"She's out for a while."

"Bad news on her brother?"

"Yeah."

Poor Jazz had been trying to find her older brother for years. To know that the sweet, kindhearted young woman was grieving hurt Olivia's heart. Why did there have to be so much pain in the world?

Hawke headed over to look at the board. "Let's see what you've got."

"Who am I working with if not Liam?"

"Me."

She wanted to say no. She wanted to tell him that he could work with Xavier, and she could work with Liam. They had planned this op together. It only made sense. But she wouldn't. Not because she wanted to be near him, though she did. But because they were good together. It should be no problem to fall into the same routine as always.

She joined him at the board and began to explain each aspect of their mission.

HAWKE STOOD STIFFLY BESIDE OLIVIA, cursing himself for being such an ass. Teasing her had always been natural and organic. When they'd first started working together, he had done it to get a rise out of her. She was just so prissy, so very proper. When she'd realized what he was doing, she'd given it back to him one hundred percent. They would challenge each other to come up with the best one-liners and zingers. Later, when they'd realized their feelings for each other, the banter had turned into a sensual, sexy game.

But to expect her to come back with something witty or sassy now was out of orbit, out of bounds, and wrong. They weren't the same people anymore, and there was too much water under the bridge to even try.

Listening to Olivia in operator mode had always been a huge turn-on for him. With her aristocratic air, proper British accent, and ethereal beauty, she looked like she belonged in a castle. She could talk about bombs, blood, guts, and ammo and make every word sound sophisticated.

Forcing his mind off what he could no longer have, he asked, "So five different buildings. You're sure we don't need more time than you've allowed?"

"I'm sure." She pointed to a row of three warehouses. "These are close together, so we can set strong enough charges on the left and right warehouse, and the middle will go up as well."

"What's the time frame?"

"The guards change shift at midnight. We go in at one thirty, take them down, and get them out of the way. Then we'll set the devices."

Hawke nodded. The goal was to cause no loss of life. Guarding warehouses filled with narcotics that killed and destroyed people's lives wasn't legal or admirable, but their primary mission was to destroy the Gonzalez cartel once and for all. These men would be interrogated. Once they'd given all the intel they could, most, if not all, would be released. Yeah, they'd likely go on to commit other illegal activities. Leopards rarely changed their spots, but that would be on them. The priority was to destroy the cartel, period.

"Where's the holding facility for the guards?"

"Two miles down the road. We'll have a van there. We'll get them in, and Kate's people will drive them away."

"How much time does that leave us?"

She was silent for a few seconds and then said quietly, "Liam and I have done several practice runs. With no imped- iments, we set eight charges and made it to the safe zone. Our longest time was seven minutes, thirty-seven seconds."

Hawke raised a brow. "No impediments?"

"Your leg."

"Will be fine."

"You were limping the other day."

"And now I'm not. I'll be fine." He didn't bother to explain to her that he'd been limping because her mother had kicked the shit out of him when he'd captured her. Underestimating Iris Gates had never been a smart thing. Even as a prisoner, she had been deadly.

Giving him a searching look, Olivia apparently saw the resolve in his gaze, because she went on, "Once the charges go off, the response time for an emergency crew is approximately five minutes."

"That's impressive."

"That's the Gonzalez influence."

Only it wasn't, not really. The more he knew about this shadow organization, the more he realized that those under its dominion controlled nothing. It might be called the Gonzalez cartel, but the people who were supposedly in charge were puppets, dancing to the tune of their invisible but powerful masters.

"We go in three days. Correct?"

"Yes. That give you enough time to create your charges and set everything up?"

"Yes. Liam and I already have everything ready. I'll just need to double-check the connections once they're in place."

"I've got to leave, but I'll be back the day before."

"Where are you going?"

"Personal business."

She jerked as if he'd slapped her in the face. He hadn't meant to be short with her, but neither did he want to have to explain. She wouldn't understand. Hell, he didn't understand it either.

Backing away from him, she said, "Have a good trip."

"Livvy…"

"No." She held up her hand to stop him. "You don't owe me any explanations. What you do on your own time is your business. Forget I asked."

Instead of doing the smart thing and leaving, he took three steps forward and stopped, only inches from touching her. Looking down at her pale, composed face, he could see the hurt she was trying to hide. And it broke something inside him. He loved this precious, beautiful woman more than life, and he had hurt her so badly.

"How did we get here, Livvy?" He touched her then, unable to stop himself. His fingers gently brushed her cheek, then her trembling lip. "How the hell did we let this happen?"

"We lost our way, Nic," she said softly. "We got careless. Took what we had for granted."

"When I was gone all those months on the job, I would go to bed every night, wondering what you were doing, where you were, what was going on."

"And I would wonder the same thing." She shook her head. "Those weeks and months of not hearing from you... I knew you were deep cover, and you were doing good work, but it just wore me down. That separation created a divide we never saw coming."

"I'm sorry, Livvy. I shouldn't have left you like that."

"It was the job. I understood." Her eyes flitted away from him as she added, "I just really needed you, and you weren't there."

"Is that why you decided what you did?"

"Yes and no. I thought we would have time to talk about it. I thought once I explained everything, you might not be totally on board with it, but that you would eventually agree. It didn't work out the way I'd planned."

"Not for either of us."

He drew her into his arms and closed his eyes at the way

her body molded against him as if she were made for him. Every soft part filled his hard angles.

"I know I've already apologized for this, but I have to say it again. I'm sorry for what I said, for the way I handled it, babe. It was the worst thing to say. I didn't mean it."

"I know that."

"I wish I had held you in my arms and comforted you. I wish I could change so damn much, Livvy."

Her smile was sad. "I know that, too." She let out a little puff of air. "I knew telling you I was pregnant would be difficult, but I thought we would get through it. I knew we might argue, but I thought we would talk it out like we used to. I didn't know it would destroy us."

Hawke held her even tighter. He had plenty of regrets in his life, but how he'd behaved that day would always be number one.

"I wish I could make things right again."

Her eyes roamed over his face. What she saw made her back away from him. Hawke dropped his arms to his sides.

"You haven't changed your mind," she said softly.

He didn't want to hurt her, but neither could he lie. "No, I haven't."

Taking a deep breath, she said, "Then I think you should go. There's nothing more for us to talk about." She turned away from him and went back to the plans for the op. "Nothing other than business."

"I'll see you when I get back."

"Wait."

His hand was on the doorknob, but hope leaped within him as he turned back to her. "What?"

"I've watched Iris's interview a dozen times over the last couple of days."

Pushing aside the crushing disappointment, he asked, "You saw something?"

"Heard something. Do you remember when Iris said we should look for the traitor among the surviving members of the team?"

"Yes. Why?" Confused, he shook his head. "I don't for a moment believe Mack, Deacon, or Trevor betrayed us. Do you?"

"No, I don't."

"Then what are you saying?"

"What if she was referring to another survivor?"

"You mean Rio or Layla?"

"Yes."

"We both identified Rio's body, and I ID'd Layla's."

"We identified *a* body in Mexico. He was wearing Rio's ring, had an identical tattoo and similar features. Those things can be faked."

Rio's body had been found badly burned and barely recognizable as human. However, the ring and tattoo had definitely been Rio's.

"The DNA and dental matched his military records."

"Records can be altered. We already know these people have deep pockets and incredible influence. Records can be changed with a keystroke."

"All right, but why not suspect Layla? She would have had the same opportunity."

"You know why not. Layla was the best of us all."

He could argue with that, but she wouldn't agree. Yes, Layla had been honorable and valiant, but no less than Olivia. Rio, on the other hand, had been the most volatile of the team. He and Hawke had gone toe to toe on several occasions. Hawke had kept him on because, despite his faults, he'd been a brilliant strategist and a deadly ally.

"Knowing Iris, she could have said that to throw us down another rabbit hole."

"Maybe, but it would explain where all the intel on those emails came from."

"I'll take a look at the interview footage again."

"Okay...good night."

Wanting to say more, wanting more than he had a right to want, Hawke turned and walked out the door.

CHAPTER TWENTY-SIX

San Antonio, Texas

His heart pounding like a jackhammer, Juan stood at the door of the hotel room. He raised his shaking hand to knock but couldn't make himself do it. If this was a trap, then he had consigned Mamá and himself to horrible deaths. She had done nothing but try to take care of him his entire life, and this could well be her reward. Nausea churned in his gut, and it took everything he had to not turn around, grab Mamá, and run.

"We've come this far, niño. There's no going back now."

Mamá had been more receptive to his plan than he had expected. He hadn't known how miserable she was or how much she regretted going along with the agreement his papá had signed. She agreed that it could be a trap but had told him he was the head of the family, and she would follow his lead.

But what if that led to their deaths?

Praying that he had made the right decision, Juan knocked three times, as he had been instructed. The door opened immediately, and a tall, broad-shouldered man with long blond hair, a gray beard, and dark glasses stood before them.

"Hello, Juan, Señora Gonzalez, please come in."

Taking Mamá by the hand, Juan led her into the room. They sat on the sofa where the man had pointed.

Juan was surprised there was no one else in the room. He had figured there would be several people here. He tried to peer into the bathroom he could see across the room, but he could see no one.

"I'm the only one here, Juan. No one else knows about this."

"So you are my 'concerned friend.'"

"I am."

"What now?"

"I give you the information you need to start a new life."

"What if I don't want a new life?"

"Then why are you here?"

"I…" He had no answer.

"Juan, let's not play games. You had a choice to make, and you made it. If you choose to back out now, I cannot guarantee yours or your mother's safety."

"But how do I know this isn't a trick? Some way to get me to give you information, and then you'll kill me."

"Because I want nothing from you. I have all the information I need to destroy the Gonzalez cartel. Which is something that's going to take place very soon. This deal is a one-time offer to get you and your mother out before that happens."

"Why would you do this for us? For me?"

"Perhaps because I don't believe you should be held responsible for the mistakes of your father."

The man turned to his mamá. "And, Mrs. Gonzalez, I don't believe you signed up for this either. You are still a young woman. You can have a life free of danger. As can your son."

Juan glanced at Mamá. Why had he never considered her happiness? She had been seventeen when she'd had him. Her marriage to his papá had been arranged between the two families. His papá had been twenty years older, and though Juan had witnessed affection between them, his mamá had never really had a choice. She had done what she had been told to do. But this could be a new start for her, too.

"Mamá?" Juan said softly.

Her eyes gleaming with promise, she said, "Juan…it would be nice to not be afraid anymore."

Something settled in his mind, and the anxiety he'd been living with lifted. He turned back to the man and said, "Very well. What do we need to do?"

The man slid a thick envelope onto the coffee table in front of them. "These are new identities for you and your mother. Passports, birth certificates, driver's licenses. All the things you'll need to start a new life." A second thick envelope joined the first one. "Your father was not a good man, Juan. I know you loved him, but he destroyed a lot of lives and did some evil things. However, one thing he did do right was provide for you and your mother. He had three different accounts set up in your name that the authorities don't know about. They are now under your new name."

Juan opened the envelope, his eyes widening at the amounts he saw on the account documents.

"As you see, you'll be starting out without any money worries. Four million in one account, three million in another, and four hundred fifty thousand in another. All the monies have been transferred to a bank here in San Antonio. A house has been purchased here in your name, Juan. You are not obligated to stay there. It's merely a place to live until you decide if you want a different one. I do recommend that you stay in San Antonio for at least a year.

"The title and keys to the house are inside the packet, as well as the keys to a SUV that's parked in the parking lot outside.

"Also, even though your documents can stand up to any scrutiny, I have arranged an appointment for you with an excellent plastic surgeon. Some light cosmetic surgery, nothing too drastic, should throw off anyone who knows you."

Juan touched the scar on his cheek. He had considered having it removed but had decided that it needed to stay. Every time he looked in the mirror, it would remind him of the hatred he should have for the people who had destroyed his life. But now, removing it sounded like the perfect solution. He wanted to rid himself of the anger and desolation that had consumed him for the past few years.

"Any questions?" the man asked.

"Will I ever see you again?"

"No. This will be our last communication. Once I leave this room, you and your mother are on your own."

"And you're sure no one can trace us to here?"

"I'm positive. No one other than myself knows anything about this."

"I don't know how to thank you."

"Live the best life you can, Juan. Don't let your father's past define your future."

The man stood and headed toward the door.

"Wait!"

He turned and said, "Yes?"

Juan wished the man would take off his sunglasses so he could see his eyes. With his face almost totally covered by the beard, the glasses, and the baseball cap pulled low, it was impossible to see any identifiable features.

"Thank you, señor, for everything."

Mamá repeated the same words.

The man nodded and opened the door. As he stepped out, Juan noticed for the first time that the man had a slight limp. The door shut before he could see anything else that might help him identify the man who'd given them this amazing chance at a new life.

Whoever he was and whatever his reason for such generosity, Juan hoped that he would make him proud.

CHAPTER TWENTY-SEVEN

Colombia

"You need more sunscreen. Your nose is getting pink."
Olivia lowered her binoculars and watched Hawke dig the tube of sunscreen out of his pack. She'd applied three coats already, but the humidity was so high, much of it had melted off.

It struck her how they'd gone back to their same routine. He'd always been the one to carry their medical supplies. From bandages, to painkillers, to antibiotics, he was always prepared for anything.

In her pack were the MREs and snacks. They each carried their own canteens.

They'd been on numerous ops together, and from the very first one, they'd started a routine that had lasted for years. They never talked about it, never planned for it. This was who they were and what they did.

Although Hawke had been on various large missions during his career, this was the biggest one she'd ever been involved in. She hadn't served in the military, but she had overseen multiple ops and had been involved in dozens of missions. Nothing like this though. Yesterday, she had stood at the door of the OZ operations room and almost gawked at what could only be termed a war room. Eve had told her that they'd added several additions to OZ headquarters since she'd left. The war room was one of them. Giant monitors covered every wall. A huge table big enough to seat a couple dozen people sat in the middle.

For an instant, she had felt out of her element, uncertain. Not the norm for her. There were several areas in her life she wasn't confident in, but this wasn't usually one of them. This was what she'd been raised to do—this was her life.

Hawke had been standing beside one of the monitors, talking with Eve and Gideon. When he'd spotted Olivia, he had waved her in. "Come on in. Make yourself at home."

She didn't know why, but the moment he'd said the words, she'd felt immediately comfortable. This *was* her element. She knew who she was and what she could do. In seconds, she had been immersed in the discussion, confident once more in her role.

The monitors had revealed the different people involved in the planning and execution of the mission. Twenty-one operatives were actively involved in tonight's coordinated attack. Seven others were in communications roles. Each person would play an important part. For the mission to succeed, every one of them was vital. By tomorrow morning, five warehouses, four cargo ships, and three drug labs would be reduced to ashes. The Gonzalez cartel wouldn't be completely broken. There were other, smaller facilities owned by them, but it would cripple them so severely that it would take decades before they would have even a percentage of the influence they had now.

This would not only be an almost complete decimation of

the cartel, but also a huge blow to the shadow organization funding them.

And with no Gonzalez at the helm, the cartel would be decimated.

"So what did you do with Juan and Priscilla?"

Not by any noticeable gesture did Hawke indicate he knew what Olivia was talking about.

"Come on, Hawke. I know you."

When Serena had announced yesterday that Juan and his mother had disappeared and that there were all sorts of urgent messages about finding them zipping through cyber-space, Olivia had known immediately that Hawke had had a hand in their disappearance. She remembered him telling her about the takedown of Hector Gonzalez and how his son had been inconsolable. She knew he'd felt bad for the child.

Her husband's extraordinary compassion was one of the many reasons she'd fallen in love with him.

Shrugging, Hawke stared at the horizon. "The kid deserved a chance. He never signed up to be a drug kingpin. His mother was forced to marry a man twice her age. She never asked for that life either. I simply gave them a chance to live different lives. What they do now is all up to them."

"Where'd you come up with the funds?"

"I may or may not have funneled some of the funds from the original bust to a few private accounts."

"How'd you explain your extraordinary generosity?"

"I lied. Said that Hector hid some funds for them. That I found them. The kid doesn't need to know his father didn't give their welfare a single thought. Juan still looks up to his papá. He already had his heart broken. I just gave him a little bit of hope back."

Her heart melted. This man who tried to be so tough and who was as deadly as they came in many ways, was a good man. She loved him, would always love him, but more important, she genuinely liked him, too.

She tilted over, nudged him gently with her shoulder. "Softy."

"Shh. You'll spoil my reputation as a badass."

She grinned at him and then caught her breath. The hot look he threw her could melt a girl's clothes from her body. They'd never had sex in the middle of an op. They'd had plenty before and after, but never during. It wasn't going to happen now, and they both knew it, but it was still amazing that after all they'd gone through and after all these years, he could give her one look, and she wanted to rip his clothes off and let him devour her.

Blowing out a shaky breath, she stood. "I'm going to check the devices again."

His eyes locked on hers for several breathless seconds before he looked away and said, "Good idea." Turning his gaze to the warehouse, he raised his binoculars.

She didn't need to check the devices again. They were ready to go. She had triple-checked them already, but another check wouldn't hurt. Especially since she needed to get her mind back on the mission. Letting herself get sucked back into these feelings again couldn't happen. Hawke had made his position clear. He wouldn't change his mind, and neither would she.

After once again checking each device connection as well as the computer links, she returned to Hawke, who was still eyeing the warehouse. The guards changed out at midnight. The plan was to enter at one thirty and disable them. The men would've had an hour and a half to get comfortable, become a little less vigilant. Once the security guards were out of the way, the devices would be placed. She and Hawke would get clear, and detonation would occur.

Coordinating timelines so that all targets would be

demolished almost simultaneously took careful planning. Each team had their own timeline for securing their target, but demolition would happen at the same time. The annihilation of the Gonzalez cartel would be over in one fell swoop.

She seated herself beside Hawke again and pulled an energy bar from her pack. "Want one?"

He took it, and as he munched, she pulled out one for herself. As she consumed the chewy bar, she said, "You know they're not going to stop coming after us."

"I know that. After today, I would imagine they'll be even more determined to find us."

"Mack, Trevor, and Deacon okay with that?"

"Yeah, as much as they can be. They'll stay hidden. This might take the heat off them, though. The contract to kill the team was a promise made to Gonzalez. With the cartel demolished, and Juan and Priscilla gone, I doubt they're going to devote much attention to it."

"I hope so. I'd love to see the guys again." She glanced over at him, noting the solemn, almost grim set to his mouth. "You going to keep working for OZ once this is over?"

"Yeah, most likely. What about you?"

"I'll go back to LCR. It's where I can do the most good."

"They're lucky to have you."

They were so polite, so civil to each other it made her want to cry. She wouldn't, though. These were the choices they'd made. He couldn't give her what she wanted, and she couldn't be what he wanted. It was as simple and complicated as that.

They sat in silence after that, each waiting for the activity to begin. There were occasional desultory comments about the weather or what kind of snake slithered in front of them. Once, she mentioned mosquitoes, and he tossed her repellant. Despite the low chatter, it wasn't uncomfortable or awkward. This was the norm for them.

At one o'clock, the check-ins began to come in. Each team communicated to the others that they were in place and ready to roll at the appointed time.

Hawke waited until everyone had checked in before replying with, "Go on my command."

Unless there was a problem, radio silence would follow until the op had been accomplished.

While she checked the devices and charges one last time, Hawke completed another check of their weapons. A text signal alerted them that the van was in place. With the help of two additional men, they would load up the tranquilized security guards and send them off. When the men woke, they would be in another location and someone else's problem.

At one fifteen, she geared up and then sat and watched as the guards finished their rounds. Once that was completed, the guards would return to their individual posts and then make another set of rounds in fifteen minutes. She and Hawke would ensure that didn't happen.

The instant the last man returned to his post, they gave each other a nod, and Hawke said, "Let's go."

RUNNING side by side with Olivia felt like old times to Hawke. Their pace matched perfectly. There was no one else he'd rather work an op with or trusted more to get the job done.

A few feet from the gate entrance, they stopped. Olivia went left, and Hawke went right. The guard in the gatehouse office was looking down at his phone when Olivia made a noise to catch his attention. He looked up to see her waving and calling out to him. Startled, he ran from the office. The instant he appeared from behind the glass enclosure, Hawke, crouched low and out of sight, shot him with a dart. Grabbing his neck with one hand, he tried to reach for his gun with the other. The powerful drug acted immediately, dropping him to the ground before he could alert his fellow guards.

Hawke glanced at his watch. That had taken thirty seconds of their limited timeframe. Livvy nodded and gave him a thumbs-up. One down, five to go.

Fortunately, the gate was low enough that they could both climb over it easily. On the other side, Hawke once again went right, and Livvy went left. They now had four minutes and fifteen seconds to take out the rest of the guards.

Over the last couple of days, they'd noted that security was lax to the point of being nonexistent in some areas. Six security guards for a facility this large was laughable, but the cartel's arrogance worked to their advantage.

Night-vision goggles on, Hawke spotted a guard at the entrance to one of the warehouse doors. Staying low, he crept closer. The man lowered his head to light a cigarette, and Hawke fired. The guard fell face first onto the pavement.

Hawke dropped a small signal light beside the guard so the cleanup team could find him with ease. Continuing on, he took out his two remaining guards without incident.

"Liv?" Hawke said softly.

"Hold on." He heard the ping of the dart gun, a grunt of pain, and then a thud. "Okay. Done."

Checking the time, he was pleased to see they had an extra twelve seconds. Clicking his earbud to a different frequency, he reported, "Package ready for pickup."

A double click was the affirmative answer. The two men responsible for picking up the guards and loading them on the van would arrive within a minute. In the meantime, he and Olivia had ten minutes to set twelve charges.

Running to the northwest corner of the first building, Hawke went to his knees and removed a small device from his pack. Placing it on the metal surface, he heard the slight click, letting him know it was now attached. He flipped the switch, and the detonator light came on.

"One," Hawke said into his mic.

Grabbing his pack, he went through his sector, attaching each device to the position they had decided would make the most impact. With each additional one, he counted off, listening to Olivia do the same with her charges.

"Done."

He was halfway to the entrance when Olivia said, "Hawke, number three isn't giving me a connection light."

That was one he'd set. "Okay. Give me a sec." He took off, racing as fast as he could back to the location he'd just left. Sure enough, the light had gone off. Lying flat on the ground, he checked and immediately saw the problem. A wire on the back had come loose. Reattaching it, he clicked the switch again, and the light came on.

"Okay, got it," Olivia said. "Now get out of there."

He didn't need to be told twice. Getting to his feet, he raced back the way he'd come. A glance at his watch told him he had two minutes, twenty-three seconds before—

On his next step, his foot twisted. His knee went one way, his foot the other. Searing shards of pain shot through his knee, and he went down.

"Hawke, you okay?"

Cursing his clumsiness and gritting his teeth, he got back to his feet, and damned if he didn't almost go down again.

He looked up, noting he had about twenty yards to go before he could even get to the outer section, then it'd be ten yards after that. Yet, he could put no weight on his left leg.

"Hawke?" Olivia's voice was quiet, but he heard her mounting tension. "Talk to me."

"Had a little accident. Get out of the blast site. I'll be there soon."

"What kind of accident?"

Dragging his leg, he growled between clenched teeth, "Just get the hell out of here, Liv. That's an order."

When she didn't respond, he blew out a sigh filled with relief. She would follow protocol. She would be safe.

He continued to drag his leg, all the while knowing he wasn't going to make it. Detonation could not be stopped. He wouldn't give up, that just wasn't in him, but a quiet calm was enveloping his senses. He'd had more time in this world than he'd thought he'd have. Didn't mean he wouldn't have liked to have decades more, but maybe this was the way it was supposed to be. Seeing Olivia, making peace with her, making love to her one more time—those had been gifts he'd never expected.

He didn't bother to look at his watch again. When it happened, it would happen. No point in—

The sound of running feet caught his attention. He glanced up to see Olivia running like a bat out of hell toward him.

"No!" he shouted. "I told you to get out of here!"

Ignoring him, her expression one of grim determination, she charged toward him. Doing his best, he tried to run toward her, shouting at her the entire time to leave.

She reached him in seconds. "Put your arm around me."

Arguing now would only get them both killed. He did his best not to give her his full weight.

They weren't going to make it, and it literally killed his soul to know that she would die with him. Because of him. Never in a million years had he wanted this to happen.

He glanced down at her. Sweat poured down her face, but there were tears, too. He wanted to say something profound, something comforting. All he could come up with was, "I'm sorry, baby. So sorry."

She didn't acknowledge his grim words. She just kept moving.

The entrance was ahead of them. His heart kicked up. Maybe they could make it. Ignoring the agony in his leg, he forced himself to move.

Thirty seconds from safety, the world exploded around them.

CHAPTER TWENTY-EIGHT

She couldn't breathe. As fiery hell rained down around her, Olivia tried to raise her head. Something was pinning her down. She couldn't draw a breath. Her ears rang, and in the distance, she could hear what sounded like explosions and fireworks going off. Once more, she tried to lift herself up and realized that what pinned her down wasn't something, but someone. Hawke.

The second after the explosion, Hawke had thrown her to the ground and then landed on top of her to try to protect her from the blast.

She tried to move his body off of her without success. "Hawke!" she shouted.

Nothing. No movement. Was he even breathing?

Fire raged all around them, scorching heat searing her skin. If they didn't get out of here, they would burn to death.

Fear gave her herculean strength. She managed to push herself up on her elbows, shifting Hawke's weight slightly. She screamed his name, calling out to the heavens to save them. The effort to move him and the terror of what was happening forced her to her limits. She finally managed to

shove him off of her. He landed on the pavement
beside her.

Getting to her knees, she made a quick sweep of the area
with her eyes. Fire virtually surrounded them, and the only
clear pathway out was in front of them. It would get them
out of the danger zone, but safety was at least twelve yards
away. Knowing she had no choice if they were both to
survive, Olivia got to her feet. She knew that moving him
could be dangerous. He could have a broken neck or internal
injuries. One thing she knew above all others was that if she
didn't move him, he would burn to death. She had no choice.

Praying like she had never prayed before, she tucked her
forearms beneath Hawke's armpits and began to pull. She
lost her grip, started over. Tugged again. Dragging a six-four,
two-hundred-twenty-pound, unconscious man even a yard
was a stretch for her. Hawke outweighed her by a hundred
pounds and some change. That didn't matter, couldn't
matter.

She tugged, she pulled, she cursed, and she prayed. And
finally, with the fires of hell falling around her, she made it to
the safety zone outside the gate. Fortunately, the explosion
had blown the gate open. Otherwise, she never would have
been able to get him to the other side.

Finally out of immediate danger, Olivia collapsed beside
him, breath wheezing in her lungs, her entire body
screaming from the strain. She allowed herself a few seconds,
and then she went back to her knees. They had to get out of
here. The fire would have been seen by nearby businesses
and residents. The emergency response time would be fast.
They had no time to waste.

She shook his shoulders, shouting his name. Hawke had
not opened his eyes. "Hawke? Can you hear me?" Tears
pooled in her eyes. "Not again," she cried. "I am not going to
lose you again. Wake up, dammit!" she shouted.

Still nothing.

Her ears were ringing, and the noise around her prevented her from hearing him breathe. Was his chest moving at all? Her hand shaking with fear, she pressed her fingers to the pulse in his neck. Yes! A good, strong beat.

She shook him again. He had to wake up! They had to get out of here. The Colombian National Police force would be arriving within the next three minutes. Their SUV was parked only a few yards away, though up a hilly path. There was no way she could carry him. His leg was hurt—she didn't know how badly—but it couldn't matter. If they didn't get out of here, they would be arrested. No one would rescue them. That had been a key agreement. For this to work, it had been decided that if anyone were caught, they were on their own. Having this lead back to Option Zero or Kate's people would destroy a lot of lives.

She shook him again, and when there was no response, she shouted directly in his ear. "Hawke! Nic!" She smacked his face, shouting, screaming, suddenly feeling more helpless than she ever had before. "Why you, Nic? Why do you always have to be the hero? Why?"

His eyes fluttered, and through the ringing in her ears, she heard him groan.

"Hawke! Yes, wake up. Wake up!"

He opened his eyes and blinked up at her. "Damn, Livvy. Did you have to shout so loud?"

Torn between laughter, tears, and smacking him again, she said urgently, "We've got to get out of here. We only have a couple of minutes before the police arrive."

Comprehension came in an instant. He pulled himself up, groaning.

"Can you walk at all?"

"Yeah." The instant he tried, he fell back on his butt with a loud curse. "Oh man, that's messed up." He rolled onto his side, put one knee down, and rose up slowly.

Olivia helped him stand and wrapped her arm around his waist.

"Let's go," he growled.

She knew he was hurting, but there was nothing she could do. It was slower going than they wanted, but they finally got into a rhythm and made it up the hill. While she opened the vehicle and threw their bags inside, Hawke leaned against the door. His face told the story. He was in excruciating pain.

She opened the back door and helped him get inside. He never made a sound, but the grim set to his jaw told the story.

The instant he was safely inside, she ran around to the driver's side, cranked the engine, and they were speeding away. Lights from the police vehicles glowed below them. Since she couldn't turn on the headlights, she kept her night-vision goggles on and maneuvered down the hill and onto a side road, away from the burning structures and away from danger.

CHAPTER TWENTY-NINE

His leg propped up on a pillow, Hawke lay on the bed. The little inn they'd been staying at was perfect for this kind of op. Small, slightly run-down, with just enough guests that no one noticed them.

With half-closed eyes, he watched Olivia. She was working herself into a fine tizzy. She marched back and forth in front of him, getting things they needed. First, it had been the ice pack from his kit for his knee. Then she'd grabbed the medical supplies. Next, it had been water for both of them. With each pass in front of the bed, she shot him a fuming look that could rival the sun.

She was injured—cuts and scrapes were on her shoulders, arms, and face—but he knew she wouldn't see to herself until she had completed her tasks. When she'd dropped her backpack onto the floor and pulled off her shirt, he'd seen the cuts and blood where glass and metal had hit her. He'd tried to protect her from the worst of it by covering her body with his. The heat had been intense, and her face was pinker than it should be. Livvy was fair-skinned and easily burned in the sun. There were no visible burns, but he wouldn't be able to see to her until she had run herself down. He would just have to wait her out.

She grabbed the ice bucket from the dresser. "I'll be back in a minute." The look she gave him before walking out the door told him she'd have a few things to say when she returned.

Hawke settled back on the bed. He had a few things he planned to say to her, too. Right now, though, he still had work to do.

Picking up the satphone, he dialed a number. Serena answered.

Hawke said, "Report."

"Victory." Their code word that all the jobs had been successful.

"Casualties?" Hawke asked.

"Negative."

No loss of life, among the operatives or the cartel's employees. That had been his biggest concern, especially for the ships. It had taken careful scrutiny and timing to ensure that the ships had the least amount of personnel on board. The people who had been there had been abducted and would be released after questioning. This hadn't been about killing people, it had been about destroying what the cartel held most dear—product and property.

For the first time in days, tension eased from his body. The operation had been big, and there were days he'd doubted they could pull it off. Major destruction without loss of life had been an ambitious plan. Anything could have gone wrong.

Something *had* gone wrong. He glanced down at his knee. He hadn't taken his pants off yet, but it was clearly swollen. It'd been his fault, every bit of it. He hadn't been looking where he was going. In his early years, he would've stumbled and recovered his footing without even thinking. But now, older and much less agile, he had to be extra careful. He'd like to be bitter about his circumstances, but he'd learned that being bitter accomplished nothing but making a person feel shittier than they already did. He accepted and moved on.

What he couldn't accept was Olivia's deliberate disobedience of his orders. She had almost gotten herself killed, and he intended to get an explanation. Of course, that would have to come after she burned off the fury bubbling inside her. He knew she was furious with him. And while he could understand her anger, that would not get her out of a tongue-lashing for not following protocol.

The door opened with a loud bang, and Hawke grabbed his gun, pointing it at the intruder. Except it was Livvy, still in a huff. She glared at the gun in his hand.

"Good way to get yourself killed, baby."

"Yeah, well, you should know all about that, shouldn't you?"

Okay, here it comes.

Surprising him, she came at him with scissors. Starting from the bottom hem, she cut his pants leg open to reveal his angry, red, and swollen kneecap. The sound she made was between a gasp and a sob.

"It's not as bad as it looks."

She jerked her head up, her eyes searing him. "Shut up."

Okay. He had enough self-preservation to do just that. Olivia didn't get in these snits very often, but when she did, he'd learned to let them run their course.

She was fighting anger and the extreme emotions that came with almost losing him. Yes, he knew she still loved him. A love like theirs never died. It hadn't saved their marriage, though, and it wouldn't save whatever they had now. Love could exist without fulfillment. It was a hollow, sad kind of emotion, but it never went away.

"I don't know how to fix this," she said softly.

"You don't have to. The swelling will go down. I'll check in with my ortho guy and see what I need to do."

Her expression stoic, she took a breath and said, "Let's see your back."

Gritting his teeth because, yeah, it hurt to move, he leaned forward and pulled off his shirt. Moving behind him, Olivia released a sympathetic hiss. He didn't know if it was because of new damage or the damage that was already there. One benefit of the scars from the fire was there was so much nerve damage, he had little feeling on that side of his back. Though he'd had to sit for hours for the tattoo of the soaring hawk, he hadn't felt a thing.

"How bad?" he asked.

"You're going to need some stitches."

"Too many for you?"

"No," she said evenly. "Just hope I don't run out of thread."

That was the last thing she said to him for over an hour as she cleaned his wounds, sewed him up, and bandaged what she could.

"You have some burns. I've put salve on them. A couple of places might blister, but the rest aren't too bad."

That was better than he'd figured. He knew there was blood, because he'd felt the warmth oozing down the part of his back he could still feel.

"How many stitches did it take?"

"Five on one, eight on another, three on another."

"Frankenstein's monster's got nothing on me."

The silence told him his little quip hadn't landed well.

She stood and silently put away the gauze and bandages.

"Hold on," he said. "We need to do you."

"I need a shower first."

"All right. But take your shirt off and let me see what we're dealing with."

She could refuse him. There was no way he could get off this bed and pull it off her. This was her choice.

Myriad emotions still gleaming in her eyes, she pulled the shirt over her head. She wore a tank top and a plain, no-frills bra, which she removed and dropped on the floor. Despite her fury and his pain, his never-ending desire for her surged through him like a geyser. If he lived to be a hundred, no matter how many other body parts stopped working, he didn't doubt that she would still be able to turn him on.

There was a small cut just above her left breast that needed tending to, but it probably wouldn't need stitches. She had another couple of jagged cuts on her shoulders and a large bruise on her midriff.

"Your ribs okay?"

"Yes. They're bruised, but nothing more."

"Turn around."

The look she gave him then told him she wasn't as immune to this as she would like him to think. She had stripped for him multiple times. Each time had always led to hours of pleasure. Even though this wouldn't be one of those times, the memories had both of them thinking of hot, sweaty nights and the sweetest, most intense pleasure that existed on this earth.

She turned, and he caught his breath. She had a couple of second-degree burns on her shoulder, a nasty, jagged cut on her lower back, and a vicious-looking bruise on her right side.

"We'll need to treat those burns."

"Yeah, I figured. A cold shower will help."

"The bruise from when I tackled you?"

"Probably."

He was surprised it wasn't worse. He'd slammed into her hard to protect her from the blast.

She stood still for several more seconds and then said, "I'll go take a shower."

Her shoulders were slumped, and he knew she was doing her best to keep it together. With Livvy, it had always been fury and then tears. The shower would soothe her physical pain, but he knew she needed those moments to deal with the conglomeration of emotions spiraling through her.

When the bathroom door closed, he closed his eyes and listened. Though the shower came on and he knew she was doing her best to stifle the sounds, he had no trouble hearing her sobs.

His Livvy was sometimes as predictable as the sunset. She had her quirks—her peccadilloes, she would call them—and a couple of nervous tics that he'd always found endearing. She chewed on her lip when she was deep in thought, which he thought was the sexiest thing ever. And she had an M&M's addiction that came out only before a major operation. He knew if he checked her bag right now, it would have a family-sized bag of Peanut M&M's right beside her extra ammo.

Those habits had—

A thought came to him, and his entire body jerked at the notion that ran through his mind. Iris Gates had had a small quirk, too. During their interview of her, she had bounced her right foot several times as if she'd had a cramp. It hadn't registered at the time, but as he thought on it now, that gesture struck him as strange. There hadn't been the slightest indication that she had been nervous. She'd been way too experienced and poised for that. Admittedly, if she had already determined she was going to kill herself, something like that could have made even the calmest, most coldhearted person nervous.

Grabbing the satphone again, he called the holding cell in

Arizona. When Bruce answered, Hawke said, "You checked under all her nails, right?"

"Yes. Other than the pill she'd hidden beneath her thumb-nail, everything else was clear."

"And her toenails?"

There was a long pause. Then he said, "Her fingernails were fake. Her toenails weren't."

"Check them anyway."

"I'll call you back."

As Hawke dropped his head back onto the pillow, the improbability of such a thing hit him. Even as odd and out of character as the foot jiggling had seemed, what would be the reason for her to have anything else hidden beneath her nails? She was dead. There was no coming back from that.

The phone rang, and even before he heard the words, Hawke knew.

"Under the middle toenail of her right foot."

"What is it?"

"Microdot. I'll get my tech guys on it ASAP. I'll call you when I have something."

"I'll be there tomorrow afternoon."

He grunted. "May take us longer."

"Tomorrow afternoon."

A huff of exasperation and then, "See you then."

Letting his mind work through the scenarios, Hawke grabbed the TV remote and pressed the On button. A TV news reporter stood in front of a large warehouse belonging to Garcia Industries, one of the shell corporations owned by the Gonzalez cartel.

He didn't bother listening to the reporter's speculation about how or why the fire started. The whole world knowing that it had been a series of small bombs was fine with him.

He clicked on an international news station and was pleased to see another story about an explosion at a port in

Cartagena that had destroyed three cargo ships, all belonging to Gomez Holdings, another Gonzalez shell company.

The shower shutting off diverted his attention. Grabbing the medical pack lying on the bed, he sat up. They both had things to say to each other, but this came first.

She walked into the room, dressed in a pair of silky-looking shorts and a cotton T-shirt. They were cheap, probably something she'd picked up at a discount store. Everything they owned during an op needed to be disposable and untraceable. The tags would have been cut out of the outfit immediately after her purchase. The cost of the clothing didn't matter, though. Silk, satin, lace, or sackcloth, Olivia would look beautiful in all of them.

Her eyes were rimmed in pink, and her skin was more flushed than before. The tension around her mouth had lessened, and her shoulders were less stiff. She'd had a good cry and was now ready for fireworks. First things first.

"Come over here and let me check your cuts and burns."

She didn't argue. They both knew how important it was to take care of even the slightest injury while on a job. A small cut could become infected, requiring medical care. Taking care of the problem before it became a problem was their protocol.

Without a hint of embarrassment, she pulled her shirt up and sat on the bed.

He carefully examined her cuts, thankful to see that they were already closing up. He gently applied antibiotic ointment to each one, telling himself it was wrong to enjoy touching her. He never wanted to see her hurt, but the feel of her soft skin beneath his fingertips was a pleasure he sorely missed. It took every ounce of will to not press his mouth against her. He could live a thousand years with this woman and never get tired of her.

Instead, he did the sensible, wise thing and treated her

wounds. After applying an aloe-based salve to her burns, his voice only slightly hoarse, he said, "All done."

She sprang up from the bed like she couldn't wait to get away from him, from his touch. Not that he could blame her.

When she turned, Hawke took a breath. Now came the part he dreaded and looked forward to the most.

"All right," he said softly. "Let's get on with it."

CHAPTER THIRTY

Olivia ground her teeth together. That was the problem with being infuriated with the one person who knew her too well. Hawke was more than aware that she was furious with him. He had kept quiet while she'd taken care of seeing to their immediate needs. He'd known that would focus her, calming her down until she could clear her head. A shower and a gargantuan sobfest had mellowed her out even more. She wanted to resent him for knowing her so well, but it went both ways. He was angry, too. If they had gone at each other while their emotions had still been flaming, there was no telling what they would've said.

Now, calmer and wiser, she opened her mouth to speak, but nothing came out. He was sitting there in pain, cut, bruised, burned, and exhausted, waiting for her to castigate him. And the only thing she wanted to do was throw herself into his arms and beg him never to put himself in that kind of danger again.

This was who Hawke was, though. She had known that from the beginning. He was a hero in every sense of the word, and to expect him to be someone else was not only unrealistic, it wasn't what she wanted. This was the man she had fallen in love with, the man she would always love. Asking him to change would be like asking the sun to be less hot. It was his nature to be this way, and she never wanted him to be different.

"Well?" He arched a brow. "I know you're fuming, so let's get it out in the open."

Instead of giving him what he clearly expected, she said, "Why do you do it?"

His brow furrowed. "Do what?"

"Always have to take the danger by yourself."

"There are a lot of people who would argue that point. I don't do anything a million other people don't do on a daily basis."

That might be true, but she wasn't in love with a million other people. She was in love with this man. The one who always put himself in jeopardy first. Hawke, who led the way.

Knowing she wouldn't get a satisfactory answer, because there wasn't one, she moved on. "The charge didn't need to be fixed. The building would have been badly damaged, maybe even demolished, without it."

"True, but it would have looked sloppy. Our message had to be clear. We came to destroy, and we did. Leaving it half-assed would have given the wrong impression."

The familiar ire began to resurge. "So you risked your life for the sake of appearances?"

"These people, whoever they are, believe they're untouchable. Our attack against the cartel is only a minute portion of who they are and what they control. If our initial offensive is flawed, we look weak and unorganized. Right now, they don't know exactly who we are or how many. We can show no weaknesses."

His argument might be sound, but it didn't diminish the personal aspect. Before she could come at him with something else, he asked, "Now, you want to tell me why you disobeyed a direct order?"

"At the risk of sounding childish, you're not the boss of me, Mr. Hawthorne." She used her most prissy, snobbish tone.

Sparks glinted in his eyes. "On this op, I am."

"So what are you going to do? Demote me?"

"If I didn't know what would happen, I'd take you across my knee and let that sweet bottom know who's in charge."

Despite the challenging and arrogant words, Olivia felt a smile twitch at her mouth. Their bedroom play had always been passionate *and* fun. Once, without warning her, Hawke had gotten it into his head that a sensual spanking would fire her up. And it had, but not the way he'd expected. She'd rolled over, jumped to her feet, and slugged him.

She'd loved her husband's dominance in the bedroom, but only because she agreed to the submission. That spanking had been unexpected and totally without her approval. They'd both learned something that day. He had never again done anything without making sure she was on board with it, and she had agreed that if he happened to do something she didn't like, a simple *no* would suffice instead of a slug to his jaw.

As the memories took her down a road she couldn't afford to go, she said evenly, "The op is over. It's done. Let it go."

He shook his head. "I'll never forget seeing you run toward me like that."

"I couldn't let you die, Nic," she said softly.

"I know that, Livvy. I know."

They stared at each other, the words unspoken but heavy in the air. Love, bright and burning, eternal. Oh sweet heavens, why wasn't it enough to destroy the darkness?

A commercial on TV, louder than the news program

Hawke had been watching, broke the spell. Olivia pulled her eyes away from him and said, "What are the news reports saying?"

"Various suppositions but no speculation yet that they're related."

That's what they'd planned. On paper, none of the targets were related to one another. All the bombs had been different. There had been no similarities for anyone to say for certain that one particular group or entity had been the cause of all of them.

"And everyone is healthy and accounted for?"

"Yes."

"So it was a success."

"For a first strike, it was a rousing success."

First strike. Yes. Because this group was much larger than a large drug cartel. Option Zero would continue to hunt them. They'd find the head of the snake and cut it off, as Ash had mentioned.

"When does our flight to Montana leave?"

"Change of plans. We're headed to Arizona first."

That surprised her, but it shouldn't have. She had been putting off deciding what to do about Iris's remains. She supposed it was time to make that decision.

"I was thinking cremation and then a—"

"No. That's not why we're headed back."

"Then why?"

He told her about what he'd suspected and how he had been proven right.

"Why on earth would Iris have a microdot beneath her toenail?"

"Beats me, but if it was important enough for her to hide it, then there's something on it we need to see."

Her tired mind spun with questions. Was this intel Iris had stolen? If so, had it been for MI6 or the shadow group?

"We won't know anything until we get it deciphered. Best to get some sleep. Our plane to Yuma leaves at two thirty."

"You need some help getting set for the night?"

"No. Swelling has already gone down."

She watched him rise from the bed and limp to the bathroom. She knew he was still hurting, but he was right—the knee looked a thousand times better than it had when they'd first arrived. He had lived with this pain for over two years. She would trust him to know when to ask for help.

She pulled back the covers and slid between the sheets. Ten minutes later, when she was just slipping into sleep, she felt him lie beside her. Without thinking about it, the movement as natural as rainfall, she turned and snuggled against his side, her head fitting into the curve of his shoulder, her hand against his chest. When he reached up and covered her hand with his, the ritual was complete.

CHAPTER THIRTY-ONE

Barely five hours after landing in Yuma, they were in the air, headed back to Montana. Since they'd detoured from their original departure plan, they were taking a commercial flight. A flight to Missoula had been taking off within the hour of checking for one, and he and Olivia had hightailed it to the airport. After settling into their seats, Hawke had barely heard the flight attendant's announcements or the muted conversations among the other passengers. His mind was too focused on what they'd learned, and the new questions that had been raised.

When they had arrived at the holding site, he'd been prepared to bully someone into getting the information from Iris's microdot. That hadn't been necessary. The young tech genius had dived into the deciphering like a shaggy dog jumps into a swimming pool on a hot day. The young man had considered it an honor to pull intel from such an old-school device. The fact that it had come from the notorious spy Iris Gates had only made the job that much sweeter.

He and Olivia had walked in the doors, and the info had been waiting for them. Hawke didn't know who had been more floored—him or Olivia. Iris Gates had always gone out of her way to be unpredictable, and she had once again achieved that goal. The information had been a treasure trove.

He reviewed the short history Iris had provided about the shadow organization. The Wren Project, as they now knew the entity was called, had been founded by Trenton Jefferson, a wealthy man from New York City who in 1922 lost his daughter, Wren, in a tragic accident. In his grief, Jefferson vowed to honor his daughter's memory by devoting the rest of his life to altruistic pursuits.

For twenty-seven years, he had kept that vow. When he died, he had no other children, and the philanthropic foundation went to his nephew, who didn't have the same altruistic nature as his uncle. Twenty-three years passed, and by the time the nephew died, the Wren Project no longer resembled what Trenton had created. By then, it was responsible for some of the most corrupt and dangerous events of the twenty-first century.

Following that brief explanation, Iris had listed fifty-three families, including many politicians and world leaders, and forty-nine companies and organizations with ties to the Wren Project.

Why had she given them this information? The woman hadn't had a moral or selfless bone in her body, and determining her motives would be impossible now that she was dead. Maybe she'd intended to send them in the wrong direction, deliberately diverting their focus away from legitimate avenues they might have pursued. Regardless, they had no choice but to look seriously at the info she'd provided. Serena and her people should be able to determine its validity.

He glanced over at Olivia, who had been dealt an even more shocking blow. Along with all the intel, Iris had included a letter to her daughter. Olivia had read it several times already, and Hawke still didn't know how she felt about what she'd read.

How did you react when a woman who should have been a caregiver, mentor, and role model revealed more truths than you'd ever wanted to hear?

Her face, pale beneath the slight pink that remained from the intense heat of the explosion, showed both shock and sadness. Her beautiful eyes shimmered with emotion, her lips trembling. It was all he could do to keep from pulling her into his arms and comforting her.

"You okay?" he asked.

"Truthfully, I don't know." Her gaze shifted to the folder of intel on his lap. "You think all of that's real, or just another of Iris's chess moves?"

"What would be the point of lying at this point?"

"To throw us off. Send us in the wrong direction."

Yes, even in death, Iris could be a dangerous, vindictive woman. Who knew what her agenda was? However, they would dig deep into the information she'd provided and go from there. If it was bogus, then they had wasted time. If it was for real, the intel was a godsend—and something others would kill to get.

Always hyperalert, Hawke was even more so now as he glanced around the cabin of the plane. They were seated in first class, which gave them some privacy, but he wasn't going to take even that for granted. They knew for certain that the Wren Project organization was huge. Just how large was anyone's guess. Anyone, anywhere, at any time, could be working for them.

"Why do you think she had a letter specifically for me?"

"You're her daughter."

"No, I was her protégée. Her lab rat. An experiment that went horribly wrong, to her way of thinking."

"Because you didn't comply. You have a mind of your own and a goodness inside you that she could never comprehend or understand."

Iris Gates loved to mess with people's minds, and she had done her very best to do that to her daughter. Fortunately, Olivia was much too strong to allow her mother's influence to control her. Hawke had already read Iris's final words to Olivia, but he took the letter from her hand and reviewed it again to ensure he hadn't missed something.

Olivia,

If you're reading this, then I am gone. I won't bother trying to give you sage advice or words of wisdom. You would ignore both. Let's face it, we're opposites in every way that counts.

Letting you go to America was our biggest mistake. You were there to gather intel, not to desert your heritage. Marrying Nicholas was your worst mistake. I wasn't surprised it didn't last.

We didn't bring you into this world to do as you please—you were born for a purpose, one you'll never achieve. That's not to say I regret your existence. As your caretakers, Glen and I learned much from you. We were harsh with you in many ways. We prepared you for the life you were intended to lead. Sadly, that didn't happen.

I won't end this on a maudlin or sentimental note. I am neither of those things. However, I will say this, and take it as you may: You've achieved something, Olivia. Own it. Believe in it. Live it. But guard your soft heart, because that's where the vultures feast.

I

"Is there a message in there that I'm missing?" Olivia asked. "Or is this just another one of Iris's mind games?"

"Actually, I think it's a mother saying goodbye to her daughter."

She swallowed hard, and he knew that despite her effort not to be, she had been moved by Iris's words. Which was sad in its own way, because they weren't particularly kind or helpful.

Hoping to make her smile, he said wryly, "Apparently, Iris was not my biggest fan."

"What? That's what you got from 'worst mistake ever'?" Though she didn't smile, her eyes sparkled with amusement. "But it was so obscure and indirect. However did you crack that code?"

He loved her sass. She was hurting but oh-so-strong. "Okay, smartass. I—"

His retort was interrupted by a flight attendant's instructions for their upcoming landing. She had a slight accent, and Hawke said, "Where do you think she's from?"

Olivia's ear for accents and languages had never failed to impress him. Hawke used to quiz her just to see if he could find one she couldn't identify.

"Ontario."

"Seriously?"

"Betcha five."

As the attendant started past them, Hawke said to her, "You have a slight accent. Mind if I ask where you're from?"

The woman's eyes went wide for a second before she answered with a brilliant smile. "Omaha, Nebraska."

Delighted that Olivia had finally been stumped, he glanced at her, surprised by her narrowed eyes. Still, she smiled and shrugged, saying, "My mistake."

"Here, dear," the attendant said. "Your jacket's about to fall to the floor."

Taking the jean jacket the woman held out for her, Olivia thanked her. The woman went on her way.

Olivia glanced over at him. "Don't smirk. It's not attractive."

Enjoying the easy camaraderie, Hawke leaned back in his seat with a sigh. A successful mission, more intel than they'd ever expected, and a safe, smooth flight back home. Some-times, you couldn't ask for more than that.

He looked at the woman sitting beside him. Yeah, some-times you could ask for more, but that didn't mean you could have it.

CHAPTER THIRTY-TWO

Missoula, Montana

With no bags to claim, she and Hawke made it out of the airport in record time. It was midday, and though the sun was shining, a definite chill was in the air. Her long-sleeved shirt was fine for now, but she had the distinct feeling she'd be bundling up soon. She draped her jacket over her shoulders as she and Hawke headed to the long-term parking lot where they had left their SUV.

Had it been only three days ago? It seemed that so much had happened in that time. Now, they were due back at OZ headquarters for debriefing. Everyone who'd been involved in the op would report in with any issues they'd had, but the meeting should be brief. From what she knew, there had been no problems with any part of the operation, other than the mishap with her and Hawke.

Out of the corner of her eye, she watched Hawke. He was in pain, though he never complained. They'd had the foresight to stop by a medical supply store for crutches before boarding the flight to Arizona. His grim countenance told her that driving was not helping his knee, but he'd given her a look when she had suggested she drive. She knew when to pick her battles. If he wanted to grind his teeth against the pain while driving the stupid SUV, then she would let him. He had promised he'd go see his doctor as soon as he had time. She intended to hold him to that promise.

She froze. That had been a very wifely thought. And she shouldn't be having those any longer. After this meeting, she would return home. That had been her plan from the beginning. Nothing had changed. When she left OZ today, she wouldn't be coming back.

These last few days of working together had felt like old times. They were still good together, able to read each other's thoughts, anticipate each other's needs. Their comfortable partnership was something she had sorely missed. She'd worked with several different partners over her career, but working with Hawke was no comparison.

It was more than the job, though. There was more, so much more, than that. There was still love and devotion between them. Still an aching tenderness that welled up inside her whenever she looked at him. Still an immeasurable attraction and connection that drew them together like a magnet to steel.

A stupid, fantastical, insane idea speared through her mind. *Could* she convince him to give them one more chance? Was she going to let go of the best thing that had ever happened to her because she was too afraid to risk rejection? With Hawke's return, she had been given another opportunity. Was she really going to let it go by without trying one more time?

She knew his issues with his father colored everything. Hawke had been beaten almost daily as a child, but the physical abuse had been only one aspect of the torture. His father had convinced his son that he would be just like him, and that mental abuse had controlled much of Hawke's life. In no way had she ever seen in him anything remotely resembling his father, but Hawke refused to believe that. How could she persuade him to try again if he still felt that way?

But didn't she owe it to them to try?

Anxiety locked her muscles, and she could practically feel the tension permeate the interior of the vehicle. Her window of opportunity to bring up the subject was closing. They were only a few miles from OZ headquarters.

He said he hasn't changed his position, her mind whispered. Just how much of a masochist did one have to be to not get the message?

But she might never have this chance again. Didn't she owe it to herself to try one last time?

The closer they got to HQ, the more nervous she became. It was now or never.

She breathed a silent prayer for courage and said, "I realize this is an inappropriate time to bring this up, but we haven't really had the chance to discuss this fully."

That part wasn't quite true—had they really discussed it at all? They'd mostly skirted the issue, but now she wanted it out in the open. One way or the other, she had to be sure. If there was no hope, then she would let it go.

"Discuss what fully?" Hawke asked.

"Us."

The look he threw her was a cross between incredulous and heated. She didn't know if that was a good thing or a bad thing.

She cleared her throat. "I was wondering if you might want to try again."

"You're serious?"

"Why does that surprise you?"

"Because of what we talked about last week. I haven't changed my mind. You haven't changed yours."

"But we could talk about it. We never did. Not really. I know I presented you with a fait accompli. That was my fault, and I take full responsibility. It wasn't planned, but if we did—"

"Livvy, baby. There's nothing I want more than to be with you, to marry you again."

Her heart almost bursting, she reached for him. He stopped her by grabbing her hand and bringing it to his lips. "I've never stopped loving you, and I never will. But nothing has changed, or will change, about having children. I do not want them."

"But if you could just—"

"Do you really want to get back together when you know that I'll never change my mind?"

"But how do you know, Nic? How can you be sure? If you would—"

"Stop it, Olivia! Don't you think I've thought about this? Don't pretend you don't know why."

The silence was thick, the entire atmosphere in the vehicle one of suppressed emotions. She swallowed past the huge lump developing in her throat and wrapped her arms around herself.

All right, that hadn't been well received, but she wasn't giving up yet. Clearing her voice, she tried a different direction. "Have you heard from Ash lately?"

"Yeah. Talked to him this morning. He'll be at the debrief today."

"That's good. Jules and the baby doing okay?"

"Healthy and happy, as far as I know."

"How's he enjoying fatherhood?"

"I didn't ask."

"I've never seen him happier than the day we visited them at the hospital."

"Yeah."

She gazed out the window, taking comfort from the beauty surrounding her. The trees were at peak fall color, their leaves every shade and hue imaginable, the mountains surrounding them majestic and untamed. It was one of those vividly beautiful sunny days in Montana, with the sky so ocean blue that it looked like the world had turned upside down. It was a day where anything seemed possible. Why couldn't this be possible?

She kept her face averted when she said, "Did you know that Ash had an abusive father?"

"Yes."

The hard, abrupt tone of that one word told her he knew where she was going with this, and he didn't want to go there with her. She forged on. If she didn't, she'd regret it for the rest of her life. It had to be said.

"He doesn't seem worried that he'll take after his father."

"Olivia…don't."

"But I—"

"The day I put my father in the ground, I swore to myself that I would never bring a Hawthorne into this world. I will not go back on that promise."

"Your thinking is flawed, and if you'd give yourself a chance to see it, you'd realize that. I've seen you lose your temper a million times. Not one of those times have you been abusive. I've seen grown men spit on you, curse you, and punch you in the face. Not once have you retaliated out of anger. I've never felt safer with anyone than with you. You are not and never will be your father."

He was silent for several seconds, giving her the stupid hope that he was actually thinking about her words. When he spoke, she realized how stupid and hopeless she was being.

"It's there, Olivia, under the surface. I can feel it. I can control it now, but what happens when someday I can't?"

"It won't happen because of who you are. I know you, Hawke. You are a good, decent man. Nothing like the man who raised you. Everyone else can see that. Why can't you?"

"You weren't there, Olivia. Every. Single. Damn. Day. He justified his behavior by saying his father did the same thing to him. It's a heritage of abuse, and I refuse to put a child through that."

"If you would just—"

He raised a hand to stop her. "No." The look he gave her was both tortured and angry. "Do you know how much it hurts me not to give you what you want? To be with you, love you, spend the rest of my life with you? I want that more than anything. But I'm not willing to risk a child's life just because of what I want."

Olivia clenched her jaw. She would not cry. There was no point. Nothing had changed. Life would go on. She would return home and figure out what the rest of her life would look like. It wouldn't include Nic, but she had lived without him for two years. She told herself that this time together had been good for her. It had given her closure. Most important, she knew now that he was alive. She needed to celebrate that fact and move on.

He pulled into the parking lot of OZ headquarters. There were half a dozen cars already here. She spotted Eve's sporty baby blue convertible and blew out a shaky breath. That was another blessing. She had made peace with Eve and the other OZ operatives.

That was something her grandmother had taught her. When life fell into chaos and everything seemed doomed, she had to count her blessings. *Look for the good, Olivia. Look for the rainbow behind the dark clouds.*

She put her hand on the door to get out. There was nothing more to say, nothing more she could do to convince him of something he wasn't willing to work for. This was it for them.

"You should find someone else," he said gruffly.

She jerked her head around and stared at him. "What?"

"Find a man who can give you what you want. Someone who will be good to you, give you what you need."

She tried to take comfort in the fact that his voice sounded like he'd said the words around a mouthful of gravel. And the expression on his face was one of torment. A part of her wanted to reach out and comfort him. Another part wanted to slap him for being so stupid and stubborn.

She spoke quietly and deliberately. "So you would be okay with another man touching me, kissing me, making love to me? Putting his seed into my body?"

He looked away, unable to face her. That was answer enough for her. She opened the car door.

"Thanks for that. It makes this much easier." She got out of the car. Ignoring the trembling of her knees, she locked them into place. Preparing to shut the door as hard as she could, she halted and said between clenched teeth, "By the way, that was not your father talking, Hawke, that was all you. You said those words. You own them."

She slammed the door and stomped away. Jerking her jacket on, she headed toward the building. She would stay for the meeting, say her goodbyes to everyone, and then she would be gone. She refused to regret anything. She had tried, and she had failed. That was all she could do. She'd had enough.

Halfway to the front porch, she stumbled. Inexplicably, her legs didn't seem to want to work. Confused, she looked around, wondering when it had gotten so dark. She could've sworn the sun was shining and the sky was blue only seconds ago. Why could she still feel the sun's heat?

Blinking rapidly, she tried to clear her vision, but darkness continued to close in, rimming the edges of her vision. Something was wrong…very wrong. She turned to look back at Hawke. Her vision was fading, but she saw the concern on his face, saw him mouth her name as he opened his door.

Her eyelids heavy, she blinked rapidly, fighting against the darkness. The darkness won.

CHAPTER THIRTY-THREE

Hawke was out of the vehicle and running before Livvy dropped to the ground. Had she been shot? He hadn't heard a sound, but the look on her face had told him something had happened to her before she collapsed.

He reached her in seconds. She lay facedown on the pavement. His own heart racing, he touched her neck, relieved to feel a strong pulse.

"Livvy...baby?"

No response.

He looked around quickly to determine if there was a threat. He saw nothing. Heard nothing.

The front door swung open, and Gideon ran down the steps. "What the hell happened?"

"I don't know. She just collapsed."

Gideon took a sweeping glance around the perimeter. Hawke knew he was looking for a sniper, just as he had. But there was no indication of anything like that. Besides, OZ had the most secure location in the world. No one within a five-mile radius of HQ got in without their knowing about it.

"Let's get her inside."

Apparently noting that Hawke could barely walk, Gideon scooped her up and headed to the door. His heart thudding with a panic he'd never imagined, Hawke hobbled after him.

Eve met them at the door, her eyes dark with worry. "What happened? Is she breathing?"

"Don't know, but she is breathing," Gideon said as he carried Olivia to the living room area.

"I've instigated protocol one security," Eve said. "The helicopter is on the way to take Liv to the clinic."

The privately owned clinic, which had a wing on the top floor for OZ employees only, was about ten minutes away. Hawke reminded himself that the best doctors in the world were available to them. Whatever was wrong, they would fix it. They had to.

Gideon placed Olivia on the sofa and checked her over for visible damage, finding nothing that would explain her collapse.

As Hawke stood beside her, Gideon checked her vitals. "Her pulse and respiration are good. Her pupils are reactive to light." He shook his head. "I see no injuries. Nothing." He glanced up at Hawke. "Did she eat or drink anything? Does she have any allergies you know about?"

"We both ate the same thing—coffee and a muffin. She doesn't have any allergies."

The sound of a helicopter closing in on them had everyone scurrying. Hawke noticed that Serena, Liam, and Xavier were hovering near the door, their expressions filled with the same worry.

Did Livvy know how much she was loved? No, not past tense. What's wrong with me? Livvy is *loved.*

"Okay, let's go," Gideon said.

Once again following behind them, Hawke barely registered that someone handed him crutches. Getting onto the helicopter with a bum knee would be no picnic, but there's no way he could let her go without him.

Once settled, he took her hand in his and held tight. It was all he could do to keep howls of anguish from erupting.

She had to be okay. There was no other option. Livvy had to be okay.

～

TWO HOURS LATER, she was still unconscious. Not in a coma. Several doctors and specialists had examined her already. So far, they agreed on only that one thing. Her body wasn't reacting the way a coma patient would, they said. All they could do was continue to monitor her vital signs and test blood samples to try to figure out what the hell was happening.

Hawke stood outside the closed door of her room. He'd been shoved outside while newly arrived doctors did another examination. Her room was filled with them. More blood was being taken. MRIs and scans were being ordered. They were doing all they could, but what if it wasn't enough?

He'd never felt so hopeless, so lost.

"Hawke, any word?"

He turned to see Ash headed toward him. The concern in his eyes mirrored that of all the other operatives who'd gathered in a room down the hall, waiting for word on Olivia's condition.

"Nothing," Hawke said.

"Come sit with me a minute."

"I don't—"

"We won't go far. Just over there. You can still see her door from there."

Feeling like a zombie, he let Ash lead him to a row of chairs across the hallway.

Once seated, Ash said, "Okay. Tell me exactly what happened today."

Hawke blinked, knowing he needed to focus. If the explanation rested in anything that had happened today, he needed to find it.

"Our flight was an early one. We grabbed a coffee and a muffin at the airport. Got on the plane. She drank some bottled water and ate half an energy bar during the flight. She was fine. Nothing out of the ordinary happened. We landed. Went to long-term parking and got the car. Drove to OZ."

"Did you talk to anyone? Did anyone come close enough to touch her?"

"No, I would have noticed that. Why?"

"I talked to the admitting doctor. He said she has no wounds, nothing that would indicate she's been injected with anything, but he said it's like she's been drugged or dosed with something."

"I opened the water for her on the plane and ate the other part of the bar. Neither of them could have been tampered with."

"Okay. When you got to OZ, what happened?"

He told himself not to think about the words, about the awful things he'd said. Things that made him want to cut his tongue out.

"Hawke?"

He knew Ash wasn't asking about that.

He refocused. "She got out of the vehicle. Put her jacket on. She walked toward the building and stumbled, kind of wobbled a little." He swallowed, the lump in his throat growing larger. He'd thought she was crying about what he'd said. He'd watched her, wanting to go to her and beg for her forgiveness.

"Come on, Hawke. Almost there."

"Sorry…sorry." He rubbed his face, focused. "She turned and looked at me. She had this really confused expression on her face. She wasn't pale or anything. Didn't look like she was in pain. She just seemed surprised, maybe shocked. And then she went down."

"So nothing out of the ordinary until she stumbled and collapsed." Ash leaned back in his chair. "If she'd been injected with something, she would've felt it."

"Yeah, and no one got close enough to—"

His mind went back to the flight attendant. She had adjusted Olivia's jacket, saying it was about to fall on the floor. Could she have tampered with it?

"Her jacket." Hawke rose to his feet.

"What?"

"A flight attendant handled Olivia's jacket. We need to find her clothes."

Ash was already on his phone. Hawke heard him give orders for Olivia's clothes to be found and treated as a possible chemical or biological hazard. The fury he felt at this possibility was drowned out by the knowledge that Olivia might not survive this. Evil people did not expose others to a weapon like this and expect them to survive.

They had to find out what it was!

The door to Olivia's room opened, and two nurses wheeled her bed out.

"Where are you taking her?"

"Radiology," one of the nurses answered.

A series of loud buzzes sounded over the intercom, and a calm male voice announced, "Possible contamination. Lockdown initiated. All employees and visitors must adhere to protocol level four."

All of that was background noise to Hawke. His eyes were on Olivia, who seemed to be sleeping peacefully through the possible catastrophe. But she wasn't sleeping. And no one knew if she would ever wake again.

CHAPTER THIRTY-FOUR

Hawke stood at Olivia's bedside, looking down at her still body. It had been two days since her collapse. Two of the most heart-wrenching, agonizingly painful days of his life. He'd take a hundred more explosions and a thousand more scars if only she would wake up.

They knew a lot more now than they had, but they still knew so little. They'd found the residue of an unknown substance inside one of the sleeves of Olivia's jacket. The flight attendant must have inserted a small patch of a genetically altered drug that had been absorbed by Olivia's skin, causing deep unconsciousness. Three elements had been identified so far, none of which on their own would cause this kind of reaction. However, another, unidentified chemical had been detected. Scientists and lab techs were working night and day to name the unknown chemical. So far, they'd gotten nowhere.

The flight attendant was nowhere to be found. The airline didn't even have a record of her employment. How the hell she'd gotten on the plane and posed as an airline employee was anyone's guess. Security cameras showed her in the

Yuma, Arizona and Missoula, Montana airports. No one had been with her and so far, no facial recognition program had been able to identify her. It was like she was some kind of evil apparition only there to serve one purpose. That purpose had apparently been to harm Livvy.

Bottom line: Someone, somewhere had created a dangerous new drug, and they had targeted the woman he loved beyond anything or anyone in the world.

All available OZ operatives were working around the clock as well. While Ash connected with every contact he had throughout the world who might even remotely have knowledge of this drug, Serena, Gideon, Eve, and Liam were poring over the intel that Iris Gates had given them. Some-where in the morass of information had to be something that could help them.

What the doctor had just told him had added new urgency to her condition and multiplied his own agony.

Douglas Steiner, Olivia's main doctor, was both a neurol-ogist and infectious disease specialist. He had multiple alpha-bets after his name and had studied biological and chemical warfare extensively. He was their best hope, but what he'd told Hawke moments ago had given him no hope at all.

Dr. Steiner's dark brown eyes behind thick glasses had been compassionate but resolute. "She's slowly dying, the chemical is working on her body like poison. Her heartbeat is slowing. She's headed toward bradycardia."

"How much slower?"

"According to her medical records, her normal rate is sixty-one. When she arrived, she was at fifty-five. Still in the normal range. Over the last day or so, it's slowed signifi-cantly. She's at forty-five right now."

"What happens if it gets too slow?"

"Her brain won't get the oxygen it needs to function, or she could have a stroke."

"What's the treatment?"

"We administered epinephrine yesterday, which increased her heart rate. However, today it's dropping again. I can give her more, but it's a temporary fix. If it gets too low, we can insert a pacemaker."

Hawke had waited, knowing that there was more.

"The pacemaker can moderate her heartbeat to an acceptable level, but it won't fix the underlying problem. Even if her heart rate returns to normal, she's still not waking up."

"But it will buy us time."

"Yes, but not a whole lot. Her respiration is slowing, too. The epinephrine has helped some, but again, it's not going to fix the underlying cause. Unless we can identify the chemical or find an antidote, we're just prolonging the inevitable."

Hawke was a stickler for straight talk and blunt assessments, but hearing those words had just about done him in. Olivia was dying, and there wasn't a thing anyone could do to stop it.

After the doctor had walked out, Hawke had pulled up a chair, taken her hand, and resumed what he'd been doing for the last two days. He had to reach her, had to make her fight. She had to return to him.

"I called McCall…just to let him know what's going on." Hawke swallowed around the lump in his throat. Having that conversation with Noah McCall hadn't been an easy one. Just saying the words outloud had almost put him down. But Livvy's boss deserved to know what was going on. Hawke and the OZ team weren't the only people who cared for her. McCall had been understandably concerned and had offered to help in any way he could.

He'd thanked McCall and promised to alert him of any change in her condition. Using that terminology scared the shit out of him. The way things were going, a change in her condition right now would be devastating.

He could not think like that. She had to wake up—there was no other option.

Hawke cleared his throat and continued, "Livvy, I know you can hear me. I know you're in there, listening. Please, baby, please come back to me." His voice was almost hoarse, but he couldn't stop. Wouldn't stop.

It had been decades since he'd uttered a prayer. His parents hadn't been churchgoers. The only exposure to religion he'd received had come when a neighbor lady, Dottie Mae Wiggins, had come by on Sunday mornings to take him to Sunday school. His old man hadn't known, or he would've put a stop to it. Fortunately for Hawke, his dad had always slept till late afternoon on Sundays, since Saturday nights had usually been spent drinking with his buddies.

Escaping his miserable life for a short while each Sunday had given him hope, something he'd desperately needed. He had learned about good and evil, right and wrong, and the power of prayer. He had never really practiced that belief, though. Figured he'd messed up too many times for anyone to really care what he wanted. But now...now he was willing to try.

For Livvy, he would do anything.

Still holding her hand, he closed his eyes and scrambled for words. In his lifetime, he'd heard eloquent and heartfelt prayers. He dug deep for something that would convey his gut-wrenching heartache, but the only words that came to his mind were, "Lord God, please, please, please."

As prayers went, it was a pathetic attempt, but he continued to say the same thing over and over, hoping he was being heard somehow, that something miraculous would occur, and Livvy would be spared.

Several minutes later, he lifted his head. He didn't know what he expected, but seeing no change, he swallowed his disappointment. After all he'd done in his life, had he really thought a higher power would be interested in granting him a miracle?

Unable to watch her lying there all alone, Hawke stood. Scooting her over a bit, he lay down beside her. Careful of the attached tubes and wires, he pulled her into his arms, pressed his lips against her silky cheek, breathed in her scent. She was warm, still vital. Still alive.

"Livvy," he whispered in her ear. "Listen to me, my darling. You have to come back. You have to. There are so many people who love you. So many people depending on you to get better. I'm sorry for what I said. I'm sorry for how I behaved. I'll give you babies, Livvy. If that's what you want. One, a dozen. However many it will take to make you happy. Just please come back to me."

He kissed her face, her lips. Taking her left hand, he kissed her finger where her wedding ring had been. They had removed it when she'd been brought here. "I loved you from the moment I heard your voice, Livvy, and I will love you until the end of time. Please, please, please come back to me. I'm begging you, baby, please."

Pressing his forehead against hers, he tried to will her to wake up, tried to will her to hear him. He couldn't stop talking. Some of it was probably gibberish. He hadn't slept more than an hour or so the last two nights. What if she slipped away while he slept? He couldn't risk it.

The ringing of his cellphone was a distant irritant. He ignored it. Nothing was going to take his mind off Olivia. Nothing mattered but her.

A minute later, another tone sounded, letting him know he had a text message.

Still holding Olivia with one arm, he slid the phone out of his pocket and stared blearily at the screen. He frowned, rubbing the tears from his eyes, trying to clear his vision, because the words from Bruce, the overseer of the Arizona facility, made no sense.

Iris Gates's body has been stolen. All medical records have disappeared. Tissue and blood samples are gone, too.

Why? What would be the point of stealing Iris's body? None of this made sense.

If Olivia could hear, he didn't want her to know this. She didn't need to worry about anything except waking up. Pressing one more kiss to her cheek, Hawke got up from the bed and went to the corner of the room. He pressed the number for the Arizona facility.

The minute Bruce answered, Hawke said, "What the hell happened?"

"Not sure. No alarm was triggered. Nothing else is missing."

"You shut down?"

"Yes. All prisoners and personnel have been moved to an alternate location."

"Cameras pick up anything?"

"Disabled."

"Fingerprints?"

"None. It was a precise surgical strike performed by people who knew exactly what they were doing and what they wanted."

"Any idea why they'd want her body?"

"No clue. I'd hoped you might have one."

He didn't.

"Okay. Call me if anything else comes up."

"Will do."

He glanced back at Olivia's still form. Who were these people? How did they get into a secure facility that only a handful of folks even knew existed? What was their agenda? They believed they could kill indiscriminately and destroy lives without the slightest compunction. And why take Iris's body? What other secrets did it hold that they hadn't discovered?

～

Slovakia

"OMAR, WE HAD A DEAL," Ash said.

"You don't know these people, Drake. They find out I've helped you, I'm a dead man."

"What do you know about them?"

"Not a lot. They've been around a long time. I've heard rumors and whispers for years, but I've never had to deal with them. Never wanted to."

There were people far more evil than Omar Schrader. The former chemical weapons dealer had actually saved lives since Ash had turned him into an OZ asset. Schrader had been given a choice between losing everything by going to prison or continuing in his role as a weapons trader with the addition of being an informant for OZ. He'd been cunning enough to make the right choice.

That wasn't to say he was reformed or remotely ethical, but he had a healthy sense of self-preservation. This wasn't the first time Schrader had dragged his feet. There was usually time for haggling and coercion. This situation was too urgent. If they didn't find a treatment soon, Olivia would die.

Schrader's contacts and associates would make most governments blanch. He knew and did business with some of the most dangerous and evil people in the world. One of those people had to know what this poison was and how to reverse its effects.

Ash leaned forward in his chair, staring the man dead in the eye. "Let me make it easier for you. If you don't help me find the antidote within the next twenty-four hours, I'll kill you." He paused and then added, "Does that give you extra incentive?"

Omar huffed. "I don't know why I agreed to work with you in the first place."

"Because you had no choice. It was either this or prison. I can still make that happen."

"You're a very unpleasant man, Asher Drake."

"Yeah, I know. And you're a real peach, Omar."

"How did the beautiful Juliet fall in love with such a rough-edged, uncouth man?"

And this was the paradox. Omar had a crush on Jules. Not only that, but Jules communicated with Omar frequently. Jules, his precious, beautiful, impossibly brave wife, had charmed the evil Omar Schrader during their first meeting. When Omar had had her kidnapped later, Ash had been threatening death, while Jules had been both exasperated and amused.

"Since she speaks fondly of you, Omar, I'd say Jules's tastes are not always the wisest choices."

"How is my sweet angel?"

Omar knew nothing about Jules's pregnancy or their new son. Keeping that information from him had been intentional. Ash didn't want him to know, and Jules had agreed. It wasn't that they expected Omar to use the information for evil purposes, but their son was way to important to take any chances with, no matter how small.

"Stop procrastinating, Schrader. Get me that intel."

Schrader stood. "Fine. I'll call you when—"

"I'm staying here." Ash nodded at the phone on Schrader's desk. "Get busy."

Shooting him a lethal look, Omar grabbed his phone and clicked some keys. When the call connected, Omar spoke in rapid Russian. The man had no idea that Ash was fluent in Russian.

Through threats and coercion, Schrader received a lead that had him punching in another number, this time speaking in Spanish.

For half an hour, Ash listened to call after call. He had to hand it to Omar. The man knew his way around the world, and he knew how to get intel.

As he was listening to another of Omar's calls, this one in French, Ash received a text from Hawke. Dread filling him, he read the message.

No change in Livvy's condition. Thought you'd want to know that IG's body was stolen, along with all records.

What the hell? What was the point of stealing a corpse?

Omar ended his latest call and looked at Ash with what looked like real regret. "My apologies, Drake. This is taking longer than I anticipated." Before Ash could issue a new threat, Omar held up his hand. "You can shoot me full of bullets, and it won't help."

For the first time since Olivia had collapsed, Ash felt the hopelessness that he knew Hawke was living with daily. Omar had been his last, best hope of finding the antidote.

Standing, Ash nodded. "All right, Omar. I believe you. You'll keep looking though, correct?"

"Absolutely. I know I can come off as a somewhat selfish man, but I'm not heartless. I know what this woman means to you and my sweet Jules."

Ash didn't even have the heart to remind Omar that Jules was not his sweet anything.

"I'll be at my hotel until tomorrow. When you get something, let me know."

"I will. I promise."

Before walking out the door, Ash turned and eyed Omar. "Have you ever heard of Iris Gates?"

"But of course. She and Glen were once two of the most feared spies in the community. Glen's death allowed many of us to breathe a sigh of relief, but Iris is even more dangerous. Why do you ask?"

Since "the community" didn't know of Iris's death, there was no way Ash would reveal that info to Omar. Although, now that the notorious spy's body had been stolen, it might be only a matter of time before word leaked out. Or perhaps her body had been stolen so no one would know she was dead.

"Why do you ask?" Omar asked again.

This he didn't mind sharing. "My friend—the woman who is dying—is Gates's daughter."

"Olivia? Oh my. I'm sorry to hear that."

"You know Olivia?"

"I know of her. I think I might have met her when she was just a teenager, still in training. Lovely girl."

And an even lovelier woman who didn't deserve what was happening to her.

"I'll do my very best to find you a cure, Drake. I promise."

Despite the fact that the man would kill him if ever given the chance, Ash couldn't help but smile. Evil had degrees, and a few evil people even had hearts.

CHAPTER THIRTY-FIVE

Helplessness now as much a part of him as bone and muscle, Hawke sat at Livvy's bedside. If there was anything he could do, anything he could give, including his life, to save her, he would. He cursed the two years that he'd stayed away from her. He cursed the times he'd made her cry. He cursed the angry words he'd said that had caused her so much pain.

If a man could die from regret, then he was living his last moments.

She wasn't going to make it. His heart was still fighting the knowledge, but his mind knew the truth. Olivia, the love of his life, was dying before his eyes, and there wasn't a thing he could do to stop it from happening.

She still breathed, but it wasn't his imagination that her respirations were shallower than before. There was a possibility she would have to be intubated soon. She might stay in a vegetative state forever, or die without ever regaining consciousness. Whatever she'd been given was an unknown entity.

He had feared she had been given the same drug that Iris

had used to kill herself, but there appeared to be no similarities between the two. They had checked that immediately, before Iris's body and medical records had been stolen.

Specialists from all over the world had been consulted, and not one of them had been able to offer an ounce of hope.

The phone in his pocket buzzed. Hawke clicked answer without looking at the screen. "Yes?"

"How's Sleeping Beauty? She dead yet?"

Hawke jerked up, his body on full alert. The voice was distorted. He couldn't even tell if it was male or female. Did he know this person? Why disguise the voice otherwise?

"Who is this?"

"You really want to spend our time talking about my identity? I would think you'd be more interested in learning how to save Olivia's life."

"You're right. What was she given?"

"Now that would be spoiling the fun. The question should be, is there an antidote? And the answer to that would be yes. However, she'll need it soon, or she'll never wake up."

"What do you want in return?"

"I don't think you're a stupid man, Mr. Hawthorne, but I'm beginning to think that Iris doesn't know you as well as she said she does. I want her, of course. You never should have taken her."

Two good things. This man—he'd assume the person was a man for now—didn't know Iris was dead. Which meant he wasn't the one who'd stolen her body. But the best news of all was that there was an antidote. Unless the man was lying. Didn't matter. Hawke had no choice but to pretend to give this bastard whatever he asked for.

"How do you want to do this?" Hawke asked.

"Simple. Bring Iris to me. I'll exchange her for the antidote that will save Livvy's life."

"How do I know this isn't a trick?"

"You don't, but what choice do you have?"

And there was the crux.

"Where and when?"

"Cartagena. I'll text you the location."

"When do we meet?"

"Friday. One p.m."

"That's two days from now. Olivia could be dead by then."

"Then you wouldn't have to deliver Iris, would you?"

Relief rushed through him. If Olivia was that close to death, no way would he delay the meeting.

"Very well."

"Just you and Iris. I see anyone else, I put a bullet in you, and your Livvy is gone forever."

"Just send me the details. I'll make it happen."

"See you soon," the voice said. The call went dead.

Whatever he had to do, he'd do it. Finding a woman to pose as Iris Gates might be tricky, but OZ had talented makeup artists at their disposal. They could make anyone look like someone else.

How this was going to play out, he didn't know. He only knew he didn't have a choice. If this was Olivia's only chance, then he would damn well take it.

The door banged open. Hawke turned, surprised to see Ash striding toward him, Dr. Steiner on his heels. Their urgent expressions filled his body with dread. What now?

"What's wrong?" he asked.

"We've got the antidote!" Ash announced.

His breath halted, and his heart leaped in his chest. "How?"

"Suffice it to say, having friends in low places sometimes pays off. I made a bargain with a weapons broker a year or so ago. Omar twisted some arms and came through."

"You trust him?"

"Not in everything. But in this, I do."

Turning, Hawke watched the doctor insert a needle into the tube going into Olivia's hand.

"How long will it take?" Hawke asked.

Dr. Steiner shook his head slowly. "I don't know. I have no clue what I've given her, but considering the options, this is her best hope for survival."

Holding his breath, Hawke never took his eyes off Olivia's face. She was so serene-looking, so peaceful. What if the drug wasn't the cure? What if it was intended to stop her heart? What if—

Livvy's eyelids flickered. The heart monitor picked up speed, and her breathing became noticeably louder.

Tears pooling in his eyes, Hawke leaned over and said hoarsely, "Livvy, can you hear me?"

She moaned slightly and then opened her beautiful eyes and looked up at him.

"Nic?" She swallowed, then whispered, "What happened?"

"Hallelujah!" Ash slapped Hawke on the back.

Hawke had never seen a more beautiful sight. He took her hand and kissed it. "You had us worried."

She cleared her throat. "I don't understand."

Dr. Steiner gently touched her shoulder. "Olivia, my name is Dr. Steiner. I'm going to examine you." The doctor looked up at Hawke. "Give us a few minutes."

Hawke squeezed Olivia's hand once more and walked away.

"Wait," Olivia said.

"I'll be right outside, Livvy. I'm not going anywhere."

The worry left her eyes, and she smiled slightly.

Feeling weak in every part of his body, Hawke walked out the door and leaned against the wall.

"Take deep, even breaths," Ash said.

Bending at the waist, Hawke did just that. The joy inside him was spiraling out of control. Olivia was going to be all right. She was going to be all right! Gratefulness flooded through him. Someone *had* been listening, and he'd actually received the miracle he'd prayed for.

Peering up at Ash, Hawke said, "I owe you, man."

"You owe me nothing. She's important to all of us."

"Where'd Omar get the antidote?"

"When I asked him, he said I wouldn't believe him if he told me, whatever that means. I didn't take the time to question him, wanting to get back here as soon as possible."

Now that the fear had subsided, the fury returned. Whoever had done this would pay.

"I got a call a few minutes ago from the man responsible," Hawke said.

"You what? Who was it?"

"I have no idea. He used a voice distorter, which makes me think I'd recognize his voice if I heard it."

"What did he say?"

Hawke described the conversation and the agreement he'd made.

"So this was all a ploy to get Iris Gates back. What are you going to tell him now?"

"To go to hell, that his ploy didn't work. I'll tell him Iris is dead, and it's too—" He stopped, realizing something. "Wait. We can still play it out."

"How so? Iris is not only dead, we don't even have her body."

"We'll get Eve to disguise herself as Iris to make this meeting. She's around Iris's height. We can turn the tables on this bastard and capture him."

"You have any idea who this might be?"

"Maybe. The person referred to Olivia as 'your Livvy.' Only a handful of people know I call her that."

"You think you're that close to this guy?"

"Yeah, I do."

"You faked your death. Maybe someone else faked theirs."

That was what Olivia had suggested, that perhaps Rio had faked his death. Hawke and Rio had never been friends. The man had been too much of a lone wolf and wild card to form attachments. But had the man gone so far off the deep end as to turn traitor and try to harm Olivia? If he had, Hawke was very much looking forward to a reckoning with him.

"Whoever it is, you'll need to be prepared for him," Ash said. "Once he realizes he's been tricked, he won't be happy."

Hawke smiled at the thought.

CHAPTER THIRTY-SIX

Looking both puzzled and elated, Dr. Steiner grinned down at her. "Your pulse, respiration, and blood pressure are normal. Your reflexes are excellent. Except for some lingering weakness, I'd say you're in excellent health. I see no reason you can't resume normal activities soon."

"When?" Olivia asked. She wanted to find the people who'd done this to her. If this drug got out into the public domain, the havoc and destruction could be unimaginable.

"Give yourself a couple weeks," he said. "Take it easy. Take walks instead of running or hiking. Eat well, stay hydrated, and get plenty of rest."

Considering she had more or less slept for almost five days, it seemed ridiculous that she would need rest, but she couldn't deny that she felt incredibly tired. The doctor's assessment was a welcome relief, though. In a few days, she should be back to normal, and she could get to work finding out who'd poisoned her and why.

She glanced over at Hawke, her heart turning over when she saw his expression. He looked like he hadn't slept in days. His eyes were bloodshot, his hair looked like he'd run his fingers through it a dozen times, and the beard that he'd been keeping closely shaved was once again shaggy.

He had been through hell, and despite the hurt she felt at their last conversation, she wanted nothing more than to go into his arms and hold on to him for dear life.

The doctor patted her shoulder in the universal language of comfort that all doctors seemed to use. "I'll see you tomorrow."

Hawke walked with the doctor to the door and exchanged a few words she couldn't make out. Dr. Steiner gave her another bright smile and then walked out the door.

"What was that about?" she asked.

His eyes somber, Hawke shrugged as he came back to her. "Just getting reassurance that you're really going to be okay. You scared the hell out of me, Livvy."

She glanced around the room, noting the blanket on the chair beside her bed. "Did you sleep here?"

"Sleep? No, but I stayed a few nights." He took her hand and brought it to his lips.

She savored the feel of his mouth on her skin for a few seconds and then pulled away. "Tell me what you know."

"Not a lot. We found the toxin on the inside of your jacket. I figured the flight attendant placed something in the sleeve when she handed it to you on the plane."

She nodded, remembering. "I didn't put it on until I got out of the SUV at OZ."

"Yeah. It was fast-acting."

"Where did the antidote come from?"

"One of Ash's informants."

"Do we know what the poison was yet?"

"No."

"So it wasn't what my mother took?"

He looked away for a few seconds, then shook his head.

291

"No. From what we could tell, the two drugs had nothing in common."

"Any idea why I was targeted? Do you think it had something to do with Iris?"

"We're not sure yet. Serena's been digging into all the intel that Iris provided. So far, she's thinking it's legit."

She swung her legs around and put her feet on the floor.

"Where the hell do you think you're going?"

"I need to help."

A giant hand landed on her shoulder to stop her. "No. Your job is to get better."

"Hawke, no. I have to—"

"Olivia, only a few hours ago, we didn't think you would make it. For right now, you need to rest."

She told herself if she'd had an ounce more strength she would have fought him. But she also knew he was right. She wasn't ready for anything remotely active yet. Each moment she felt stronger, but she knew she wasn't close to being a hundred percent. Collapsing again would help no one.

Sighing, she put her feet back on the bed. "Fine. But I want to know what's going on in real time. Okay?"

"Of course. Now get some rest." Hawke pressed a quick kiss to her forehead and walked out the door.

She watched him go, frowning at his quick exit. She blinked her suddenly heavy eyelids, but a part of her feared going to sleep. What if she didn't wake up?

That was her last thought for the rest of the night.

OLIVIA SIPPED her tea and breathed in the first quiet she'd had all day. After eight hours of undisturbed, natural sleep, she had woken feeling almost normal. Her day had been filled with doctors, tests, and visitors. It was now early evening, and this was the first time she'd had to allow herself to think about what had happened.

She remembered everything. When the dizziness first hit, she had been confused. Darkness had closed in around her, but she could still feel the heat of the sun on her face. Her body had felt weightless, weak. At that moment, her every instinct had been to turn to Hawke. A voice inside her had told her to look at him one last time. If she were going to die, she wanted his face to be the last thing she saw.

She also remembered what he'd said before she'd gotten out of the car. As arguments went, it had been a mild one, though it had been no less devastating. The only one that came close was the argument two years ago that had crushed her heart. This one had left her without hope.

Why she had continued to go down that path she couldn't say. Hawke had made it clear from the beginning how he felt about having children. Hoping he would somehow change his mind had been both naïve and stupid.

Telling her to find someone else—that hadn't been him. Yes, she knew he wanted her to be happy, but actually saying the words he'd said hadn't been Hawke. Her husband had a strong possessive streak. She knew the thought of another man touching her would destroy him. She had seen his face when he'd uttered those words, seen his regret and pain. Problem was, even though he hadn't meant them, he had said them.

They hadn't had an opportunity to talk much since she'd woken, what with the steady stream of visitors. Eve and Serena had brought toiletries, clothes, and her favorite brand of tea. Liam had brought magazines and a box of candy. Gideon had brought flowers. Hawke had been by multiple times, but he hadn't stayed long. She thought maybe he was making sure she hadn't fallen back into a deep sleep.

No one would tell her anything about what was going on.

Every question she'd asked had been met with, *You don't need to worry about that now. Just get better.* She would get better once she had answers. Being treated like an invalid wasn't going to work.

The only piece of news had come from Serena, who'd told her the flight attendant they suspected of putting the patch on her jacket had disappeared.

Other than that, she knew nothing. She wanted to know what else they'd learned. Was the Wren Project, the shadow group Iris had named, behind her poisoning? If so, what had they hoped to accomplish? Was it because of the Gonzalez cartel's destruction or something else? Was it because of what had happened to Iris? Was it retribution?

No one had been by for almost an hour. She'd looked for her phone earlier and couldn't find it. If she needed anything, she could use the Call button, but a nurse couldn't tell her what she needed to know.

Her feet touched the floor, and she stood, sliding her feet into the tieless sneakers beside the bed. Her legs were a little wobbly in the beginning, but they found purchase, and she felt stronger with each step. Eve had helped her shower earlier, and after brushing her teeth and dressing in a pair of sweats and a long-sleeved T-shirt, she'd at last begun to feel human again.

She glanced in the mirror on the wall. Despite the makeup she'd applied earlier, she was still a little pale, but not too much so. She pulled her long hair into a low ponytail and pinched her cheeks to add a little more color. That would have to do. She was determined to leave this room and find out what was happening.

Opening the door, she peered into the empty hallway. She knew this was a special wing created specifically for Option Zero employees. She'd been here before, but only as a visitor.

From what she remembered, at one end of the hallway

was a nurses station and reception area. At the other end, there was a waiting room and a small chapel. Since the area was limited to OZ personnel, it wasn't large, but why did it feel so deserted?

She headed toward the nurses station, willing her legs to stay strong. By the time she made it to the desk, she was sweating and felt as if she'd run a marathon, but she also felt triumphant. Unfortunately, when she got there, no one was around. Standing in the middle of the hall, she called out, "Anyone here?"

The sound of raised voices coming from the other end of the hallway caught her attention. Turning, she slowly headed that way. A door on the left with a Meeting Room sign above it was closed, and she distinctly heard Hawke and Gideon shouting.

She twisted the knob and pushed the door open to reveal a conference room. Several OZ operatives were sitting around a table, while Hawke and Gideon were standing within inches of each other, looking as if they were about to brawl.

No one had noticed her, so she stood quietly and listened. She had a feeling this was the only way she would get some answers.

"You have no plan, Hawke," Gideon barked.

"Everything's going to have to be fluid until we can figure out what we're up against."

"In the meantime, Eve is expected to stand in for Iris Gates without knowing what they want with her. For all we know, they'll kill her on sight."

"She'll be protected."

His face dark, Gideon shook his head. "You can't protect against an unknown entity."

"Oh for heaven's sake, Gideon, we do it all the time," Eve said. "It's not like this is my first rodeo."

Gideon glared at her over his shoulder. "Maybe so, but we have no idea who these people are. There could be hundreds...hell, thousands of them. How do we know you and Hawke won't be walking into a bloodbath?"

"Maybe Olivia could tell us some of her mother's characteristics or traits," Serena said. "Eve might be able to look like her, but to be more convincing, it would help if she could mimic some of Iris's mannerisms."

"No," Hawke said. "Olivia stays out of this. She's been through enough. This doesn't concern her."

"Shouldn't I be the one to make that judgment?"

All eyes turned to Olivia. Myriad emotions played across everyone's faces—surprise, guilt, embarrassment. Hawke was the only one who looked angry.

He strode toward her, and she could easily read the intent in his expression. He was going to try to put her back in her room, back in bed. That wasn't going to happen.

She stood her ground, refusing to retreat. "What's going on? And why is Eve planning to impersonate my mother?"

"That's not—"

"Don't you dare say this doesn't concern me, because it obviously does."

"You're right, Liv," Ash said from across the room. "Now that you're here, why don't you join us? We'll fill you in."

Shooting Hawke a challenging look, Olivia headed to the nearest chair. Even though she was infuriated that a meeting had been taking place without her, she couldn't deny she wished the chair were a little closer. Her legs were beginning to feel like overcooked pasta.

Hawke reached out to help her, and she shook her head. She had to do this on her own. When she reached the chair, she rolled it away from the table, dropping into it with more gratitude than grace.

"How are you feeling?" Ash asked.

"Better. Still a little weak, but I'm feeling stronger every second." She glanced around the room. "Now, who's going to tell me what's up?"

All eyes went to Hawke, who blew out a ragged sigh. "Fine. We can use your input."

In short, terse words, Hawke told her about the call he'd received while she'd been unconscious. Even though they'd gotten the antidote on their own, the plan was to proceed with the meeting in hopes of capturing the person who'd offered the cure in exchange for Iris.

Her brows raised in challenge. "Doesn't it make more sense for me to stand in for Iris—I look just like her after all —rather than trying to fool them with Eve, who'd have to wear a ton of makeup?"

"No," Hawke said. "You're not strong enough to go on this op."

"Yes, I am," she shot back.

His face rigid with anger, Hawke came toward her. Before she could stand, he was turning her chair and pushing it out the door with her in it. "Excuse us for a few minutes," he growled over his shoulder.

The instant the door closed behind them, she was on her feet. "What the hell, Hawke?"

"You are not going on this op, so get that out of your head."

Infuriated, she snapped, "You are not the head of Option Zero. If I want—"

Using one finger, he pushed her, just hard enough to have her plopping back into the chair because of her unsteady legs.

Springing back to her feet, she snarled, "Your Neanderthal tactics are not only pissing me off, they won't work. I will not back down from this." She glanced down at his leg, which she could tell was still hurting him.

"Should I kick you in the knee to prove you're not fit to go either?"

"That's different."

"In what way?"

The anger in his expression dissipated like smoke, leaving only pain and fear. "I almost lost you, Livvy," he said softly. "I can't go through that again."

There were so many responses she could give, so many she wanted to give. She wanted, with her entire body, to leap into his arms and hold on to him for dear life. But she couldn't. Hawke had made it clear numerous times that what they'd had was over. It was time she accepted that.

"I think you're the one who doesn't understand, Hawke. You don't have me to lose anymore."

Only by the slight jerking of his body could she tell that her arrow had hit its mark. She told herself not to feel guilt. He'd basically told her the same thing repeatedly. Still, it took everything she had not to reach out to comfort him.

"Very well." His tone was now coated in ice. "Come back in and get involved, but remember, if you screw this up, it's not just your ass on the line. It's everybody's."

He opened the door and walked back inside, leaving her to push her chair back into the room. She knew everyone had heard their argument. It wasn't as if they'd lowered their voices.

She pushed the chair back to the empty space at the table and sat. Out of the corner of her eye, she saw Gideon slide a hundred-dollar bill toward Eve. Raising a brow, she looked at them both. "Really, guys?"

Gideon had the grace to look sheepish, but Eve only grinned and said, "Gotta support my girl."

The amusement giving her a much-needed lift, Olivia turned her attention to the front of the room, where Hawke stood, his face impassive.

"Before we go any further, Olivia, you need to know that your mother's body was stolen."

BEING an asshole was becoming a 24/7 thing for him. He'd known those blunt words would shock and wound her. Not only that, he'd said them in front of the whole team. And now, that whole team stared daggers at him.

He could justify his actions by telling himself that if she couldn't handle the news, then she sure as hell couldn't work this op. But he was honest enough to know part of the reason he'd said them that way was because she had hurt him when she'd said she didn't belong to him anymore. That had knocked the breath from his body.

So he'd hurt her right back. Yeah, definitely dickwad territory.

"Stolen?" Olivia said. "When? How?"

"I got the call yesterday morning. It was a professional job. Not only her body, but all her medical records were taken, too."

She'd been pale before, but now all color had leached from her face. Still feeling like a jerk but knowing he had to move forward, he said, "Since the players have changed, let's review the details for Olivia's benefit."

"Wait," Olivia said. "If the people we're meeting aren't the same people who stole Iris's body, then who are they?"

"We don't know," Hawke said.

"Where and when is this exchange supposed to take place?"

"One p.m. tomorrow, at a warehouse in Cartagena, Colombia."

"One of the cartel's that we missed?"

"No. This is an abandoned warehouse outside of town. There's no connection to the Gonzalez cartel."

"What was the plan before I came in?"

"Eve, disguised as Iris, and I were going to go in, and the team would have the area surrounded and wait for my signal to attack."

Olivia turned to Gideon. "And you don't like that plan?"

"Didn't say I don't like it. I just think it's too dangerous."

Eve rolled her eyes at Gideon's assessment.

Hawke knew exactly why Gideon objected. What these two felt for each other was obvious. But would they ever figure out that they were made for each other?

He and Livvy had thought the same thing—that they were made for each other. Maybe that wasn't even a real thing, though. Maybe it was as simple and as complicated as two people who cared about each other enough to want to work on their relationship together. Somehow he and Livvy had gotten lost along the way.

"Do we or do we not believe this person is connected to the Wren Project?" Olivia asked.

"Who else would want Iris Gates back and be willing to hurt Olivia to make that happen?" Serena said.

"I'd say there are a lot of people who'd like to get their hands on Iris Gates," Gideon said.

And that was the question. If this was the Wren Project, did they want Iris back because she was a valuable asset, or did they want her back to find out what she'd revealed during her captivity? Did they plan to kill her once they learned what they wanted? Not that any of that mattered— the woman was dead.

"We've been reviewing the intel that we got from the microdot found on Iris," Serena said. "So far, all the info contained in the documents seems legit. All the people, businesses, and organizations mentioned do exist, and there's some shadiness surrounding them."

"So do we now think Iris was a good guy?" Eve asked.

"No," Olivia said. "She was involved in hurting Hawke."

Weird, but he felt a small easing of his heart at her emphatic words. What that said about their relationship he didn't even want to consider.

"Okay, let's get back to the plan." Hawke clicked a remote, showing a photo of a warehouse. "Here's where we're going in Cartagena." Giving Olivia a sharp-eyed glance, he added, "And I have a new idea about how we can play this."

CHAPTER THIRTY-SEVEN

Cartagena, Colombia

The Killer walked around the perimeter of the warehouse for the third time. Everything had to be perfect. Everything had to go just right. He would get only this one chance, and he didn't plan to blow it on something he'd missed. He'd been a perfectionist all his life, and it had always paid off. This time would be no different.

Iris would be coming back home. He felt a little thrill about that. She had been his one constant for so long, he couldn't wait to see her again.

Would she be glad to see him? Certainly not. Surprised? Most definitely. Getting the best of Iris would be the ultimate reward. He owed her many things, and many of those things he'd been fantasizing about for years.

Plus, he would finally get to meet Hawke in person. He'd fantasized about that for years, too—meeting him and then killing him.

How had Hawke convinced Olivia to marry him? He was a man without any real connections, without seemingly anything going for him other than being some kind of badass spy. Hell, he could beat that kind of man with his eyes closed and one hand tied behind his back. And Olivia had actually married the prick?

Hawke would be expecting a setup. And it was, but not in the way he might imagine. He had every intention of saving Olivia's life. It had never been his intent that she would die this way. The lifesaving drug was stored in a safe-deposit box at a bank in Alexandria, Virginia. Once he had what he wanted, he would use Hawke's phone to contact the people he worked with so they could get to the drug and save Olivia's life.

The ring of his cellphone brought him back to the mission. He didn't have to check the screen. Only one person knew this number.

"Is it set?" a gruff, heavily accented voice growled.

"Yes."

"And?"

"We're ready."

"You won't get another chance, you know."

"I'm well aware."

"I want her head. You can have the rest of her."

What he would do with a headless corpse wasn't something he wanted to think about. The deed would be done, and his debt would be paid. A part of him knew he would mourn the loss of Iris. At one time, she had meant everything to him.

The voice on the phone said, "You're still not off the hook. The Gonzalez fiasco will follow you for the rest of your life."

They had chosen him as the scapegoat for all that had gone wrong.

His assignment had looked simple enough. A restlessness had been seen in Juan Gonzalez, and he'd been told to take care of the problem. He'd thought that scaring the hell out of the kid would work, thought Juan would quiet down and do what he was told. All the fool had to do was buy his expensive toys, fill his belly with gourmet food, and sleep in a mansion fit for a king. Who wouldn't want that kind of life? Instead, Juan and his mother had disappeared. People throughout the organization were looking everywhere, but so far, they'd found nothing.

In the grand scheme of things, Juan and his mother weren't important. They'd been silly, meaningless pawns. However, their disappearance had been just the first phase of the destruction that had followed. The Gonzalez cartel had been decimated. Someone had to be blamed. It pissed him off that the responsibility was being laid at his feet, but he'd do what he must to repair the damage.

"What do I have to do to pay off my debt?"

There was a slight pause, and he wondered if the man was really thinking this through, or if he just liked to torture him. He figured it was the latter.

"Send me Hawke's head, too."

That would be easy. Chopping off the head of a dead man would be no problem. Before he could feel the slightest relief, the man added, "We'll consider that your first down payment."

The line went dead.

Determination driving his steps, he walked the perimeter again. This had to go perfectly. He would get only one chance to take them both out. A dozen men would assist him.

Iris Gates and Nicholas Hawthorne would not walk out of here alive.

CHAPTER THIRTY-EIGHT

F ive miles from the meeting site, the team stopped their SUVs to prepare. Hawke figured there would be lookouts close by, so this seemed a good distance to finalize their plan.

The sun beat down on Olivia as she exited the passenger's side of the large, specially designed SUV. Humidity had made a mess of her hair, so while the team gathered for one last review of the plan, she quickly braided and pinned the locks into something cooler and more manageable. It might be just a short drive ahead, but as their traveling accommodations would be cramped, it was going to be a hot, humid one.

"All right," Hawke said. "Let's check weapons and comms one more time. We know what we're here for. Anyone we can keep alive, let's do it, but not at the cost of any of ours." His eyes targeted each team member. "Got it?"

He waited to get a nod of agreement from everyone and then continued, "Comms good. Weapons ready."

With Sean, Jazz, and Xavier still out, the team was smaller than usual. Also, everyone had agreed that Ash should sit this one out, too. Jules needed him, as did their new son. If this was going to get hairy, not one person wanted Ash in danger. Telling the head of Option Zero this had not been well received, but he had eventually given in.

Serena was sitting this one out, too. She and Sean were partners, and she had never worked a mission without him. With all the intel Iris Gates had provided, she and her people were working overtime to delve deeper into the Wren Project. She would be their key to unlocking the identities and motives of these people.

The team now consisted of Eve, Gideon, Liam, Hawke, and Olivia. After reviewing the aerial footage of the warehouse, they had all agreed that having a smaller team could work to their advantage. There were few hiding places in the surrounding area. It was an ugly, open space, and approaching without being spotted was going to be a challenge. A tower stood in the middle of the warehouse area, and they anticipated guards would be posted at all four corners. Sneaking into the warehouse would be impossible unless they took the guards out first. Fortunately, they had an expert marksman on the team.

Olivia felt her energy surging. She was still weaker than she'd like, but the rush of adrenaline was giving her a much-needed boost.

"Okay," Hawke said. "Let's do this."

Gideon rolled the dirt bike down from the SUV as Eve gathered her gear. Handing the equipment bag to Gideon, she hopped onto the bike, then took the bag that held her sniper rifle and hung it crossways over her back. Giving Olivia a wink and a nod, she roared off.

"Let's go," Hawke said.

The back of the SUV swung open, and Olivia and Hawke slid inside. The door slammed shut, and the engine started. She heard the other SUV start, too, and drew in a breath. Even though she had originally balked, she now agreed that this really was the best plan. They had no clue what this person wanted with Iris. He could intend to take her back home or kill her. Until they knew his intent, this was the safest way.

"Comfy?" Hawke asked.

"Oh yeah. You?"

"Sure." His reply was wry. "I've always wondered how sardines feel."

She did feel a twinge of sympathy for him. Not only was she several inches shorter and much lighter, but she also didn't have a sore knee. Even though he'd given up the crutches a couple of days ago, she knew his knee was still painful. Being crammed inside a holding area, no matter how large it seemed, couldn't be easy on him.

"Not far now," she whispered.

"Yeah. How are you feeling?"

"Better. Stronger."

"Okay, guys." Gideon's voice came through their earbuds loud and clear. "You're about a quarter mile from the warehouse."

Olivia's hand went to her weapon in her holster. Even though she couldn't see Hawke, she heard him move and knew he was doing the same.

"Your SUV is coming into the gate," Gideon said. "The warehouse door is wide open. The sensors have been programmed to stop about ten feet inside. Godspeed, you two."

The self-driving SUV slowed, and in her mind's eye, Olivia envisioned it driving through the gate. Sounds outside changed, indicating the SUV was now driving into the warehouse. Nothing had stopped them yet.

"Stay still until we're completely stopped," Hawke said quietly. "Unless they blow us up, we're covered."

On that last reassuring note, they waited. The SUV traveled for several more feet. A second before it stopped, two shots were fired, and the windshield shattered. The question of whether they wanted to take Iris alive had been answered. If Olivia and Hawke had been in the front seat of the SUV, they'd be dead now.

The rest of the SUV was bulletproof, but they had swapped the windshield for regular glass and had placed two life-size dummies in the driver and front passenger seats.

Only seconds after the initial shots, weapons fired all around them, bullets pinging off the SUV.

The noise was deafening. No part of the vehicle was spared. Never had she been more thankful for bulletproof shields. How many men were out there? It sounded like an entire army, but rapid-fire weaponry often sounded like that. It was possible they would be facing more men than they could take, but they had known that from the start.

The instant the gunfire ceased, Hawke whispered, "Ready?"

"Yes."

With that, Hawke flipped a switch, and the SUV's backend swung open. They jumped out. Before their feet touched the floor, they were shooting. Men scattered, diving behind posts and old machinery. Olivia continued shooting, taking down two men, one after the other. Bullets flew everywhere, but as long as they stayed behind the SUV, they were protected.

The shooting slowed and then stopped completely. Olivia peered around the tail end of the vehicle. She spotted four men on the ground. She glanced around to see that Hawke was searching the area from his position at the front end of the SUV.

"You see anyone?" she said into her mic.

"No," he replied. "You?"

"Just bodies."

The muzzle of a gun suddenly pressed against her head told her their ploy hadn't worked as well as they'd hoped.

"Drop your gun, mate, or Iris gets it through her pretty skull."

Two things struck her simultaneously. One, the man thought she was Iris. Even though she hadn't bothered to try to look like her mother, she resembled her enough. They were about the same height, weight, and had similar hair color, so it was a reasonable assumption. Especially since this man believed Olivia was unconscious in the hospital.

The second thing that struck her was even more astonishing. She knew this man.

In fact, she knew him all too well.

HAWKE DROPPED HIS WEAPON. There was no way he would try to talk their way out of the situation with a gun pressed against Olivia's head.

He didn't know the man who held her. All this time, he'd been thinking it could be Rio. But this man, with his gleaming bald head, beady brown eyes, and hulking, body-builder physique, bore no resemblance to his former teammate.

"Quite the reception you planned for us," Hawke growled.

"You as well." The man smirked, obviously taking his words as a compliment. "I must say the dummies in the front seat was quite a brilliant move."

"Since you clearly have us at a disadvantage, how about taking that gun away from my wife's head?"

The man jerked, startled. "Your wife?"

Taking advantage of his distraction, Hawke pulled a gun from the holster at his back. Not wasting time, Olivia whirled, knocked the gun from the man's hand, and punched him in the nose.

The man staggered back, cupping his nose and cursing.

Both of them now in control again, Hawke and Olivia stepped forward together, their guns aimed at the man who'd set this up.

Before Hawke could demand answers, Olivia glared at the man before them. "What the hell do you think you're doing, Simon?"

"Simon?" Hawke said. "As in your ex-fiancé, Simon?"

He'd never met Simon Swift, the man Olivia had been engaged to before she'd moved to the States. Olivia had told him plenty, though, and none of it had been good. The man was a sleaze and an opportunist. As far as he knew, Swift was still working for MI6, but this was no sanctioned operation. Was the man a rogue agent or something more evil?

"Where's Iris?" Simon glared at Hawke. "You double-crossed me."

"Oh gee, Simon, we're sorry." Olivia was at her sarcastic best. "I apologize that I'm not lying in a hospital room, barely clinging to life."

"You always were so dramatic, Livvy."

Hawke glowered at the bastard. That was why the man had called her Livvy. It had been his nickname for her, too.

"Her name is Olivia, asshole."

Rolling her eyes, she said, "Seriously, Hawke?"

Hawke shrugged. Might be petty, but he wasn't going to apologize for that.

Simon's eyes roamed around the SUV. "Where's Iris?"

"Since we have two guns to your none, how about we ask the questions?" Olivia said.

"Come on, Livvy. You know me better than that."

Four men stepped out of the shadows, three guns pointed at Hawke, one at Olivia.

Hawke held his tongue. They had reinforcements as well. Eve would have taken out the men on the watchtower by now. Gideon and Liam would be close by. He would call them in when it was time.

As if she'd heard his thoughts, Eve said quietly in his earbud, "Took out two on the tower, one on the roof, plus one hovering near the front."

"Good enough," Gideon answered. "Come join the party."

Hawke heard her switch on the dirt bike. "Roger that. On my way," she said.

His tension eased. The team would come in on his signal, but for now, he intended to get some answers.

"Are you working for the Wren Project?" Hawke asked.

Only the slight stiffening of Simon's shoulders indicated the question had startled him. "I don't even know what that is."

"You're not a very good liar," Hawke observed.

A smile played around Simon's mouth. "Fooled Livvy into thinking I was marriage material. I must say I don't think she did much better."

"No one is good enough for Olivia."

"If you say so."

Olivia huffed out an exaggerated sigh. "The next thing you guys will be doing is sharing cute tidbits about my personality. Can we get on with this?"

The noise of Eve's bike in Hawke's earbud reassured him she was getting closer. As soon as she joined Gideon and Liam, he'd call them inside.

"All right, Simon, you want to tell us what all this is about?" Olivia asked.

"No, I don't think I do." He glared at Hawke. "We had a deal. You didn't keep your end of the bargain."

"The agreement was the antidote in exchange for Iris. I no longer need the antidote, as you can see."

"Maybe so, but I still need Iris."

"Why?"

"That's none of your concern," Simon snapped.

An odd crashing noise sounded in Hawke's ear, followed by a small yelp and then silence. He cut his eyes over to Olivia. Her brow furrowed, and her eyes narrowed. Yeah, she'd heard it, too.

"Eve," Gideon said. "You okay?"

No answer.

"Damn," Gideon said softly. "Stryker, you're closer to her entry point. Find her."

"Already on my way."

Simon waved a hand in front of Hawke's face. "Are we just going to stand here and stare at each other? I need to know where Iris is, and I need to know now."

"Shut up," Hawke snarled, focused on what was happening in his ear.

Looking startled, Simon seemed to struggle with a response.

Seconds later, Liam gasped Eve's name, then said, "Gideon, you need to get here now." The urgency in his voice was apparent.

"On my way," Gideon said.

Olivia looked at Hawke like she wanted to run out of the building. Unfortunately, that couldn't happen with five guns pointed at them. They'd have to play this by ear.

"Steady, baby," Hawke said quietly.

"Baby?" Simon said. "Are you two back together? I was assured that would never happen. You were supposed to be dead, Hawke."

"Sorry to disappoint you. Shall I say the news of my death was greatly exaggerated?"

"I'll make sure that doesn't happen this time."

Before Hawke could respond, he heard Gideon say softly, "Oh, beautiful girl, what have you done to yourself? No, Eve, sweetheart. Look at me. Don't close your eyes. Look at me."

A whimper came from Olivia. Doing the only thing he could for now, Hawke grabbed her hand and tightened his grip to show her he understood. She squeezed his hand in acknowledgment.

"I've got to get her some help, Hawke," Gideon said.

"How bad?" Hawke asked.

"Bad."

"Go ahead. Liam, you go, too," Hawke said. "We've got this."

Gideon and Liam cut off their mics. All Hawke could do now was pray that Eve would be all right and that he and Olivia could handle this thing with Simon as quickly as possible.

"So, are you going to deal with me, or are you going to continue to talk to the voices in your head?"

Simon's petulant tone grated on Hawke's nerves. "Was he this whiny when you dated him?" he asked Olivia.

She shrugged. "I don't think the years have been kind to him."

"Very funny," Simon snarled. "But keep in mind I only need one of you to talk. I can shoot the other and still get what I want."

Ignoring the threat, Hawke asked, "Why don't you tell us why you want Iris back so badly?"

"Because she's important to me, of course." He sent Olivia a smug smile. "After you left, she became something more."

"Simon…seriously? No way would Iris sleep with you."

"Of course she didn't. That wasn't what I meant. She was my mentor, my friend. She taught me so much."

"Oh, get over yourself. Whatever you think you had with Iris, I assure you it meant nothing to her. She used you."

Instead of being insulted, Simon's smile was filled with pride. "Well, of course she did. And I used her. People like us don't do love and devotion." The smile turned mean. "You should have known that from the beginning, Livvy. It would have saved you a lot of trouble when we first started dating."

"Thanks for the life advice. Now tell us about the Wren Project. Are you working for them, or are you solo?"

"Livvy...really? You're acting like you have some kind of control here. You've got several guns pointed at you. I could end you with one word."

"Might I remind you, there are two guns pointed at your head. We could just as easily take you down."

"My men would shoot you."

"True, but you'd be dead, too. So there's that. Besides, you still want answers, don't you?"

"Doesn't mean I won't kill him." Lifting the gun he'd been holding at his side, Simon pointed it at Hawke's head.

"You're just a ray of sunshine, Simon," Hawke said.

Releasing his hand, Olivia stepped in front of Hawke. "You hurt him, you get nothing from me."

Hawke wrapped an arm around Livvy and pulled her to his side. She would not put herself between him and weapons.

"Tell me where Iris is, and I won't have to hurt either of you."

"Who said we know where she is?" Hawke asked.

"I know you captured her in Mexico."

"How do you know that?"

"Camera feed."

Since Hawke had been wearing a ski mask, Simon couldn't have known the identity of her captor.

One of the men aiming his weapon at Olivia said, "I owe the girl a few bruises. She busted my nose."

Olivia's body tensed, and she released a growling sound.

"What's wrong?" Hawke asked.

"I recognize his voice. He's one of the men who attacked me in my apartment."

"Then he's yours," Hawke said.

"Damn straight," Olivia said softly.

That answered the question of whether Simon had been responsible for the attack on Olivia. Just as Hawke had figured, they'd been looking for Iris's whereabouts.

"I'm tired of this shit," Simon snarled. He pressed his gun against Hawke's forehead. "Tell me where she is!"

From the dark depths of the warehouse, a female voice said, "She's right here."

Ignoring the gun at his head, Hawke twisted around and could only gawk at the woman standing a few feet away.

For a dead woman, Iris Gates looked amazingly healthy.

CHAPTER THIRTY-NINE

L ife no longer made sense. All the things Olivia had thought she knew, had been sure of, had gone up in smoke. Her mother was alive, her ex-fiancé had tried to kill her, and Eve, her beautiful, precious friend, was injured, and Olivia had no idea how badly, or if she was even alive.

How the hell had things gotten so twisted?

Showing he was made of sterner stuff than she was, Hawke let out a little laugh. "Iris, you never fail to make an impression."

"Thank you, Nicholas," Iris said.

Dressed in black cargo pants and a thin black T-shirt, Iris not only looked healthy and vibrant, she also appeared to be supremely pleased with herself. A small, satisfied smile twitched at her mouth, but her eyes were just as cold and evil as they had always been.

"I don't suppose you want to tell us how you faked your death. Especially considering an autopsy was performed on your body."

"Have to admit, that did sting a bit." When no one reacted, she laughed. "Come on. Where's everyone's sense of humor?"

"Sorry, I lost mine when I was ten years old," Olivia snapped.

Why she'd said that she didn't know. Bringing up the beating she'd received at the hands of this woman served no purpose. Except it likely made Olivia look weaker than she already felt.

"I'm not going to apologize for that, Olivia. You learned an important lesson that day."

She couldn't argue that point. She'd learned multiple lessons. And every time she looked at her back in the mirror, she was reminded of them.

Out of the corner of her eye, she saw Iris move her hand and show four fingers. Before Olivia could figure out what that meant, there were four pops, and the four men holding guns on her and Hawke went down. Her mother had obviously brought her own reinforcements.

Simon stared at the dead men in horror. "What did you do, Iris?"

"My job, dear boy," Iris said mockingly. "You've been bad, haven't you?"

"I could say the same to you, Iris. There are lots of people looking for you."

"And you thought you could bring home the prize and make Daddy proud?"

Daddy?

Olivia stared at the man who looked nothing like the man she had once been stupid enough to consider marrying. Back then, Simon had not only been on the thin side, but he'd also had a full head of curly blond hair. Other than the familiar facial features and eye color, she wouldn't have recognized him if he'd passed by her on the street.

And how was it that Simon's father was involved? He had told her he was an orphan and had been raised by a series of foster families. It was one of the things she'd felt a kinship with him about—she'd felt like an orphan herself for much of her childhood.

"Father is disappointed in you, Iris, as am I."

Iris clutched her chest dramatically. "I'm crushed to my very soul."

Olivia was beginning to feel like a third wheel. There was obviously some history here she had known nothing about. When they'd been together, Simon had done everything within his power to get her parents' attention and approval. After they'd broken up, she'd given little thought to what kind of relationship he'd maintained with them. It had apparently expanded. Had Iris recruited Simon into the Wren Project?

No matter what their history was, she wanted answers. Looking at Simon, she snapped, "Did you kill Layla Templeton and Mario Kingston?"

The smile Simon gave her was one she remembered well. "Wouldn't you like to know."

"Yeah," Hawke said as he pressed a gun against Simon's head. "And it'd be in your best interests to drop your gun and answer the question."

"Fine," Simon growled. Jerking his head away, his gun thudded on the floor. "I didn't kill either of them."

"Who did?" Olivia asked.

"Your pal Rio killed Layla," Iris said.

Both Olivia and Hawke looked at her. "So the body in Ixtapa wasn't Rio's," Olivia said.

"No. Disguised to look like him. Being dead gave him the freedom to move about the world. You'd know something about that, wouldn't you, Hawke?"

Hawke gave her a nod of acknowledgment. "As would you, apparently."

Iris grinned. "It is quite freeing, I must admit."

"Why did Rio kill Layla?" Olivia asked.

"That was his assignment. To take out your team." Iris shrugged. "He was my informant and gave me intel about your team. His job expanded."

"You ordered him to kill us?" Hawke asked.

Looking surprisingly insulted, Iris shook her head. "Absolutely not. He was just supposed to feed me intel. Once your team disbanded, he was no longer useful to *me*." Iris shifted her gaze to Simon. "Someone else decided Rio could still be useful."

"Rio's still alive?" Olivia asked.

"No," Simon said. "He outlived his usefulness."

Olivia looked between Iris and Simon. They talked about killing people as if it was just an everyday, ordinary event. To them, she supposed it was.

"As interesting as it is to see how screwed up you two are," Hawke said, "Olivia and I have a job to do. You're both coming with us."

Ignoring the gun Olivia had pointed at her, an arrogant, mocking smile flashed across Iris's face. "Really? You're going to take both of us in?"

"You really want to test our skills against yours, Iris?" Hawke asked.

"No, I actually don't, Nicholas. As much as I disapprove of your relationship with my daughter and how you've treated her, I admire your skills. However, there's only one way this can play out."

"And how is that?"

Iris pulled a gun from behind her back and fired, hitting Simon between the eyes. He dropped to the floor at Olivia's feet.

Iris stood smiling in the midst of the chaos. The fact that she'd gunned down a man in cold blood didn't seem to faze her one iota. Simon had been evil, without a doubt. He had used Rio to kill Layla, and then when Rio was no longer useful, he'd killed him, too. And he'd come close to killing Olivia.

But this woman, this entity who'd given birth to her, was something else altogether.

"What?" Iris said, staring at the guns that Olivia and Hawke were both pointing at her. "You're going to kill England's most-prized spy? The woman who survived her own autopsy?"

She shook her head, her eyes deadly serious. "I don't think that's something either of you want to take credit for. You won't like the outcome. And you, Olivia? Holding your mother at gunpoint? Have you lost all sense of who you are?"

"I know exactly who I am, Iris."

"No, you don't, darling, but that's okay. Although, after all I've done for you, a modicum of gratitude would not be inappropriate."

"What exactly have you done for me, Iris?"

"Other than give you life? Well, let's see. I got you away from that sick bastard." She nodded at Simon's body.

"How did you do that?"

"By arranging for you to go to America."

Olivia didn't doubt that for a minute. She'd always wondered how a young, relatively inexperienced agent with almost no field experience had been selected to join an elite US black ops team. She hadn't questioned it, though, because she had so desperately wanted to get away from anywhere where her parents had influence. Little had she known that their influence spread much farther than just MI6.

"And I kept you from being assassinated when Gonzalez put out a hit on your team."

"By making it appear that I was a traitor?"

"You're alive, aren't you? And, just a few days ago, I saved you from dying."

Ash had said that Omar Schrader, his asset, had implied

that no one would believe him if he told them where he'd gotten the antidote. He would have been right, considering they'd thought Iris was dead.

"So how did you fake your death?" Hawke said.

"You don't really expect me to give away all of my secrets, do you?"

From what Olivia could tell, her mother had only ever been a conglomeration of secrets. And how stupid was it, with all she knew about Iris and the mountain of information she still didn't know, that she was actually glad she wasn't dead?

Iris huffed out a little sigh. "All right. I'll admit I had a bit of help. You'll likely learn soon that a couple of your medical people in Arizona have disappeared. They were of great assistance."

"Did you kill them?"

Iris shook her head as if disappointed in Olivia's question. "Seriously, darling?"

Olivia shrugged. "It's a reasonable assumption. Murder doesn't seem to faze you."

"I think you'd be surprised what does and does not bother me. But that's a conversation for another day."

"So where do we go from here, Iris?" Hawke asked.

"You're going to let me walk out that door."

"Uh, yeah, I don't think so."

Iris gave her lilting little laugh. "Really, Nicholas. I allowed you to capture me once. I don't plan on doing it again. I gave you the intel. What you do with it is up to you."

"You *allowed* me?"

"Of course. Do you think I just happened to meet with Gonzalez's people that night? I had the intel fed to you so you would come to the meeting place and take me."

"For what purpose?"

"To give you the information you found on the microdot under my toenail, of course."

"Was there ever a dead body in the first place?" Olivia asked.

"Of course there was, darling. It just wasn't mine."

"Who was it?"

Instead of answering her question, she said, "You'll be hearing from an attorney soon, Olivia. He has something for you. I suggest you hear him out."

Before Olivia could ask anything else, Iris dropped something from her hand. A noxious gas exploded, burning Olivia's eyes and throat. Hawke grabbed her arm and pulled her away. She knew her mother was escaping, but smoke filled the area, and she couldn't breathe, could do nothing but cover her face and try to get away from the fumes.

Seconds later, the smoke evaporated. And Iris was gone.

CHAPTER FORTY

Hawke and Olivia sat in a bank of chairs in the hospital waiting room. They had dragged themselves there a couple hours ago, looking as shell-shocked and ragged as they felt. Once Iris had fled, there'd been no reason to remain at the warehouse. Everyone else was dead.

He evaluated the mission and decided it had been a halfway successful op, though he knew he was being generous with that estimation. They had gotten some answers and some justice, but they still had more questions than answers.

Those things would have to wait. Eve was in the ICU. It hadn't been a bullet that had taken her down, but the dirt bike. When she'd wrecked, she'd been thrown from the bike and landed on her back. With a broken collarbone and leg, three cracked ribs, and a concussion, she was in better shape than they'd feared, but she was still in serious condition.

He and Olivia had finally stopped coughing. The smoke bomb Iris had used as a distraction to get away had stung like hell. They'd both gotten checked out, and other than lingering, irritating coughs that should go away in a couple days, they were told they would be fine. Since he'd practically had to carry Olivia into the hospital, Hawke wasn't so sure about that. She hadn't completely recovered from being poisoned. This additional trauma had pushed her to the point of extreme exhaustion.

The ER doctor had assured him that her vitals were good, but he'd agreed that several weeks of complete rest would be in order. Hawke had an idea for that, but considering the way he'd behaved, he had grave doubts that she'd go for it. Didn't mean he wasn't going to try.

A message chimed on his phone. Pulling it from his pocket, he expected to see a response from the cleaners he'd texted with orders to dispose of the bodies and erase all evidence of violence at the warehouse.

Hawke cursed softly as he read the text.

No evidence exists at the location. Someone got here before us.

Hawke responded, *You're sure? Blood, bullet holes, shells. Nothing?*

The reply came in an instant. *There's no indication that anyone's been here in years.*

Iris Gates had struck again.

Who did this woman really work for? MI6, the shadowy Wren Project, or someone else? Every time he thought he had her figured out, she threw a new wrench into his theory. He still didn't know how she'd escaped the facility in Arizona, much less how she'd faked her death. Or the identity of the body that had been autopsied. Hell, he wasn't really sure there had been an autopsy. He had confirmed with Bruce that the med tech from the holding site that had pronounced Iris's death had mysteriously disappeared. Additionally, a coroner's assistant had apparently vanished as well.

Every time he had an answer, ten more questions popped

into his head. He wasn't sure they'd ever know the whole truth.

From the corner of his eye, Hawke watched Olivia. She was three shades past pale. Dark circles beneath her eyes and the downward turn of her mouth told him she was almost at the end of her strength. How could he blame her? In the last two weeks, she'd learned her deceased ex-husband wasn't dead. She'd been beaten and drugged. She'd learned that her mother was a likely traitor, although that was up for debate—maybe. And she'd thought her mother had committed suicide.

To top it all off, she had almost died from some kind of experimental sleeping drug, and oh yeah, her mother was still alive. Not to mention that Simon Swift, her ex-fiancé, had been responsible for a lot of what had happened to her.

Just one of those things might destroy a weaker person, but Olivia Gates was not weak in any way, shape, or form. She was at the end of her fierce reserves, though, and since Hawke was responsible for much of her pain, he was going to do his best to repair the damage he'd caused. If she would let him.

"How are you feeling?" he asked.

She sent him a half smile. "Like a balloon with several pinpricks."

"Come away with me."

"What?"

"I talked to Ash. OZ is shutting down for a few weeks. He's taking time off to spend with his new family. Gideon's going to stay with Eve while she recovers. Liam is going on location with Aubrey for a documentary she's filming. Xavier and Jazz are still trying to run down more intel on her brother."

"And Sean's gone," she said sadly.

"Yeah." Hawke took full responsibility for that. He'd called the man numerous times, leaving more than one message to apologize for what had happened, hoping to absolve Serena of all blame for the secret she'd kept. So far, he'd heard nothing back.

"Serena's going to spend some time with her family in Wisconsin."

"What about all the intel Iris gave us? All the things we've gathered?"

"Serena's people will continue to dig. There's nothing concrete on anything. Hopefully, by the time everyone comes back, we'll have more to go on."

She nodded slowly and said, "Where do you want to go?"

His heartbeat picked up its pace. "Remember that little shack in Bermuda?"

Her laugh was soft, husky. "You mean the place you called the love hut?"

"Yeah."

"Okay," she said softly.

The heaviness he'd been carrying around for the past two years eased. He'd screwed up so badly, but if she would let him, he would do his best to make up for past sins. It wouldn't erase the past and the hurt he'd caused, but hopefully it would help.

He sent a text to confirm what he'd set up a couple days ago. It helped to have friends in the intelligence community who didn't blink an eye at such a request. They would have everything ready within hours of his request.

Olivia's phone pinged with a text, and she let out a little huff of a sigh.

"What?" Hawke asked.

She held out her phone so he could see the screen.

Three things:

No need to call cleaners. It's done.

The attorney is Lydell Stitwell. Take his call.

Live well, Olivia. Whatever that looks like to you.

I

"She's something else," Hawke murmured.

"She's definitely that."

"What do you think the attorney's about?"

"I have no clue. Every time I think I know my mother, she shows me a different person."

His phone signaled a text. Figuring it was confirmation of their getaway, he looked down. It was from the same number Iris had just used to text Olivia.

Hurt her again and the next time you'll blow up for real.

Yeah, Iris Gates was definitely unique.

He texted back, *Understood.*

No answer. He hadn't expected one. She'd probably already pitched the burner phone. Besides, what else could he say? He couldn't guarantee he wouldn't hurt Olivia again —that was who he was. But he would do his best to mitigate any further pain.

Standing, Hawke held out his hand. "Let's go see Eve and then find a place to crash for the night."

"Sounds good."

Holding hands, they walked out of the waiting room toward Eve's private room. Gideon had told them she was unconscious, but Hawke knew Olivia wanted to see her friend even if she wasn't awake.

Pushing the door open, he was surprised to see Liam standing in the middle of the room. The bed was empty.

"Where's Eve?"

"That's what I'm wondering." He handed a piece of paper to Hawke. "I found this on the bed."

I'm taking Eve away for a while. She's in good hands and will have the best medical care. Will be in touch.

G

"Where would he have taken her?" Olivia asked.

"Beats the hell out of me," Liam said. "He seemed worried earlier, but I thought that was normal, considering. But he said nothing about leaving. I stepped out to call Aubrey. Wasn't gone more than ten minutes. When I got back, they were gone."

"Did you try calling him?"

"Yeah. Went to voice mail. I left a message." From the look on Liam's face, it hadn't been a polite one.

"Where would he take her?" Hawke asked. "And why?"

"Wherever he took her, she'll be safe," Olivia said. "Gideon would never let anything happen to her."

Hawke couldn't argue with that. Eve and Gideon had been together for as long as he could remember. If there was anyone who would look out for Eve's best interests, it was Gideon.

"I agree." He gave Liam a quick nod. "We're out of here."

Pulling Olivia with him, Hawke walked out of the room with three things on his mind—food, sleep, and kissing the beautiful woman beside him. Not necessarily in that order.

Whether that beautiful woman would be in agreement was another matter. He was going to do his best to convince her.

CHAPTER FORTY-ONE

Bermuda

Olivia stretched her long limbs, luxuriating in the sheer loveliness of doing absolutely nothing. The sun beat down on her bikini-clad body. On the table beside her was a deliciously decadent piña colada, and if she raised her head, her view was an azure ocean stretching for miles. Foaming white waves curled gently toward the shore, beckoning her.

They had arrived on the private island three hours ago, and she was already feeling the tension seep from her body. Their original flight had been delayed for two days by a phone call from the attorney Iris had told her to expect.

After the call, she and Hawke had chosen to fly to London to meet with him immediately. They'd sat in the attorney's office and stared wide-eyed and openmouthed as Lydell Stitwell had explained about an inheritance she could have never anticipated.

"Your grandmother Maggie was a very wealthy woman. You were her sole heir."

"I don't understand. My grandmother has been dead for over twenty years."

"Yes, well…" He'd cleared his throat and glanced down at his papers, apparently unwilling to meet her eyes.

"Do you have her death certificate?"

"Um…yes. I believe so." He'd shuffled through some pages and then pushed an official looking document toward her.

Her hands had been shaking so hard, Nic had had to hold the edge of the certificate so she could read it. For so many years she had wondered if Iris had been responsible for Gran's death. Seeing the official cause of death was determined to be a stroke was only slightly helpful. While it was true that her grandmother had suffered two mini strokes while she had lived with Olivia and her parents, Olivia couldn't help but believe that a broken heart had contributed to her death. Her beloved grandmother had deserved so much better.

"Why wasn't I contacted before?" she'd asked.

"We were told that you couldn't be found." He'd smiled as if everything was now fine. "I'm pleased that we're finally able to settle this matter with you."

The *matter* was more than she could ever imagine. Her grandmother had indeed been a wealthy woman, and she had left her entire estate to Olivia. There had been no mention of her mother or any other relative in her will. The money— just under seven million pounds, or the equivalent to about seven and a half million dollars—plus stocks and bonds in varying amounts—was more than enough to distribute among many other people. As a minimalist, Olivia had never considered money to be a high priority. She made a good living working for LCR, but her needs were simple. Much of what she earned went into the bank and to various charities. Now, she had more than she'd ever dreamed.

In addition to the money, she was now the sole owner of

two houses—one in Milan, Italy, the other in the exclusive area of Camden in London. The houses had been maintained by an endowment, and according to Stitwell, both were move-in ready. For a woman who'd only ever felt at home in a little house in Virginia, and that had been for only a brief moment in time, the idea of owning two homes was a bit overwhelming.

She and Hawke had walked out of the attorney's office and stood on the streets of London, both of them in total shock. Then, because it was all so incredibly ridiculous on all accounts, they'd burst into laughter.

An hour later, they'd boarded a plane Hawke had chartered and flown to Bermuda. A short taxi ride had delivered them to the docks where a boat had been waiting to take them to the private island. Years ago, when she and Hawke had first married, they had stayed here for a week. It had been glorious, and she was happy to see that nothing had changed.

While she basked in the sun, Hawke was checking in one last time with OZ, and then he would be hers for the remainder of their time here. What would happen after that, she didn't know. They were together for the here and now, and that was all that mattered.

They both needed the rest, and she refused to allow worry over the future to mar the present.

A sound behind her had her looking over her shoulder. A slow smile spread over her face. Hawke, wearing nothing at all, appeared before her.

"Um…so clothing is optional?"

Grinning, he gestured to the empty beach. "No one around for miles."

She'd never been shy about her body, but running around nude, even with just Hawke as an audience, was asking a bit much for a modest soul like hers.

"Maybe tomorrow." Holding out her hand, she said, "Come lie beside me, you handsome stud."

Chuckling, he dropped down onto the lounge chair beside her. Taking her hand, he leaned back on the chair and sighed. "That's the stuff."

"Yes, it is. Everything okay at OZ?"

"Yes. Other than the intel that OZ is running on-site, they're officially shut down for the next few weeks."

"Has Ash talked to Gideon? Does he know how Eve is? Where they are?" The way Gideon had mysteriously swept Eve away, without telling them where and why, still made no sense.

"Ash has talked to him and apparently gave him an earful. Gideon apologized for the haste and the secrecy, but he said he just wanted to get her away as quickly as possible so she could start healing. Which was the vaguest kind of bullshit I've ever heard. But that's all he'd give him."

"How is she? Can we talk to her?"

"Gideon would only say that she's had surgery on her shoulder already. Says it's going to be a long, slow recovery."

She noted the shadow of concern in his eyes. "There's something else. What is it?"

"Nothing really. Just a bit of a mystery."

"What?"

"Ash said that both Eve's and Gideon's location trackers have been deactivated."

That was huge. One of the requirements to work for OZ as an operative was to accept a tracker inserted in your arm. Operatives were often deep cover, and having the ability to track them was imperative when they needed aid. When she had left OZ, she'd had hers removed. She knew that Hawke had had his taken out right before he had disappeared.

But those removals had made sense—they'd no longer

been OZ operatives. Gideon and Eve, however… "Are they not coming back to OZ?"

"I asked the same thing. Ash was a little sketchy on details, but he said he believes they'll both be back after Eve's recovery."

She trusted Gideon. She knew there was no one who cared more for Eve than he did. Still, the situation seemed odd. "I wish I could see her, talk to her, hear in her own words how she's doing."

Hawke squeezed her hand. "I know. We'll give them a few days and try again."

"Okay." She turned her gaze to the peaceful beauty before her and asked wonderingly, "Do you think Iris has turned over a new leaf? Maybe softened a bit?"

"Your mother is the most manipulative and conniving person I've ever met, so no, I don't think she's changed. There's a reason for everything she does—even if it appears to be good. I don't think Iris has it in her to be any different than who she is."

That was likely true. It amazed her that she'd even consider that her mother could be softening. Hawke had her pegged right. Iris Gates was an opportunist in every way. Sociopaths didn't switch to being Good Samaritans. Iris always had an agenda.

"Okay, here's the deal," Hawke said. "Beginning right now, there is no OZ. There is no Iris Gates. And there is nothing evil under the sun. There are no past hurts or pain. It's just you and me…Livvy and Nic." He glanced over at her, love and hope simmering in his eyes. "How does that sound?"

"Perfect," she replied softly.

She closed her eyes and, still holding his hand, fell into a peaceful, dreamless sleep. Vaguely, she felt arms beneath her and knew she was being carried. She opened her eyes as soon as they entered the air-conditioned house. This place was the perfect getaway spot, filled with everything two people could want.

Nic carried her to the bedroom and then stopped to let her take it all in. The phone call he'd made to Ash hadn't been all he'd been up to. Flower petals were strewn on the hardwood floor and bed. A table held a bottle of her favorite wine, two glasses, and a tray of tropical fruit. Soft, romantic music played in the background.

"This is beyond perfection," Olivia said.

"Just like you," Nic growled and laid her on the bed.

She looked up at him, loving the dark passion in his eyes. Cupping his face with one hand, she said quietly, "This is like all my wishes coming true at once. When you were gone… When I thought you were dead, I prayed every night that you'd return to me. I prayed that one day, I'd be in your arms again. My prayers have been answered."

"I want all your prayers and wishes to come true, Livvy." With that, he covered her mouth with his and began a slow, sensuous seduction. His mouth and hands were everywhere at once, caressing, touching, molding. In minutes, she was breathless, panting. Need rose within her. Nic was doing everything in his considerable power to arouse her beyond her ability to think.

Urging him softly, she said, "I want you, Nic. Please. Now."

Kissing his way up from her feet, he stopped at her core and looked up at her, his eyes heavy and glinting with the same heat boiling within her. "Soon, my love. Soon."

His mouth was on her, licking, kissing, teasing. Olivia groaned, raising her hips, needing, wanting. This was too much…it wasn't nearly enough. It would never be enough. Just when she could take no more, when she could feel everything rising within her about to be torn apart, he stopped. Before she could protest, Nic rose up and slid inside her, going deep, going forever. Nothing mattered but this. Only and always this…

When she finally recovered a shimmer of her senses, she gazed up at him. His face was fierce, his eyes gleaming with passion. He was still moving, still thrusting.

A moment of clarity hit her like a rocket. She whispered urgently, "Nic…wait. You're not wearing a…"

"Shh," he growled. "I know." Lowering his mouth, he plunged his tongue deep and thrust hard one final time.

A sob catching in her throat, she wrapped her arms and legs around her husband's body and gave him all that she had to give.

IF A PERIOD of time could be captured and replayed on repeat for the rest of his life, it would be this time he was spending with Livvy. Not a minute, not a second went by that he didn't feel absolute peace. Perfection couldn't begin to describe it.

The first day set up a routine they followed each day since. Long, breathless hours of being in each other's arms, sun, sand, delicious food that he and Livvy prepared together, and the sheer joy of being alive. In the mornings, they would walk on the beach, come back for breakfast, and then laze around. Snorkeling became their afternoon activity. In between all that, they talked, they laughed, they shared silly, inane stories. The future was never mentioned, and the past was in the rearview mirror. The only thing they had was the present, and his intent was for them to concentrate only on that.

Not since that first time making love had they mentioned birth control. They both knew what was happening, what could happen. It was what he wanted. He couldn't change who he was, but he could give her this. When she had been near death, when he had thought he would lose her, he had made her a promise. He wanted this for her.

After a sweaty, mind-blowing hour of incredible morning sex, they were lying side by side, facing each other. He had never seen her look lovelier or more relaxed. Sun, good nutrition, and hours of restful sleep had given her skin a healthy, golden glow.

He remembered the first time he'd seen her, and while he'd thought then that she was the most stunning creature he'd ever seen, she was even more so now.

Caressing his jaw, she asked softly, "What's that smile for?"

"I was just wondering how you keep getting more beautiful."

"Well, I'd say it has a lot to do with being thoroughly and passionately cared for."

"You are definitely that, my love." He grabbed the remote lying on the nightstand and clicked a button. "Remember this?"

The music swept through the small house, its gentle strains giving him the best kind of chills. The memories it invoked bringing a smile to his face, he watched to see if she recognized the significance.

Beautiful blue eyes sparkled, telling him before she said anything that she remembered. "'Musetta's Waltz.'"

"That's what was playing the first night I held you in my arms. I fell in love with you at that moment."

A teasing smile lifted her mouth. "I always thought it was my voice you fell in love with first."

"Your voice turned me on and made me want to sweep you away and take you in every way possible, but it was the feel of you in my arms that made my heart recognize yours as mine."

"You're mine, too, Nic. Always have been…always will be."

He kissed her softly and said, "What about you? When did you know?"

"Same night, of course. But it was your sexy drawl that got me. Drew me in like a magnet."

"Wait. My drawl? I was using a British accent at the time."

Her soft laughter sent shivers through him, spreading warmth to every region of his body.

"Your accent was almost perfect, my darling, but I heard a slight Texas drawl, and it was the sexiest thing I've ever heard in my entire life."

"Oh yeah? How about this?" Crawling on top of her body, Hawke proceeded to growl every sexy, dirty, enticing thing he could think of.

"Okay, okay. I surrender. This is ten times sexier."

Cutting off her laughter with his mouth, he proceeded to show her that he could do more than just speak the words. Deeds were so much better than words anyway.

CURLED UP IN HIS LAP, her head on his shoulder, Olivia had never known peace such as this. Every muscle in her body was languid. Every fiber of her being felt alive and sated. She had loved this man for a long time, and these days together had reminded her why they'd been so happy for that short period of time after they were first married. Their every intent had been on making the other one happy. That had been their primary focus. It wasn't until they'd allowed other things to interfere that the trouble had begun.

Here, now, it was just the two of them. Nothing intruded. Nothing prevented them from giving each other their undivided attention. Maybe it wasn't real life, but for now, it was exactly what they both needed.

She had no idea if Nic knew she was ovulating. Her cycle was as accurate as Big Ben. She knew she could very well be pregnant already. They hadn't talked about the possibility. There was no need. They were both adults. Both knew where unprotected sex could lead.

She wanted his baby. And he was doing his best to give her what she wanted. She knew nothing had changed for him. Not really. He still didn't want children. It was what they had agreed to before they were married. He had been adamant, and so had she, about not wanting children. After her childhood and then seeing the evils in the world, the last thing she'd wanted to do was bring an innocent child into it.

Not once had she ever anticipated that she would change her mind. Until she had.

Nic never had. She doubted he ever would. That was no longer a problem. If she were blessed with a baby, she would raise their child with all the love she had inside her. She would tell her child about Nic, about what a wonderful man he was and how he was out making the world a safer place for them all. Her child would never wonder if he or she was loved or wanted.

Nic shifted, and she stretched with an answering groan. They were both gloriously nude. When the time came to wear clothes again, she was sure they would feel confining and uncomfortable. For almost ten days, she had been running around naked without the slightest degree of embarrassment. Nic made her feel safe and loved—and so very, very happy.

Long fingers combed through her hair and then smoothed it down, petting her. He was always touching her, caressing her. It was like he couldn't get enough of her, as if he wanted to create memories that would last a lifetime. Just like she did.

This couldn't last. They had only a few days left, and though they hadn't talked about the future, she knew it was on his mind, as it was on hers. Living in the now could last only so long.

"You've grown pensive. What's on that beautiful mind of yours?"

She looked up at him, loving him with everything in her heart, soul, and mind. If she told him the truth, the idyllic days would be over. They wouldn't argue, there would be no harsh words, because nothing had changed. But the bubble they were living in would pop. There was no way she would destroy their paradise when they still had a few days to revel in it.

"I was thinking about getting a tattoo."

At first, there was surprise and then intrigue. His eyes glinted with heat. "Is that right?"

Adjusting her position, she straddled his hips and lowered herself onto him. He slid inside her, and she sighed at the delicious sting of his entry. Biting his earlobe, she whispered, "Where do you think it should go?"

"Umm, I don't know." He grabbed her bottom and squeezed. "However, I'm particularly fond of this part of your anatomy."

"Yes, so I've noticed." She rose up slowly and then dropped again, the lovely, hot friction making her swoon with delight. "Why don't you show me what else you're fond of?"

"With pleasure." Surprising her, he grabbed hold of her butt to keep them connected and stood. Walking over to the bed, they bounced on it together, and he demonstrated in a most delicious way what his favorite parts were.

· · ·

Three days later

The *whomp-whomp* of whirring helicopter blades woke him. Instantly alert, he glanced over at the empty place beside him, and his heart dropped. Livvy was gone. He wasn't surprised. Their time together was over, and she hated goodbyes. Especially ones where there would be only tears and pain. She had made the smart choice and left before that happened.

He spotted an envelope on the dresser across from him. His name was scribbled in Livvy's stylish and distinctive handwriting.

Hawke dropped his head back onto his pillow. Did he even want to read what she'd written? Hadn't they said everything that could be said? Given each other all they could give?

Unable to put off the inevitable another moment, Hawke got up and grabbed the note. It was short, simple, and so very Olivia.

Nic,

You will always be my one and only love. Thank you for these glorious days.

Yours, Livvy

He tried to work up anger that she'd leave him like this. Why couldn't he be enough for her? Why couldn't they go back to what they'd had when they'd first married?

He knew the answers to those questions, and there wasn't an ounce of anger in him. The promises they'd made at the beginning of their relationship had been between two young, idealistic people who'd thought they had the world in the palms of their hands. But people change...needs changed.

Livvy needed something he couldn't give her, not completely anyway. So she had gone to live her life, and he would live his. Happily-ever-after endings were a rarity.

His and Livvy's wasn't meant to be one of them.

CHAPTER FORTY-TWO

Four months later
LCR Headquarters
Alexandria, Virginia

Olivia drove through the hidden entrance and parked in LCR's underground parking. This was her last stop. Her SUV was loaded with only the items that meant something to her. Everything else she had donated to a nearby women's shelter. She had never felt at home in that apartment. It had been a place she'd stayed, living in limbo until she could start living again. That time had finally come. She was now ready to move on to the next phase of her life.

The last few months had been a whirlwind of activity. She had visited both houses her grandmother had left her. The homes had given her insight into the woman who'd meant so much to her. The emotions had sometimes been overwhelming, but they'd been sweet, too. She'd gone into her grandmother's closets, and there had been the slightest scent of amber, Gram's signature fragrance. Memories of those three years Olivia had had with her had risen up as if her grandmother had been embracing her.

She still wasn't sure what she would do with the houses. They were beautiful, and caretakers were doing an excellent job of upkeep. At some point, she'd decide, but for right now, she didn't see a need to change anything.

Thanks to her grandmother's generosity, she had been able to purchase a lovely beachfront home in Marco Island, Florida. Sun, sand, and crystal-clear blue water held a special place in her heart. Every day when she looked out the window, memories of that joy would sustain her, giving her the strength to carry on.

Noah McCall had been pleased that she wanted to continue working for Last Chance Rescue. It had felt good to make that decision. An LCR satellite office was in Tampa, about three hours away. Operatives Dylan Savage and Cole Mathison oversaw the operations. For the time being, her responsibilities included interviewing potential clients and gathering intel for various missions. At some point, she might resume fieldwork, but for right now, this was perfect for her.

To make things even better, Dylan and his wife, Jamie, and their two children lived only half an hour from her new home. Cole and his wife, Keeley, and their four children were just a few miles farther. She already had a built-in family close by.

It felt good to be able to think of them that way. For so long, she'd held herself apart from everyone. Even when she knew she'd be happier creating friendships and relationships, she hadn't been able to do that. All of that was different now. *She* was different.

Olivia got out of her vehicle and headed into LCR head-quarters. Noah and several team members were in Bolivia on a rescue mission, but Noah wasn't the person she had come to see. She needed to talk to a wise and impartial person, someone who could identify with her issues, but would be able to give her a willing ear without judgment.

Samara McCall met her at the front door, a delighted smile on her face. Noah's wife had a way about her, as if you could tell her anything, and nothing would shock her. Petite, with long dark hair and beautiful sapphire eyes, Samara was the epitome of what LCR stood for—compassion, determination, and everything good. Though she was likely incredibly busy being the mom of two children and a full-time LCR counselor, Samara gave no indication that she had anything else on her mind other than Olivia's visit.

"Olivia, it's so good to see you. How are you feeling?"

"Thank you." Olivia smiled at the other woman. "I'm fully recovered."

"I'm so glad. When Noah told us what happened, we were so worried for you."

She led Olivia to her office, a uniquely individualized area filled with color and dozens of photos of the McCall family. "Come have a seat. Would you like something to drink? I was about to make myself some tea."

"That would be lovely."

While Olivia settled herself in a chair, Samara went to the kitchenette in the corner of the room and poured steaming water into a small teapot. She brought the tray over to a serving table and handed a cup to Olivia. "Fix it the way you like. I'm a three-teaspoons-of-sugar kind of girl."

Olivia prepared her tea and took an appreciative sip, feeling herself relax even more. She had called Samara yesterday, desperate to talk. So few people knew about the real issues between her and Nic. There was a reason for that. She wanted no one to take sides. But she also wanted someone to hear her out. She wasn't even sure she wanted opinions. She just needed someone to listen.

"Before we get started," Samara said, "I want to assure you that whatever we talk about goes no further than this room. Not only would I never tell anyone, Noah would never expect me to tell him anything."

"Thank you." She had known that but appreciated Samara saying so.

She took another sip of tea. "It's hard to know where to start. You're the only person I would even consider talking to about this."

"Start where your heart tells you to."

She nodded, took a breath, and it was no surprise to her that she started at the very beginning. "Nic and I met in Germany, when we were both undercover. I was working for MI6. Nic was working for a deep-cover intelligence agency in the US. Neither of us knew the other was an undercover agent. The attraction was instantaneous."

There was no way to describe just how explosive that attraction had been. First, his mesmerizing voice, then his incredible eyes, his smile. By the time she'd gone into his arms to dance, she'd already been halfway in love with him.

"It was the briefest of meetings. We shared no personal information, but it made an impact on both of us. Since I didn't know his name or anything about him, I didn't think I'd ever see him again. A few months after that, an assignment became available in the US that I volunteered to fill. It was a chance to work with a covert agency as a liaison. For a lot of different reasons, I jumped at the chance. I was still fairly inexperienced and didn't think I'd get the job, but I did."

The fact that Iris's machinations had put her in that position would only cloud the issues she wanted to discuss, so she kept that part to herself.

"It wasn't until I arrived at the facility that I realized Nic was in charge of the team."

"So he knew who you were in Germany after all?"

"No. He really didn't. It was one of those weird coincidences that occasionally happen. When he learned I was being assigned to him, let's just say he wasn't very keen on the idea."

A smile played around Samara's mouth. "There were fireworks, I imagine."

Olivia laughed softly. "Oh yes, plenty of them, but we soon started working well together. The team was exceptional, and it was perfect for a while."

"What changed?"

"We were on an op. We had turned an arms dealer into an asset. My assignment was to protect the asset's son."

As concisely as possible, she explained how that had been a life-changing mission for her. Not only had it been her first solo mission, completely separate from her team, which was working in another part of the world, she had finally acknowledged the immensity of her feelings for her team leader. He had been Hawke to her at that time, and she had fought that attraction for as long as she could. When she'd been separated from him, she'd felt as if she were missing a piece of herself.

He had arrived unexpectedly one day to break the news to her that her father was dead. He'd held her in his arms and commiserated with her when she'd realized she couldn't grieve for a man she'd had little affection for. He'd told her about his own father that night—about the beatings, the abuse, and his mother, who had abandoned him to such a fate. They had bonded by sharing a few horror stories from their childhoods.

A connection that had already started was knit together that night. He had kissed her for the first time, and that was when she'd learned that he had been fighting the same feelings for her. He had left soon after, but the promise in his eyes had given her hope that when the mission was over, they would explore these new feelings.

Days later, the mission had gone sideways. An army had descended upon the tiny island. Eighteen people had been killed, and twelve others had been injured, including her. Tomás, the child she'd been protecting, had been a bright, energetic seven-year-old, and Olivia had done everything in her power to keep him safe, including covering his body with hers when the bullets had rained down on them. In the end, Tomás had been the only one not injured.

When she glanced up at Samara, she realized she'd stopped talking and had gone down a rabbit hole filled with memories.

"Sorry. Got lost there for a moment."

"Just take your time. We're not on the clock."

She nodded her thanks. "After the attack, we knew we had a mole. The team disbanded, but Nic and I stayed together. We took the jobs we wanted to work, got married, bought a house."

That one sentence couldn't in any way convey the absolute joy she and Nic had shared during that time. Eighteen months of perfection.

"I approached Noah around that time and offered my services to LCR. Nic ran some of his own ops without me, but it was still good. We were doing what we loved, but we still made time for each other."

Their separations had been few and far between. When they had been without each other for more than a couple of days, their reunions had been deliciously passionate.

"A few of Nic's friends contacted him about joining Option Zero. Both of us were intrigued and agreed to come on board. I wanted to continue my work with LCR, too, and that wasn't a problem.

"Everything worked fine for a while. Then Nic started

working a difficult op. He was deep cover, completely dark. He excels at that type of work, but he was gone for long periods of time. At first, it wasn't a problem, but the longer he was away…" She shrugged. "I don't know… I could tell when we did see each other that we were drifting apart."

Something had felt as if it were missing then. She hadn't been able to put her finger on it, and she had told herself it was nothing. And then something had happened on an LCR op that had turned her life upside down, showed her who she was and what she wanted.

"Do you remember the Fleming kidnapping case?" Olivia asked.

Samara nodded. "The one in Reno. The newborn stolen out of his crib?"

"Yes. When we found him…" She paused for a long while, and Samara allowed her the silence, giving her the chance to work out the words in her own time.

Olivia cleared her throat. "Before we married, Nic and I both agreed we didn't want children. There were a lot of reasons, but the number one reason was because our childhoods had been horrific. Nic grew up with an abusive father, and my childhood… Well, it was unorthodox, to say the least. The last thing we wanted to do was bring a child into the world and be rotten parents.

"Nic was adamant about it. So much so that I'm not sure, even as much as he loved me, that he would have married me if he'd had the slightest inkling I would change my mind about wanting children."

"But you did."

"Yes. When we made the agreement, I really didn't believe I would ever feel differently. My job was too demanding. I would never be able to be totally devoted to a child, the way a parent should be, and I never thought I'd want to be off work long enough to have a child. All the things you tell yourself when you're young and you don't realize that your priorities can change.

"And then, during the Fleming op, everything changed."

Olivia closed her eyes as she remembered the event as if it were yesterday. It had been one of the most defining moments of her life.

The mission had been relatively simple. An emotionally disturbed woman had broken into a couple's home and stolen their newborn right out of his crib. Even though local authorities and the FBI were immediately involved, leads had dried up. The couple had asked LCR to assist. Through an intricate web of contacts, they were able to locate the woman and the baby only a few miles from where he had been stolen.

Olivia had been in on the rescue. She was the one who'd picked up the baby. The moment she'd held that precious infant in her arms, an ache unlike anything she'd ever felt before had developed within her, almost choking her with emotion, with need. She had known in an instant what she wanted—it had been something she hadn't even known she was missing. She wanted a child with Nic. A baby created from their love for each other. Someone with his features and hers blended into an individual she would love into infinity. In her mind's eye, she could already envision the tiny little human who would stand for everything good and beautiful their love represented.

"When I returned home after the op, I went to see my doctor. It was time for my birth control shot. She told me I could go off my birth control, but Nic and I should use protection for about three months until the birth control was out of my system.

"Nic had just gone back to his deep-cover op when I left to work on the Fleming case, so I wasn't expecting him back for months. I had it all planned. When he did come home, we would talk about it, and I would convince him to change his mind. I believed I could explain what I was feeling...why I was feeling it, and he would understand, and that would be that."

She closed her eyes as tears threatened. She'd had it all worked out in her mind. Unfortunately, what she'd envisioned and what had occurred were the exact opposite.

"He came home much earlier than I anticipated. And we did what we always did when he came home."

She couldn't even work up a blush as she remembered how hot they'd been for each other. She'd been asleep in bed when he'd appeared beside her. She'd been so elated to see him, it had never occurred to her that they needed to use protection.

"He got called out only a few hours later when something broke on the case. I never once thought about birth control, and I never got the chance to tell him what I was feeling. We didn't get to discuss anything."

"You wouldn't be the first person who's forgotten about protection in the heat of the moment," Samara said dryly.

"No, I guess not. I just never thought there would be such a devastating outcome."

"You became pregnant."

"Of course. Isn't that the way tragedies always work? The thing you want most in the world occurs at the worst possible time? I couldn't get word to Nic to let him know what was going on. No one could. He was purposely off the grid. When he finally came home, I was two months pregnant. He found me in the bathroom throwing up. Needless to say, when I told him why, he didn't handle it well."

Up until then, she didn't think she'd known real pain. Not like that. It had been horrible. She had made excuses for his behavior simply because it had hurt so much. The things he'd said, the way he had looked at her. It was as if she hadn't known him, as if a stranger who looked exactly like her kind, loving husband had come into the house and behaved in a way Nic would never have acted.

"He was, as I guess you can imagine, furious. I barely got the chance to explain what had happened. He ended up leaving. I honestly didn't know if I'd ever see him again. A few days after that, I miscarried."

She had been numb with shock, overwhelmed by an agonizing grief for the tiny, precious being she had never gotten to hold or kiss. She had never been able to tell him how very much she already loved him. Not that she had known the sex—it had been too early. But something inside her had told her the baby was a boy.

"Nic came back. I thought it was to talk. At least that's what I'd hoped. He didn't know about the miscarriage. I was hurting and angry. I told him he didn't need to worry about the baby any longer."

It had gotten so ugly. Both of them had been hurting, and they'd done their best to damage each other. Both had succeeded.

Even after all this time, it still hurt to think about that day. She had sworn she would get all of this out of her system. She had to say the words. If she didn't, they would continue to fester and hurt. Even though she had forgiven him long ago, she had never said this out loud, and if nothing else, it needed to be said so she could purge it from her soul.

Her voice was so thick, she barely understood her garbled words. "He asked, 'Did you get rid of it?' He called our baby *it*. As if our child was nothing. As if he had no soul, no heartbeat. As if our son hadn't been alive only days before. My child…our child. As if he hated him."

A box of tissues appeared before her. Olivia gratefully took one and dried her eyes.

"When the people we love say awful things," Samara said

softly, "the hurt can be a million times worse. But I think you already know that he was speaking to you from a place of pain, don't you? The things we say from pain are often the most untruthful, but also the most hurtful."

"I know that now. I didn't then. It just hurt so bad."

"Have you forgiven him?"

She had—or at least she believed she had. Was she still harboring resentment? She knew he hadn't meant the words. He had, in fact, apologized the moment he'd said them. She had been in too much pain and turmoil to listen, to forgive him then. He had apologized several times since then, but had she been holding on to the pain? Using it to keep him from hurting her again?

No. After seeing his pain, his struggle, and knowing the reasons why, she knew she had forgiven him.

"Maybe if other things hadn't happened, we might have been able to get past it. But our old team was being targeted. Two of our team members were dead, and three others had barely escaped with their lives.

"We knew we were going to have to do something if we were going to stay alive. Our plan was simple enough. The rest of the team would go underground. Nic would fake his death and go deep cover to find out who was targeting us. It would appear to my OZ team that I was responsible."

"I'm sure everyone was angry with you."

That was an understatement.

"It seemed like the most sensible way to keep them from digging too deep into his death. It should have worked perfectly."

"But it didn't?"

"No. Nic was supposed to reach out to me, but I didn't hear from him. No one we knew heard from him, at least that I knew. I could only assume he was dead. There was no other explanation."

"But he came back."

"Yes."

"You've had several shocks over the last few months, haven't you?"

More than Samara would ever know. Nic's horrific injuries, Iris's supposed death and then reappearance, Olivia's own brush with death. So many things had worked against them. Tried to destroy them. But that wasn't why she had come here today. All the other things that had happened, even as monumental as they had been, paled in comparison to her feelings for Nic and what their future held.

Olivia felt as if she'd been walking the edge of danger even before she had learned to walk. Every movement monitored, every step evaluated. It had been her life, *all* of her life.

She hadn't chosen that life—it had been chosen for her. And she had gone along with it, accepted it. She had been good at it and had enjoyed many aspects of it. And if she had to do it all over again, maybe she wouldn't change a thing.

But that wasn't what she wanted—not anymore.

She had come to a new phase in her life. She wanted the mundane, the ordinary. She wanted what might look boring to many people. She wanted to argue about who ate the last cookie in the cookie jar or who put the empty milk carton back in the fridge. She wanted soccer matches to conflict with dance classes and homework assignments that kept everyone up all night. She wanted weekends when the kids jumped on the bed and demanded pancakes for breakfast, big dogs that slobbered all over her sneakers, and family vacations that were hectic, wild, and memorable.

She wanted a life well lived. And she wanted that life with the man she loved.

That wasn't what he wanted, though. Nicholas Hawthorne was the very definition of a hero. Courageous, kind, ethical, and strong. She didn't want to change him. She loved him for exactly who he was, what he was.

Whatever decisions he made, whatever changes he decided upon, if any, had to be because he wanted them. Not because she wanted them.

"Olivia!"

Jerking back from where she'd gone, she said, "Yes?"

A brilliant smile lit up Samara's face. "Oh my gosh, you're pregnant!"

Joy rushed through her body, flooding her with a blessed, beautiful satisfaction. "Yes," Olivia said softly. "Nic and I took some downtime after everything was wrapped up."

"And it happened then? But did he…"

"Yes. He knew I wasn't on birth control."

"He gave you what you wanted."

"Yes." She just wished he wanted it, too.

"That's a step in the right direction, isn't it?"

"That's what I keep telling myself."

"I'll tell you a secret few people know. When I fell in love with Noah, I learned he didn't want children. He had, in fact, gotten a vasectomy."

Hope leaped within Olivia's heart. She had seen Noah with his kids. She knew he adored them and was completely devoted to his family.

"How did you convince him to change his mind?"

"I didn't. He made up his own mind. He knew I wanted children, so he had the procedure reversed."

It had happened for Samara and Noah, could it happen for her and Nic? How could she convince him that he would make a wonderful father? She didn't know. The only thing she did know was that he was going to be a father. Whether he wanted to be involved was entirely up to him.

"Does Nic know he's going to be a father?"

"Yes. I sent him copies of the ultrasound."

She refused to hide anything. Even though he had done this for her, given her the baby he knew she wanted, she intended to make sure he was aware of everything. There would be no secrets. Even if she never saw him again, he would know what was going on with his child. She would send him photos, videos, pictures of school projects, and report cards. He would know his child, even if he never *knew* his child.

There would never be secrets between them again.

"Have you heard from him?"

"No."

"And?"

Olivia smiled, knowing it likely looked sad, but it wasn't, not really. She was at peace with her decision.

"And," she said quietly, "I'll wait forever if I have to."

CHAPTER FORTY-THREE

Marco Island, Florida

The house, made of wood, stone, and brick, had five bedrooms and four-and-a-half baths. A large porch wrapped all the way around to the back, where a glistening pool separated the house from the white-sand beach. It had an open floor plan, a gourmet kitchen, and a giant bonus room on the third floor designed to accommodate a large family. It wasn't the largest home in the neighborhood or even the fanciest, but the welcoming exterior gave only a hint of the warmth within. To Hawke, it represented the beauty that was Olivia Gates.

Not that Olivia had shown him around the house. Instead, he had toured the home when she'd been gone. Breaking in had been easy, which reminded him he needed to ensure her locks were changed. They were good, but they could be better.

Stalking his ex-wife had never been on his radar. Stalking in general was creepy and wrong on so many levels. Although, was it technically stalking when the one you were watching not only knew you were there but openly invited you inside?

Olivia had a routine, one Hawke had become accustomed to following. Around six thirty each morning, the shutters would be pulled back, the front door would open, and Olivia would appear on the porch. She would stand there, looking directly at him, sometimes for a full minute, sometimes less. Then she would turn and go back inside.

At seven, she would take a run or walk on the beach. At eight, she would return home, prepare breakfast, and eat in the sunroom attached to the kitchen.

Her day varied from there. Recently, she had been receiving furniture deliveries. Last week, when the baby furniture truck had arrived, Hawke had watched with great interest, trying to determine what she'd purchased and picture where she might place each piece in the nursery.

The day he'd received the ultrasound photos had been one of the most painful and exciting days of his life. He had stared at the images a million times. One moment, he was railing that they existed. The next, he was thanking God they did.

Yeah, he was about as screwed up as a man could get.

He knew what she was doing. Knew that she was putting no pressure on him to be involved, but wanted him to know what was going on because, dammit, he was the father of her child.

On the bad days, he would hear his father's voice, remember the bitter hatred in his eyes. Cooper Hawthorne had been born with a hatred of people in general. He'd died, hating his son most of all. His last words were a testament to that.

You're just like me, boy. Stop trying to pretend you're not. You get yourself a kid or two, and you'll see. We ain't no different.

Hawke had tried to deny that all of his life. Had gone to

great lengths to make sure he never ended up like his old man. And what had he done two years ago when Livvy had told him she was pregnant? He had turned into the bastard. No, he hadn't hit her, but he might as well have.

And then, when she'd told him he no longer had to worry about the pregnancy, he had gone full Cooper Hawthorne on her.

Did you get rid of it?

Those words reverberated through his brain like a stabbing knife. That's how he'd referred to their child…his baby. If that hadn't shown him who he was, nothing could. Those words had been classic Cooper Hawthorne. If he had ever wondered if his old man's blood ran through his veins, he had learned the truth that day. He was most definitely his father's son.

Two days after he'd uttered those words, his life had blown up. Layla was dead, his other team members had barely escaped with their lives, and his marriage was on life support.

Divorcing Livvy and then disappearing to try to find the killer of his friends had made the most sense to him. It had been a hellish two years. Every part of his being had missed her and what they'd had, but he was still the same man. Still convinced that having a child should never happen.

And now his life had come full circle. Or had it?

He felt as if he was on the precipice of heaven. He could literally see it shining before him. But to get to heaven, he had to turn his back on all the preconceived beliefs he'd held on to for so long. If he made a mistake, did the wrong thing, it wouldn't be him who suffered, it would be Livvy—and his child.

Heaven had never looked so enticing or so far away.

THE SKYLIGHT above her bed poured sunshine into the room. Olivia opened her eyes and looked up into blue skies. Even though the skylight was intended for the sitting area of the room, she had deliberately placed her bed beneath it so she could wake up to sunlight. She never wanted to go back to darkness again.

Sitting up, she waited to see how her morning was going to go. After several minutes, she determined that it was going to be a rare day of no morning sickness. She brushed her teeth, combed her hair, and donned running clothes. Standing sideways, she looked in the mirror at her growing belly, smiled, and rubbed it lovingly. "Good morning, sweetheart," she whispered.

On her way downstairs, she noted with pleasure how the house was coming together. It was a conglomeration of what she and Nic had had in their first home together and new items she'd purchased. Though there were still plenty of bare spots, she refused to rush through filling the house. She planned to live here a long time and was determined to purchase each item deliberately.

She opened the plantation shutters, allowing sunlight to shine throughout the downstairs. Two of the most delightful features of the house were the numerous windows and the open floor plan. When the shutters were open, natural light flooded the entire first floor.

She headed to the kitchen, another favorite part of the house, with its multitude of cabinets and the large island in the middle. She envisioned future homework assignments getting lost on that island beneath breakfast dishes, newspapers, and whatever else busy families accumulated. She smiled at the image.

Sipping a cup of herbal tea, she inhaled the subtle scent of jasmine as she continued with another morning routine.

Opening the front door, she stepped out onto the porch.

For several long seconds, she stood there and stared at the SUV parked across the street. Then, just as she did every morning, she went back into the house to begin her day.

After a brisk, refreshing walk on the beach, she made herself a light, healthy breakfast and then turned on soft music to fill the silence, refusing to feel lonely. A spark of sadness threatened, and she fought it back.

Maybe because she wasn't alone—not really.

After cleaning up the breakfast dishes, she took her tea and walked back to the window. The dark SUV was still there. He never tried to hide from her. She knew he was there. He knew she knew. He never came to the door, never got out of his vehicle. He was just there.

She hadn't heard from him since she'd left Bermuda. She hadn't tried to hide from him. With his resources, she knew he'd had no problem finding her. She had wanted him to know where she was.

Unconsciously, her hand went to the gentle swell of her belly. She was well, and the precious life inside her was well. And the man on the outside…was tortured.

She wanted to go to him, reassure him it would be all right. Tell him she knew to the depths of her soul that he would be a good father. But he needed to believe it himself. Her trust in him wasn't lacking. It was his belief in himself that he had to come to terms with.

It hadn't been easy living without him, wanting with all her heart to share the excitement and joy of having their baby inside her. She wanted him there to experience each little milestone, and yes, sweet heavens, she had wanted someone to comfort her while she was throwing up and hold her when the nausea finally passed. She had never wanted to do this alone, but she refused to not do it just because she was uncertain. Other than her love for her child and for the stubborn man sitting in his SUV, nothing in life was certain. She had missed out on too much already.

Whether he wanted to share this with her or not was all up to him.

This had been going on for months. Holidays had passed. She had spent a lovely Thanksgiving at Cole and Keeley's house and enjoyed a delicious Christmas dinner at Dylan and Jamie's home. She had watched each family, seen the love, the devotion, and yes, the messiness. Both Dylan and Cole led dangerous lives, but their commitments to their families were a testament that it could be done, and done well.

No, she knew it wasn't as easy as it looked. But the hard things were often the most worthwhile.

Turning away from the window, she resumed her day, determined to continue to live the life she had planned. No matter what happened, what decision Nic made, she would enjoy the life she was creating.

She just prayed that, someday soon, that life would once again include the father of her baby.

HAWKE GRIPPED the steering wheel and stared at the house, trying to will the front door to open. She was late today. For the tenth time in less than a minute, he glanced at the clock on the SUV's dash. It was almost seven fifteen. Olivia was usually downstairs by now, having opened the shutters and given him a pointed look from the porch before continuing her routine. It was something he counted on.

At seven twenty, he was out of the SUV and striding toward the house. Something was wrong. He knew it. He pulled on the glass door and cursed. Of course it was locked, and he sure as hell didn't have time to pick the lock. Grabbing a flowerpot filled with geraniums, he slammed it into the glass. Avoiding the jagged glass, he unlocked the door. The solid wood door was another matter but not for a man determined to get inside. It took three slams with his shoulder before a crack appeared and one more before he could break the damn thing down.

The instant he was inside, he yelled, "Livvy!" Taking the stairs three at a time, he was in her bedroom in seconds. The sounds coming from the bathroom told him exactly why she was running late.

OH SWEET HEAVENS, having her head in the toilet wasn't exactly how she had wanted to see Nic again. She had over-slept this morning, and her morning sickness had come later than usual.

Without a word, he pulled her hair back with a large hand as his other hand gently patted her shoulder for comfort.

Deciding that it was over for the time being, Olivia flushed the toilet. A cool, wet hand cloth appeared before her eyes, and she gratefully accepted it.

"Okay?" he growled softly.

"Yes. Better. Thanks."

When she went to stand, he tried to lift her in his arms. "No. Wait." She went to the basin, rinsed her mouth, and then grabbed the mouthwash. Vomit breath was so not sexy.

Once that was done, she turned and smiled at him. "It hit later than usual."

Without speaking, he picked her up and carried her back to bed. Laying her down, he pulled the covers over her and helped her get her pillows settled.

"I'll be right back."

She nodded and closed her eyes, too afraid for him to see the want and need in them. She told herself this was noth-ing. He had come out of concern, not because he had changed his mind. Getting her hopes up would be ridiculous.

Five minutes later, he was back with a cup of steaming chamomile tea and saltine crackers.

"You're going to need new doors."

She had heard him—how could she not? He'd busted down her doors to get to her. She decided it was good to be married to a man who could bust down doors.

"I'll take care of it," he added.

She took a sip of tea and nibbled on a cracker, trying to determine if her stomach was going to cooperate. And while she did that, Nic continued on as if it hadn't been months since they'd talked to each other.

"Have you heard from Eve lately?" he asked.

"A couple of days ago. She sounds better…"

"But?"

She shrugged. "I don't know. She doesn't sound like Eve. Something's going on with her and Gideon, and I can't get a fix on it."

"Yeah, I agree. I talked to him last week, and he was more closemouthed than ever."

"He's apparently going to stay with her until she's fully recovered."

"Did she say where she is?"

"No. I asked, and she said it's best for everyone if no one knows."

"What the hell does that mean?"

"I don't know." She smiled slightly. "Those two have been circling each other like prizefighters in a ring for years. It's about time they finally admitted their feelings."

"They're both as stubborn as mules."

She wasn't going to point out that the epitome of stubborn was sitting on the bed in front of her.

"So you're definitely staying with LCR?"

"Yes. There's a satellite office in Tampa. I'll go there if I need to, but for right now, I'm doing intel gathering, which I can do here at the house."

"It's a nice house."

"I'd give you a tour," she said dryly, "but I know you've already had one."

He didn't look the slightest bit guilty.

"You feeling better?"

"Yes. Thanks. It usually only lasts a few minutes."

Nodding, he stood. "I'd better go."

Before she could say, *Don't go*, or *Want some breakfast?* or even *Have a nice day*, he was gone.

Half an hour later, three men arrived to replace her doors. Nic was conspicuously absent.

A NEW ROUTINE began after that day. At six thirty each morning, Nic would appear in her bedroom. He'd place a cup of tea and crackers on the nightstand. If it was a nonvomiting day, he'd chat with her for a few minutes, and then he would leave. If she had morning sickness, he'd hold her hair back while she vomited, wipe her face, and then carry her to bed. Tea and crackers would appear, and then he'd stay with her until she felt better. Then he would leave.

Their conversations were rarely of a personal nature. He told her he was working on some things for OZ, that they were continuing to gather intel on the Wren Project, but so far, it was still just a conglomeration of information with no real solidity. Since the organization had been around for over a hundred years, it was going to take time and a lot more digging before they would be able to act on what they'd found.

She told him she'd noticed he wasn't limping. He told her he'd had some minor surgery on his knee, and it was better.

He mentioned he was staying at a hotel close by. She didn't invite him to stay with her. She knew it would cause awkwardness between them, and that was the last thing she wanted.

The routine went on for several weeks, and she supposed it might have gone on longer if her little princess hadn't decided to say hi to her parents. Days later, she still got weepy over the memory of how Nic had reacted.

They'd been discussing a new computer virus protection defense system that Serena had created. The woman was a technology genius and could have made millions either selling her own software or working for tech giants in any capacity she wanted. Instead, she chose to stay with Option Zero, fighting evil.

Nic had been in the middle of talking about Sean and his stubborn pride when the sheet over Olivia's belly had moved. He had jerked back as if he'd seen a ghost.

It had been the first time the baby had moved, and she had been thrilled to be able to share the beautiful moment with Nic. Overjoyed with delight, she had taken his hand and gently placed it on her belly beside her own, allowing them both to feel their precious child inside her.

All the color had left his face, and then, without a word, he'd gotten up and left the house.

That had been three days ago, and she hadn't seen him since. He was no longer sitting outside her house. No longer coming inside to help her while she was sick.

He was gone, and she had no idea if he would be back.

CHAPTER FORTY-FOUR

Hawke parked a few yards away from Olivia's house. It was his first time back here since he'd walked out after feeling their child move beneath his hand. Behaving like an ass had apparently become his full-time job.

Describing how he'd felt was impossible. The absolute reverence he'd experienced was by far the most humbling moment of his life. This precious, beautiful child had been created from the love he and Olivia shared. Barely an instant later, that sacred moment had been swamped by incredible shame.

Just a few months back, he'd arrogantly told Juan Gonzalez to not let his father's past determine his own future. But wasn't that exactly what Hawke was doing? He'd allowed Cooper Hawthorne control over his thoughts, his feelings. Despite all his posturing, all his protests, and all his damn denials, he had allowed his old man to take charge of his life. The bastard was long dead, but had been alive and well inside his brain.

The day his father had died, Hawke had sworn it would be the last time he would allow him any kind of influence.

He'd been twenty years old and had taken leave from the Navy to come say goodbye. A part of him knew it was to make sure that the old man was really gone for good. There'd been no love or an ounce of affection between them. He didn't know if there ever had been. After his mother left, it had been endless days of pain, of verbal and physical abuse that seemed to have no beginning or end. It was just there.

When he'd gotten big enough to defend himself, the beatings had turned into full-fledged fistfights. He and his father had gone at it, breaking furniture, denting doors, destroying everything in their path trying to best each other. The day he'd won his first bout had been the first time his old man had looked at him with even the slightest amount of respect. Of course, that respect had been combined with a loathing that had been a part of Cooper Hawthorne for as long as Hawke could remember. The man had hated everything and everyone, but he'd had a special hatred for his wife and son.

After he'd ensured his old man was in the ground, he'd gone looking for his mother. Since she'd left, he'd alternated between a deep hurt and fierce resentment. She had left him alone with that bastard. Any love she had given him had seemed like a lie. Through the years, he had forgiven her, acknowledging that if she had stayed, his father would have eventually beaten her to death.

Since he was due back to his post in Iraq the day after his old man's burial, and didn't have the time to go searching himself, Hawke had placed a call to a private detective. He'd thought it would take the PI a few days or more to locate her. In his mind, he'd envisioned letting her know that Cooper was dead and she no longer needed to be afraid. He'd naively thought they could have some kind of relationship.

Hawke had been sitting in the airport, waiting for his flight when the PI had called with the information. It had taken the man less than an hour to find out that three days after his mother walked out on him, she had been found dead of a heroin overdose in the next town over. The PI had sent him the police report, which showed that Cooper had been informed of his wife's death the day after she'd been found. He'd never shared that information with his son.

If that didn't show him who Cooper Hawthorne was, nothing could. She had meant nothing to his old man, and neither had his son.

On his next leave, he'd found where she'd been buried. It'd been just a marker with her name, Gina Hawthorne, engraved. No mention of who she was, or what she had been to anyone. Cooper hadn't even had the decency to buy her a headstone. Hawke had purchased one for her, had *Beloved Mother* engraved on it, finally making peace with the woman who'd given him life. Gina had been twenty-nine years old when she'd died. Way too young to allow her demons to destroy her. Maybe she hadn't been the best mother, but he had some good memories. She'd made him a birthday cake once, and let him lick the empty bowl of icing. They'd watched cartoons together in the mornings. And he remembered the times she'd stood in front of him, keeping him from being hit by his old man.

His mother had been stuck in an impossible situation, and Hawke refused to allow any bitterness to take away the good she'd done. Cooper Hawthorne had been the demon in both their lives, evil to the core.

And somehow, someway, Hawke had allowed himself to believe what the bastard had constantly told him. The man who had lied, stolen, cheated, and beaten his wife and kid to a bloody pulp—the scum of the earth if there ever was one— had been inside his head, telling him who he was and what he would be.

No. Fucking. Way.

"Get out of my head, old man," Hawke snarled. "I am not you."

With that, Hawke got out of the SUV and strode to Olivia's house. He didn't stop until he was on the front porch. He didn't need to knock. Livvy had seen him and had opened the door. She had been watching for him, waiting for him to be the man she needed—the man she knew him to be.

"I want to be your husband, Livvy. I want to be the father of your babies. If you'll let me."

"You already are, Nic," she said softly. "I never signed the divorce papers. We're still married."

More grateful and humbled than he'd ever been in his life, he pulled her into his arms and buried his face in her neck. Holding her as tightly as he could, he whispered roughly, "I'm sorry, Livvy. I'm so very sorry. For everything. The things I said, the things I've done, not done. All of it."

"Shh. I understood. We understood."

He went to his knees and pressed his face to her belly. "I'm sorry, angel. I promise...I swear... I'll be a good father to you."

"She knows that, too."

He looked up at her. "She?"

"Yes. She."

He kissed Livvy's belly and then stood. Wrapping his arms around her again, he kissed her with all the passion, hope, and commitment he had in his heart. For the rest of his days, he would strive to be the husband she deserved and the father his children needed. He had been given a second chance at heaven, and this time, he would never let it go.

EPILOGUE

O n a bright, sunny Florida day, Maggie Nicole
Hawthorne made her appearance. Her exhausted
mother glowed with happiness, and her father had tears in
his eyes as he met his sweet princess face-to-face for the first
time. Watching her big, strong husband hold their tiny,
precious daughter in his arms was a moment Olivia knew
she would relive forever.

"She has your nose," he said.

Filled with both elation and exhaustion, Olivia smiled up
at the loves of her life. "And her father's dark hair."

He grinned. "But hopefully not his big feet." His eyes
swept over her. "How are you feeling?"

"Considering our baby girl weighed in at a healthy seven
pounds and three ounces and decided she wanted to meet
the world butt first, surprisingly good."

When the doctor had realized the baby was breech, it had
been a few tense moments. The worry in Nic's eyes had been
belied by his encouraging words and soft kisses as he'd held
her hand. She had been prepared to do this without him, but
she thanked God she hadn't had to do it alone.

"Did you let everyone know?" she asked.

"Yeah. Talked to Ash. He'll tell everyone. Offered his congratulations and said he, Jules, and Josh are looking forward to meeting Maggie Nicole."

"I was thinking we could call her Nikki," she said softly.

His eyes glinting with emotion, he said gruffly, "I like that."

"What about Noah?"

"Called him, too. He and Samara send their best. They're coming down to Tampa in a few weeks. He said they've been accumulating baby gifts from LCR people all over the world."

Olivia breathed a sigh filled with sheer joy. She had a beautiful, healthy daughter, a husband she loved more than life, and an extended family with LCR and OZ, most of whom were some of the toughest, most wonderful people in the world.

Her eyes blinked heavily, and Nic leaned over and kissed her mouth softly. "Get some sleep. Nikki and I will be right here when you wake up."

Olivia fell asleep with a smile on her face, knowing that when she opened her eyes again, her precious family would be waiting for her.

～

The other side of the world

ON THE PHONE in her hand, the blond woman watched the little family in the hospital room. She noted Olivia's serenity and Hawke's happiness. She nodded slowly and whispered, "Good for you, Olivia."

She deleted the app she'd used to hack into the hospital's security cameras. Removing the SIM card, she broke it in half, then in quarters. With quick efficiency, she dismantled the burner phone. She'd distribute the pieces throughout the city as she went about her day.

Satisfied, Iris Gates went back to work.

THANK YOU

Dear Reader,

Thank you so much for reading Heartless. I sincerely hope you enjoyed Hawke and Olivia's love story. I fell in love with both of them and hope you did, too. If you would be so kind as to leave a review at your favorite online buy site to help other readers find this book, I would sincerely appreciate it.

Next up in the OZ series is Ruthless. I'm only a few pages into the story, but Gideon and Eve have already told me some amazing secrets. Can't wait to discover more from them.

If you would like to be notified when I have a new release or a special sale, be sure to sign up for my newsletter *https://christyreece.com/sign-up-newsletter.html*

To learn about my other books and what I'm currently writing, please visit my website *http://www.christyreece.com/*

Follow me on:

Facebook *https://www.facebook.com/AuthorChristyReece*

Twitter *https://twitter.com/ChristyReece*

Amazon *https://www.amazon.com/Christy-Reece/e/ B002K8S34A?ref=sr_ntt_srch_lnk_2&qid=1606762009&sr=8-2*

Goodreads *https://www.goodreads.com/author/show/2741576. Christy_Reece*

Bookbub *https://www.bookbub.com/profile/christy-reece?list= author_books*

Want more of Hawke and Olivia? Check out Their Beginning on my website *https://christyreece.com/book-heartless-deleted-scene.html*

OTHER BOOKS BY CHRISTY REECE

OPTION ZERO Series

Merciless, An Option Zero Novel

Relentless, An Option Zero Novel

GREY JUSTICE Series

Nothing To Lose, A Grey Justice Novel

Whatever It Takes, A Grey Justice Novel

Too Far Gone, A Grey Justice Novel

A Matter Of Justice, A Grey Justice Novel

A Grey Justice Novel Box Set: Books 1 - 3

LCR ELITE Series

Running On Empty, An LCR Elite Novel

Chance Encounter, An LCR Elite Novel

Running Scared, An LCR Elite Novel

Running Wild, An LCR Elite Novel

Running Strong, An LCR Elite Novel

LCR Elite Box Set: Books 1 - 3

LAST CHANCE RESCUE Series

Rescue Me, A Last Chance Rescue Novel

Return To Me, A Last Chance Rescue Novel

Run To Me, A Last Chance Rescue Novel

No Chance, A Last Chance Rescue Novel

Second Chance, A Last Chance Rescue Novel

Last Chance, A Last Chance Rescue Novel

Sweet Justice, A Last Chance Rescue Novel

Sweet Revenge, A Last Chance Rescue Novel

Sweet Reward, A Last Chance Rescue Novel

Chances Are, A Last Chance Rescue Novel

WILDEFIRE Series writing as Ella Grace

Midnight Secrets, A Wildefire Novel

Midnight Lies, A Wildefire Novel

Midnight Shadows, A Wildefire Novel

ACKNOWLEDGMENTS

I am beyond blessed with many wonderful and supportive people in my life. Writing can be such a solitary endeavor, and I could not do what I do without the following people:

My husband, Jim, who loves and encourages me in ways too numerous to mention. Thank you for the laughter, for bringing me goodies to keep me going, and for handling a million things that I take for granted. You are, and will always be, my one and only love.

My beautiful mom, who inspires me everyday.

My incredibly precious fur-babies who bring me smiles and more love than I ever thought possible. I would mention all their names, but I would run out of room!

The amazing Joyce Lamb whose copyediting and fabulous advice are always on-point.

Kelly Mann of KAM Designs for her gorgeous cover art.

The Reece's Readers Facebook groups, for all their support, encouragement, and wonderful sense of humor.

Anne, my super reader, who always goes above and beyond in her advice and encouragement, and knows just what to say to keep me going.

My beta readers, Crystal, Hope, Alison, Kelly, and Kris, who offered great suggestions and much-needed encouragement.

My proofreaders Susan and Kara, who found those things I missed even after reading the manuscript a thousand times.

Linda Clarkson of Black Opal Editing, who asked just the

right questions to fill in those pesky story holes to make the book so much better.

Special thanks to Hope for her help and assistance in a multitude of things. Your generous heart and thoughtfulness are so very much appreciated.

To my all readers, your support means the world to me. Thank you for your patience and encouragement as I continue to learn my way around these secretive and complex OZ characters. I hope you love them as much as I do!

ABOUT THE AUTHOR

Christy Reece is the award winning, NYT Bestselling Author of dark romantic suspense. She lives in Alabama with her husband and a menagerie of pets.

Christy loves hearing from readers and can be contacted at *Christy@ChristyReece.com*.

DISCOVER THE ACTION-FILLED WORLD OF OPTION ZERO

Beneath a barrage of bullets and destruction, six men defied death and betrayal to form an unbreakable bond of friendship and loyalty. Though the people responsible sought to destroy them, in the end, they only made them stronger.

And like a Phoenix rising from those ashes of destruction, Option Zero was born.

Both hated and respected, OZ works under the cover of anonymity. They have free rein—as long as they don't get caught. If that ever happens, they'll be tried and convicted without help from any government.

Receiving intel from multiple sources throughout the world enables OZ to do things ordinary citizens could never accomplish. But they're living on borrowed time. Many have tried to take them down, and at some point, someone will succeed. It's a price they're willing pay.

The warriors of OZ will stop at nothing to achieve their objectives.

MERCILESS
Option Zero
Book One

Somewhere between darkness and the dawn lies a truth that could get them killed.

Years ago, Asher Drake lost everything he loved. He had followed the rules, done the right thing, and was repaid with betrayal. Now, as leader of Option Zero, he plays by his own rules and handles things a different way. Ash knows he might not live to see another day, but one thing is certain, he will fight till his last breath for what's right.

Out of dark desperation, Jules Stone became someone else. Having experienced the worst of humanity, she battles her demons by fighting for those who can't fight for themselves. But the shadows linger. When an opportunity arises to pay a debt, Jules accepts the offer, hopeful that the shadows will disappear forever.

Secure in the knowledge that power is the ultimate weapon and truth is only a matter of perception, an enemy watches, waiting for the perfect moment to strike.

Putting aside the pain of the past, Ash and Jules must join forces and fight their demons together before the darkness becomes permanent and destroys them both.

DISCOVER THE MYSTERIOUS WORLD OF GREY JUSTICE

THE GREY JUSTICE GROUP

There's More Than One Path To Justice

Justice isn't always swift or fair, and only those who have felt the pain of denied justice can truly understand its bitter taste. But justice delayed doesn't have to be justice denied. Enter the Grey Justice Group, ordinary citizens swept up in extraordinary circumstances. Led by billionaire philanthropist Grey Justice, this small group of operatives gains justice for victims when other paths have failed.

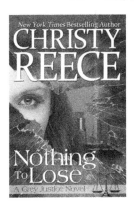

Nothing To Lose
A Grey Justice Novel
Book One

Choices Are Easy When You Have Nothing Left To Lose

Kennedy O'Connell had all the happiness she'd ever dreamed—until someone stole it away. Now on the run for her life, she has a choice to make—disappear forever or make those responsible pay. Her choice is easy.

Two men want to help her, each with their own agenda.

Detective Nick Gallagher is accustomed to pursuing killers within the law. Targeted for death, his life turned inside out, Nick vows to bring down those responsible, no matter the cost. But the beautiful and innocent Kennedy O'Connell brings out every protective instinct. Putting aside his own need for vengeance, he'll do whatever is necessary to keep her safe and help her achieve her goals.

Billionaire philanthropist Grey Justice has a mission, too. Dubbed the 'White Knight' of those in need of a champion, few people are aware of his dark side. Having seen and experienced injustice—Grey knows its bitter taste. Gaining justice for those who have been wronged is a small price to pay for a man's humanity.

With the help of a surprising accomplice, the three embark on a dangerous game of cat and mouse. The stage is set, the players are ready…the game is on. But someone is playing with another set of rules and survivors are not an option.

DISCOVER THE THRILLING
WORLD OF LCR ELITE

A Whole New Level Of Danger

With Last Chance Rescue's philosophy of rescuing the innocent, the Elite branch takes the stakes even higher. Infiltrating the most volatile locations in the world, LCR Elite Operatives risk everything to rescue high value targets. Unsanctioned. Off the grid. Every operation a secret, danger-filled mission. Led by Noah McCall, LCR Elite will stop at nothing, no matter the cost, to fulfill their promise.

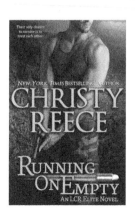

Running On Empty
An LCR Elite Novel
Book One

The Danger Has Only Begun

Having survived a brutal childhood, Sabrina Fox believed she could handle anything. That was before she watched the love of her life die before her very eyes. Brokenhearted, her emotions on lockdown, she finds purpose and hope as an LCR Elite Operative rescuing victims from some of the most volatile places in the world.

Covert ops agent Declan Steele is used to a life of danger and deceit, but when the one person he trusted and believed in above all others sets him up, he'll stop at nothing to make her pay. Finally rescued from his hellish prison, Declan has one priority—hunt down Sabrina Fox and exact his revenge.

Trusting no one is a lonely, perilous path. Sabrina swears she's innocent and Declan must make a decision--trust his heart or his head. As memories of their life together returns, he realizes just how treacherous his torture had been and the target of his revenge shifts. But when Sabrina is taken, retribution is the last thing on his mind. With the assistance of Last Chance Rescue Elite, Declan races to rescue the only woman he has ever loved before it's too late.

Made in the USA
Monee, IL
27 October 2022

16689096R00229